ENEMY STAND
TRIDENT RESCUE
BOOK SIX

A.L LIDELL

SONIA

"Here is to the first first-year resident to be published in *Breakthroughs!*" Sonia raised a margarita and clinked her friend's glass. Around them, the North Vault's speakers blasted music across the dance floor, large screens alternating between zooming in on dancing guests and patching the feeds of the professional dancers of both genders twisting lithely atop lit pedestals. The three bartenders danced with the beat as they flowed expertly through their domain. If not for the fact that Sonia hated the man who owned the place, the North Vault would be perfect. She grinned at Win. "A small step for Dr. Winafred Carrell, a large step for victims of rare diseases everywhere. What's your secret?"

"I hacked China and big pharma."

Sonia winced. Win was probably only half kidding. Possibly quarter kidding. Outwardly, with her shiny golden curls, perfectly drawn facial lines, and petite stature, she looked like a doll. Gorgeous and tiny and delicate. What she lacked in physical presence, she made up for in spades on the darkweb. Though only a few people in the world knew who she was.

"Right," said Sonia. "Doctor Carrell and Ms.—what's your moniker again?"

Win sipped her drink. "Nothing you need to worry about, counselor. But if you are in the mood to talk laws and rules—and let's face it, you are never not in the mood to talk about laws and rules—tell me you found some loophole to get me out of the ER rotation?" She gave Sonia a pleading look as if Sonia had some mythical power over either Colorado state law or the administrative policy of Denton Memorial Hospital. "I'm a geneticist. Give me a blood sample and a computer and I'll get you the world. Give me a screaming patient with a broken arm, and I pass out. So me being in the ER is a lose-lose proposition for everyone."

"And none of that has to do with Sith's best friend being your attending?" Sonia asked. She'd only met Win's older brother Sith a few times, the last being at Sonia and Win's college graduation. He was in the SEALs, and leave was difficult to come by.

"Matthew Jennson? Oh, it has everything to do with Jennson," said Win. "I've no idea why he left the joyful military world of crawling around battlefield mud, because he clearly thinks that to be the superior lifestyle. Speaking of the devil. Or, asshole."

Sonia followed Win's glare to a tall black-haired man joining a group of other former military types at the corner of the bar. Denton had a collection of them. Casey McKenzie—the North Vault's proprietor and former Delta operative—was currently holding court. In addition to Casey, Sonia's boss Liam was also there as was Cullen Hunt who ran Denton Memorial. The men greeted each other with low grunts and Casey slid Matthew a drink across the top of the polished bar.

"The superiority complex does seem to be endemic to the Tridents," Sonia murmured.

"Tridents?"

"The cabal of special forces guys in Denton Valley. They all know each other, train together, and act as pains in the ass to various degrees. I don't know how the nickname started, but they ran with it. I mean Liam's company is literally called Trident Security and Rescue. The Tridents are like a mix of gods and the mafia around here, and it doesn't hurt that they either own or run all the major businesses in the area. Anyway, back to Matt Jennson, what's he doing?"

"Oh, it's Matthew, not Matt." Win rolled her eyes. "Besides confusing the ER with a bootcamp?—I swear he takes a perverse joy out of seeing if he can't make me cry at least once a day." Her shoulders sagged, energy and the will to fight leaving her like air rushing from a punctured balloon. "I see enough of him in the hospital, I'd rather not deal with it on a night off. We should find a different place for drinks."

"And yield ground to a bunch of idiot men? No way in hell," said Sonia. "In fact, that is going to be our new motto. *We shall survive, we shall grow, and we shall never yield to idiot males.* Especially ones who think they are god's gifts to humankind."

Win smiled shyly, but raised her glass in a toast. "Survive, grow, don't yield." Her eyes sparkled as she took a sip of her drink and pulled out her phone, typing furiously.

"What are you doing?" asked Sonia.

Win kept her attention on her screen. "Hacking the Vault's camera feed to the screen. We could put the Tridents' nose hairs up there instead of the dancers."

"Don't." Sonia snatched Win's phone away. "Seriously, are you twelve? That's, you know, illegal."

Win threw up her hands. "If you are going to play rule-keeper, put that legal mind of yours to getting me the hell out of the ER."

"Well, does anything about this rotation violate medical ethics?"

"Forcing a geneticist to work in the emergency room? It violates *my* ethics." Win gulped from her drink and waved it between them. "You know what they have in that place?"

"Patients?"

"Exactly! Living, breathing, talking *patients*. With feelings, and complaints, and convoluted stories that don't actually make any sense and then change whenever Jennson walks into the treatment room."

"Have you talked to your brother?"

"Twice. His knee jerk reaction is that Jennson can do no wrong, because brothers in arms and all. I finally got Sith to admit that he has no idea why Jennson left the navy, for all the good that does me."

"I could talk to Liam," said Sonia. "Since I'm in his legal department I see a lot of him and he has sway. But, honestly? It might do more harm than good. Bullies smell blood in the water, so if Matthew knows how much he is getting to you, he could just double down."

"Good point. What's worse is that Ivy West-Keasley, the other ER attending, is on bed rest with preeclampsia. It will be months until she is back." Win growled under her breath, then focused on something behind Sonia's shoulder. "Speaking of our favorite people, yours has separated from the pack."

In the mirror panes built into the decor behind their booth, Sonia saw Casey's approaching reflection. Tall and broad shouldered, he wore a designer black suit that cost more than Sonia's monthly apartment rent. The expensive cloth was tailored perfectly to his chiseled body, and somehow made his blond hair and gray eyes even more stunning. The bastard *was* beautiful. Beautiful and arrogant and self-centered. But that's not what made Sonia's blood boil every time she ran into him.

Casey McKenzie had made a point of humiliating Sonia in court last year, manipulating and playing her for his personal amusement before the whole world. To add insult to injury, Casey didn't even practice law in civilian life. He'd swooped in for a single case that involved his cousin, turned Sonia's reputation and self-esteem inside out, and swooped out again to do what he liked—run North Vault Night Club.

She glanced at the door. Maybe Win's idea of getting out of this place wasn't a bad one.

"Survive, grow, don't yield to idiot men," Win whispered.

Right. Sonia straightened her back.

Casey snatched a whiskey off a passing waiter's tray and wrapped his long fingers around the glass as he sauntered over to Sonia and Win's booth. He moved with an easy, confident step, the fingers of his free hand tapping his thigh in rhythm to the music. Waiters and patrons shifted slightly to clear a path for him. A parting of the sea. No wonder the prick had an oversized ego.

"Good evening, Winafred. Counselor. Shouldn't you be over at the courthouse, dazzling the jury?"

"At eleven at night? If you have trouble reading the arrows on that expensive watch of yours, get yourself a Disney one with a numbers display."

"At any hour. From what I hear, you plea out most cases these days." His sultry voice was a caress that made Sonia's thighs tingle, even as she contemplated possible ways to cut off his balls. He swirled the whiskey in his glass. "If you need help, all you need to do is ask. I'm at your full disposal."

"I want your help about as much as I want an STD."

Casey's gaze roamed over her, lingering with deliberate drama on her small breasts and wide hips. "I'd not recommend the latter myself, but to each their own."

"You are disgusting," Sonia told him.

"I am no such thing. That's not just my personal opinion, by the way. I've several references who could vouch for my—"

"What do you want, McKenzie?" Sonia asked, cutting him off.

"Oh, many things. At the moment though, sex."

Sonia blinked. "With who?"

"With you, obviously," said Casey. "Did you imagine I came to you for help getting someone else into my bed? I don't usually require assistance in that regard, your case notwithstanding."

Win made a small snorting noise.

Sonia choked on her sip of margarita. He was serious. In that absurd, arrogant mind of his, Casey was serious. "Are you… Are you out of your mind?" she asked. "Why would I want to have sex with you?"

Casey motioned to his body, as if showcasing the perfection. "Because everyone does." His brows pulled together. "It vexes me that you don't share the general opinion. Is it the suit?"

Sonia rose, collecting her clutch, and slapping a twenty on the table to cover drinks and tip. "No, McKenzie. It's not the suit. Or the music. Or me. It's you. Really, it's just you."

Sonia held her ground, making sure Win could walk safely behind and to the exit before turning on her heels and joining her friend. Once outside, she gave Win a sideways glance. "That wasn't yielding," she said. "That was making a deliberate decision to retreat."

"No argument here." Win touched her arm. "Are you alright, Nia?"

She took a breath and let it out slowly. Win was one of the few people in the world who knew what Sonia's father's business partner had done to her that day during their senior year of college. Simple conversation didn't usually trigger that buried part of her, but Casey had a way of making even words feel like roving fingers.

"I'm fine. McKenzie and his quest for another notch on his bedpost are not going to ruin this evening for either of us." She linked her arm through Win's and steered them toward her apartment. With the wind ruffling Sonia's hair just enough to caress without being downright cold, it was too nice of a night to bother with an uber.

A flock of motorcycles zipped passed as they walked, the star-filled sky twinkling brightly. "One thing I love about Colorado is that I can see the little dipper," Sonia said after a while.

"Goes well with the bikers," said Win. Indeed, there seemed to be more motorcycles out than usual on the streets. Maybe some club had a ride out or whatever they called it when they put on leather and rolled out in a herd of helmets and wheels. "The ER will have some donors tonight."

"That's morbid," said Sonia.

"It's Darwin's Law. Natural selection."

Turning off the main road, Sonia steered them toward the first floor apartment she was renting in a three family house. She was the only tenant there currently. The top floor required more repairs than the landlord was willing to invest in, and the family from the second floor had moved a month earlier. Sonia missed their familiar faces, but she did sleep better without the three teenagers stomping around like elephants. Liam paid a good salary, but with her student loans—and the other debts she'd had to take on after she cut ties with her parents—this place was all she could afford.

"You've got mail," Win pulled a shiny postcard from the mailbox while Sonia struggled with the front door lock. "You are cordially invited to a week-long cruise aboard the *Belle Nuit*, sailing from

Newport, Connecticut. Staterooms starting at only ten thousand dollars."

"What a bargain. Marketing companies could save themselves a great deal on postage if they went by something beyond my occupation for targeting criteria. Plus, Connecticut? Why would I go from Colorado to Connecticut for a cruise?"

"Because it's a special reunion for Yale Law grads and you miss your classmates that much?" said Win.

"We just graduated a few years ago." Sonia shook her head. Some of her classmates came from serious money. "Someone probably wants to show off and rub elbows. Either that or try to poach each other for their firms."

"So what should I do with this?" Win waved the postcard in the air.

Sonia shrugged. "The recycling bin is just inside the door. File it there."

"Will do." Win paused on the inside of the door and then grinned. "You know, this cruise sounds like exactly the kind of thing idiot men would be at. So staying home is actually a strategic decision, and I for one salute you."

CASEY

Casey awoke to the first rays of dawn light streaming through his bedroom window and falling over the dark sheets of his bed. That, and the tell-tale sound of his phone vibrating. This early, it had to be Briar. Casey sat up. He was between two women, both as naked as he was, and still asleep. Ana and Brittany. Most likely. Or were they both Ana, just spelled differently? There had been three women in the bed originally, all from last night's evening at the North Vault, but one of the ladies had left before they fell asleep.

None of them were Sonia Dancer, however. No, that pitbull seemed more likely to castrate him than enjoy him. Which was… unsettling. Especially because he couldn't get her out of his head. Hell, he'd gotten hard last night just watching Sonia's hips as she walked out on him from the North Vault. If he could only have a night of fun with her, he was sure he'd finally be able to evict the woman from his mind.

Casey slipped out of the sheets carefully so as to not disturb the sleeping beauties and pulled on a pair of gym shorts before heading out.

"Where are you going?" one of them moaned softly. Ana. Yes, that was certainly Ana.

"To see what has a burr under my brother's hide," Casey said, letting his gaze caress her gorgeous curves one more time. "There is coffee in the kitchen."

At least there should be coffee. Briar usually started a pot. Not because he cared about Casey's guests, but because he wanted them out of the penthouse sooner than later, and guests plied with coffee typically moved faster than those who weren't.

Casey inclined his head in farewell to the women, though Ana had already fallen back to sleep. By the time he and Briar were done with training, the women would be gone. At least until the evening, when they came to the Vault again. He might invite one over again... No. Probably not. It was easier to keep fun as just what it was. No complications. No miscommunications.

Grabbing a bottle of water, Casey made his way over to the small gym that had started its life in the penthouse apartment as a formal dining room. Now, mats lined the floor and walls, and a punching bag hung from a reinforced ceiling beam. Briar was there already, kicking the life out of said bag. Casey watched him in the mirror, his twin's body identical to his own except for a few tattoos. And the scars. Those were equal, but not the same—though many had come from the same source. He grabbed a set of pads.

Briar stopped, wiping his face with the bottom of his shirt.

"Put those back," Briar said. "Hunt wants us. All of us."

"For what?"

Briar grunted. "How would I know? Got the same text you did."

Casey pulled out his phone. So that morning's alert hadn't been from Briar after all. Not that the text had anything more to offer, but its very existence was interesting. Cullen Hunt was the Trident's unofficial leader. If he was mustering everyone, hopefully it meant someone needed to get their arse kicked.

That would scratch an itch.

Casey tossed the kicking pads back to their spot and went to change.

An hour later, Casey slid into a leather seat beside his brother at a large conference room table. Faces he'd become familiar with since moving to Denton Valley were already there. Liam, Eli, Kyan, Aiden, Tara. Cullen's wife, Sky, was there too. Sky had about as much to do with combat as Casey did with dancing the ballet, but what she lacked in ability to assault a bunker, she more than made up for in her knack for getting information. It usually made everyone feel better to not know how she did it.

Casey adjusted his cufflinks and reached for the stainless steel kettle in the middle of the table. At least someone thought to brew coffee. He started to pour himself a cup—only to realize the dark liquid inside was actually tea. "Has England invaded?" he demanded.

Eli brightened and pulled the kettle toward him. "Not yet, mate." Eli's crisp British accent filled the room. "But when they do, I'm coming for your piano first."

"Right. Thank you everyone for coming," Cullen said before Casey could retort. He stood and surveyed them all with a penetrating gaze. "Though you should know that you aren't actually here. Because the Denton Valley Police Department would never approach a group of civilians to ask for help. Nor would the Tridents ever stick their noses into things we've no legal authority to mess with. Are we clear so far?"

"Crystal," said Casey. Wherever this was going, he already liked it.

The others nodded solemnly.

The door opened before Cullen could continue, and Matthew Jennson slipped inside. The doc was still in his scrubs, and rubbed fatigue from his face as he found an empty seat. "Sorry I'm late."

"You aren't," Casey drawled with a lazy smile. "Since we aren't actually here."

Matthew blinked then shrugged and reached for the faux coffee pot. Casey pushed an empty cup toward him and watched the doc make the same discovery he had minutes earlier.

"What the ever loving fuck is this?"

"Seems to be a hello from across the pond," Casey supplied.

"Right then, what are we not here to discuss exactly?" said Eli. "Besides the American Revolution."

"Satan's Armada," said Sky, taking control of the room and giving Casey a withering glare.

He grinned back.

Sky clicked on the large screen behind her, where a slideshow of bikers began to play. "The Armada is an OMG—an outlaw motorcycle gang. Similar to the Hells Angels but newer. They recently expanded into Colorado, bringing with them exactly the trouble you'd expect. Then, about a month ago, the Armada decided Denton Valley to be a good location for a chapter. Denton Valley Memorial has already felt the effects."

Across the table, Matthew nodded. "Two stabbings last night alone. Prospects trying to earn their way up the ladder."

"The Armada appears to have a point system to reach full patch status." Sky clicked to the next slide. "Wounding a member of a rival club is five points. Killing him, ten. Going to prison to protect a chapter gets you a lifetime of support. Then, there is the business part of things."

The screen changed to a show pictures drugs, guns, and women, many with bruises and hands tied behind their backs. Casey sat up straighter, exchanging a silent look of fury with his twin. They were both all too familiar with the bruises part. Had seen them too many times on their mother growing up. Those hurt more than the ones they received themselves.

Casey blinked, forcing himself to focus on Sky's briefing. He didn't look at Briar, but could feel his radiating tension beside him.

"The Armada doesn't just ride around on motorcycles making a nuisance of themselves, they run drugs, guns, and yes—women," Sky was saying. "A full scale international business, complete with an attorney to keep them out of prison."

"They sound like a job for the feds." Liam tapped his finger on the polished table. "Much as I like Denton PD, they are out of their league on this."

"They know," said Cullen. "They also know that Denton Valley isn't going to be a priority for anyone, not with the larger cities in play."

"So the locals can't deal with it and the feds won't," said Casey. "How can we help?"

"Not by going out and kicking the ass of every biker you see," Liam said, throwing Casey a hard look. "Just in case that entered your heads."

Casey raised his hands in innocence, though a good brawl was appealing. Briar grunted.

"Liam is right," said Cullen. "Taking down the Satan's Armada requires something bigger than a show of force to a few bikers or whatever arrests of low-level grunts the local PD can make. We need to get inside their operations, identify key players and money movements. Stop this at its source. Or at least make the Armada's continued presence in Denton Valley a very bad business decision."

"Intelligence on who is who is sketchy," Sky said apologetically, and shifted the screen again. Headshots of three bearded men in leather jackets and one clean-cut younger man appeared before them. "This is all we know of the possible leadership cadre. The dirty looking ones are bikers themselves, and the fourth—Nero—is an up and coming attorney who keeps the law away. He was working in Detroit for a while, but has been meeting with the president of the Armada's Denton Valley chapter. He might be heading this way."

"What else do we know about Nero?" Liam asked.

"Twenty eight years old. Yale graduate. Still lives in Detroit, but passed the Colorado Bar earlier this year." Sky pulled screenshots of Nero's social media posts. Closeups of girls, jewelry, and private jets filled the feed. "Filthy rich and likes to show it. But he is careful online. Nothing about business."

"Looks like he's gearing up for vacation." Eli pointed to a photo of Nero holding a shiny advertisement for a cruise ship cutting through turquoise waters. Below the image, Nero's comment read *See you on the Belle Nuit.* Eli clicked his tongue. "Open sea and alcohol gets people talking. If there ever was an op more crafted for our Casey McKenzie, I'm yet to see it. McKenzie even speaks legalese."

Casey leaned in to read the fine print on the ad. "Much as I appreciate you voting me off the island, that's a reunion cruise and I, alas, did not go to Yale Law."

Liam stared at the screen, then walked over to Sky's computer and flipped back to the slide show, finding what little she had on Nero's bio. He made a clicking sound with his tongue then blew out a long tense breath. "McKenzie didn't go to Yale, but we do know someone who did."

SONIA

"The *Belle Nuit* reunion cruise?" Sitting in Liam's office, Sonia split her attention between a copy of the shiny postcard she'd just recently tossed into the recycling bin, and a smug looking Casey McKenzie who she wished to send along the same route. "Yes, I received the invite. I imagine hundreds of people did, my year, plus the one before, and after. Didn't they?" Her attention, which had been snagging on Casey's presence, now focused entirely on Liam.

Was that mailing a trap of some kind? In addition to her work with Liam, Sonia had been putting in hours at the understaffed prosecutor's office. It was entirely possible that she had more enemies than she knew about.

"The marketing company sent over six hundred invites," Liam said firmly, as if catching the direction of her thoughts. He leaned his forearms against the edge of his desk. Unlike other executives of multimillion dollar companies, Liam's office was a working space not a power play one, with leather chairs worn from many conversations and a myriad of computer screens in active use. Now though, Liam's attention was on her, not the displays. "There is nothing to suggest you were singled out for the mailing."

So why am I here?

"I've no intention of going," said Sonia. "If you were worried about me being gone for a week all of a sudden."

"Thank the gods," said Casey. "I can only imagine what a disaster it would be for Rowan's multimillion dollar enterprise if they were to lose your invaluable legal service for a few days. The whole thing would implode."

Liam gave Casey a *shut the fuck up* look and turned back to Sonia. "First of all, you are entitled to vacation time. And the fact that you've taken none of it since you started here is a conversation I've been meaning to have with you separately," Liam said in that voice he sometimes got, the one filled with unyielding dominance. "Since we are on the topic, you will either schedule some days off for yourself, or I will schedule them for you. Leave it to me to somehow keep Trident Security and Rescue from collapsing in your absence. Am I clear?"

Sonia swallowed. "Yes. Thank you, sir."

Liam leaned away from her, and the aura of dominance eased. His voice softened, "In this case, however, the question about the *Belle Nuit* reunion cruise is entirely for my benefit. And before we go any further, I want to make it clear that what I might ask of you is entirely and completely voluntary."

She ran her hands along her pencil skirt, then caught herself. Casey was probably marking every move she made. Every sign of nerves that he could exploit later for his own amusement.

Liam laid out a series of photographs on the desk. They were all of a man in his 20s, slightly built except for a bit of a belly hanging over a tailored suit. He had a receding hairline, eyes as dark as his hair, and face that had a vaguely familiar feel. "Do you know this man?" Liam asked.

Sonia took a closer look at the photo, running a finger along the smooth photo paper. Her memory stirred with a distant haze. The face, the clothes, they were familiar, but not obvious. An actor perhaps? Someone she'd caught on a show? Or was it a professional encounter?

"His name is Nero, if that helps," said Liam. "At least that is what he goes by now. He might have preferred a different name when you went to school together."

"Which one?"

"Pre-school," said Casey.

Sonia ignored him. Didn't even rise to the bait of demanding to know what he was doing here beyond the obvious endeavor of being a pain in the ass. Dealing with Casey would have been easier if he were stupid or at least didn't look like a Greek god made flesh. Unfortunately, he was neither of those things. Especially not stupid. He was brilliant. And manipulative and arrogant. And he took sheer unadulterated pleasure in making her look like a fool in the courtroom, the one place she'd fought so hard to conquer.

"You would have met him at Yale Law," Liam said, cutting into Sonia's thoughts. "You may not have known him personally, given the size of the class."

Sonia forced her mind away from Casey and the memories of the courtroom games he'd played with her at last year's trial. Away from the absurd invite to his bed he made at the North Vault. If Liam brought her here, it was important and she owed him nothing less than her full attention and expertise.

She looked at the photo again, examining the man's features against her memories from Yale. *Ah.* Yes. Nero. She remembered now. The kid who'd preferred the strange name even back then. "I placed him now. He was never a friend, but we shared some classes and faced each other in moot court. If you need me to reach out to him, I can certainly try—but I don't know that he'd take my call any more readily than yours. Less so given your position."

"Positions can be creatively shifted," Casey said, a wicked gleam in his eyes as he tasted the word. "Let's not get all hung on a single possibility."

Her face heated, her good intentions of not taking Casey's baiting snapping like a ripped rubber band. "Is there a reason you are here, beyond a desire to give me a headache?"

"Most certainly. I'm here to propose to you in marriage," said Casey.

"Can you shut up for a minute, McKenzie?" Liam demanded.

"I could, but what would be the fun in that?"

Liam pointedly turned his chair away from Casey and faced Sonia directly. "No call is needed. However, Nero appears to be the new council for a chapter of the Satan's Armada that has been hazing Denton Valley, and we'd like to see if he wants to share some insight about his clients."

"He couldn't do that," said Sonia. "Attorney-client privilege."

"Oh, for fuck's sake." Casey threw a pen into the air. "The Satan's Armada rapes, murders, and traffics drugs all around North America. And you think Nero's primary concern is the ethics board?"

"It would be mine."

"Which is why you don't represent an outlaw motorcycle gang and he does," said Casey.

"Would you shut up," Liam hissed at Casey, then reined his voice in as he caught Sonia's gaze again. "We don't need you to call Nero. We were hoping to leverage your class standing another way—by having you accept the invitation to the *Belle Nuit*. The cost would be covered, of course, as would your time."

Sonia stared at her boss. "You want to send me on a ten thousand dollar cruise on the long shot that I can get Nero to disclose privileged information?"

"Ocean, help us all if you try that," Casey said. "We'd have better luck sending a dentist to win over the candy lobby." He stretched out his legs, the muscles shifting beneath his tailored suit as he crossed one ankle over another. As perfectly at ease here in Liam's office as he was at the North Vault and the courtroom. "Chatting up Nero would not be part of your duties. All you do is accept the invitation and show up. And bring a plus one."

"Plus one?" The moment Sonia said the question aloud, she realized the answer. Realized exactly which plus one was on the launching pad. Casey's earlier off handed comment about a marriage proposal clicked morbidly into place. "You want me… to bring you onto the *Belle Nuit* as my *husband*?"

"That's too much paperwork," said Casey. "A fiancé will do just fine."

Despite all her time in court, all her training to find words when she had none, all she could do was blink at the men. It went without saying that they didn't look the part. Casey was a beauty incarnate. Broad shoulders, sculpted muscles that no clothes truly hid, and powerful lethal grace. Sonia was, well, a pencil with hips.

You are a fat ass on a stick, Sonia-baby, so don't pretend you aren't enjoying this. Don't pretend I'm not doing your cunt a favor.

Sonia pushed down the voice from that phantom memory with a practiced breath and focused on the absurd proposition the men were laying out before her. She and Casey were a problem that went far beyond looks. Sonia practiced law. Casey practiced making a mockery of it. Casey's idea of a good evening involved debauchery. Wine, women, and song taken to new heights. Sonia preferred a friend or a book. More importantly—most importantly—to Casey, Sonia was little more than a toy. The one time they had worked together, he'd played with her like a cat toying with its food. Humiliated her. And she'd been unable to stop him.

Sonia's hands gripped the hem of her skirt, her stomach turning over.

"I'm fully aware that what we're asking is well beyond your job description," Liam was saying in the background. "Once you bring Casey into the events, he will take care of engaging with Nero and I trust him to ensure your safety. Even so, I will not fault you for one second if you say no. No pressure. No judgment."

Of course there would be pressure and judgment. It was already there, sitting beside Liam with a smirk on its face.

"Don't you prefer someone more qualified to go?" Sonia pulled on a mask of pure courtroom professionalism. "Someone like Tara who could take on my identity."

"It's only been a few years. People will expect a familiar face and recognize one that doesn't belong." Liam gave her a look he probably thought was reassuring. "As far as qualifications go, you've all the credentials we need. Which does not mean you have to say yes. I'm asking whether you'd be willing to go, not telling you to."

"Of course you are the only ticket we have onto the *Belle Nuit*," said Casey. "And our best shot at getting a violent gang off Denton Valley streets. But sure, no one will think less of you if you decide you are too much of a coward to subject yourself to a week on a luxury cruise where you need to do nothing but enjoy the spa."

"Enough, McKenzie," Liam snapped, releasing that leash on his power again. "Either keep your mouth shut or wait in the hall."

Casey closed his mouth, but when he turned his face from Liam, Sonia could see his lips pressing into that hint of a smile. Red flashed before her eyes. The prick was doing it again. Shoving her around. *Survive, grow and don't yield.* That was the motto she and Win had agreed on.

She glared at Casey, letting him see a hint of her fangs.

His smile only grew.

"Tell you what, I'll sweeten the pot." Ignoring the promise of murder now darkening Liam's face, Casey leaned forward toward Sonia. "You get to publicly break-off our engagement right on board. Leave me behind in the dirt. That itself should make the trip worth it for you."

For the first time in her life, Sonia agreed with him. "When you put it that way," she said, her heart still pounding with fury as she faced Casey, "it would be a pleasure to assist this operation."

MATTHEW

"Sir, you need to move Winafred Carrell the hell out of the ER before she kills someone," Matthew leaned his hands on the edge of Dr. Yarborough's desk, "or lets them die. That's more likely, but same end result."

Yarborough, who oversaw both the ER and surgical departments at Denton Memorial, leaned back in his chair. He was a former SEAL himself and, though it had been decades since he served, had an aura of military competence and command about him. Now, he studied Matthew with an unreadable expression. "That would certainly be an unfortunate outcome. And where would you have me move her to, Dr. Jennson?"

"Anywhere that doesn't have living people. The arctic circle comes to mind, but pathology is a solid second choice." The tiny, golden-haired fairy of a doctor was driving him insane, which in fairness was a short trip. Especially on no sleep. "I assure you, that she wants to be in my ER as little as I want her there."

He'd told Sith as much on the phone yesterday. Win didn't belong in the ER. It was that simple. Sith had told Matthew that he didn't give two fucks which department his little sister was in, so long as she was alright. And that he'd cut Matthew's balls off and roast them with chestnuts if she was not. Then Sith started prying into Matthew's sudden departure from SEAL Team Six's medical support and he'd ended the conversation quickly.

"I didn't realize your happiness was a metric on my training matrix," Yarborough said with a mildness that Matthew knew better than to interpret as anything but solid steel. "Or hers either."

Matthew read the unspoken order to check himself, and followed it, getting his hands off Yarborough's desk and draping them behind his back instead. In theory, one of the perks of being an attending was an end to the sadistic shifts the residents endured. In reality, leaving Win alone in the ER—even with him a phone call away—was not happening. Still, Matthew shoved his fatigue down into irrelevance and addressed Yarborough again only when he had full control of his voice. "My happiness or lack thereof is irrelevant, sir. However, the efficient operation of Denton Valley's emergency room is material. Dr. Carrell is an award-winning geneticist, with an expertise in research not clinical application. Her background is being underutilized in the ER setting. Meanwhile, she is taking up a slot in the ER that requires someone with clinical experience."

Hell, Matthew would take anyone who wasn't afraid of blood. The lunch lady at the cafeteria was starting to look like an attractive choice.

"I propose," Matthew continued, "that it would be better for general patient outcome—"

"What is better for general patient outcome," Yarborough said, cutting him off, "is a hospital raising a cadre of young residents into fully capable doctors. We are too remote and critical to allow interns to specialize, no matter how much teaching might inconvenience their attendings. You've not worked with civilians prior to taking this post, is that correct?"

"Yes, sir. I served with special operations medical support since the start," Matthew said stiffly. "The last few years were with SEAL Team Six."

"You do much teaching on SEAL Team Six, Jennson?"

"No, sir."

"Many women on that team?"

Matthew raised his chin. He knew the dress down routine well, having been on both sides of it more times than he could count. Knew that it too shall pass. "No, sir. None."

"How about first year residents, brand new doctors with all the expectations and none of the experience? Many of those there?"

"No, sir. We deployed only with seasoned personnel."

"Then maybe Dr. Carrell isn't the god damned problem in this equation, Jennson. Maybe I've more tolerance for a young doctor thrown into the deep end than I do for an attending who can't work out a way to teach her to differentiate her ass from her elbow. And maybe, just maybe, you should cut your losses and get the hell out of my office right now before I come up with a more creative way to get my point across. One thing to know about my department is that there is no bell here for you to ring because you find the job too difficult."

"Understood, sir." The suggestion that Matthew was somehow shirking his duties hit like a physical blow, reverberating through Matthew's body. He waited for Yarborough to dismiss him, then turned on his heels and walked out, keeping a rein on his emotions until he was well out of sight and range. Only then, in the privacy of a fourth floor locker room, did he allow himself a few minutes to brace his hands on his thighs and pull the shattered pieces of his dignity back together.

Ten minutes later, Matthew was walking back into the ER. Unlike the trauma hospitals in combat zones, everything around him was clean and spacious, blue and green colors moving about the sea of mostly quiet patients. Yarborough had certainly gotten one thing right, Matthew belonged here as little as Win did. But he had no other place to go.

"Dr. Jennson," Michelle, a skilled charge nurse who was the real power house behind keeping the ER operational, set an intercept course for him as she spoke. She also had years of experience keeping new doctors and nurses from killing patients, which currently made her the more valuable player of the two of them. Now, her brisk pace told him that the matter was urgent. "You'll want to check room three. Fifty-four year old male with chest pain and shortness of breath."

Matthew started to bay three at once. "EKG?"

Michelle handed him the iPad. "ST elevations."

"Fuck. Sorry." He flipped through the chart as they walked. "Win already saw him?" He found his own answer to that a moment later—a two page book report detailing the man's history going back to his grandmother's stubbed toe. Speaking of his forced protégé, where the hell was she? Matthew surveyed the ER, finding Win with her nose buried in a high-powered laptop, typing furiously and occasionally making some calculation-like gestures in the air with her index finger.

Fifty bucks said she'd gotten hold of a new batch of blood sample results and was now running some simulations on their genetic markers. Exactly the sort of activity that saved lives in an emergency room.

"Dr. Carrell," Matthew pitched his voice over the ER, making Win flinch. "With me, please."

Win ruefully put away her laptop and trotted over, her face weary. She didn't just dislike him, she was afraid of him. Granted, he'd yelled at her a few times, but it had always been for a good reason and he never punished her beyond a raised voice. Then again, that had been enough to send her into tears. He truly had no idea what to do with her. Win was six years younger, tiny, delicate, and shy. Happier with her computer than with patients and afraid of blood. God help him.

"Talk to me about the possible MI in three," Matthew said.

"Fifty-four year old man developed chest discomfort earlier today," Win kept her eyes on the data on her iPad as she spoke. "No history of cardiac disease, non-smoking, in good physical shape. He got nitro and baby aspirin. I ordered cardiac labs but—"

"What does he look like?" Matthew interrupted.

"Umm... Black hair, medium build. Is that what you mean?"

"I mean," Matthew said through his teeth, "does he look sick or not sick?"

"I..." Win swallowed. She had no idea. "His vitals are stable."

"Not what I asked." He pulled away the curtain to bay three to find an athletic middle aged man sitting on the edge of the bed. Pale face.

Sweat-beaded forehead. Extended jugular veins. Tripod position. Yeah. Sick. "Hello, Brian, I'm Dr. Jennson," Matthew said by way of introduction as he pulled the stethoscope off his neck to listen to heart sounds. "I understand you are having chest pain?"

"Just a bit of pressure really." Brian rubbed his arm. "Started feeling it toward the end of training. I do triathlons and today was a run day. I was going to let it sort itself out, but..." he shrugged. Frowned. The heart monitor attached to him beeped in alarm. "Oh god."

Brian grabbed at his chest.

Stethoscope abandoned, Matthew rushed forward and caught the man before he could fall off the table. Brian's eyes were wide open, his body a dead weight in Matthew's arms. On the still screeching monitor, the wave pattern changed to wide erratic curves. *Fuck!*

"V-fib on the monitor," Matthew announced. A heart attack at fifty-four in a man who took damn good care of himself. It wasn't fair. It was ugly. But Matthew wasn't going down without a fight. "Michelle, call a code team." He lay Brian flat on the bed and yanked the gown off his chest. "It's a witnessed MI and a shockable rhythm. We can still reverse this, people."

A code alert sounded, people rushing toward the bay to offer assistance. Matthew picked up the defibrillator paddles, a nurse already ready with conductive gel.

"Set the charge to one-twenty and prepare to start CPR as soon as I shock." His orders filled the room. He spoke slowly. Clearly. "Carrell, you'll manage the airway. Get your intubation kit ready. Someone draw up a milligram of epi and be ready. We're going to run this one in steady steps."

A quiet electrical whine sounded as the defibrillator dialed in the electricity. "Clear," Matthew called. Everyone stepped away from the table.

Everyone except Win, who was scrolling through her iPad as if the answer to Brian's life was buried in his genetic history.

"Carrell, do you have a death wish?" Matthew snapped.

"What? Oh!" She stepped away.

Matthew suppressed a growl, but this wasn't the time. "Shocking at one-twenty." He discharged the first round of electricity through Brian's chest, the man's body jerking slightly. "Shock delivered. No pulse. Start CPR."

A tech stepped into place over Brian's chest, beginning compressions. Matthew pressed two fingers against the carotid artery to check their effectiveness. On the other side of the patient, Win was yet to take control of the airway as he'd ordered, and one of the nurses had moved in to breathe for the patient in Win's stead.

"Dr. Carrell, are we distracting you from a good book?"

Win looked up from her iPad, her face pale. For once, the dread in her large hazel eyes had nothing to do with him. "He... The patient has a Do Not Resuscitate order on file, Dr. Jennson," she said so quietly she could barely be heard over the equipment. "We can't do this. Any of this. We can't save his life."

The tech doing chest compressions faltered. "What?"

Matthew shouldered the man out of the way and took over. "The DNR isn't valid. Brian came to the ER because he wanted help. If he wanted to die, he'd have gone to the morgue."

Win's throat bobbed. "But the advance directive—"

"Put down your god damned electronics and get control of your patient's airway before you kill him, *Doctor*." Despite his best efforts, Matthew's patience had finally reached the end of its tether. "Michelle, call the cath lab. Tell them we are coming up."

"Dr. Jennson," Michelle said his name with emphasis. She turned to Win, who now clutched the iPad against her chest and looked to be on the verge of tears. "When was the DNR signed?"

"Two... Two months ago, at this hospital," said Win. "With a witness. Do Not Resuscitate and Do Not Intubate orders. Both valid."

Michelle snapped her fingers. "I remember him now. Brian's wife had leukemia. She was here on her last day—we ran the code for an hour trying to bring her back. He watched it all, then asked about advanced directives. Poor man." She shook her head. "Looks like he went forward with his decision."

"Relive history later, call the cath lab now," said Matthew. Given the totality of the circumstance, he gave Brian two out of three odds of walking out of Denton Memorial.

Michelle blew out a long breath, her tone changing to briskness. "I'm sorry, Dr. Jennson, but the patient has a valid order. He does not wish heroic measures to be taken to save his life." She touched the elbow of the nurse providing ventilations, pulling her off the task.

Brian's oxygen levels plummeted.

Fury spilt into Matthew's blood, his heart pounding as loudly as the beeping monitors. They were holding a man's life here, not a fucking document. A man who'd come to them for help. Who was young and vibrant. Who could beat this if only his doctors stayed with him and fought.

And yet, Win and Michelle and everyone else in the room, all they saw were papers. Fucking papers and lawyers and legal documents. Matthew wanted to roar at them all. How many times had he fought for the slimmest chance when soldiers lay bleeding on his table? Had given his all to buy them just one more breath and one more hope, when all the textbooks said there was none? And here, now, when there was chance and hope a plenty, these people—these fucking civilians—wanted to stand by and do nothing?

Did they even hear the absurdity of their words?

Matthew glared up at Win, the one who opened the gates to this path of hell. The one who went looking—looking—for a reason to keep from saving a man's life. Because she thought the answers to the universe lay in her iPad.

Matthew let the full force of his wrath show in his eyes as spoke to Win directly. "Brian," he purposely used the man's name, "Brian was upset two months ago. He was grieving. But when he came in today, he did it because he wanted our help. Look at him. Look. At. Him! He is a human being, not a print out of whatever genetic code you think in."

Win stepped back.

Matthew finished the hundred compressions and grabbed the intubation kit from the cart, shoving Win bodily out of the way and slipping the tube inside.

The monitor beeped again, the waveform on the cardiac monitor shifting from ventricular fibrillation to a flatline. The monotonous note of asystole cut through the silent room.

"One milligram epinephrine IV," Matthew ordered.

No one moved.

The hammering in Matthew's heart became a drumroll that echoed through his bones. His hand closed around the edge of the table.

"Brian doesn't want to die. He wants to run the triathlon he was training for this morning." Matthew breaths came hard. "I don't give a flying fuck what that iPad says, Win. We save people's lives here. So you are going to put down your damn toy, push the epi as ordered, and keep this man from suffocating to death or I swear I am going to make your life a living hell whose fury you are yet to see. Am I clear?"

Win gripped her iPad like a security blanket. Her face was pale, her wide, hazel eyes rimmed with silver.

He stared her down, the monotone beep of the monitor was the only sound in the room.

"Persistent asystole," Michelle announced into the silence as if they didn't know how to read an EKG.

Matthew gave the patient two breaths of oxygen, pushed the epi himself, and continued compressions. Running a code alone was idiocy, but he'd done it before. In a world where they didn't have people standing around worrying about attorneys. On the table, Brian's body shuttered beneath the force of the compressions, the ribs giving way. Ninety eight. Ninety nine. One hundred.

He moved back to the airway, to deliver the oxygen, to check the pulse at Brian's neck in hopes that the epinephrine had done its job. It hadn't. Not yet.

"Get on his chest," Matthew snarled at Win. "That's an order."

"No," Win whispered.

Matthew's arms dropped away from the patient as he whirled on Win, towering over her, invading every inch of her space with his presence. He loosened that internal leash he usually held on his power and let the full impact of his years in the special forces, of giving orders that would send men to their deaths, fill his voice. "Start. Compressions. Now."

Win swallowed again and looked beyond him, to where the monitor still declared its verdict and the patient lay helpless on that table, with only the doctors around him standing between him and the end. Win's voice shook. "Time of death, 14:23," she whispered.

The words hit him like a blow. Matthew didn't need to look over to know that Michelle and the others were already turning off the equipment and disconnecting the leads. The world pulsed around him, like a bubble between him and the little doctor who'd planted herself on the wrong side of his wrath.

"That man didn't have to die today," Matthew snarled at her softly enough that only she could hear the words. "Fortunately, you were here to ensure he did. I hope you remember his eyes each time you close yours."

Without waiting for her retort, he grabbed the iPad from Win's hands and shattered it on the floor before walking away.

Matthew was halfway across the expanse of the ER when he tasted the first faint traces of sulfur. Just a hint, but it was enough. His stomach tightened, fear conquering the fury still pulsing though him. He twisted quickly, focusing on the door to the stairway, calculating how much time he still had. Auras were already floating in his vision. That fourth floor locker room was the best place to go, if he could make it. He took the stairs two at a time, slipping down the back corridor into the rarely used locker room and then into the far handicapped stall, the one where the door went all the way down to the floor.

Shit. Shit. Shit. Sulfur was coating his tongue now and the auras had turned colorful. Pulsing. Matthew had just enough time to ensure that the door was locked and lowered himself to the floor before the seizure gripped fully.

SONIA

One thing Sonia knew was that no matter how much Liam promised that Casey would be on his best behavior, the only one who was truly capable of setting the boundaries was Sonia herself. Not to mention the fact that Casey's notion of best behavior had little objective value.

The key, she decided, was to get their new partnership started on the right foot. To set the tone on the outset, while they were still on equal footing. This was her chance to set the ground rules and stop Casey's inevitable bullying and taunting before it started. Last time she and him worked together, Sonia had been caught off guard by what to expect. Now, she knew better. And now, he *needed* her.

To that end, Sonia was taking the initiative. She'd invited Casey back to Trident Security for their initial strategy session and now waited in one of the small formal conference rooms for the man to arrive. The room she reserved was close to her office and one she used regularly with attorneys and clients. Her turf. And since she had the home field advantage, she could also capitalize on it by setting up her things on the slightly more comfortable side facing the door, leaving Casey the visitor's side of the table.

It was all subtle, and likely not something Casey would ever even notice, but it wasn't for him. It was for Sonia herself. A subtle shield against the man who could reduce Sonia to uncertainty with a single raised brow.

The door opened and Sonia jumped at the noise, despite having been expecting company.

"Did I scare you?" Casey gave her a lazy grin from the door. Like her, he wore a business suit. Unlike hers, his cost several thousand dollars and enhanced every line of his unfairly perfect features.

You are a fat ass on a stick, Sonia-baby.

"Not at all." Sonia stood, running her hands over her pencil skirt to straighten it. "I'd expected the receptionist to tell me when you came, but she must have overlooked the request."

"I told her not to bother." Casey strode in like he owned the room. "Coming to tell you I'm here just to have me walk in a moment later seemed like a waste of time."

Sonia's jaw tightened. He'd countermanded her instruction to reception and reception listened to *him*. Pulling herself together, she reached inside herself for the mask of the courtroom and pointed to the empty chair she'd designated for him. "Thank you for coming, Mr. McKenzie."

"Mr. McKenzie?" He strode forward, hands in his pockets, muscles rippling beneath the expensive material. Amusement danced in his gray eyes and every one of his steps radiated that catlike predatory power that mocked Sonia's with every beat. Especially because it made her thighs clench despite herself. Casey titled his head, studying her. "Surely there is a more appropriate way to address your beloved fiancé?"

"It is an appropriate way of addressing my partner in an operation my boss asked me to participate in," said Sonia. "But to your point, yes, how we address each other in public is on the agenda of things for us to discuss. Please sit."

"There is an agenda?"

"Yes, of course." Sonia opened her leather portfolio. She'd prepared for this meeting as she would for any important conference, with everything printed and labeled with small, colored flags. But she wouldn't be giving the prick the time of day until he sat his toned ass down in the chair.

Casey must have sensed the line in the sand, because he pulled out a chair and sat across from Sonia, his hands folded in front of him on the table. He even reined in that perpetual smirk into something that resembled professionalism. Good enough. At least it was a start.

Sonia pulled the first sheet of paper out from her stack and slid it across the table. She'd thought for several hours last night about how to best present this part and decided to go with the straightforward approach.

"As we will be portraying two people intent on future marriage, there will be an expectation that we know basic facts about each other," she said. "I have prepared this life-resume for your reference. If you could prepare a similar document for me by close of business, I can review it by—"

"You dislike cooking shows," Casey said, interrupting her as he picked up the document and read off of it. "You try to watch all the Yale Bulldog games, especially when they face the Harvard Crimsons. Your favorite popcorn is Smartfood, though you only allow yourself to indulge in it when said Bulldogs are kicking the Crimsons' ass. Actually, no," he squinted at the page. "When the score difference swings in Yale's favor."

Sonia's skin heated. It sounded perfectly appropriate when she wrote it, but the way Casey read the list, enunciating every word, made her feel like a fool. Sonia captured a stray lock of hair that had escaped her bun and pushed it behind her ear. "I have full faith in your ability to read. There is no need to prove it."

"What's your bra size?"

Sonia's head snapped up. "What?"

"What's your bra size?" Casey repeated, utterly unphased. "And panty size, too. It's not listed here. As your fiancé, surely I'd have purchased little unmentionables for you on occasion. It would be awfully strange if I didn't know what size to acquire, wouldn't it?"

The warmth in Sonia's cheeks turned to full heat. The worst part of it was that Casey wasn't wrong. But the notion of sharing those numbers with him, of listing them out on a piece of paper... Sonia disliked sharing her measurements with salespeople trying to help find her a pair of jeans, sharing them with Mr. Sixpack was a bridge too far. "I will advise you of those numbers later," she said, holding on to that tether of professionalism for dear life. "For the moment—"

"I have an idea *for the moment*." Casey picked up Sonia's carefully composed resume, the one she'd assembled line by excruciating line, and ripped it. The expensive linen paper made a whooshing sound as it tore.

"What- "

"This is stupid," said Casey.

It was all Sonia could do to keep herself from flinching, to keep the sudden stinging in her eyes from becoming something more. She pulled her papers back toward herself, the carefully typed notes going back into the leather portfolio.

"You'll want to get some tape," she said, her attention fully on her task. "I'm not printing that for you again. And I'm not going to verbally go over what I've already taken time to write up in a memo."

Casey leaned forward, interlacing his fingers on the polished table top. "I'm not writing down a list of hobbies, favorite colors, or sexual positions for you."

"I never wrote down- "

"Likely because you've no imagination. Either way, if you are interested, I'll let you borrow a few books."

There they went again. Same old ground. Sonia rallied herself to try reason one last time.

"I need to seem as if I know you," she enunciated each word as if speaking to someone slow of mind. "Given how little interest I actually have in the subject, it would make it more efficient if you simply gave me a list of characteristics I should know. This whole thing isn't my idea of a good time, please don't make it harder than it is."

"Oh, for hell's sake," Casey threw up his arms. "Why don't we try something a little more practical, counselor. Spend two days with me. Find out if I'm even more irritating than you think I am. Otherwise you might spend all that energy being upset about the wrong vice of mine. Think about it. You'll be able to tell the world how truly awful I am as opposed to merely obnoxious."

Sonia didn't answer.

Casey's voice changed, taking on one of those rare notes of reason. "If you can't stomach spending a couple of days with me in Denton Valley, you are not going to be able to keep up any kind of façade on a cruise ship trapped in the middle of the ocean."

That, Sonia had to admit, was actually true.

As if sensing the shift of her thoughts, Casey pressed in on his advantage. "It would also be helpful if my fiancée could tell Briar and me apart. It's easy enough when Briar is being Briar, but you'll be surprised what we can pull off if the occasion calls for it."

Sonia had all but forgotten about Casey's twin, who usually kept to the shadows. A quiet contrast to Casey's exuberance.

"Maybe Briar should be going with me instead," she said.

"Talking up pricks at parties is Briar's definition of personal hell," said Casey. "So I can see why you like him. That said, he will be aboard. One of the passengers who isn't part of the reunion crowd. This isn't a high risk operation, but it's better to have backup and not need it than the other way around."

Sonia ran her fingers along her leather portfolio. Eleanor Roosevelt once said that no one could make you feel inferior without your consent, but Casey seemed to be an expert in just that. Because no matter which way she turned his point over in her mind, it was reasonable.

"Alright," she said, "so you showcase the entirety of your life to me in forty-eight hours?"

He nodded.

"And then, you follow me around like a lost puppy for two days in return?"

"I'm never lost," said Casey. "And I'm certainly no puppy. As for your life, I think I've got it down. There is only so much time I need to spend sitting in a law library to know that it's a miserable type of existence."

Sonia gave him a vulgar gesture that she hadn't used in a while.

Casey only grinned. "We have a month to get ready. Why don't we start with something simple. Like dinner. With food. And alcohol."

"I prefer not to drink."

"I prefer that you do drink," said Casey. "Spending time with your sober state is giving me a headache."

She took a breath. Compromise. They needed to compromise. "Fine. Dinner tonight."

"And then two days playing house at my apartment."

She let that go and leaned forward. "Fine. But in exchange, you are going to brief me into the *whole* operation, including whatever you know of Nero and the outlaw motorcycle gang the Tridents are going after."

Casey's brow lifted. In surprise or respect, Sonia didn't know. But then he shook his head, his blond hair swaying with the motion.

"That's Liam's call. He is the one who brought you into this, and only for the limited scope. Which in this case, is to be window dressing and my ticket into the dirty little world Nero runs." For once, Casey's voice held no condescension. If anything, he sounded somewhat sympathetic. "The Satan's Armada aren't nice people, and when shit hits the fan, you should be beyond any suspicion. My gut feeling is that Liam told you little of the criminal side of things on purpose. He doesn't want any impression that you may be aware of Nero's dealings. The best way of concealing knowledge is to not have it in the first place."

"I think this is the first time today that you and I are in complete agreement," said Sonia. "Liam is an overprotective mother bear. Why do you think I didn't press the point when he was in the room?"

Casey snorted.

She laid her palms flat on the table, her back straight. "I've no intention of being window dressing. So you are going to need to learn to work with some new rules of engagement. We go into this as partners. Actual partners, not the bullshit you pulled at Tara's trial last year. You share everything with me. No lying. No keeping me in the dark of your plan. And in return, I get you into the cool crowd. I play the too-dumb-to-live fiancé, and introduce you around like a bee spreading pollen. I go to your parties and dinners and follow you around to take note of your greatness." She paused. "Take the deal, counselor. You aren't getting a better one."

"And if I say no?" Casey's voice was utterly neutral.

Sonia shrugged, leaning back in her seat. "Then we go onto the *Belle Nuit*, where you get to enjoy all the spa treatments you'd like while I go to my reunion without you. Who knows, maybe you can catch Nero over a pedicure and talk him up that way."

Silence stretched between them, and Sonia realized that throwing down the gauntlet had felt good.

Casey weighed her with his gaze.

She had no idea what he might be looking for, or whether he found it, before he spoke again. "If Liam finds out about this little pact, we are both going to be grounded faster than we can say 'just kidding'. If you can handle that, handle keeping all this from your boss, then… then I will pick you up for dinner tomorrow night."

CASEY

"You look like shit," Casey told Matthew as he circled him in the sparring ring while Briar caught his breath from the previous round. Matthew's blond hair was plastered against his forehead and there was an icy fire blazing in his blue eyes. The doc wore a pair of gym shorts and no shirt, the panes of his muscled abdomen shifting as he adjusted his fighting stance.

"Less talking, more fighting," said Matthew.

Casey lowered his level, sweeping his foot viciously at Matthew's leg. Matthew jumped over the assault, but gave up his right side. Casey punched his ribs. Hard.

Matthew grunted, but kept fighting in the same vein as he'd started the round. Hard and reckless. As if this were a brawl. The doc was usually a precise striker, but today he seemed to be in the ring as much to take a beating as to dole one out.

They'd all been there, and would be again. Casey had no problem obliging if that was what his friend needed. He just wasn't certain that was all Matthew needed this morning.

The doc swung and Casey took the hook on his torso, moving in so close that the attack lost some of its power. He grabbed Matthew's sweat-slicked shoulders and yanked him down into his knee-strike.

Casey felt his knee connect against hard muscle and heard Matthew's breath catch from the impact. Casey's own breathing came in hard puffs now, his heart keeping the beat of the fight like a metronome.

Matthew was still doubled over. Casey cut a quick glance at Briar. His twin nodded. Not giving the doc a chance to recover, Casey threw him to the ground.

To his credit, Matthew rolled with the throw, managing to get on top of Casey and straddle his chest before trying to pummel his face into pulp. Thank fuck they wore gloves. It still hurt, but at least nothing would break. Most likely.

Finally catching one of Matthew's arms, Casey flipped the man off of him and danced back again, waiting until they were both standing to re-engage. Kick. Move. Block. Again. Again. Fast and brutal and without a moment's reprieve. Leather gloves hit sweaty flesh, feet struck against blocks of coiled muscles. Casey's own lungs burned.

Matthew ducked beneath Casey's defenses and came up with a right hook that hit home. Casey's head rang, blood trickling into his mouth.

"Keep your fucking guard up," Matthew snarled.

Casey wiped his mouth with the back of his hand. So that's how it was going to be, was it? He dropped down in a wrestler's shot, taking Matthew's legs out from under him. The moment the doc fell onto the mat, Casey was on him, pressing his shin viciously over Matthew's ribs and digging his knee into the doc's vulnerable solar plexus.

Matthew's lips pulled back, pain drawing the lines of his face.

Casey grabbed and pulled up on Matthew's head, cinching the pin down further. "So," he said, his voice deceptively casual for the fight they were having. "What did you fuck up?"

Matthew punched him. Or tried to. He wasn't in much of a position to do anything.

"You kill someone?" Casey asked.

Matthew gathered his strength and last bits of air to attempt to shove Casey off. He'd have managed it too, if Casey hadn't chosen that moment to jump over to Matthew's other side and jam his other knee into the doc's ribs.

Rage fluttered over Matthew's face.

"Time," Briar called.

Casey didn't move. This fight wasn't done. Matthew wasn't done with whatever it was he needed to work out.

"Let him go," Briar ordered.

"I'm performing a public service," said Casey. "Doc's half asleep. If he's not killed anyone yet, he will shortly. Do you know what kind of sharps and drugs they let him play with at the hospital?"

Matthew took advantage of Casey's talking to throw him off, but instead of re-engaging, walked off to the edge of the mat. Bracing his hands on his thighs, Matthew drew in big gulps of air. His glassy eyes finally focused, taking in Casey's bloody lip.

Matthew swore.

Casey shook it off. "It's nothing."

"Let me see." There was too much guilt in the demand. Whatever was eating Matthew was far from the sparring ring. Even after the match they just had.

Casey waved him off. "Keep your hands to yourself, Doc."

Briar eyed Matthew critically and reached for his headgear. "Again?" he asked. An equivalent of "anything I can do to help?" in Briar's world.

Matthew started to nod, then looked at the clock and cursed. "I need to get back to the ER before goldilocks starts wandering the floor unsupervised." He pulled off his headgear and gloves, and started to unwrap his wrists. "Is Dancer on board with the *Belle Nuit* plan?" he asked over his shoulder.

"Of course she is," Casey drawled. "What woman wouldn't want to be my fiancée? Or man for that matter."

Briar snorted. "A smart one."

Matthew kept his attention on the few things he was packing up. "I re-read the intel from Sky. That's the best way forward." He straightened. "I'm on shift tomorrow morning. Eighteen hundred?"

Briar muttered an agreement. Casey blocked Matthew's way out. A last ditch attempt to get at whatever it was they hadn't worked out on the mat. "What's going on, Jennson?"

For a moment, Matthew looked like he was going to say something. Then he just shook his head and pushed past, heading for the door. "I'll see you tomorrow."

Casey watched Matthew disappear out the door of their small gym. He'd shower back at the hospital. "Denton Memorial should be charging him rent," he said, then turned to Briar. "Fifty bucks says he lost a patient."

"Hundred says he's in love," Briar replied.

Casey winced and got back into the sparring ring, this time to face his twin.

***

AFTER CASEY and Briar wrapped up their morning workout and spent a few hours on the business logistics needed to keep the North Vault running smoothly, Casey turned his attention to the upcoming evening and the trial by fire dinner date he had with Sonia Dancer. Pulling out his laptop, Casey opened the browser to look for a restaurant. On the couch beside him, Briar was working on beefing up security around the club. Satan's Armada's roaming of Denton Valley's streets was becoming an issue, especially for the women. The bikers seemed to think of females as utility instruments put on earth for their pleasure and service.

It reminded Casey of his father. He wondered if Briar had made the same connection, but was smart enough not to ask. Benjamin McKenzie didn't ride a motorcycle, but that was where the differences ended.

Shoving away those thoughts, Casey focused on the decision at hand. Specifically, finding a place that the counselor might enjoy enough to overlook her dislike of him. "You think lobster?" he asked Briar. "Or steak?"

"How the fuck would I know?"

Casey made a noise with his throat and scrolled down the list of top rated restaurant reviews. "Small and intimate or large and famous?"

"Again, how the fuck would I know?"

"Maybe I'm looking at this wrong. Do you think the counselor would prefer a formal dress kind of place or something more casual? Sweater and jeans?" She'd look delicious in either one, especially if it showed the curve of her hip a bit.

"I think she'd prefer a spot in frozen hell so long as it's without you," said Briar.

"Fair point," said Casey. "Surf and turf at a Chez Loupe then. Nothing says I'm a man of taste like a good cut of meat and a better glass of wine. And I know the chef." He knew the chefs at most of Denton's top restaurants actually, but Loupe owed him a favor. If anyone could harmonize the evening, it would be him. Plus, the French knew how to do dinner.

"Don't take her to bed," Briar said, his attention squarely on his computer screen. From the furious typing, he was arguing with someone.

Casey raised a brow at his brother. "Strictly business. We are preparing for Operation Finding Nero." Not that he'd mind running his hands over the counselor's hips if she were interested.

Briar closed his computer. "I'm serious. She's one of Liam's people and he'll tear your balls off. And mine too for good measure."

"I'm offended."

"You are peaked because you've found the one woman on earth who has no interest in fucking you. And I'm telling you to not mess with her. She'll get hurt. We'll get hurt. Everyone will fucking be hurt."

Casey made the reservation, clicking the keys with more force than required. "I wouldn't hurt her," he said, all traces of amusement gone from his voice. Annoy, tease, flirt—sure. But not hurt. He'd never do that. The fact that Briar even voiced as much aloud was insulting.

* * *

SONIA WASN'T WEARING an evening dress when Casey picked her up on the small street filled with poorly maintained, multi-family homes. She wasn't wearing jeans either. No. Sonia Dancer had come to dinner in a business suit. Either because she didn't actually own other clothes or because she had no concept of how people dressed for an evening out. That at least, was one problem Casey knew how to solve. Her choice of domicile on the other hand... He shook his head.

The building looked run down, even by this street's standards, and the top two floors were completely dark. "You live with vampires?" Casey asked. He hoped so, because those would be the safer creatures in this neighborhood. "Doesn't Liam pay you a decent wage?"

"My neighbors on the second floor moved out about a month ago," said Sonia. "The landlord is still looking for occupants."

"Maybe there is a reason no one rents here."

"Maybe there is." Sonia adjusted her pencil skirt. It suited her well, though. Casey looked forward to seeing her in something looser, seeing that hair of hers released into the wind from the bun she kept it jailed in. Like she kept everything in. Except him.

Him she kept utterly out.

"Have you ever been drunk?" Casey asked, turning onto the main road.

"No," said Sonia. "Have you?"

"Of course. Many times. Why haven't you?"

She shrugged. "It has never been an interest. I do drink. Just not to excess."

"And high?"

"Have I ever been high? Of course not. I imagine I don't need to bother asking you the same question." There was a note of reprimand in her voice. "Where are we going?"

"McDonalds."

"Really?" asked Sonia.

"There is a happy meal toy I've been dying to get my hands on." Casey cut her a glance, looking for a smile and a roll of the eyes. For something.

Sonia pressed her lips together. "Is this how you intend to spend our entire time together? By criticizing where I live and answering my questions with quips?"

Well, this was starting out marvelously.

"Tell me about Nero," said Sonia. All business. Just not the business they needed to be in this evening.

Casey considered his options as he pulled onto the freeway. Fine. Maybe if he gave her a taste of what she wanted, she'd at least consider trusting him. "New player on the scene, arrived as an attorney for the Satan's Armada as they started to grow in numbers exponentially over the past year. There is speculation that in addition to keeping them out of prison he also assists with running the back end of the business."

"What's the back end of the motorcycle club?"

Casey reined himself in from taking the opening. "Guns mostly. Some drugs. Prostitution."

"And Nero, he is a biker as well?"

"As far as we know he is just a paid suit with access to information. Hopefully, one who doesn't share your aversion to alcohol and will be happy to chat." Casey checked his mental map and made a sharp turn, having nearly missed the street he sought.

Sonia gasped as the car took the corner like a champ, her long fingers gripping the seat. "Was that necessary?"

"No. But it was entertaining." Casey spotted the boutique he wanted and pulled up to the curb at its door. "We can talk about Nero later."

"Where are we?"

"At a magical place called a store. Here, they have things called clothes that are not business suits. With the help of Roma and a small miracle, we might be able to find something that resembles dating attire for you." Casey got out of the car and shook hands with the young man, Roma, who was already coming out to greet them.

"Casey!" Roma grinned, flashing the kind of smile that ensured his bed never stayed empty. He scanned Casey unabashedly, probably undressing and dressing him in a new outfit in his head. He was welcome to it. The Italian had impeccable taste and was the only one in Denton who Casey trusted blindly with his wardrobe. And now, with Sonia's. "What will we create this evening?"

"I've a challenge for you today," Casey said, flinching as Sonia slammed the car door. He inclined his head toward her. "Sonia, this is Roma, the owner of the aptly named Roma Viale. Roma, this is the praying mantis I need you to make over into something that hides her nature. And do be careful—she takes joy in castrating anyone who comes too close."

Roma smiled at Sonia, his perfect white teeth flashing.

Sonia did not smile back. If anything, for the first time since he'd met her, the counselor looked positively terrified.

SONIA

Sonia, who'd gotten out of the car on instinct, now felt her hand tighten on the door handle. Two men turned to look at her, undressing and redressing her with their eyes. Two beautiful men, each a perfection in his own right, though they were as different from each other as branches of law.

Against their explicit agreement, Casey hadn't brought her to a restaurant. He brought her to Roma Viale, a high-end exclusive boutique that even Sonia had heard of. It was a personal service kind of place where they probably hemmed your socks for you—not that Sonia could afford a pair of socks here. And even if she could, the boutique catered to the kind of bodies one saw on magazine covers and Victoria's Secret ads. Tall women with mile long legs, tight hips, breasts large enough to complement the perfect package, and perfect faces that gave sirens a run for their money.

Sonia checked none of those categories. She knew it. And Casey, observant as he was, knew it, too. Was this another one of his jokes then? A bit of amusement at her expense? If his usual jests were just annoying, this one... this one hurt. Even if he didn't know how much Sonia hated shopping for clothes, which never—*ever*—looked the way they were supposed to on her, he sure as hell knew she wasn't a runner up for the catwalk caliber men and women Roma Viale made clothing for.

"Shall we go inside, Bella Donna?" Roma asked, his understated exquisite shirt a perfect compliment to rich tanned skin.

Bella Donna. It wasn't even funny anymore.

"I'm sorry, there appears to be some misunderstanding." Sonia gathered all the dignity she could muster. Her hand was still on the car door, her palm turning sweaty. "I'm not going to be doing any shopping today."

"Then we shall simply enjoy ourselves with your makeover." Roma flashed that smile of his, his italian accent coating each word in honey. "I've a dress that I'd be delighted to swathe you in."

Sonia's stomach clenched. Unlike Casey, Roma was probably trying to be kind, but she'd learned the hard way that nothing on her looked the way it did on a model—or a hanger. No clothing maker ever sat down to design garments for fat asses on sticks. Sonia ordered all her things online, from a few sites that seemed to fit misfits, and tried everything on in the privacy of her bathroom.

The only thing more humiliating than proving even Roma couldn't put lipstick on this pig, would be doing it in front of Casey, whose body could make a trash bag look good.

Realizing that Roma was still looking at her expectantly, Sonia managed a smile that didn't reach her eyes. "Thank you for your hospitality," she said. "I'm sorry for wasting your time."

Roma frowned as if she'd personally wounded him.

Casey frowned as if she were an obstinate toddler protesting zipping up a winter jacket.

"Excuse us," he told Roma. Walking over to Sonia, he gripped her by the upper arm and walked her a few steps away from the car. Her skin seared where he'd gripped her, all her attention flowing to that spot of sudden contact. It wasn't a bruising grip, but it was firm.

He let go of her arm only to square off, blocking her escape route to the car. With his feet shoulder-width apart and broad arms crossed over his chest, he took up all the air between them. He was so close that she could smell his earthy aftershave, the heat of his body trailing over her skin. Her arm still tingled where he'd gripped her.

"What's with you?" Casey demanded quietly. "You'd think I brought you to the dentist."

No it wasn't. Sonia could handle the dentist a lot better than she could a full body mirror.

"This isn't what we agreed to," said Sonia.

"Yes, a monumental deviation from an agenda. Let's chalk this one up to my desire for efficiency." He gave her a half smile. "And my curiosity over how you'd look in a few of those lacy things Roma keeps in the back."

She knew what he was trying to do, but that cocky smile had the opposite effect on her. She wouldn't wear "lacy things" in front of a mirror in the dark, much less a living human. Much less a living god. She appreciated that Casey didn't rub her appearance in her face, but this, pretending she wasn't what she was, it turned decency into absurdity. And it hurt. "Not funny."

"Wasn't a joke," said Casey. "Come on, Counselor. Company credit card and a delicious personal designer. It will be fun."

She shook her head.

Casey's jaw tightened. "Let's. Go."

An order this time.

"Let's. Not." Her nostrils flared. She no longer cared whether Casey was indeed enjoying a joke at her expense, or simply didn't understand what it was like for someone who didn't share his physique, or was now simply flexing his alphahole muscles. She wasn't doing this.

Her heart quickened. Phantom voices spoke in her memories again. Phantom hands ripped her clothes. Phantom lips sneered in disgust.

Don't pretend I'm not doing your cunt a favor. No one else would touch that fat ass.

Sonia, honey, I'm not saying you are making it up, but perhaps you misremembered something? You were drinking a bit. I've been partners with Robbins for a decade. He isn't that kind of man. And if he was interested in a college girl, frankly, he could hire one that looked like a centerfold of a playboy. Why would he go after you?

Sonia blinked and the phantoms dissolved, replaced by Casey still towering over her and glowering in irritation.

She didn't care how irritated or annoyed he was though. She already felt naked. Humiliated by a makeover that hadn't even happened, the hidden cringes on Casey and Roma's faces as an expensive skirt ripped at the seams over Sonia's hips. The sad fact was that Casey, who probably had his entire apartment lined with mirrors just so he could look at himself, would never understand the emotions going through her. Giving up all pretense of being composed, she stepped around Casey and yanked on the car door.

Locked.

Sonia's breath quickening to match her heart. She yanked the door again, feeling Casey come up behind her. She could hear his breath, feel his presence at her back. Images that she knew had nothing to do with the now flashed through her body. Things that weren't going to happen, but could. A locked car. A dark night. A man who could break her into two wanting—insisting—that she try to wiggle herself into lingerie for his amusement. She knew none of it was real, but the shame, the vulnerability, that was visceral enough to scramble her thoughts.

Sonia yanked the handle again and again, pulling with all her might. The door swung open suddenly and Sonia fell backwards onto her ass. She stared at her hands, half expecting to find a broken off piece of ferrari in her grip. Her gaze cut to Casey, who was looming over her again, a keyfob in his hand.

He'd unlocked the door.

"The car is innocent in all this, you know," he said. His voice was straining for amusement, but it wasn't there. He held out his hand to help her up.

Sonia ignored it and rose. "Take me home. I want to go home right now."

"What's going on?" he asked. "What the hell just happened?"

"I want to go home."

Casey tightened his jaw, a muscle straining along the side of his face. Despite the evening, she could make out each one of his features, from the ferocity in his gray eyes to the wisps of dirty blond hair fluttering in the wind. All of his attention was on her, gripping her as firmly as his hands could.

Humiliation drenched Sonia from head to toe. She was making a fool of herself. She wanted to run. To go back to her quiet street and empty house and dark apartment and hide. She reached for her phone to call an Uber only to realize that she'd left her clutch in the car.

Casey followed her gaze. Saying nothing, he gave Roma an apologetic shrug and walked around to the driver's side.

Sonia stayed where she was.

Casey leaned over. The passenger's door was still wide open. "Are you going to get inside?"

Sonia hesitated, her attention on that clutch.

"If you can't tolerate so much as being in the same car as me," Casey said quietly, with none of the lightly amused notes Sonia was used to, "then there is no chance of us pretending to be together on a cruise ship in the middle of the ocean." There was no accusation in his even voice. No anger. No emotion at all. Just a cool statement of fact.

If Sonia hadn't felt like an absolute idiot before, she certainly did now. Face blazing, she got into the front seat, her hands gripping her clutch.

"I'm sorry," she said as Casey put the car into reverse and angled them back out onto the highway. His eyes stayed on the road. Still not angry, like they should have been. Just… hard.

"You don't really have to take me home," said Sonia. "We can still go out to dinner as we planned."

"I'll take you home," said Casey.

Shit. "No need. Really. I changed my mind."

"I've lost my appetite." Casey pressed down on the gas, the powerful car gobbling up the fuel.

Sonia let out a long breath. "So that's it? I don't want to go shopping on your schedule, and now you want nothing to do with me? You're going to end this whole operation before it starts?"

Casey cut the wheel, pulling the car over onto the wide shoulder and breaking to a hard stop beneath a large highway light. Sonia doubted he chose the particular spot at random. She was certain of it as he turned to her, his entire face clearly visible while the tension crackled between them. Slowly, deliberately, Casey shifted the car into park and twisted toward her.

"I don't care whether you want to go shopping or not," said Casey. "I don't care whether you find me pleasant company or not. Hell, I don't even care if you stay up at night conjuring the many new ways you can think of cutting off my balls and shoving them down my throat." His jaw tightened, that muscle clenching along it again. "What I do care about, is you looking at me like you think I'm going to backhand you across the face. So no, Counselor, I don't have any appetite left for the evening."

Before Sonia could respond, Casey shifted the car back into drive, skidding off from a stop to seventy-five miles an hour as fast as the engine would take him. He didn't say another word to her as he found his way back to her house and opened the door to make sure she got the hell out.

SONIA

"I feel like an utter idiot." Sonia told Win as they ate in the small staff room at Denton Memorial's ER. Sonia wasn't technically supposed to be there, but it was the only place she could catch Win most days—and so she'd sweet talked the hospital's legal team into getting her a staff badge in return for a promise to help with the occasional legal overflow. She adjusted her chopsticks and dove into the beef lo mein, still in its carton. "What am I supposed to do now?"

"Have you talked since?" Win asked. She was chomping down on fried rice like she'd not eaten in days. Between the ER and her own research, which Win insisted on continuing even while she served her time here, it was possible she hadn't. Even now she had her laptop balanced on her lap and was splitting her attention between it, Sonia, and the food.

Sonia winced. "We texted."

Win put down her carton. "It's been a week. The cruise is at the end of the month. Are you still going?"

"We are." That was as far as their texting had gone. Yes, they were still going. No, Casey's suddenly busy schedule didn't allow for dinner just now. Yes, they'd work things out on the fly. "He's a professional, so he isn't going to scrap the whole op because I hurt his feelings."

She had hurt his feelings, Sonia realized that night after Casey had dropped her off. She'd typed out an apology text several times, but each attempt sounded even more awkward than the last, so she'd finally given up.

Win pointed at Sonia with a pair of chopsticks. "First, you are no idiot. Absolute or otherwise. Given what you've been through, a little jumpiness when someone invades your space and wants you to take your clothes off is an understandable reaction."

"Casey doesn't know—"

"It's none of his business," Win said. "And second, it is highly debatable who exactly should have egg on their face. Because from where I sit, the big bad Delta guy is potentially compromising an operation because someone looked at him the wrong way. If that's not stupid I don't know what is." She popped her chin up, punctuating the last statement.

"Your talents are utterly wasted in medicine, Win. You should have been an attorney."

Win scowled. "So long as I'm not required to stick needles into people or carry severed limbs to the OR, I'm ready to sign up for the LSAT exams tomorrow. I actually gave a patient a blood bath trying to find a vein earlier today. There was... a great deal of unhappiness on all sides of that." Win put down her food and stretched her back. She was tiny, one of those people who didn't put on an ounce of weight no matter how badly she ate. If Casey wanted to take someone to Roma Viale, he should have taken the petite doctor.

Sonia realized she'd said her last thought aloud when Win shook her head, her golden curls shifting behind her. "I look like I'm twelve. Like I actually had to get scrubs from pediatrics—they keep some around for the kids. You know how patients stare at me when I walk into a treatment room?" she shuddered. "I had one lady yesterday who wouldn't believe I'm a 'real doctor' even after I showed her my ID."

Win glanced out the door, her gaze going to the electronic monitor the staff here seemed to live by. To Sonia's eyes, the place seemed to be running at a slightly slower bustle, as evidenced by the fact that they'd managed a whole ten bites without interruption. Still, every time a new line got added to the screen or someone seemed to set course for the staff room, Win seemed to jump in her seat a bit.

Matthew had Win running scared, and Sonia liked none of it.

"With the cruise fiancé thing, it will work out, hun," Win continued. "It's only ten days. You can do ten days standing on your head. And you are both too professional and too stubborn to let this dumpster fire spill over into your work, not when it counts."

"I'm not stubborn," said Sonia.

"Oh, let's see. You won't touch a penny of your dad's money on principal, worked all through Yale Law, graduated at the top without all those fancy tutors everyone else hired, *and* got yourself hired into a top security firm in Colorado."

"That's not stubbornness," said Sonia.

"Technically no, it isn't," said Win. "The stubborn part is that I'm pretty sure you did it all just to spite your father."

Sonia stuck her tongue out.

Win snorted.

"How are things here?" Sonia asked, changing the subject before Win could offer any more diagnosis. "Is Matthew being the usual level of arrogantly unbearable, or is it tipping more toward narcissitically horrible?"

"We're definitely in the horrible. Matthew pretty much hates everything about me. And I hate everything about this place." She frowned into her half eaten rice. "There is so much pain here. People arriving in pain, us causing more pain, everyone rushing about in hoards from one room to the next as if it's all a big zoo exhibit. Even when everything goes well, I don't like it. And when it doesn't... It's even worse when it doesn't. What I don't understand is why Matthew is even here. Clearly he'd prefer to still be putting on tourniquets and squatting with snakes somewhere."

"What does Sith say?"

"He's got no idea either."

Win's screen beeped and she looked down, surprise and glee filling her face. "Well, well, well."

"What is it?"

"Can your attorney self put on a set of earmuffs for a sec?"

Sonia pantomimed putting on a headset.

Win's eyes sparkled. "This whole why is Matthew even here thing has been eating at me. So I decided to do a little investigating. Point of information—watch who else is around when entering a pin into your phone and for heaven's sake don't allow connections to unsecured networks. Anyway, the man is as quiet online as he is in person, except for a little foray into a dark web pharmaceutical forum which I just caught."

Sonia shook her head. "Are you telling me Matthew Jennson is buying drugs on the black market?"

"Drug, not drugs. At least so far. Lamotrigine."

"Is that like cocaine?"

"Nope. It's an anti-seizure medication. Simple to get on the up and up." Win raised a brow. "Unless you don't want anyone to know you have seizures."

"Shit," Sonia whispered. "Remind me never to get on your bad side. What are you going to do with that?"

Win's gaze hardened. "I don't know yet. I don't even know whether the meds are for him or someone else. But I've more teeth than Matthew Jennson thinks I do."

"Fred, bay five," Matthew's voice rang through the ER. The man himself leaned halfway out from behind a curtained compartment a moment later. His gaze found Win quickly, as if he'd been zeroed in on her location earlier and was now simply pressing the trigger. "Motorcyclist against concrete. You can guess who won."

"That's not my name," Win said, but the words were not nearly loud enough to breach the distance between her and Matthew. She looked back at Sonia and shook her head. "He thinks it's funny."

"I don't get it."

"Winifred—aka, Fred." Win sighed. "He's been on a kick with that for days. The louder the better."

Anger rose inside Sonia. She stood up, flanking Win toward bay five.

"You can't come with me," Win hissed. "There is a patient in there. It's not a bring a friend kind of thing."

"I'm not coming with you to see the patient. I'm coming to have a chat with a certain resident about the hospital's hazing and harassment policy." Sonia straightened her staff badge, her heart already pounding a steady beat against her ribs. It was one thing when an arrogant ass pushed her own buttons, but when one came after Win, it was a different matter altogether. "I may be unable to change the ER rotation policy, but I certainly can slap a censure on a certain loudmouth attending. There is nothing like a threat of rising malpractice insurance costs to make people think twice about bullying others."

"You don't have to," said Win, but there was a grateful note in her tone.

"I want to. Trust me." Sonia pulled down her sweater as she walked. She wasn't in her usual business suit battle armor, but the anger roaring in her blood was making up for that well. "Plus, I'd rather stop this before you snap one day and use some hacker nuclear option."

As they neared the treatment room though, Matthew's voice reached them again, this time from the other side of the curtain. It was quieter, but no less harsh. With a start, Sonia realized that Matthew was now berating the *patient*. Her brows rose as f-bombs filled the air, along with a graphic description of what happened to other imbeciles who rode motorcycles without a helmet. She didn't doubt that he was accurate—or that Denton Memorial was about to get sued.

She put an arm out to stop Win. "Wait. It may be better if you hang back a moment. Does he talk like this to patients often?"

"To patients? No," Win shook her head, talking as softly as Sonia had. "I mean he's always direct, but he usually saves the dressing down for me."

"He talks to you like that?"

"Not the swearing," said Win. "At least not usually. Sith says it's a military thing."

Matthew shoved himself out of the treatment bay, fury hanging around him like a nuclear cloud. Tall, muscled, and confident, he looked like someone Hollywood would stick a stethoscope on for a romance film. Except for the attitude, which was closer to the Full Metal Jacket genre.

"Can I help you?" Matthew said, spotting Sonia at Win's side.

"Actually, I thought I could help you." Sonia bladed her body to put herself between him and Win while simultaneously cutting off his escape path. "I'm Sonia Dancer, an adjunct for Denton Memorial's legal office, and—"

"I know who you are, Dancer," Matthew said, cutting her off. "But if you could take whatever riot act you were about to read to me and read it to your *fiancé* instead, we would all be much obliged."

Sonia blinked. "Your pardon?"

Matthew yanked open the curtain to the treatment bay behind him, revealing Casey sitting on the bed's edge and holding a wad of bloody gauze to his forehead. He was dressed in a pair of jeans and torn jacket, both covered with mud and blood. Everything about Matthew's recent rant took on a new perspective.

"What happened?" Sonia asked.

Casey's gray eyes, filled with pain and irritation, took her in. "Borrowed Aiden's bike. Hit a rock. Fell." He turned back toward Matthew. "Doesn't the hospital have rules about visitors?"

Matthew's lips pulled back, showing his teeth. "Ms. Dancer is an adjunct of our legal office, you see. She has full access to the ER. So no, asshole, you get to hear what she thinks of your brilliance in as much detail as she wishes to share." He turned to Sonia. "Did you know that helmetless motorcycle drivers are a top source of organs for us around here?"

Sonia was still putting the pieces together, but for this one isolated moment, she was actually on board with Matthew. Casey could have hurt himself badly. Did hurt himself. And seeing him there, on a hospital bed, with blood coating his face and clothes... Sonia didn't like it at all. Especially because she now longed to run her fingers along Casey's skin, ensuring he was alright for herself. Not that she would give in to it. "Why didn't you wear a helmet?"

"I don't own a bike, why would I own a helmet?" Casey said.

"Aiden—" she started to say.

"Aiden's didn't fit. Can you save your insightful questions for some other time possibly?" said Casey.

What was it with men cutting her off? "Next time, feel free to do the genetic pool a favor and splatter your brains completely," she snapped.

Behind her, Matthew snorted.

Casey glared at him.

"She isn't wrong," Matthew said.

"How fast were you going, Mr. McKenzie?" Win asked, taking a look at Casey's wounds and wincing. "Do you remember?"

"It's Casey. And no, I don't. Not fast enough for Ms. Dancer's preference, clearly." He gave Win one of his smiles as she helped him out of his shirt, revealing a scattering of shallow, but impressive scratches along his shoulder blade—and a lithe chiseled body that made heat rush along Sonia's skin. With the exception of the cuts and an impressive collection of scars, smooth skin covered a six pack along his abdomen and stretched taut over his pecks. A set of intricate tattoos coiled around Casey's left bicep and Sonia wondered whether Briar had the same one, or if she'd found that difference between the twins.

For a moment, Sonia was unable to help but imagine what that body might feel like next to hers. Touching. Holding. Twining around her own. She didn't dare look down to the bulge in Casey's jeans. If the rest of him was any indication as to what hid there... hell. It was enough to moisten a set of panties.

So long as it all stayed safely in her imagination at least. In reality, Sonia wasn't sure that her body would be quite so receptive to a man's touch. Not anymore.

Win braced her small hand on Casey's chest as she examined his shoulder blade and he shifted to give her better access. "You have a good touch, Doc."

A muscle twitched along Matthew's jaw. A small movement, that was there and gone in an instant. "On the odd chance there is actually something between your ears, I'm sending you for a head CT," he said roughly. "Fred, draw some blood. A lot of blood."

Win paused her exam to frown at Matthew. "What are we testing for?"

"Check him for lyme disease and lupus for all I care. Just draw the labs. Personally." Matthew turned on his heels and stalked away.

Casey's attention swung back to Win, who'd now stepped away from the bed and scowled at the opening through which Matthew had just left. "So," he asked, "are you good at drawing blood?"

"No," said Win.

"Yeah. That tracks." Casey swung himself further onto the bed and held his arm out to her.

Win stayed where she was.

Casey gave her an encouraging nod—though the movement made his eyes glaze in a flash of pain. "I don't mind the extra prodding, especially if I can talk you into some advice afterwards. Or a shot of whiskey."

A hint of a smile touched Win's lips. Yep, Casey's signature charm had won another one to his side.

"I'm not drawing labs just for the sake of tormenting you," Win said. "If Jennson is so hell bent on it, he can do it himself. As for the pain meds, didn't he give you any yet?"

"What do you think?" said Casey.

"I think someone needs to slap him upside the head and I'm too short to reach," said Win. She picked up the iPad. "I'll check on the CT scan and see about getting you something for pain. Give me a few minutes."

Left alone with Casey, Sonia let out a slow breath. The coward inside her wanted to follow Win out, but she was mature enough to take a step toward him instead. Even if he was shirtless and masculine and—for once—not making her look like an idiot in front of everyone. A low bar for manners, but it was Casey.

"Are you alright?" she asked.

"I'm fine." He closed his eyes, leaning his head back against the head of the bed. "Jennson is being an overprotective hen, but he is pissed not worried. He gets like that."

Sonia wondered whether Casey knew why Matthew might be ordering seizure meds on the down low, but it wasn't her information to share. She stepped closer to the bed. "What were you doing anyway?" After a week of terse text messages, it was strange to be having a normal conversation. Strange but good.

"Wanted to see Denton from the bastards' vantage point. In case it helped understand something about them." He shrugged, his eyes staying closed as if the light hurt. "The bike turned out to be less cooperative than I expected."

Her brows rose. "You've never ridden before?"

"Not at all."

"Good god, Casey," Sonia realized that she'd gripped his shoulder only when his eyes popped open, his gaze cutting to where her fingers wrapped around his warm skin. Her mouth dried, a touch of heat kissing her face. It was all she could do to keep from yanking her hand away and calling even more attention to the touch. "Matthew is right. That really was stupid."

"Look at the bright side," Casey's gray eyes caught hers. "If I'd killed myself, you wouldn't have to go on the cruise with me."

The words hung between them. A not question that was really a question.

Sonia pulled her hand away and straightened her sweater, which was just fine to begin with. "I wouldn't dream of depriving you of a week of partying in the name of the greater good."

A corner of his mouth twitched. "You'll be partying right along with me, Counselor."

Nothing about that sounded appealing. She cleared her throat. "Do you want me to call Briar to pick you up?"

Casey started to shake his head then thought better of it. "He's not around. I'll drive back."

"Like hell you will," Matthew came back into the bay, a suture kit in hand. He grabbed a fresh pair of gloves from the box and pulled a tray table over to him, starting to lay out his things atop a blue drape.

None of it looked appealing, though Matthew's hands moved with an easy competence. "With a concussion you aren't staying home alone overnight either."

"You can come sleep in my bed," Casey told him.

Matthew didn't break stride as he drew up lidocaine from a vile and stepped around to get a good angle on the wound. "No dice. You aren't driving and you aren't staying alone. I'll admit you if I have to."

Casey's face remained stoic as Matthew injected the anesthetic, but his hand tightened on the bed. "I'm not staying here, Jennson," Casey said tightly.

"I'll stay with him." The words left Sonia's mouth before she could think too long on the offer. It was the only logical course of action. They needed the time together anyway, and if Matthew thought Casey needed someone in the house, then he needed someone at the house.

Casey cut a glance toward her. "I do have a very comfortable bed," he crooned.

Prick.

Ignoring him, Sonia made a point of turning to Matthew. "What should I know? I'm not a doctor, but doesn't it seem that gagging this patient might be medically necessary?"

CASEY

Well, at least something good had come from his motorcycle escapade, Casey decided as he lay in bed and listened to the sounds of Sonia moving about the apartment. He'd woken up some time ago, but had stayed where he was. In part, due to a still pounding headache. In part because he liked hearing her walking around, opening cabinets, and making coffee. He still remembered how it felt when she'd touched his shoulder in the hospital. Hell, that alone had been worth Jennson's reprimand.

Sinking his head back into his pillow, Casey let himself pretend that, just as with yesterday's touch, the counselor had stayed at the penthouse because she wanted to, and not from a sense of obligation. Let himself taste how *that* morning would go.

Casey strode into the livingroom to find the counselor on the leather couch, her legs curled under her. She wore his shirt, which she had slept in, and it had ridden up just enough to show off that delicious curve of her thigh. Casey's cock gave a little twitch of appreciation. It liked seeing her in his things. It would like seeing her out of his things even more though.

"You've something that belongs to me." He slid his hands into his sweatpants' pockets.

Sonia looked up. Her hair, for once freely unbound, framed her enticing face. "No," she said, her tongue flicking between her lips. "No, I don't think so. Finders keepers."

He strode up to her, lifting her from the couch and sitting her atop the polished top of the baby grand. She squeaked, but her eyes dilated as they settled on him. Her mouth parted slightly as his gaze roamed over her and realized that beneath his shirt, Sonia wore nothing. Her nipples pebbled beneath the fabric.

Casey hardened. With a short intake of breath, he let his hands roam from her waist, along her hips, and the inside of her thighs.

"What are you doing?" Her voice was breathless. Moisture gleamed on the inside of her very naked thighs. Delicious, sweet moisture that he was going to feast on for breakfast.

"It's just like you said, Counselor," he murmured, pushing her back until she was indeed open for him. His mouth watered. "Finders keepers. And I've found you."

Casey groaned and swung himself off the bed, barely making it to an icy shower before finding release. What kind of sorcery did the woman have over him that he came like a teenager from just thinking about those curves? About all of her, truly.

Finishing up in the bathroom, Casey frowned at the road-rash that still stung his shoulder blade and pulled on a shirt and sweats in homage to that morning illusion of finding Sonia in makeshift pajamas. It was technically possible that she still wore the shirt he'd given her to sleep in last night. Possible, but not probable. He shook his head at himself and walked out into the living room.

Sonia wasn't there, but the twenty five pages of discharge instructions now scattered on the kitchen island provided evidence of her recent presence. Probably the first time those things had been read by anyone. No, not just read, but highlighted. As if the same damn thing wasn't printed in generic form for every patient just to cover the hospital's ass. From the quick glance Casey took, his injury put him at moderate risk of everything from paralysis to pregnancy. According to the lawyers.

He hated lawyers. Even if he was one himself.

Meanwhile though, where was the counselor herself? Casey

cocked his head, listening for sounds throughout the apartment and followed them to the last place he'd expected to find the woman—in his gym. Interesting. He walked quietly toward the place and stopped at the door.

She *was* still in his shirt, though it was tied up at her waist. Unfortunately, she had pants on beneath—the same jeans she'd come into the hospital in last night. Not exactly workout attire, but then, Sonia fit into the gym about as well as those jeans did. She was standing next to the punching bag and Casey winced as she punched it. Bag one, Counselor zero. She did it again, though it was more of a push this time, and the bag swung on its chains.

Casey came up behind Sonia on soft feet just as the bag was swinging back toward her. "Boo."

Sonia jumped, yelping in surprise. Not quite the same squeak that her illusion had emitted in his morning imagination, but still entertaining.

The bag finished its swing, striking Sonia with a thump and taking away what little passed for her balance.

Casey stepped back, letting Sonia fall onto her ass on the mat.

Sonia glared at him, her chest heaving slightly and her face still pink from the startled shock. "Prick."

"Mmm," Casey said with agreement. He wiggled his hand. "But at least I have all my fingers intact to do all sorts of things. Whereas the way you were going, well, if we were really about to be married, we'd have fewer options for the wedding night."

"Prick," Sonia said again, though her brows pulled together slightly at his words. She'd been listening. Knew that something about her punches was off.

Casey pulled Sonia to her feet and reformed her fingers into a fist, this time keeping the thumb on the outside. He spun her around so that her back was to him. She smelled of ocean breath shampoo from the guest bathroom and had her hair pulled back into a ponytail that tickled against his chest. Sliding his hand along Sonia's arm, Casey guided her through a punch. One that had some chance of hurting the other guy more than it hurt her.

Training others was a Briar thing, but Casey disliked that Sonia possessed not even the basics of self-defense in her arsenal. Not that she was paying much attention to him. No. She was too busy being, well, uncomfortable. Her breath hitched when he touched her, her muscles stiffening despite a valiant attempt to keep them moving. As if it was all she could do to keep from trying to bolt.

Casey leaned his mouth down to Sonia's ear. "Do I frighten you, Counselor?"

"In your dreams," said Sonia.

Well, that was bullshit on all counts. "You are many things in my dreams," Casey said right back into her ear. "Afraid isn't one of them."

"You are a prick."

"Oh, very much so." Casey held his ground. "It's the third time you said as much in as many minutes. Tell me, do you not know many other words or does your mind naturally head down toward that one?"

Not even a smile in reply. Sonia's muscles tensed and relaxed, then tensed again.

The two of them were not compatible. Not if even such a minor intrusion into her space set her on edge. Plainly, something had happened in her past. And just as plainly, she was now lumping him into the same category with whatever bastard had hurt her. And that —*that*—set him on edge in return.

Casey's teeth ground together so hard that his jaw cracked, his pounding headache pulsing through him. He wasn't his father. He would never be his father. Ever.

"Are you alright?" Sonia twisted within the brackets of his arms and frowned up at him. Her palm pressed flat against his chest. "Casey?"

He blinked, realizing that he'd gone as rigid as the little pitbull he'd been teasing. His heart hammered against his ribs hard enough that she could probably feel it. Shit.

Shoving his own memories down down down, Casey raised his chin and gave Sonia a lazy, arrogant smile. "Of course I am. I'm not the one who got knocked on his ass by a punching bag."

"No, that honor fell to a loose stone on the road." She gave him a feral little smile of her own, her teeth showing. She was no longer afraid, though they still stood close, her hand still pressing against his chest. "I remember the same thing happening to me when I was learning to ride a two-wheeler. In kindergarten."

He growled softly in response, but didn't move away. Casey was hyper aware of every inch of his body that Sonia's palm covered. Of the way his breath disturbed the few loose wisps of her hair. The quiet room vibrated with intensity, his heartbeat now seeming to echo off its walls. Just a few inches between his mouth and her still parted lips. Just a dip of his head and he'd get a taste of her.

It might as well be a mile. With a pack of attack dogs and rocket launchers.

Sonia's fingers reached toward his temple, grazing a slow path along his cheek. "How is your head?"

"Thick and empty," said a voice from the door, Briar striding into the gym.

Casey and Sonia stepped away from each other quickly.

"Why the fuck are you back early?" Casey asked Briar. He wasn't sure if he wanted to thank his brother for the interruption or kill him for it.

Briar grunted. A wave of his hand encompassed Casey from head to toe, as if to say *because of you, asshole.*

"Did Jennson call you?" Casey crossed his arms over his chest. "I'm going to rip the doc apart limb from limb."

"Actually, I called him," said Sonia. "You say so many stupid things that it's hard to tell what's normal and what's concussion caused. I needed a baseline."

Oh good, they were back to that.

"They both called." Briar turned on his heels, leading them all back to the kitchen. The space was open and large, flowing directly into the living room. There, in addition to the leather couches, Casey and his brother had installed a wet bar. Casey's baby grand piano held a spot near the window. It was a smaller version of the one at the club.

Casey recalled the prominent spot that piano had played in his earlier daydream and hardened.

Briar headed for the coffee.

Casey headed for the bar. "What would you like?" he asked Sonia.

"The stronger the better."

"Why?"

"You are a pain to deal with sober, I'm hoping for a reprieve if you are drunk."

Briar held a cup of steaming coffee out to Sonia. She took it and settled onto the leather couch, now looking like someone in the waiting room for a divorce attorney. Prim, proper, and on a mission. She even pulled her hair back into that bloody neat bun and pulled his highlighted discharge paperwork toward her. Casey poured himself an old fashioned.

"You aren't supposed to drink alcohol with a concussion," said Sonia.

"Any blackouts overnight?" Briar asked. "Memory gaps of anything since the fall?"

"Unfortunately not," said Casey. He turned to Sonia before his brother could ask any more prying questions. "And since you are in such a tell-all mood as to call Briar, maybe you can finally enlighten me as to what you have against clothes."

"I've nothing against clothes. I wear some every day in fact." Sonia then turned from Casey and asked Briar instead, "Do you have triple antibiotic cream? That goes onto his back and shoulder this morning."

Briar pulled a tube from the bottom drawer and lobbed it over to Sonia.

"Take your shirt off," she told him. "And yes, you are about to say *you first* and then we go back and forth a while. But can we just skip all that because my coffee is getting cold?"

Touché. Casey pulled off his shirt and sat down on the spot on the couch that Sonia indicated, trying not to think of how much he wanted to feel her hands brushing along his skin—even if it was just to put on some goop. Truly, there was something absolutely wrong with him.

Sonia's salve saturated finger slid gently over the abrasions. At least she had no problem touching him. Her breath brushed against his back, waking him lower down all over again. Shit. This was absolutely not the time. He looked over his shoulder, found Sonia deep in concentration, and prodded the bear.

"I was thinking that you would look good in Dior. Red silk, maybe. With a slit along the thigh and a tailored top. What say you?" He could already see the way her breasts would fill out a well cut bodice. And if it were cold outside... Well, that would be even better.

"I'd say that you are a pig."

"And yet you agreed to marry me." He picked up his drink and took a sip. "You should wear whatever clothes the Sonia who is desperately in love with Casey would wear. As we both agree you are not *that* Sonia, I doubt you have anything in your arsenal. If I was actually marrying you, you'd certainly dress differently."

"And why would that be?" She recapped the antibiotic lotion and tossed his shirt into his face.

"Because obviously I wouldn't marry someone who has no taste or style. What do you think she should wear?" The last was directed to Briar.

"Kevlar."

"We are weeks away from trying to worm our way into a large-scale criminal enterprise," Sonia said to Casey before he could reply. "Do you think you could get control of your cock long enough to stop mind-dressing me in skimpy outfits and concentrate on the matter at hand?"

"The first smart notion I've heard all morning." At the kitchen island, Briar was deep into his laptop. "I'm sending the ship's schematics to the printer, in case anyone cares how to get around. We -" Briar's phone rang, cutting off whatever he was about to say. He glanced at the screen. "Liam."

Casey glared at Sonia. "Did you call him, too?"

"Hello, Rowan," Briar answered the phone. "You are on speaker."

"Nero just changed his reservation," Liam's hard voice said over the line. No preamble, just business. "He's boarding tomorrow. I hope you assholes still remember how to pack shit quickly."

Casey straighted, his attention now fully on changed terrain. From the slight shift in Briar's posture, he knew his twin had hit that internal switch as well. That quickly, everything else quieted, Casey's full attention was now on the voice coming from the phone and the implications of Liam's every word.

"Do we know why?" Briar asked. The reunion wasn't for two weeks yet.

"No. Maybe he'll stay through to the reunion and maybe not. And no idea who he is going with either. So change of plans. Casey, you'll need to make friends on your own. I'll wave Sonia Dancer off. Too many unknowns to risk taking her."

"I'm here too, Liam." Sonia strode over to the table where Briar had the phone. "And I'm still the only in to Nero. Just because—"

"Sonia, my apologies for the language," Liam's tone shifted slightly from his military staccato to smoother civilian notes, but remained no less firm. "We appreciate the flexibility, but there is a world of difference between attending a large law school reunion and walking into a likely crime heads meeting in the middle of an ocean. Casey and Briar will take this one."

She opened her mouth to protest. Casey slammed his palm over it.

"Received and understood," he said into the phone even as Sonia bit him. "We'll be airborne tonight."

Briar disconnected the line. Casey yanked his hand away, examining the skin for blood. "Ow."

Sonia glared, fire flashing in her eyes.

Casey turned toward her, his hand forgotten as he leveled the counselor with an assessing look. "There is no way on this side of hell that Liam Rowan will give you his blessing to go. Lesson one of tactical operations, know what battles not to start."

She huffed slightly. "I am still the best connection to Nero that we have. Nothing has changed on that front."

"Everything has changed," said Briar. "You were needed to get into a party. There is no more party."

"Nero is a party boy," said Sonia, her voice becoming more insistent. For all their back and forth, she'd been set on this operation it seemed and was hurt to be benched. "You've read his dossier. There will be a party. And Casey having a fiancée gives him more leeway to come and go. Plus, if Nero isn't coming for the reunion, he's coming for either fun or business. And his kind of business includes trading women as sex toys. If there are women there, you'll need me to talk to them. To make them feel safe."

Briar's face remained unyielding, but he tapped two fingers on the table. A signal between the two of them that meant he agreed. Casey did too, and he sympathized with Sonia's disappointment, he really did, but the tactical part of him also knew that she wasn't ready. With two weeks to get comfortable with him and then a hundred familiar faces around the ship she might have been able to pull off the fiancée gig, but as of now? No.

Sonia turned to Casey. "I know I'm not a commando, but I can still help. We made a deal, McKenzie. Partners. You don't get to back out now."

Casey blew out a breath. She had him there. But some things were still a bridge too far. He walked to her and there was no humor in his eyes as he put a finger under her chin and tilted her face up to meet his gaze. "This is a different game now, Counselor. The clothes, the touching. Me taking up your space. You can't handle it and we both know it."

She flinched.

Casey nodded and let go.

Sonia grabbed his wrist, that pitbull determination blazing in her face so brightly it could have powered the entire Denton Valley. "Wait. You were right, what you said at the Vault the other night. All I'm doing these days are plea bargaining cases. Even at the prosecutor's office. I want to do more. I want to do this."

"You will do more, Counselor," Casey said softly. "But not on this one."

"I can do it. The touching, the flirting. I can do it. Just give me a chance." Her hand tightened on his forearm. "Please. Just give me a damn chance."

Casey weighed her with his gaze, then snapped it toward his brother. "Close the window shades," he ordered his twin, then turned back to Sonia. "Alright, Counselor. Let's play some make belief." He reached for her shirt.

SONIA

Sonia's heart raced so quickly that a wave of dizziness washed over her before she gathered herself together. A test. This was a test and she hated, hated, hated tests, where everything rode on perfection. At Yale, she was the first one in the library and the last one out. Studying. Getting it right. Fearing the day, an instructor surprised her with a question. A pop quiz was a monster of nightmares. An impromptu practical in sensual contact? Yeah. Not her thing. Especially not with her body.

Casey fingered the hem of her shirt.

Sonia swallowed a shaky breath, lest she failed before even getting started. She understood what Casey wanted to do, and why. She even knew he was right. And everything inside her trembled regardless.

"Here are the ground rules, kitten," Casey leaned his head down to whisper into her ear. He was so close that if he moved just a fraction of an inch, his lips would brush her skin. His warm breath tickled and goosebumps erupted over her body. "I'm going to enjoy your body a bit. Looking and touching. But we'll call this the PG-13 version of the show."

It took Sonia a second to find her voice. "What's PG-13 in your world?" Anything starring Casey was R rated by normal people's standards. Or should be.

He chuckled softly. Sensually. "I don't get to play with any pink parts."

Play with pink... oh. Sonia felt the tops of her cheeks flush slightly.

Behind them, Briar closed the curtains with a rustle of fabric, then planted himself at the kitchen island with his laptop. There and present, but not part of their little game. A chaperone. Sonia didn't know whether to be grateful or embarrassed. Not that her body much cared about whatever logical conclusions she was trying to draw for herself.

"As much as I like seeing you in my clothes, I'm going to peel this shirt off you," Casey said.

No. Don't.

Casey stopped, as if he'd read the shout in her mind. His hands lifted off her. "Yeah. I didn't think so."

Shit. She failed. Not two seconds in and she failed. Sonia's stomach clenched. She hadn't realized how badly she wanted in on the operation until it was yanked out from under her. How badly she needed to feel that she could make a difference in people's lives. Casey had been willing to go around Liam and Cullen and all the Tridents to give her that chance. And she'd let it slip through her fingers.

"Please." Sonia caught Casey's wrist before he could back away. "Please give me one more chance."

"I don't get off on torment." His voice had a bite. "I don't hurt women that way."

"I know." She met his eyes, making sure he saw the truth there. She knew Casey wasn't her father's business partner, and she knew this was a game. Plus, sex didn't scare her in itself. She'd had it since the assault. Hadn't enjoyed it, but she'd had it. But always in the dark. Under the covers. "I *know* you won't hurt me. That's not... I'm not afraid of that."

"Then what is it?" Casey demanded.

Sonia bit her lip.

His eyes softened. "You need to start talking, kitten. The way you looked a minute ago, it might have given a lesser man a complex."

"A lesser man?" Sonia half chuckled, her tension easing just enough to close her eyes for a heartbeat and then blurt out the truth. "I… look like me. And you look like you. And this difference is about to become painfully obvious."

"By me looking like me you mean… what exactly?" A hint of mischief sparked in Casey's eyes. A cat suddenly with a mouse too juicy to let go. "Do tell. Are we talking height or shoe size?"

"You are a prick."

Stepping back up to Sonia, Casey took her chin into his hand. "How about you get to decide what you find attractive, and you extend me the same courtesy." He winked. "And for the record, Briar looks exactly like me and I've never had the urge to bed the bastard."

At the island table, Briar grunted.

Alright then. Taking charge of her nerves, Sonia met Casey's dancing gray eyes and lifted her arms. Both as an invitation and access to relieve her of her shirt.

"This is supposed to be the pleasurable part, you know," Casey murmured as he pulled the shirt off in a single, confident motion. Of course he did. He'd been undressing women every night for years. Probably multiple women. All who looked like they walked off a modeling photoshoot.

Sonia willed herself not to flinch as he took in her body. With the shirt gone, there was nothing to hide the softness above her jeans and the small breasts pushed up with a plain beige bra.

Fat ass on a stick, that's what you are. A sneering voice reminded her. *Disgusting.*

"Beautiful." Casey traced his fingers along Sonia's ribs, his calluses scraping against her skin.

A lie. Albeit a kind one.

The bottom of Casey's t-shirt rode up as he shifted his arms, offering a glimpse of his hard abs, of sweats hanging off the crests of his hips. He began making lazy circles that made their way toward her breasts and Sonia breathed in the hint of soap in his scent as she gasped softly.

Her entire body was alert to his touch. To his bare foot, now nudging her legs further apart as he watched her face. The mask of a cool smile that she'd summoned for him and was determined to keep.

Then he brushed the underside of Sonia's too small breasts and her nipples bunched together, peeking through the thin fabric of her bra. Sonia inhaled as Casey's fingers brushed over the buds. Despite his lethal grace, despite everything she expected of the renowned playboy club owner, Casey's touch was feather light.

Her body sang its pleasure, making it hard for Sonia to control the reactions that Casey's touch roused in her. She felt her core warm, felt wetness pool between her legs.

A smile pulled at the corner of Casey's lips. With a gentle tug, he pulled the top edge of her bra down far enough to take a look inside. "Delicious," he murmured, as much to himself as to her. "All the things I can do with these breasts, kitten. I could keep myself entertained all night."

Sonia's jaw tightened. "You don't need to do that. Let's stipulate that you know how to lie through your teeth and leave that out of the test."

Casey's hand stopped moving, his brows pulling together as he shifted his focus to her face. No arrogant smirk. No shrug of the shoulders to say *you got me, Counselor*. Just a penetrating gaze and a slight, surprised tilt of his head. "What do you think I'm lying about?" His hand slipped down again, grazing the skin along the top of her belly.

Her belly, for god's sake.

Sonia's face heated, humiliation gripping her. This wasn't fair. Not part of their deal. He didn't get to change the rules half way through.

She stepped away, crossing her arms over her chest and stomach. "Are you purposely being an asshole now as part of this little test, or does it just come naturally to you?"

"The latter usually," said Casey. "But at the moment, I really am trying to decipher what kind of nonsense is in your head. You think I'm *lying* about liking your body?"

"Of course you are lying. I have a mirror and a set of working eyes."

That tilt of the head deepened as Casey stared at her like a curious owl. His gaze darted over her shoulder for a moment to where Sonia knew Briar was sitting, then returned back to her, as inquiring as before. "You're serious, aren't you?"

Before she could tell him to stop fucking around again, he shook his head. A rueful chuckle escaped his chest. "So that's it?" he snapped his fingers. "That's the reason you don't want to go clothes shopping?"

Closing the distance between them, Casey pulled Sonia's hands away from her body until it was exposed to him again. "You are exquisite, kitten." He met her eyes, his intensity consuming all the air around them. "Would you like to know exactly what the sight of you half naked is doing to me? Really, all you have to do is look down."

Before she could stop herself, she did just that. Her gaze fell to where Casey's hand settled along the curve of her hip, and then breached the short distance of space between them.

God. The bulge in Casey's sweatpants had doubled in size and was now pulsing in a steady rhythm. For her. He was aroused for her.

"Yeah," Casey said softly. "That's what you do to me, kitten. That's exactly what the sight of you does to me." He brushed his thumbs over her peaked nipples, sending zings of excitement through her. Her sex clenched hard, beads of moisture slipping into her panties.

Casey leaned forward, brushing his lips over her ear again. "Turn that brain of yours off, kitten. Just be here. With me. And take my words at face value for once. Or better yet, just take the truth for what it is." He hooked his fingers beneath her bra straps, teasing them off her shoulder. "Your body makes me long to do so many deliciously dirty things to you. The kind of things that would turn that little blush absolutely crimson."

His hands roamed over Sonia's breasts and ribs again, then he brushed his mouth over her shoulder. Her neck. Her jugular.

Sonia's body vibrated, each nerve firing at once. Fear and pleasure. Vulnerability and safety. Arousal and erotism and disbelief. She grabbed onto Casey as the cocktail spilled into her blood, heating her from the inside out. Casey's lips brushed over hers, and she opened her mouth for him. He suckled on her lower lip. God. More. She wanted more. So much more.

Casey pulled away, his hands still moving along her skin. His thumbs traced her jaw and down her neck. "I'm going to push you a bit," he whispered, watching her face. Watching all of her in a way that no one ever had. "I won't hurt you. I promise. It's just a game, alright?"

Sonia's mind was a haze. Too many sensations, too many firing nerve endings flooding her. She nodded to him without knowing what he said.

He took hold of Sonia's arms and slipped them down to her sides then reached around and unhooked her bra, letting the whole thing finally slide right off and to the floor. Cool air brushed exposed skin. "Yes. Even better." Casey licked his lips as he watched her breasts soften. "Mmm. I love you hanging loose like that."

He turned her then, until her back was to him. Fortunately, she wasn't facing Briar, who was still at the kitchen island. Some chaperone he was. And yet... Was it wrong that—even as embarrassment filled her—the knowledge that someone was there, that he could see and hear Casey playing with her made Sonia even wetter? It made no sense and yet there it was.

She felt Casey's body behind her, his undeniable hardness pressing into her backside as he held her against the muscular wall of his body. His feet moved between hers, pushing her legs wide, wider, wider still. His arm wrapped around her waist in an iron tight grip.

This is the best day of your cunt's disgusting existence. You should be thanking me on your knees.

Don't please. Please stop.

So that's your slutty fantasy is it? I see how it is.

"Breathe, kitten," Casey's voice cut through the haze of memories. "I'll touch, but nothing more. I promise." His voice was gentle and yet unyielding in its sincerity. He rubbed slowly along her belly, not nearly as taut as his abs. Then dropped lower, skimming the top of her jeans.

Sonia's breath caught. With her feet held apart by his own, and his arm tightly around her, she could do nothing but feel him along her skin. His fingers brushing along her waistband. His breath caressed the back of her neck. His hardness pressed against her proof that the primal part of him liked what it was feeling.

"You are beautiful," Casey said into her ear. "If I could, I'd lay you out on my piano as my own personal feast. I'd make you scream in pleasure. Over and over. I think I could come just from the sound of you alone. From the taste of you."

He flicked the top snap of her jeans open. Though the pants stayed in place, the awareness of what could be was electrifying.

Something flew open inside Sonia's soul, her mind shutting down the memories of all other men, of everything that wasn't now. Casey's hand cupping her backside. His firm touch. His pulsing cock. A wave of need rushed through her, making her sex clench and her clit throb in response as his hand teased closer to its destination.

Her hips pushed themselves back against him, toward the free hand that he now had roaming along the inside of her thigh. Even through her jeans she could feel its warmth and strength, making it hard to keep from begging for it to go higher—to where she was sopping wet and aching for him beneath her clothes.

"Mmm," Casey hummed into her ear as he closed his grip around one thigh, lifting it to press against his own hip as if claiming her for himself alone.

Sonia had never wanted anything more than what Casey was offering in that moment: pleasure like no other before it. One she didn't know was even possible for her. She slid her hands along his arms, her head tilted back to expose her neck.

The need inside her tightened into a bundle of sensation that made her clit throb harder. She could feel the rising climax, the waves of it gripping her body and mind. She needed to come. Needed it so badly it hurt. Sonia's hips undulated and a strangled sound escaped her body. Just one brush of his fingers a few inches higher and she would get the friction she needed to tumble into the abyss.

Another second of this torment, another breath, and she might beg after all. Sonia bit her lip to keep quiet.

Casey's hand roamed higher. Massaging. Feeling.

Her arousal was so thick it no doubt seeped through the fabric of her jeans by now. One more inch. One more inch and he'd make her explode. One more inch and she'd come right then and there.

Casey stopped. His breathing was ragged against her back and his powerful thighs seemed to vibrate with tension, but he stopped.

Sonia panted.

Waited.

Nothing happened.

She turned toward Casey slowly, the arm he had around her waist loosening enough to allow the movement. The man stood with his feet shoulder-width apart, his muscles taut and straining but not moving, except for his hands that now came up to rub soothing circles on her bare back.

A hell of a bad consolation prize.

She shuddered.

"We are done," Casey's voice was strained, but unwavering. A bead of sweat rolled from his mussed hair and trailed along the strong angle of his jaw. "Let's get you some water. Let's get us both some water."

Water? It took a few heartbeats to process Casey's words. To accept them.

He'd stopped. It had all stopped. But she... she wasn't done. She shook her head as her muscles trembled.

Casey gathered Sonia against him. "I know," he whispered into her ear. "But I promised it would be nothing more than touch. I don't break my promises. That little bit about me you can always trust." He held out his hand, and Briar tossed a blanket over to him, which Casey wrapped around Sonia's shoulders.

Sonia wanted to cry. "Did I pass your test?" she whispered, looking anywhere, but at him.

"Yeah." He smoothed her hair. "Yeah, kitten. You passed with flying colors."

MATTHEW

"Fred is fine, Sith. The biggest threat to her continued existence is currently me, and I promise to give you notice before I stuff her head first into a latrine." Matthew balanced the phone between his shoulder and ear, while at the same time scanning through charts. The one problem with a best friend who'd saved your life multiple times, was that when he asked you to watch over his little sister you didn't say no.

"Denton Valley has latrines?" Sith asked from… from whatever country he was currently in. Matthew was no longer privy to such info.

"Not yet, but I may dig one just for that. Have you told her about the deployment?"

A pause. "No. I'll… There is no point."

Matthew nodded, hearing everything Sith wasn't saying. Wherever his team was going, this was the time to reach out and make sure the families at home were all set should things go badly. He and Sith had gone through the routine before, though it had always been together. So Sith knew all about Matthew's parents and legacy of military service, and Matthew knew that Sith had raised his little sister, called her Fred, and would turn the universe over for her.

If something happened to Sith because Matthew was no longer with the team… Matthew clamped down the thought. Something was more likely to go wrong if Matthew *was* there—there and seizing when he was supposed to be providing cover fire. "I'll tell her I talked to you and that you are out of comms range," he told Sith. "Call when you get back."

"I'll call when I'm back," Sith echoed. "If she needs anything—"

"She needs a god damn spanking," Matthew said as Casey's chart from two nights ago popped onto his screen. "Which I'm going to deliver—professionally speaking. But as far as life outside the hospital, such as it is for a first year, I've got you both. Go."

"Word to the wise, Jennson," Sith said, "do not let her get at your fucking electronics, or you will regret it."

"Does she chew wires?"

"I'm serious. Gotta go."

Hanging up, Matthew sent one more mental *godspeed* to his friend, before returning to his chart review. Win hadn't even drawn the labs he ordered on McKenzie. He pressed the heel of his hand into his eye and rubbed. Was she screwing around because she thought being Sith's sister gave her special privileges, or did the concept of doing what she is told simply hold no meaning to her? Either way, it drove Matthew insane.

Win drove Matthew insane.

He flipped through the rest of the charts. In general, her paperwork was immaculate. Actually, it was so thorough that Matthew fought to contain a growl at the thought of how long each painstakingly detailed narrative must have taken and what that time could have been used for instead. When it came to medical cases, Win's judgment went well beyond a first year resident. Hell, he'd pit her against many of the attending physicians he'd worked with and put all his wagers on the petite doc. She had such an ear for hearing heart murmurs and leaking valves, that cardiology had come down more than once for covert recon to see if she might be worth poaching.

What Dr. Win Carrell seemed incapable of doing—besides quietly ignoring him—was remaining fully upright at the site of blood. Nor did she seem inclined to improve on that particular deficiency.

Catching sight of the charge nurse, Matthew walked out from the staff room and fell in step beside her. "Michelle. How are things looking?"

Michelle didn't break stride or even pause the quick inventory she was conducting. "Asthma in three responded to albuterol, lung sounds clear bilat, ready for discharge. Diabetic in five doesn't know how to control his sugar and will need to be admitted. Dr. Carrell called a cardiology consult for the chest pain in five and neurology for possible stroke in six. She completed the heparin checklist, it's out of the permissible window. Oh, and she suspects yellow fever for the kid in room B. She has him isolated."

Matthew just stopped himself from cursing. "Yellow fever?" Talking about hearing hoofbeats and thinking zebras instead of horses. Typical first year creativity—and the type of thing Win should have come to him to discuss. "The kid hasn't been out of the country. He doesn't even have a passport for fuck's sake." So much for not swearing. But he had tried.

"That's what I thought too, except Dr. Carrell took a look at his phone. Don't know how she figured it out, but apparently it had been co-located with another phone that had very much been in Africa. Long story short, there was a girl involved and the kid didn't want to tell his parents. Once he was alone, the full story came out and it matches all the timelines."

"Fuck," Matthew said again, this time with a note of appreciation. He'd missed that. But Win should have told him. "What about the football player with the deformed wrist and the head laceration?"

Michelle continued her inventory. "I'm sorry, Dr. Jennson, you'll have to check the charts. I don't have the entire ER memorized for you."

Translation: Win hadn't seen either trauma and Michelle was too smart and experienced to get into the middle of that mess.

Right. Adding another thing to his list to chat about with Win, Matthew changed course toward where he could see a lion's mane of golden hair beside a computer terminal. Win had the rolling stool up all the way, her fingers moving across the keyboard faster than Matthew could track. Scrolls of data flowed over the screen.

"Hello, Fred."

Win jumped in her seat, a small gasp escaping her chest. He'd not been trying to be stealthy, but the woman had as much situational awareness as a starfish. Matthew didn't know why that graded on him, but it did.

Win released her gasped breath. "That's still not my name." She turned back to the monitor.

"Where are Casey McKenzie's labs from yesterday?" Matthew asked in a quiet voice that usually sends subordinates seeking cover.

"Didn't draw them." Win continued typing. There was a second and much larger tower at the computer station, one that hadn't been there before. "They were not medically necessary."

There was a pregnant pause as Matthew's blood pressure rose point by point with each heartbeat. He'd given her a direct order. He was her boss, her attending, the doctor who signed off on her charts and held the reins of her residency. She didn't get to override his medical decisions. If this happened in the field, he'd have her up at three in the morning for PT every day for a month at best and at the brig at worst. But here in the hospital…

Matthew took one step toward the power outlet and pulled the plug on Win's computer terminal.

"Are you insane?" she twisted on her chair toward him, her hair framing her face like a living flame. She was sexy as hell when she was furious, and she was very furious just then. "That's a ten thousand dollar machine and I was in the middle of running a simulation that had *twelve hours* of data."

"And I'm in the middle of running an emergency room, not a data mining operation." Matthew crossed his arms over his chest. "I told you to draw labs. I want to know on whose authority you decided otherwise." Slow, well enunciated words that had the nursing staff all deciding they had urgent business elsewhere.

Win seemed to finally process that it was just the two of them now, and that Matthew had that cold look about him that usually meant he was about to yell. They both knew he could bring her to tears if he wanted.

He crooked a finger toward her. "A moment of your time in private please, Dr. Carrell." Without waiting for her answer, he led her toward the back of the ER to one of the empty isolation rooms, which was as much privacy as they could get on a short notice. Matthew held the door open for her, then followed her inside.

Win looked at him wearily. She was flame and vinegar when she had a computer with her, but separated from that lifeline and vulnerability washed over her. Matthew leaned his hip against the bed rail, deciding where to start. Better go with Sith first, because she wouldn't be listening to him much later.

"Sith called," he said and held up his hands quickly as Win's whole body went taut with panic. "He's fine." Not a lie. He was fine when they spoke. "But they are going dark on comms for a while, so don't be surprised if you don't hear from him for a bit."

"For how long?" Win's voice became so thin that Matthew had a stupid urge to draw her against him.

He made himself shrug instead. "Not sure. But If you need something in the meantime, let me know."

"I'm fine. Thank you."

Matthew took a step forward before he could stop himself and touched Win's shoulder. "I mean it. This is Matthew, Sith's best friend talking, not your attending. You need something, you call me. Got it?"

She looked up at him, their eyes meeting for several silent heartbeats. It wasn't Sith's first deployment, and—like Matthew—she knew everything that wasn't said. Everything that Matthew tried to shrug off as no big deal. She reached up to where his hand was still on her shoulder and squeezed once. He felt the warmth of that touch long after she let go.

Sith was one fortunate bastard to have someone care for him as much as Win did. Matthew's family didn't even meet him at the airport when he returned.

Pulling herself together, Win stepped back and raised her chin.

"What I need is for someone to have a chat with my ass of an attending who unplugged an important simulation."

Right. Matthew crossed his arms. "That attending wants to know what happened with McKenzie's labs?"

"They didn't need to be drawn," said Win.

"Wasn't your call." His voice hardened. "Or did you think it was?"

She blew out a long breath, opened her mouth as if to say something, then shut it again.

"Say it," Matthew commanded.

"It wasn't medically necessary," she said again.

Matthew moved in, but it wasn't to comfort. Not now. "The code. The do not resuscitate order. I was out of line for what I said to you at the end. But as for what I was doing, I'll go to the mat to fight for a life every day of the week. You want to do battle on that, bring it on. What you do not get to do, is go against my medical orders. And you don't get to avoid trauma patients because their pain and blood makes you queasy."

Win's mouth pressed together.

"For the record, I order labs on all significant traumas and certainly on all concussions. A fact you'd know if you didn't avoid them."

She looked up in surprise. Win Carrell didn't like being wrong. "I'm sorry."

She meant it. Matthew knew she did. But it wasn't going to change what came next.

"I'm changing your assignments," Matthew said flatly. "From now on, you are on Denton Memorial's trauma service. No more medical patients, no long consults with cardiology and neurology, no looking at charts more than you look at patients. You will personally address every trauma that walks, rolls, and crawls through Denton Memorial's doors. And if we have none, you will round on the admitted patients for follow up. By the time you are done, I expect you to set broken bones and lay stitches with your eyes closed."

Win's eyes widened. "That isn't fair."

"I never said it was. I said it was happening. I suggest you get some spare scrubs to change into if yours get bloody." He let that sink in too and almost felt bad for her. Almost but not really. "Start with the football casualty in bay one. When I looked in, the wrist was grossly deformed, so put on your game face before going in."

"Please, I—"

"Let me know when you finished your initial exam," Matthew turned toward the exit. "I will walk you through setting the bones." And probably scrape her off the floor as well. As many times as it took.

SONIA

With the decision that they were going—that they were all going—made, the penthouse broke out into mission prep, military style. Briar and Casey moved with crisp efficiency, never stopping to think about what they might need or where that something was located. The utter opposite of the frantic rushing about Sonia usually fell into when leaving for an airport.

"You know Liam will have all our hides for bringing you along, right?" Casey nudged Sonia aside as he laid out empty bags in a neat row along the floor. Briar came by next to drop pre-packed bundles into each.

"Liam employs me, he doesn't own me," said Sonia. "The decision isn't his."

Casey looked at her sideways, "Yeah. You just keep telling yourself that." Beneath his amused expression, there was no trace of the man who'd been so intimate with her just moments earlier.

Of course not. That had been an act. Make believe. Plus, Casey played with partners all the time. Women. Men. Several at once. In her many visits to the Vault, she'd seen him bring all sorts of guests toward the elevator leading from the club to the penthouse above.

They all looked nearly as good as Casey himself did. She was just a tool. A game piece on a strategy board.

"Wheels up in two hours." Briar cradled the phone between his shoulder and ear. He'd pulled on a pair of jeans and shirt, a contrast to the Prada suit that Casey had slid into like a second skin. "That's fine," Briar told his mystery coordinator on the other end of the line. He turned to Sonia. "Apple or android?"

"For what?"

"For you." Briar sounded impatient.

"I have an android." She extended her phone to Briar.

He gave her cracked screen a disgusted look and walked back toward his bedroom. "IPhones. Set three up plus my usual suite. Yeah, with tracking." The closed door muffled the rest of the instructions he was rattling off.

"That brick you call a phone is staying here," said Casey. "We are taking clean electronics. Two hours until wheels up."

"Unless one of you is a cross dresser, I need to go home and get my things." She had never packed for anything in two hours. Two days was more her style. But she wasn't about to share that bit of info with the two overachievers ready to invade a small country at a moment's notice.

"Not happening." Casey readjusted the bagged items to whatever order he had in his head. "I already have Roma putting a suitable wardrobe together for you, and we'll have someone on the ship touch up the alterations."

Sonia bristled.

As if he'd seen her do it, Casey turned to her, unraveling himself to his full dominating height. Arrogance and amusement were gone as he lifted a brow. Daring her to object. She got the message. She was under his command for this op, and she could either get in line or stay home.

She understood. Had agreed. But it was still hard to swallow her pride and nod—yet Casey refused to release Sonia's gaze until she did just that.

She wasn't used to his serious side. It was both scary and sexy as hell.

Fortunately, before Sonia had to unpack all that happened in the span of a few moments, Briar reappeared again. He had one gun in a shoulder holster and three more in a hard case, which he twisted to his brother. Casey examined them all, signaled his approval and strapped the smallest of the pistols to his ankle.

"How do you intend to get weapons onto a cruise ship?" Sonia asked. "Don't they have metal detectors or something?"

"Or something," said Briar.

"Ships have people," Casey drawled, now back to his cocky arrogant self. "And people like money."

"You are bribing shipboard security?" Sonia's question came out in a squeak.

"Of course he is." Briar secured another gun to his body. "Cover story?"

"Party drugs for a party boat," said Casey.

"Have enough?"

"Checking. Yeah. We're good."

"Good."

Illegal. Illegal. Illegal. Sonia returned to the couch and busied herself with her phone, committing important numbers and email addresses to memory as she fought to keep her thoughts and nerves off her face. The law was nothing but a set of suggestions to the McKenzie brothers. Or worse, a set of taunts. Whereas she had never so much as cheated on a test or stolen a candy bar from a store. She stopped at stop signs on empty roads, and read all the slides on the stupid online refresher classes that everyone else just clicked through. This thing, it was going to be out of her league in more ways than Casey's touch.

"Limo is here," Casey said.

Sonia jumped. "Already?"

He held his hand out to her. "Last chance to stay home, kitten. Or not."

Stay home, everything inside Sonia's mind demanded. But she didn't want to stay home anymore. So she took Casey's hand.

The limo made a smooth ride to the airstrip, driving all the way to the runway where a private jet was already waiting. The crew greeted Casey and Briar with a familiarity that spoke of frequent flights. Sonia had known Casey and Briar were wealthy—one only had to look at what they'd done with the North Vault, the penthouse, and the sportscars to put as much together—but she was only now realizing how deep their pockets ran. It was as unsettling as everything else they'd thrown at her in the past twenty-four hours. Another chasm between them that they'd have to pretend to have bridged.

Aboard the jet, Briar disappeared into the cockpit with the pilot while Casey led Sonia toward the back, where two sets of seats faced each other. He slid into one, accepted a drink from the flight attendant, and sprawled back with accustomed comfort.

Sonia sat on the edge of the seat opposite him and buckled her belt without having to be reminded by the flight attendant.

Around them the plane hummed quietly to life, everything smooth and in order as it accelerated up the runway and into the air. Briar was still in the cockpit. For all she knew, he'd been the one responsible for the lift off. Casey followed her gaze toward the front of the plane and nodded, then turned his attention back to her, a predator deciding on how to best enjoy his dining experience.

"On the off chance that you've never lied before, let's do a little practice," he said.

"You are a brilliant man who I admire with my whole heart," said Sonia. "How was that?"

Casey grinned, but the smile faded quicker than it usually would. "Why are you on the *Belle Nuit*?"

"To get some time alone with my fiancé before reunion week."

Casey winced. "We'll work on it. What do I do?"

"Umm. Run a nightclub?"

"Oh for gods' sake, can you at least make the truth sound truthful?"

"You must have been a dream at witness prep," said Sonia.

"Excuse me for the interruption," the flight attendant, Marianna, came up to them again. She smiled at Sonia, showing off perfect make up. "Your wardrobe was loaded before you arrived, but I took the liberty of setting aside an outfit before stowing it in case you wish to change?"

She didn't, but given that Casey was wearing Prada, staying in a pair of jeans and tied up t-shirt was unlikely an option. She followed Marianna into the back, her stomach tightening at the sight of a red dress, already out of its garment bag.

At Marianna's direction, Sonia stripped off her jeans and shirt and let the flight attendant help her into the gown. She braced herself for the inevitable, knowing the fabric would either strain over her too large hips or sag from the too small chest. When the back zipper closed easily and snugly instead, Sonia blinked.

The dress...fit.

Light silk fabric hugged her bodice then flowed gracefully off her waist, the material cool and smooth against her skin. There was a slit on the thigh, too, just as Casey had alluded to in his musing. Marianna pulled out a needle and thread, hiding the straps of Sonia's bra, then laid a matching silk scarf over Sonia's arms.

Marianna pulled out several shoe boxes. "They sent three sizes over to see which felt best."

Sonia slid her feet into a set of red pumps, which were comfortable despite their high heels. "What sort of sorcery is this?"

"Italian," Casey called from the other side of the partition.

"May I help with your hair and makeup?" Marianna asked.

"Well, it's either you or me," Casey called again. "We certainly can't entrust Dancer with it."

"Can you mind your own business?" Sonia called back, but sat on the chair Marianna indicated and let the woman work.

A half hour later, Sonia didn't mind the mirror the flight attendant had pulled out as she stared at a reflection of a woman she'd never met before. Marianna had worked Sonia's hair into a crown at the top of her head with strands hanging down to frame her face. Understated makeup made her eyes look big and the kind of gorgeous she knew they weren't. And the dress—feminine without being flimsy, sensual, but not lewd. She looked...

"Delicious," Casey purred, coming up behind her. His eyes roved over her appreciatively in the mirror. "You look absolutely delicious." He extended the pronunciation of the last word, as if tasting the syllables. "Only one thing is missing now."

Reaching into the inside of his jacket pocket, Casey pulled out a small box. Sonia had a moment to catch the gold pressed lettering on it before Casey popped it open to reveal a large diamond ring that picked up every bit of light in the cabin and shone like the sun itself.

Sonia's mouth dried. That ring cost more than a car. Not just her run down thing, but a really nice car. She'd never touched a piece of jewelry this intricate and expensive, much less worn it.

"Will you marry me, kitten?" askedCasey into the mirror.

"No," said Sonia.

"I didn't think so. You are too smart for that." He took her hand, running his fingers over her ring finger. Casey's calluses traced along Sonia's skin, igniting every nerve they touched. Turning her hand palm up, Casey placed the ring into the center and closed her fingers around it. "See if you can figure out what goes into what hole."

Sonia felt the heat rush to her face, saw her skin flush in the mirror's reflection. Casey saw it, too. And grinned. His hand ran up her back, along the exposed upper half of her spine, and the heat dove deeper. Into her core. And belly. And thighs. But then Casey gripped the back of Sonia's neck, the hold just shy of being painful.

"One more thing, kitten." He leaned in, his lips almost brushing her ear. "I am a very jealous kind of man. Which means you don't stay with any other male in any room alone. Ever. And you do what I tell you to do, when I tell you to do it. Are we clear on that?"

Sonia swallowed. The woman staring back from the mirror, who was her but not her, swallowed, too. "So I'm marrying a rich, jealous asshole who thinks of women as property?" The cabin shifted about, but Sonia had no doubt that it was Casey's intense stare and not turbulence that was behind it. Her voice sounded steadier than she felt. "I see I'm a poster child for healthy relationships."

"Outlaw motorcycle gangs aren't an equal rights type of organization, Counselor," Casey said with a gentleness that was more disturbing than his signature arrogance could ever be.

SONIA

*B*riar came out of the cockpit just as they were about to land. His gray eyes surveyed the plane, stuttering as they swept across Sonia. He blinked and moved on. "Not bad, Dancer."

"That's a high compliment," Casey clarified.

Sonia didn't know what to do with that. Before she could figure it out, the plane came in for its landing and the wheels bumped the runway. A limo was already waiting, though this time only Casey and Sonia got in. Briar would be making his own way now, their electronic eyes and ears on the ship. They rode to the embarkation point in silence and Sonia's palms were sweating by the time they arrived. The driver opened the limo door and Casey splayed his hand possessively on Sonia's bare back as he steered her to the ship.

Sonia was overdressed. She knew it from the moment she got out of the limo to find the other passengers in casual clothes as they mounted the raised ramp, their fancier things packed away. Not her though. She was on display from the very first step, small breasts, large hips, and a dress that made every man turn his head and stare. Casey gave a vicious glare to a pair of men whose eyes stayed too long on Sonia's breasts, and they nearly tripped over themselves hurrying away.

"You enjoy doing that, don't you?" Sonia muttered.

"Oh, absolutely."

Casey's hand was hot on Sonia's back, guiding her firmly through the deck and crowd, disappearing only long enough to place hundred dollar bills into the hands of various ship staff who now hurried forward to open any doors arising in their path, no questions asked. When Casey wanted to make a statement, he didn't hold back.

"Mr. McKenzie, Ms. Dancer," a young man in a black suit with the ship's logo pinned to the lapel appeared in their path just as they reached the stateroom deck. He had an air of competence around him despite his youth, and his curly brown hair, captured with a leather thong, extended down to his shoulders. "I'm Duane, your butler. Is there anything I can get you to make you more comfortable?"

Casey placed an order for room service, with a filet mignon and lobster dinner, champagne, and chocolate covered strawberries to get them started in the evening. Another hundred dollar bill tucked into Duane's suit pocket followed the instructions and the butler bowed before striding off to fulfill the demands. Casey pressed a keycard against the stateroom lock.

Sonia had been on a cruise once before, with her family before she walked away. That stateroom was nothing like the luxurious suite that opened before her. Instead of small ports, floor to ceiling windows made up the outer wall, the ocean rippling forever beyond the glass. The floor was a plush carpet. Towels, twisted and folded into the shape of sea creatures, lay atop the white down comforter with sprinkled flower petals adding splotches of color. The bed, which was the main attraction of the space, sprawled with elegance. The one single bed. Because they were engaged.

The door closed.

Casey's hand disappeared from Sonia's back immediately. Walking over to one side of the bed, he plopped down and put his hands behind his head, his eyes closing. "We can get away with staying in the stateroom tonight, while Briar gets himself settled. Enjoy the dinner when it comes, I've got some thinking to do."

"Easy to get lost in thought when it's unfamiliar territory."

"Very much so," Casey agreed, disappearing into his own thoughts. The show was over for the night.

Sonia was obliged to remain in her fancy clothes throughout the evening—it was either that or keep opening the stateroom door in the lingerie that Casey's concierge shopper had packed for her. If there was a pair of sweats or jeans somewhere, she was yet to find it. Something to purchase at one of the overpriced shops.

Food was delivered. The rest of their endless luggage, courtesy of Roma. Random people stopped by to offer their welcome and services, the word of Casey's free hand with hundred dollar bills plainly having spread quickly. Duane came to offer turndown service, took one look at Sonia's overwhelmed face and beckoned her to the washroom to show where comfortable oversized bathrobes hung in a hidden closet. He took it upon himself to press the *do not disturb* button on the door before leaving.

"Duane," Sonia called, and the young man paused inside the half open door. "Thank you."

He gave her a small bow. "My pleasure, Ms. Dancer."

Contrary to Sonia's expectations, Casey made no remarks about the single bed. When it was time to sleep, he'd put on a pair of sweat pants and nestled himself on his side, leaving plenty of space for Sonia to settle in on the other. "You can have the blanket," he said, turning his back to her. "I'm hot as it is."

She didn't take the bait.

The following morning, Casey insisted that those lacey little lingerie pieces she'd very much *not* worn be tossed about the room before their departure. Sonia pulled on the simplest sundress she could find among her new things—a white number that looked plain on the hanger and yet managed to shine when worn—and pulled her hair back into a bun.

Casey regarded her critically. He was already in a light colored Armani suit, a silk shirt coating the sculpted muscles beneath. "You are fired."

"From being your fiancée?"

"From dressing yourself," said Casey. "I'm going to have someone from the beauty salon come up in the mornings to coordinate your clothes and find some hairstyle that doesn't make me feel like I need to write a brief." He checked his phone. "Breakfast awaits."

They made a tour of the breakfast options before settling on the largest buffet and finding a table far away from the food. Taking turns going up to the spread, they each took a different route, eyes moving between the tables. Casey called it situational awareness. Sonia called it these-people-all-look-the-same-and-I-can-barely-find-my-way-back-to-my-chair.

She was on her third buffet trip, staring at the smoked salmon crackers beside caviar sandwiches as if unable to make up her mind, when a hand with a gold ring reached across her line of sight to pluck one of the mimosas beyond the platter.

"Well, if it isn't Ms. Dancer," a familiar voice from the past sent a jolt through Sonia's spine.

Sonia jerked around, knocking Nero's mimosa right over his crisp white shirt.

Her heart shoved against her ribcage. "Nero," she stared at the mess she'd just made and said with no acting whatsoever, "what the hell are you doing here?"

"Taking a morning mimosa bath, it seems," Nero chuckled and shook his head. He was slightly pudgier than she remembered, a paunch of a belly overhanging a pair of expensive slacks. He was Sonia's height, slightly short for a man and, despite only being in his late twenties, showed that receding hairline she'd seen in the photos.

Sonia shook her head, motioning to his drenched shirt and splattered sport coat. "I…I'm so sorry. I didn't see you sneak up on me."

"I'm rarely accused of stealth, but I'll take the compliment." He winked.

"Please do." Sonia recovered herself, though her heart still hammered. First contact. She needed to get this right. Both for the op, and to prove her value to Casey and Briar. She bit her lip and handed Nero a new mimosa from the tray. "Really though, I didn't expect to see you here for a couple of weeks."

"A set of impromptu business meetings." Nero waved his hand

toward the other end of the dining room, where his table must be. "It's my new business strategy—if work won't leave me alone for vacation, then I just bring it along with me. Same boring crap, but at least I can do it over a mimosa." A corner of his mouth lifted. "Just not usually by way of bathing in one. And what about you?"

"She is here with me." Casey's voice cut in with a harsh possessive arrogance. Coming up behind her, he put an arm around her waist and pulled her close against his body. The hard cut of his muscles pressed into Sonia's back, the restraining arm iron hard against her belly.

Nero frowned slightly. Not helpful given that they were just starting to talk.

Sonia tried to step from Casey's grip, but his arm refused to budge. "Is something amiss, kitten?" Casey asked her.

She put her hand over his and covertly dug her nail into a soft part beside his thumb. "Not at all. I've just run into an old friend." She hoped her nail managed to draw blood. "Casey, this is Nero. We went to law school together. Nero, Casey McKenzie is—"

"Her fiancé," Casey shifted Sonia to his other side and puffed out his chest slightly, looking down at Nero from his greater height. He extended a hand to shake Nero's, his other extricating itself from Sonia's nails to caress the nape of her neck. "It's a pleasure to meet you, Nero." His tone said it was anything but a pleasure. What the hell was the man doing? He focused on her neck again. "I thought the reunion was not for a couple of weeks yet?"

"I've some clients to entertain so I brought them along." Nero's gaze weighed Casey from head to toe, then turned to Sonia. His attention snagged on her massive ring, then brushed against her breasts before finding her face again. "It is wonderful to see you again. Would you like to join us for breakfast? I'm sure your fiancé wouldn't mind letting old friends catch up."

Now that was more like it. Take that, military men. Sonia beamed at him. "It would be my ple-"

"She is fine, thank you," Casey cut Sonia off mid-word for the second time. "We were just finishing up and have an appointment with the concierge. Excuse us."

Sonia's teeth ground against each other. Yes, she'd found Nero first. Or he found her. Whichever way it happened, Casey needed to stop being a sore loser and get on board. She plastered a smile onto her face and stepped away from him. Hard. "Don't be rude, sweetheart. I've not seen Nero in years and have just ruined his shirt. The least I can do is accept his invitation."

"Duane," Casey raised his voice, calling over their butler. Sonia had not realized the man was even here, but sure enough Duane appeared beside them a moment later.

"Sir?"

"Please have a new shirt delivered to my new friend's stateroom immediately. A 36 short, I believe?" He glanced down at Nero, then nodded to himself in confirmation before reclaiming Sonia's waist. This time, his fingers dug into her hip nearly hard enough to bruise as he forced her away.

It was all Sonia could do to keep that fake smile on her face as Casey force marched her out of the room. Anger seared every nerve in her body. Cooperation? A team? Only the knowledge that ripping into Casey in public would jeopardize everything kept Sonia holding her tongue until the door of the stateroom once more shut behind them.

The moment it did, Casey shoved himself away from her as if pulling back from a stove. He strode to the window, his hands bracing the back of his head as he stared silently into the ocean. The muscles of Casey's broad back bunched and spread as he drew deep breaths, his knuckles turning white where he pressed his fingers into his hair.

Sonia marched up to him.

Casey turned to face her.

She slapped him.

He let his head turn with the blow, doing nothing to defend himself. Haunted gray eyes met hers for a moment then looked away, settling back on the waves. Haunted. Not self righteous or cocky or angry even.

"You are more than welcome to do that again," he said without turning back. "As many times as you need." There was the thinnest thread of humor in his voice, as if he tried to reach into that well of his usual arrogant confidence, only to find it dry.

Sonia frowned. Crossed her arms over her chest. "That was some high handed assholery back there," she said finally, with less bite than she'd originally intended.

"Yep. I learned from the best." Soft words, aimed at the ocean beyond. "If you liked act one, you'll love what this circus we got ourselves into has in store next."

She took a calming breath, willing herself back to reason amidst this spinning mess. Whatever game he was playing was plainly hurting him as much as her, but she saw zero point to it no matter which way she turned the events. "Why did you do that?" she asked. "I had an invite to Nero's breakfast table. To meet his friends. Find out what he's been up to. That's the whole point of this op, and that's the whole reason I'm here on this ship. To be bait."

"And bait you were." Casey gathered himself together with visible effort and walked over to where a decanter of whiskey had been left on the counter. He poured a knuckles' length into two glasses and offered her one. Sonia shook her head. Casey drank from his.

"Nero will come after you again. He'll want to prove that his cock's bigger than mine," Casey told her. "But no matter how breakfast had gone, Satan's Armada wouldn't ever let a woman into their inner circle. And even if they did, that's not where any of us want you. You aren't here to gather intel on Nero, Counselor. You are just here to facilitate a connection to me."

Before she could reply, he cocked his head to the side as if listening to something, then tapped his ear. "Copy. Powering up." He tapped his ear again and pulled a laptop from a safe.

"Earbud with a connection to Briar," Casey said in answer to Sonia's unspoken question. He cocked his head again, displaying the device to her. Even knowing where to look Sonia had trouble picking out the small flesh colored object fit inside the ear canal until Casey pulled it out and laid it on the table. "Briar has tapped into the ship's security camera feed. He traced Nero back to his table and is working on the facial IDs of his companions. We'll have photos and bios as soon as he does."

Sonia rocked back on her heels. She understood some of where Casey was coming from. Some. But she was still pissed. "I take it this was another reason you wanted to walk away this morning?"

He nodded. "Better to wait until we know who we are dealing with. This is a ship. No one is going anywhere."

"You could have just told me all this, you know," said Sonia.

"I did. Back in the plane. I told you that you were never going to be alone with any man here."

Sonia was going to punch him. Right in the nose. Except it would probably break her hand. She shook her head and sat on the edge of the bed, processing what Casey had said. *Everything* he'd said. For someone who was so certain that he'd done everything right, Casey was still paler than she'd ever seen him. Shaken.

She walked over to take the second drink, not to sip it but just to have something in her hand as she asked, softly. "Who was your teacher?"

He glanced at her, his gray eyes for once betraying that she'd struck her target.

"You said, you learned from the best," Sonia pressed. "So who taught you the ins and outs of being an asshole? Is that a specialized course in Delta now—a follow up to *Marking your Territory 101*?"

A muscle ticked along Casey's jaw. "No. That would have been my father. He liked to practice what he preached, so there was no shortage of practical exercises." Casey drained his whiskey, setting the glass down with a click. "I'm going to take a shower. Briar is sending the files to the laptop. Try and remember to not use a highlighter directly on the screen."

MATTHEW

Matthew found Win in the back of the L-shaped supply closet. She didn't want to be found of course, and most especially by him. Little did she know that Matthew had already scouted all the nooks in the ER and beyond where one might find privacy and that he couldn't care less what she wanted.

"It does get better." Matthew leaned against the opposite wall of shelving from where Win crouched, her forearms braced against her knees. She was still pale, but managed to glare knives at him. They'd had a gruesome car accident that morning, the young female driver arriving with a full scale evisceration and yet somehow both alive and screaming.

Win took one good look and rushed out of the trauma bay to empty her stomach in the nearest restroom. And once she was done, Matthew had made her hold those hanging guts with her hands all the way up to the operating room and scrub in for the surgery. The nurses had also been instructed to hand over all blood draws and IV line starts to Win and she was giving patients and—herself regular—blood baths as she figured out how exactly to occlude the vein when changing tubing.

Win got to her feet. "I'm fine." Aka *Fuck you, Jennson.*

"Good. The lab dropped one of the tubes from the patient in four, so you'll need to redraw the blood and we've got a full waiting room. So if you are done feeling sorry for yourself, please rejoin the rest of us on the floor."

Her jaw tightened, but she said nothing.

Matthew gripped her eyes, no mercy in his own. *Come on, Fred. Swear at me. Tell me to go to hell. Tell me what hits you so hard. Give me something to work with.*

She didn't. Win had three modes when it came to Matthew: outright insubordination, tears, and this—a wall.

Fine. He'd been telling the truth. She'd get desensitized to the trauma and blood and pain eventually. At which point she could pass this rotation, go back to her computers, and be out of his hair. He bladed his body to let her pass. "Remember, you are starting IV lines, not amputating limbs," he said. "You've had a line before. Nothing but a short sting. Stop making a mountain out of the procedure."

She glanced back at him over her shoulder. "No."

"To which part?"

"I've never had an IV. Never had a reason to."

"What?" He fell in step behind her. "You have been to the ER before, right? As a patient."

"Of course not."

"A broken arm from the monkey bars, a concussion from tree climbing, stitches from a bike tumble? You were a child at some point in your life, weren't you?"

"Pain and suffering isn't some virtue or right of passage. There is more impact to be made by counteracting genetic malformations before they affect quality of life than in patching up holes. So tell me what I need to do to get out of this purgatory and go back to addressing the former while you bask in the latter."

Matthew shrugged and quickened his pace. "The board has been updated. You can find your patients there." He stopped as Michelle intercepted the pair of them coming out of the closet. He looked at the charge nurse pleasantly. "Something interesting?"

Michelle's expression never waivered. "Thirty-eight year old intoxicated male, came in with a stab wound to upper extremity. You might want to examine him before the ranting upsets the rest of the ER."

Matthew took the iPad chart from Michelle's hands and placed it into Win's. "All yours, Dr. Carrell. Bay seven."

He watched Win walk toward the corner bay then parked himself at the central hub and pulled up the latest chest X-rays radiology had uploaded from a suspected pneumonia. "Why do you work in emergency medicine?" he asked Michelle.

"Someone has to make certain the doctors don't kill the patients. Don't you even think of using my labels for your notes." She slapped his hand away from what Matthew thought was scrap paper, but was actually an overturned set of barcoded stickers.

Matthew snorted. "And do these attempted homicides happen often?"

"At a teaching hospital? Oh, every June. And most months after that." She gave Matthew a look that said he was not off her suspect list. She nodded to the chest X-ray still on his screen. "What's the verdict?"

"Diffuse pulmonary effusion. Significant infiltrates on the right side. Consistent with pneumonia. Let's start on—"

"Get your filthy hands off me," a slurred male voice hollered through the emergency room. "I want a doctor."

"I'm sorry, I just—" that was Win's voice, cut off by the sound of something crashing.

Matthew sprang out of his chair and vaulted over the counter barrier separating the staff-only area at the center of the ER from the perimeter treatment bays. A sprint around the equipment and he was yanking open the curtain to treatment bay seven before anyone could utter another word. It was only Michelle's gripping his wrist —god only knew how she got there nearly as quickly as he did—that stopped him from breaking noses first and asking questions later.

His heart beating a steady, lethal beat against his ribs, Matthew surveyed the space. There were two men inside, both overweight, bearded and wearing leather vests. The patient's vest and shirt were halfway off to reveal a bloody puncture wound in his right deltoid—and a walnut sized hematoma at the crook of his left elbow, where Win must have punctured the vein all the way through when trying to draw blood. The second man, with *TANK* stenciled on his leather vest, had Win backed up into a corner.

"What is going on?" Matthew's voice was deadly cold. He cleared the room in three large steps, hooked his arm around Win's waist and pulled her from the corner to a space behind his back.

"Finally, a gods damn doctor in this place," Tank snarled. "Get that slut out of here."

Matthew grabbed Tank's wrist and twisted. The asshole dropped to his knees with a curse.

"I don't believe I heard you correctly," said Matthew. "I believe you were thanking Dr. Carrell for attending to your friend—" Matthew scanned the patient's clothing to see if he too had a conveniently stenciled nickname. He didn't. But he did have *Satan's Ride* tattooed on his knuckles. "Satan."

Satan took a moment to realize Matthew was talking about him, then slid to his feet and growled, showing uneven teeth. He had the glazed look of pain and alcohol. "Look what that whore did to me." He stuck out his arm.

"I don't see anything," said Matthew, adding just a little more torque to Tank's wrist. "You've two choices at the moment. Get your ass back on the cot and stay there, or get thrown out."

Satan snarled.

Tank jabbed the finger of his free hand toward Win. "That fucking bitch deserves -"

"She is mine." Matthew jerked Tank's wrist, driving the man face first into the corner of the cabinets. There was a crash and a grunt and a splash of blood as Tank's lip split open. Behind him, Win gasped. Letting the asshole go, Matthew advanced on Satan, keeping his body well between his and Win. "You, on the other hand, I don't give two shits about."

Satan pointed to his stab wound. "I'm not going anywhere until you fucking fix this."

Matthew crossed his arms. "I imagine that's a good idea. Puncture wounds are a bitch for infection. You could lose that arm if we do this wrong. Then you'd be riding around with an amputated stump. Can you even handle a motorcycle then?"

Satan eyed him warily, probably trying to muddle through the intoxicated confusion. "Well now, Doc, that's why I'm here, ain't I?" He stepped back and planted his ass back on the bed. "You have to fix it up. It's the law."

Matthew pulled a bottle of alcohol from the countertop, unscrewed the top and emptied the entire half-liter into Satan's wound. Then he stood back, while the biker's blood curdling scream echoed off the ER walls.

"That was disinfectant," Matthew's lip curled back. "I'll come back when I have the time."

"Wait, you can't leave me," Satan said between gasps while Tank recovered enough to climb slowly to his feet. "I need fucking help."

Matthew shrugged. "Of course I'll help. When it's your turn. I'm busy with a more important case, and Dr. Carrell seems indisposed just now." Keeping his body blocking the bikers, Matthew waited until Michelle and Win cleared the treatment bay before walking out himself. "Michelle—"

"I'm already calling security." She waved her phone. "I'll also give legal a heads up. I could be wrong, but assault is against hospital policy."

Matthew didn't care, not as he turned to Win and scanned every inch of her. The little doc had her arms wrapped around her shoulders and her breaths came in short, quick bursts. He longed to run his hands over her body and ensure for himself that she was alright, but when he took a step toward her, Win retreated.

Matthew stopped dead in his tracks. He'd scared her.

"Call Sonia Dancer," Matthew told the charge nurse without turning around. "She picks up legal overflow and hates me anyway."

"She went with Casey and Briar," Win said distantly.

"You've got to be kidding." He shook his head. Liam was going to have all three of their hides for that, if Cullen didn't beat him to it. But that wasn't Matthew's problem. His hands moved at his sides. He didn't know how to make this better for Win. Sonia was gone, Sith was dark, and he wasn't someone Win wanted around.

He softened his voice. "Are you alright, Fred?"

"I'm fine."

Bullshit.

He held his hand out to her.

She pressed her arms tighter around herself.

He let his hand fall. On the other side of the ER, security was already escorting Tank out, and another uniform was now keeping an eye on Satan. "Alright. You've been on for sixteen hours. Go home and get some sleep. We've got everything handled here."

"What was all that about losing his arm?" she asked.

Matthew shrugged. "It's not impossible. Our discharge paperwork says you can die from a paper cut, so it must be true." He let the corner of his mouth twitch up, begging Win to join in on the joke. She tried. Failed.

No, he was the one who failed. Failed her. Failed Sith. Everything inside Matthew screamed to keep her in his sight, but he'd not earned that. "Go home. Sleep. Alright?" He held her gaze until she nodded, then waited until she got her things and fell into step beside her.

"What are you doing?" she asked.

"Walking you home. Or to your car. Or to a unicorn, if that's how you get to work." He should have known this answer before now. Some job he was doing watching Sith's sister.

"We can't leave the ER without either of us," said Win.

"I don't care."

"I do." She looked over at him and there was nothing in her gaze that said Matthew was welcome anywhere near her. Now or ever. The force of that punch caught Matthew off guard. "I will see you tomorrow, Dr. Jennson."

Matthew waited long enough to see that Win was heading toward the staff parking lot side of the building, then marched himself to the security desk. He was probably being paranoid, but he didn't care.

"Bert," he read the rent-a-cop's name off the tag, "are you able to pull up the cameras in the staff lot?"

"Yep." Bert continued working on his crossword puzzle.

"Well?" Matthew counted to five in his head. "Bert, turn the goddamn staff lot cameras on."

"Why?"

"Because I said so," Matthew snapped before getting a hold of himself. "Because I want to make sure Dr. Carrell gets to her car safely."

Bert smiled, showing bad teeth. "Oh, that pretty little doctor? Want to see which car she goes to, eh? Not my first day."

"No. I truly just want to see that she is safe," Matthew ground out. "Fuck, aren't you supposed to be rotating the views anyway?"

Bert sighed, took a sip of coffee, then finally picked, making it clear the entire time that he was doing Matthew and the universe a hell of a favor. Each movement felt slow as molasses and Matthew fought the urge to shove Bert out of the chair.

Bert frowned at the keyboard, muttering. "Control, shift five. No. Control, shift six. Wait, wrong button. Here we go. Control, shift six. There we go."

"Well?" Matthew pressed.

"Hold your horses. I have to move…" Bert frowned. On the monitor before him, a half dozen motorcycles had gathered together, Tank gesturing wildly in the middle of them. The Satan's Armada was parked in the middle of the staff parking lot where Win was headed.

Shoving himself away from the monitors, Matthew sprinted for the door.

WIN

Win was on the dark web before she'd even cleared the ER, jumping through a chain of VPNs before logging into a chat forum. She didn't have anything to say, but she'd find something to read there. Or discuss. Or calculate. Anything to steady her shaking nerves. She was cold, inside and out, the sound of the metal tray crashing against the floor kept ringing over and over in her ears.

Get that slut out of here.

No. No. No. Win clicked on a post advertising new zero day malware. Not her market, but it was entertaining. A little green dot at the bottom of the screen announced notifications. Matthew had bit on a post *@DocPhantom42*, the personna she usually went by, had made about anti-seizure drugs. She hovered over the message then switched away from the screen. She couldn't think about Matthew right now. About the ER. About whether becoming a doctor had been a colossal mistake.

Get that slut out of here. Get us a real doctor.

Win knew she was outside only because the chilly evening breeze kissed her cheeks. Without looking up, she pulled out her keyfob and pressed a key, the familiar sound of her Toyota Corolla's answer just around the corner putting her at ease. A few more steps and she'd be in her car. Twenty minutes later, at home in her bed. Playing Fortnite, while another set of screens ran some simulations she couldn't get out of her mind.

"Looks like someone finally tossed the trash out," a man said from behind her.

Win jumped, dropping her phone. She'd not realized anyone was here. Sith was always on her case about situational awareness. She turned, coming face to face with a man in a leather biker jacket.

"I don't know you," Win said, her heart picking up its pace. She reached down to pick up her fallen phone, now realizing that the biker wasn't alone. "You're mistaking me for someone else."

A combat boot slammed down atop Win's phone just as her fingers grazed it. The fifteen hundred dollar device shattered into shards. Someone laughed. Many someones.

"Well, fuck me," Tank separated from the crowd and stalked toward her. His lip still bled from where Matthew had slammed his face into the cabinets. What was he still doing here? Win's eyes darted from Tank to the hospital entrance, then to her car. Run back or run forward?

She sprinted for the car.

Tank lunged as she tried to rush past him and grabbed Win's hair. Pain rushed through her scalp. Still holding her hair, Tank punched Win in the stomach.

It took her a moment to register that she'd been hit. For the first time in her life someone had *hit* her. She froze, the shock of it gripping her. For a heartbeat, she felt nothing but utter terror, an inability to draw breath. And then the pain came.

Win screamed.

Tank clamped his hand over her mouth. It was bloody from where he'd wiped it over his lip. "Let's put that mouth to better use," he growled and slipped his grip down to her jaw, pressing with bruising force. "On your knees, whore."

Win clawed at the hold, digging her nails into Tank's hands.

"I said, kneel." He kicked her knee. Something popped and pain shot from the joint, which no longer held her weight. She dropped to the pavement. Another kick. A boot in her ribs. Agony echoed through her bones and she screamed again, though she didn't know whether any sound came out. Her ribs were on fire. She gasped for breath. From the ground she could see the razor blade's edge worked into the toe of Tank's boot, could feel the blood soaking her shirt. His foot pulled back.

Before Tank could hit her again, a male figure in blue scrubs was on him in a flurry of blows too fast to follow. Tank stumbled backwards into one of his biker mates, both men falling to the ground. Without breaking stride, Matthew twisted and extended a crisp back kick into a third attacker. Win had no idea how Matthew had even known the man was there, how he could keep track of everyone coming at him. Yet, now that he'd reached his battleground in front of Win, Matthew's movements seemed to slow down, as if he had all the time in the world to execute each perfect strike. A kick to the gut. A turn. A punch that crushed a nose in a spray of blood.

A bald biker who'd been standing back until now, threw himself into the fight just as Tank lumbered back to his feet. A flash of a silver blade shone in Baldie's massive hand.

"Knife," Win bellowed to Matthew. He somehow had the wherewithal to hear her and nod, and to draw something shiny of his own from his scrubs. A scalpel, now held flipped along his wrist.

Tank barreled forward. "You are dead, all of you," he shouted. "That whore, you, this entire fucking sham of a hospital."

Matthew ducked under Tank's punch and swept the biker's leg out from under him. Tank's knife hand came down. Matthew bladed his body off center, letting the swing go by him. And then he slashed his own blade across Baldie's still moving forearm.

Arterial blood sprayed. Baldie fell. Even the other bikers froze at the sight of the pulsing crimson.

An approaching siren wailed in the background, more voices and shouts rushing toward the lot. Security. Or cops. Win wasn't sure.

"Ride out," Tank ordered and the five who could still move jumped onto their bikes, leaving Baldie clutching his wound on the pavement.

Engines revved. The Satan's Armada zoomed out of the hospital parking lot like a vicious snake. Tank, who was the last to leave, cut his bike right by Matthew. "You will pay. You all will." Then he spat on the ground and rode right into the onrush of security guards who barely had time to throw themselves out of his way.

Matthew barked an order to security to deal with Baldie, and then he was in front of Win. His body blocked everything but the moon rising behind him as he crouched before her, his face impossibly calm. He wasn't even breathing hard. Not like she was.

"You are safe now," Matthew said. His blue eyes seemed to glow, the moon backlighting the wisps of hair ruffled in the wind. "Win, you are safe."

She tried to peel herself off the pavement, but her body screamed and her leg wouldn't move. She shook.

"It's alright. I've got you." He scooped Win into his arms, one hand coming under her knees and the other bracing her back as he lifted her easily against his chest. He smelled of sweat and masculine musk and spicy aftershave. He smelled of warmth. Of safety and brutality all in one.

Win clung to his scrubs, her hands gripping the fabric as if she'd fall otherwise. She saw the garage door, the large entrance and exit signs, the stairs. The tile floor and the approaching sliding doors of the ER.

Michelle was on them as soon as Matthew took one step into her domain. "Isolation two," she ordered Matthew, turned to direct several other patients—including Baldie—to curtained bays on the other side, then fell in step beside them. "What do you need?"

Like Matthew, Michelle's voice was calm. She reached out to squeeze Win's shoulder.

"Portable X-ray. Ultrasound for FAST."

"Sonography is already in there. Yarborough is on his way, too."

Matthew opened the door with his back and carried Win inside. It was quiet, an oasis from the zoo beyond. Matthew lowered Win to the bed and brushed her hair off her face. His own hair was plastered to his forehead with sweat.

"How are you doing?" he asked.

Win felt the absence of his body against hers, the distance leaving her empty and alone and scared all over again. She couldn't breath in easily, not with the pain along her ribs, and there was something very wrong with her knee. The boot that had hit her in the lot now struck again in phantom memory, though the jolt of pain as she shifted was real.

"I'm fine," she whispered.

He made a sound in the back of his throat. Michelle appeared with a gown and a pair of trauma shears to help get Win's scrubs off. Matthew's movements as he checked Win's injuries were as precise as his fighting had been. Gentle but firm hands brushed over her body, calling out a clear FAST exam, a deep laceration along her ribs, and then... nothing when he got to her leg. X-ray arrived and snapped their films, but Matthew didn't throw them up on the room monitors.

"What's happening?" Win caught Matthew's wrist and he stopped at once, giving her his full attention. "What's wrong with my leg?"

"A minor dislocation. We'll take care of it once we get some pain meds into you. But maybe just this once I won't make you watch." A corner of his mouth lifted. "Your first time as a patient, right?"

She didn't see the humor in it at all. Her body trembled.

Michelle approached with an IV set, took one look at Matthew's face and handed it over to him without hesitation. Win had never seen the charge nurse do that before. In fact, no one except Matthew was touching Win, as if the doctor was a wolf unwilling to let anyone near its dinner. He'd let Michelle help Win into a gown, but that was as far as it went. The exam, the blood pressure, even the blanket covering her was put there by Matthew's hand and no one else's.

Now, he swiped an alcohol prep over the vein in her elbow, and Win's entire body went rigid.

"Look away," Matthew said. A soft order. Win turned her head. His hands were sure as he gripped her arm, the needle sliding in with a barely felt pinch.

"How did you do that?" Win asked.

Matthew was already securing the IV tubing with pieces of tape

Michelle handed over. "A shit ton of practice," he said. "Once you start a few dozen in a moving motorcade, in the dark, with your hands so cold you can't feel your fingers, you gather some confidence."

"Jennson," Dr. Yarborough came up beside them, the only one Matthew seemed willing to let that close to the bed. "Did you want to reduce the knee yourself?"

Whatever temporary calm Win had enjoyed disappeared. She knew what that meant. How much that hurt, no matter what pain meds Matthew was already pushing into her IV line. She pressed herself into the mattress as if she could somehow escape the coming fate, Matthew's too attentive gaze following her every move. Pain and fear rushed through her, as she lay there, as vulnerable as in that parking lot.

Matthew crouched beside Win's head, their faces eye level. "It's a patellar dislocation. The good news is that once the kneecap slides back into place you'll feel a hell of a lot better. You already know the bad news."

Pain. A hell of a lot of pain. "Do it." Win's mouth was dry.

Matthew nodded, but instead of getting up, only said over his shoulder. "Dr. Yarborough, if you don't mind?"

Win blinked. Matthew wasn't going to do it himself? He always performed reductions, even when others called for assistance from ortho. "Why—"

"So that I can be a friend instead." Matthew sat on the edge of Win's bed and took both her hands in his. His grip had a reassuring confidence that leaked through the connection into Win's cool skin. *You are safe. I've got you.* "Watch my face, not his hands. And breathe."

"I'm starting now," Yarborough said. Win's hands tightened on Matthew's as pure blazing agony exploded in her leg.

Win arched, screaming, gripping Matthew's hands so hard the bones rubbed. He didn't flinch, didn't so much as shift that lifeline gaze away from hers. "I've got you," he said over and over, his voice like a metronome. Tears of pain rolled down her face.

Matthew didn't have to turn around to know when it was over.

"Thank you, everyone," he said, his eyes still only on her. "I've got it from here." He brushed the back of his hand over her wet cheeks.

Doors opened and closed. People left. All except one.

"You have until the end of this case, Jennson," Yarborough said quietly.

"Thank you, sir."

Win swallowed, processing the words through the haze of pain and drugs. "What happens then? What happens when he is done taking care of me?"

"I presume I'm suspended," Matthew answered, that eerie calm never leaving his voice.

"What?" She tried and failed to sit up. "Why?"

"Assault with a deadly weapon and probably a half-dozen other hospital policies."

"More than half a dozen," said Yarborough. "And yes."

Images of Matthew slamming Tank into the cabinets, floated in Win's mind. Then Matthew moving like a deadly predator amidst the bikers in the staff parking lot, a living wall between her and them. "He was protecting me." Win did manage to get to her elbow this time, though the gash along her ribs flamed in protest. She found Yarborough's face. It wasn't angry, but it was hard. Win shook her head at him. "Everything Matthew did, he did to protect me. He saved my life. You weren't there. He -"

"I know what he did, Win," Yarborough said not unkindly. "Dr. Jennson went well beyond the level of force that was either necessary or acceptable. He knows it. And he knows he'll be punished."

CASEY

Casey lay in bed, staring out the window at the star-filled sky. The ship rocked gently and the even sounds of Sonia's breathing said that she was asleep. That made for one of them. Casey blinked, clearing one picture from his mind only to replace it with another. The downside of having a photographic memory was that Casey remembered everything in picture perfect detail. The skill made it easy to pass the bar exam and pull up the files Briar had emailed earlier. It also made it easy to, well, pull up the files Briar had emailed.

Nero was indeed here with a cabal from Satan's Armada, one where he wasn't the top dog. No wonder he'd changed his plans to come to the cruise early—it was a chance to rub shoulders, to go beyond whatever position he already had access to. There were five men total in their group. Nero, Mammoth, Razor, Popeye, and Patriot.

Mammoth was from New York, Briar's intel had said and had a passion for exerting his dominance. Except in his mind, it wasn't dominance if the victims were willing. At least three women had been taken to the hospital with injuries after encountering him, all quickly dropping charges after their initial confessions. That meant there were at least another dozen that had never gotten medical help.

Razor was the Armada's sergeant at arms from the Denver chapter. Two counts of rape allegations, enough assault and battery incidents, usually in confrontation with another biker gang, to make Casey question how the man had any brains still left in his head, and Casey's personal favorite—an unconfirmed rumor that Razor was in charge of the Armada's sex trafficking arm. Briar got nothing on Popeye and Patriot. Oh, and it seemed the five brought along their own entertainment in the form of women. These were mostly confined to their stateroom unless needed.

Casey's freedom with hundred dollar bills had gotten the Armada's notice, too. They didn't know who he was yet, but knew enough to appreciate that he had both money and power. He'd get into their circle with that. All he had to do was become his father.

Casey shut his eyes. This wasn't what he'd signed up for, not originally. Chatting up one asshole at a party was a far cry from making himself at home inside their perversion. But few plans survived first contact. So he'd adjust. He always did.

To his right, Sonia stirred and rolled over onto her other side, now facing him. Casey watched her sleep, letting the steadiness of her gentle breathing calm his own. She was his lifeline in the middle of this mess, and she had no idea.

The ship rocked beneath another wave and the cabin tilted, pushing Sonia toward him. She shifted around to regain balance without waking, and ended up curled against his side. Her breath brushed his shoulder, every place her body touched waking to her presence. Casey drew a shaky breath, not daring to move. Not willing to give up the connection even if it wasn't real, especially when Sonia's sleeping mouth curled into an easy, content smile.

Sonia was *good*. Naive sometimes, but beautiful and kind and ferocious and good. A moral compass that Casey could always trust to point north. Maybe that was the secret as to why she was so utterly immune to his charms—because deep down in her soul, she knew she was too good for him.

As if to prove his own point, Casey lay still all night, lest his slightest movement remind her to turn away.

He rose before Sonia woke, carefully extricating himself from the bed. She muttered in discontent, but fortunately remained asleep, avoiding uncomfortable questions as to how long exactly she'd been pressed against him and just how little he'd done to correct the situation.

Once Sonia was up, they spent the first part of the day flashing money around the ship, Casey making it a point to always pay cash even when a credit card or room bill was preferred. Especially when it was preferred. Casey was creating the image of a club owner with the kind of money one preferred to keep out of the bank. They'd also started planting details about their home base of Denton Valley, Colorado, which was Nero's target location if Sky's intel was right. Each bit of info, each denial of access to Sonia, was another bloody piece of bait.

That evening, Briar finally put the Armada cabal at a reception room in one of the cruise ship's larger halls. Duane had rejected the idea of bringing up someone from the beauty salon to help Sonia dress and style her hair and makeup, offering his own services instead. Casey had caught enough of Duane's covert glances to know that the young man's personal preferences did not lie in the female direction and the offer was genuine. Since Sonia seemed more comfortable with Duane than anyone else around, the issue was for once settled to everyone's satisfaction.

Duane had dressed Sonia in a deep blue evening gown that left one shoulder exposed. A swirl of swarovski crystals coiled down the bodice, drawing the eye to the delicious curve of her hip. Duane pinned half her hair up with matching barrettes and teased the rest to hang in sensual locks that framed her face and neck. The mascara he'd put on for the evening made Sonia's already large eyes even more incredible, and it was an effort of will to avoid gawking at her as Casey slipped into his tux.

"I think we need to have a chat with Duane," he muttered. "We want to draw a bit of attention, not bring down the whole god damn ship."

He held out his arm and she took it. The contact reminded him of the way she'd inadvertently curled up against his side overnight, and his trousers suddenly pressed uncomfortably tight against his crotch. Casey swallowed and shifted his weight, trying to discreetly adjust himself.

"Something wrong?" Sonia asked. And the fucked up thing was that she wasn't joking. She truly had no idea how she looked, what she did to him.

"Show time, kitten," Casey said to her by way of answer and led them into the reception hall. The *Belle Nuit's* crew had outdone itself. The hall was awash in sequins, glitter, and glamor. Waiters bearing silver trays of wine and champagne flitted about, neatly avoiding the women in their sparkling dresses and men in tuxedos. The lights were dimmed with the exception of the crystal chandeliers hanging above the dance floor and pseudo candles on the tables lining the perimeter. These were set with fine crystal, sterling silver, and sea-foam plates for the munchies.

The star of the show however was the pianist, in a long tailed coat playing the grand beauty.

It made Casey long for his own piano, and with his eyes closed, he tilted his head to the side listening to the music. Bach. And done well.

"You need a moment alone with the piano?" Sonia murmured to him under the sound of clinking glasses and low rumble of conversation.

"I wouldn't say no," Casey murmured back just as quietly. "Though I'd take a moment alone with not just the piano."

"Funny." Her eyes surveyed the room, and Casey knew the moment that she spotted Nero. Her back had pulled straighter, shoulders rolling back as if about to address a jury. "I'm going to go talk to him."

"No need." The notion of Sonia rubbing shoulders with that piece of shit didn't sit well at all, no matter what school they'd gone to together. "He'll seek me out eventually."

She gave him a look that somehow managed to go down her nose at him despite her being shorter. "We are in a public place and it looks strange if I'm avoiding a classmate when I'm here for a school reunion." She rose up on her toes to whisper into his ear, the slight scent of the ocean clinging to her. It made him go stiff all over again, although he knew she was only doing it to bring her lips close to his ear. "Deal with it. Go lick the piano if it makes you feel better."

"Sassy," Casey managed to say, but his hand tightened on her forearm. "Be careful, kitten. You know who his friends are."

She nuzzled his neck before stepping away. "Go. Play."

With a swish of her dress, Sonia disappeared through the crowd and Casey made his way to the bar. He signaled the bartender for a top shelf old fashioned as he watched Sonia's reflection in the mirror. Briar was keeping an eye on them both through the cameras set up in his stateroom.

Really, Sonia was right. It was fine to mingle here. It was safe. It was... it was just so damn hard to watch Nero kiss her cheek then say something that made Sonia throw her head back and laugh. An easy, familiar sound that probably meant the man had shared an old joke, a connection of a type Casey would never share with the counselor. Nero was very probably a piece of shit, and he certainly represented pieces of shit, but that didn't take away the fact that once upon a time he and Sonia had worried about the same exams and shared notes and walked the graduation stage together.

"What the fuck's going on?" Briar said into Casey's earpiece. *"You look like you've spotted a gun I'm not seeing."*

Casey made an upright circle motion with his drink to signal to big brother that all was well and forced himself into a chat with the bartender. He lasted all of five minutes before turning back, only to find Sonia and Nero no longer at the sidelines.

Casey straightened at once, eyes searching the room. He was about to signal a question to Briar, when he spotted the pair walking onto the dance floor. In the mirror's reflection, Casey could see them chatting away as Nero put one hand on Sonia's waist and grasped the other with his palm. She let him. They swayed out of rhythm to the music.

Nero was truly a terrible dancer, especially as he tried to twirl Sonia around beneath the pianist's rendition of Billy Joel's Piano Man. Sonia tripped. Tripped and laughed, the pair of them nearly crashing to the floor together before saving each other in the nic of time. They reclaimed their portable hug, laughing and talking and going right back to their off beat dancing. As if nothing happened.

Red colored the sides of Casey's vision.

"STAND DOWN, BRO," Briar said in Casey's earpiece. Casey shut the damn thing off.

"Is there something wrong with your drink, sir?" The bartender inquired.

Casey looked at his untouched glass, drank the whiskey in a single gulp, and put it back onto the bar top. He was moving forward before he even realized what he was doing. The intelligent part of him knew full well that Briar was right. That he needed to stand down, cool off and let Sonia do her thing. But the rest of him was having none of the rational thoughts. His core, instincts, and cock couldn't care less about plans and conversations, or anything except the fact that a short, filthy sleazeball had his hands on Sonia. That he was making her laugh. That he was going to drop her on the floor in another moment.

Casey reached the pair just as Nero was attempting another ill-fated spin, his mouth moving quicker than his feet.

"Excuse me." Casey caught Sonia's elbow before she could fall, but it was Nero who he glared down at from his greater height.

Nero's nostrils flared and he raised his chin.

"You don't mind if I cut in, do you?"

"Casey," Sonia started to say, but he didn't listen. Couldn't. Not when Nero's fucking pants had a pulsing bulge in the front.

Shouldering the smaller man aside, Casey took Sonia into the frame of his arms. Casey's right hand splayed on her back, feeling the lithe body beneath the blue satin, his other taking her hand. The Piano Man was still swirling over the dance floor, the *one two three, one two three*, of the viennese waltz as clear as crystal. Casey's eyes drifted closed for a heartbeat, savoring the notes and he let one more measure go through him before looking right at Sonia and stepping forward.

Casey's thigh brushed between her legs as he set them spinning.

She followed beautifully, her body responding to the cues from Casey's frame. Within seconds of the connection, Casey knew Sonia had some dance training, even if not the classical kind he and Briar had gotten in the posh military school they'd been sent to. Unlike her usual self, the dancer inside Sonia was open and willing, taking joy in every step and turn and spin.

Throughout the dance floor, people caught in the spell of the music paused to watch. Their dance was like a beacon to the world, like a first dance at a wedding. Casey's eyes drank in Sonia's face as, secure in Casey's arms, she glided over the polished floor. Her own eyes were half shuttered, a smile on her face as she responded to the siren's *one two three, one two three* call.

Casey could feel how the music filled her, releasing all the energy she had kept locked inside. It filled Casey with a haze of euphoria.

They circled the guests and the waiters, conquering each meter of empty space that parted before them. And then, when they were right in front of Nero's nose, Casey spun them both. Their inside legs pressing together, their arms in perfect frame, their hair whipping behind them as they went faster and faster in a chase of the song.

The pianist ended the piece with an easy flourish and the crowd around them clapped. Casey released his hold on Sonia's waist, both their chests rising and falling from the speed and exhilaration. Open joy still shone on the counselor's face as the energy of the room filled the air around them.

With a small bow to the gawking crowd, Casey led Sonia off the dance floor to a quiet corner of the room. On the way, he grabbed two water bottles from a waiter's tray and opened one before handing it to Sonia.

She took a long drink. Casey tried not to think of what that mouth, wrapped around the neck of the water bottle, would feel like around other things.

"What was that?" Sonia asked when she'd finally drunk her fill. She still had that high haze of the dance about her, but reason was now returning to her intelligent gaze.

"A viennese waltz."

She cocked a brow. "You know what I mean."

Of course he did. He was an idiot, but he wasn't stupid. "Not in the least."

She shook her head, but at least seemed to be in too happy of a mental space to be truly considering ways of castrating him.

"Nero and I were talking about Denton Valley, by the way," she said. "He looked you up. Knows about the North Vault. Between that and probably the cash you've been throwing around like candy, he wants to talk. Or at least he did, before you decided to start another pissing contest with him."

Casey cringed and was glad he'd turned off Briar. Across the room, Nero sat with his four companions, three of whom had women beside them. The thunder in the short man's eyes said he'd marked the humiliation and was still stewing over it. Shit.

"Let's go make amends," Casey said, glumly.

"Can you behave?" Sonia asked.

He knew she wasn't joking, and pulled himself together. "I can. Unfortunately, behaving in this case doesn't mean what most people think it means. Come on."

A hand between Sonia's shoulder blades, Casey guided the pair of them to where Nero sat stewing. Nero bristled at their approach, but Casey put up his free hand in a gesture of surrender.

"I come in peace," he said, sprawling on a chair and asking the waiter to bring everyone a new round of whatever they were drinking. Sonia went to take a seat as well, but Casey pulled her onto his lap instead, his hand toying possessively with the slit in her dress. "Seeing my woman so free with you put a burr under my saddle." He winked at Nero. "I'll ride it out of her later."

Nero regarded him for a moment and then threw his head back and laughed, the other men at the table joining in.

MATTHEW

Still in the ER's isolation room, Win opened her glassy eyes and blinked at Matthew. With all the pain medications he had given her, she had been out for several hours and was now beginning to stir. Her large eyes peered at him warily.

"Matthew," she whispered.

"Yeah." He felt a tug of something deep in his chest and desperately wanted to brush a lock of hair away from her face. Instead, he took one more glance at the monitor and disconnected the blood pressure cuff. "How do you feel?"

Win shifted her gaze away, her eyes suddenly distant, as if she were looking out at a faraway horizon. "I'm not sure," she murmured. "Strange. Like I'm looking out someone else's window."

"That would be the oxy," Matthew said. "I gave you quite a bit." More than he'd usually order. But she'd been so hurt and frightened that he hadn't had the heart to tackle the long row of stitches along her ribs without another dose. "Don't move too quickly. You are more sore than you think."

He could still see the horrible bruises covering her small frame, the fractures in her ribs that the biker's boot had left behind.

The door to the treatment room opened, Michelle stepping inside. "What's the plan, Dr. Jennson?"

Right. The ER needed the room back.

"I'll take her home," Matthew said. Michelle opened her mouth in protest and Matthew quickly raised his hands in a placating gesture. "My home, Michelle. I wasn't going to leave her by herself." With both of them being on Satan's Armada's shitlist, he wouldn't have sent Win home alone even if she wasn't hurt. "I'm aware that I'm an idiot, but I'm not that big of an idiot."

"You aren't an idiot," said Win from the bed. "But you are big. And pretty, too. And very fit. Like my brother." She turned her head to Michelle. "Matthew was a Navy SEAL. A lot of them look like that. They are often assholes, but they are nice to look at, you know?"

Fuck. For both their sakes, Matthew really hoped Win would remember none of this once the narcotics wore off.

The charge nurse cleared her throat. "You break it, you buy it, Doc. I'll put in the discharge paperwork. Do you need anything?"

"I'm good." Matthew's backpack was already full of medical supplies to cover the care Win would need. And a few more things. Possibly enough to run a miniature trauma center from his living room. Better safe than sorry.

He glanced toward the wall separating them from the main ER. "How are the Armadeers?"

"The original stabbing has been discharged," Michelle said with her usual efficiency. "The arterial bleed got two units of blood and went up to the OR. He's stable now."

So Matthew hadn't killed the asshole. That was probably a good thing. Probably.

He noticed Win struggling to get off the bed and put his arm out to stop her. "You won't get far walking right now. What do you need?"

"My computer."

"We'll get it before we go."

She resumed her escape attempt. Yeah. He should have been more conservative with the pain killers. "I need to check the forums," Win explained. "You should change your phone pin, Matthew. Four eight seven six. It's the same as your door access code at the hospital. I know because I looked over your shoulder. Four eight seven six. You shouldn't reuse pins. And be more careful about shoulder surfing."

Matthew grimaced. That was his phone pin alright. Trust Win to remember his pin, but forget the fact that she had cracked ribs and a recently dislocated patella. "We'll bring your laptop. For now, let's get you a pair of scrubs to go home in."

"I'm not going to your house," Win said. "I don't like you even if you are pretty. And you don't like me. You are just doing it because you are Sith's best friend. I'm going home. To my home. Alone."

"You can't walk," Matthew reminded her.

Ignoring him, Win started to slide off the bed. Michelle moved to intercept her, but he put an arm in the nurse's path. He didn't feel like arguing with a high Win for the next hour, so gravity could make his point for him.

The moment reality conquered pain meds was crystal clear. Win's bad leg buckled as it took her weight, her body arching as if a bolt of lighting shot through it. With a gasp of pain, Win fell to the floor, barely getting her arm out in front of herself to stop the fall. Matthew winced. That had to hurt. Win whimpered, lowering the rest of the way to the linoleum as she panted.

"It's a good thing you are so short," Matthew crouched beside Win and slid his arm around her to ease her into a sitting position. Between her hospital gown and her now wild hair, she looked like a half tamed lion cub. "Only so much damage you can do falling from no height at all."

She didn't smile. She gripped her ribs and gulped short bursts of air, as if afraid of drawing a full breath. Her shoulders curled in on themselves. Fuck. He'd meant to prove a point the way he would have in the SEALs, and instead he'd only proved that he was an asshole who'd let her get hurt. Again. Just as he had when he'd sent her into the biker's room, then again when his loss of self-control had painted a target on Win's back.

"I'm sorry, Win," Matthew said into her hair. He was sorry. Not just because Sith was going to rightfully kick his ass from here to the underworld. "It will be better tomorrow when the swelling goes down. I promise."

To Matthew's surprise, Michelle patted *his* shoulder before leaving. "I'll get all her things together, and make sure the pharmacy has the prescriptions filled for you."

Win lifted her face, which was now only inches from his own. She leaned into Matthew freely, trusting him to keep her from falling again. The scent of citrus shampoo drifted from her hair. A perfect scent and one that somehow roused a protective instinct inside Matthew that he didn't think he was capable of feeling so intensely. This time, he was unable to stop himself from brushing back the locks of Win's golden hair and tracing his thumb along her cheek bone.

"You'll be alright," he whispered.

Win's throat bobbed as she swallowed. Capturing his wrist in her hand, she pressed her cheek against his palm, rubbing like a cat against it. "You saved my life."

"Your life shouldn't have been in danger to begin with." Matthew pressed his forehead to Win's, every fiber in his body suddenly aware of the connection. It was hard to breathe. Harder to form words. "I have you now. You are safe and I'll make sure you stay that way. I promise."

She shifted, just slightly, but enough to bring her mouth in-line with his. Her lips parted, her minty breath hot on his skin. She tangled her hand in the fabric of his scrubs. "If I didn't hate you so much, I'd want to kiss you," she whispered. "And I don't think I hate you."

A shudder went through Matthew, his whole body tightening at the siren's call. He was hard. Painfully, pulsing hard. And he wanted so so badly to taste her.

Win pushed her mouth toward his.

He pulled back, twisting to scoop her up off the floor and back into bed. "You do hate me," he reminded her and himself both. "It's the oxy that's having other ideas."

WIN

Win awoke in a large bed. Not hers. Cool crisp sheets pressed against her aching body and a thick, luxurious down comforter embraced her from above. She vaguely remembered Matthew driving her from the hospital to his place and fortunately recalled nothing of how she'd gotten out of her hospital gown and into the man's oversized shirt that she now wore.

She tried to sit up and quickly gave up on that idea. Not because she couldn't, but because everything hurt. Her ribs, her torso, her leg. She remembered the rest of yesterday then, too. Puncturing the biker's vein so badly that the hematoma had grown to a goose egg before their eyes. The bikers' answering fury. Matthew having to bodily intervene. She remembered blissfully scrolling the dark web when the assault came. Then Matthew again. Moving like a predator, a wall of pure muscle and violence between her and death.

Things after that became hazy, with the notable exception of sheer agony when Dr. Yarborough set her knee while Matthew kept her from leaping from the bed. A Navy SEAL, she was not.

"Good morning."

Win startled to realize that Matthew was in the room with her. He pushed himself up off the floor and rubbed his face. From the looks of it, he'd slept there, his back braced against the wall. Win sure as hell didn't remember that arrangement. There was something about Matthew's presence that made her feel safe, even as every taut line of his lethal body screamed danger.

He still wore his scrubs and, even after a night spent on the floor, looked like a model off a fitness poster. Coiled muscle shaping the fabric, the shadow of scuff along his jaw, blue penetrating eyes. Loose cotton bottoms that hung off the crests of powerful hips.

Shit. Win had a crush on her brother's best friend. Worse, she had a crush on her attending. Who didn't like her. Shoving those inconvenient little realizations into a deep dark pocket, Win pushed herself into a sitting position. "Good morning." She winced. "What are you doing here?"

Matthew stretched then studied her with unnerving intensity. For a moment, Win thought he would reach a hand out toward her, but then he didn't. "How do you feel?" he asked.

"Fine."

He blew out a long breath, as if her answer disappointed him. It probably did. In her place, Matthew would have been up already, pain or no pain. So would Sith. Instead of spouting the obvious lie, they would have pushed through. Up and dressed and making coffee, testing their body's limits. And here she was, still working up the courage to get out of bed. Pathetic.

Win had never been strong and tough like Sith was. That had been their father's greatest disappointment, when he'd still been alive that is. Not only did his promised second son turn out to be a premature infant girl, but a small, weak, cowardly girl to boot. Sith never echoed their father's words, but Win knew he'd chafed at having to delay joining the Navy to watch over her. And now Matthew was stuck with that billet.

She pulled herself together. "What's the final damage tally?"

"Two rib fractures, both stable," Matthew answered with his usual SEAL efficiency. "A fifteen centimeter laceration on the left chest. I closed that up. Right patella dislocation that reduced without complications."

Win felt herself blanche slightly at the memory of that pain.

"All in all, it's not as bad as it could have been. You'll be fine."

In other words, stop feeling sorry for yourself and get on with it.

He pointed to the floor with his chin. "You should get up. The movement will be good for the leg." He paused, adding more softly. "I won't let you fall."

The words felt laden with meaning. Of course they were. Matthew wanted the same thing from her now as he had in the ER. Grow a spine, get over the petty discomforts, and get the fucking job done. Like he would. Like any SEAL would.

She summoned up that stoic face her father demanded when she'd fallen off her bike or gotten hit with a ball. "Of course. I'll meet you in the living room."

"Yeah, we aren't playing that game again," he said. She had no idea what he was talking about. Matthew stepped forward and held out his hand. "Let me help."

"I don't—"

A loud bang cut suddenly through the room, followed by a cascade of smaller tumbles. *Thump bom bom bom.*

Panic shot through Win. She jerked. Gasped. Blazing pain seared through her broken ribs.

All at once it was happening again. The metal tray falling down, the yelling, the fighting. She felt the biker's boot connect with her side and steal her breath. Heard the pop inside her knee. She smelled blood. Tasted it. Her whole mouth filled with copper terror.

"Win. Win!" Matthew's voice broke through the haze, his strong hands on her shoulders, pulling her to face him. His blue eyes gripped hers like they had in the lot. Held. "You are safe," he said firmly. "You are here with me. You are safe."

The secure feel of Matthew's hands hauled Win from the flash of memory. She clutched his shirt, breathing in his scent. Feeling his warmth seep into her through her thin shirt. She knew that she should let go. That it was ridiculous not to. But she couldn't. "I'm sorry," Win whispered against Matthew's muscled chest.

Matthew hesitated and then, instead of letting go, wrapped his arms around her instead. "I've got you." His breath whispered against her hair. It was just an embrace yet it felt more intimate than any connection she'd shared, and it left Win more vulnerable, too. Especially as she realized she was trembling. God, Matthew must think her an utter coward.

"I'm sorry," she said again.

"You've nothing to apologize for."

Lie. She had everything to apologize for. From falling apart to getting him into trouble. She remembered Dr. Yarborough making that part clear, too. He wasn't happy with Matthew's choices and there would be punishment.

Matthew stroked Win's hair. "May I introduce you to our assailant?" he asked.

"Huh?"

He pulled Win away and gave her a hint of a smile before stepping away and walking around to the other side of the bed. Win turned around to find a large bookshelf standing on that side of the room. Books stood in military-neat rows everywhere except for the top shelf, which was in disarray. And on the floor, sitting atop a pile of fallen books and decorations like a fire drake guarding its trove, sat a small black kitten.

"Meow," the tiny fire drake with glowing green eyes announced.

"Mind your manners, cat," said Matthew.

The fireball, which was as black as a cartoon Halloween drawing, jumped into Matthew's arms, scampered along his shirt, and perched on his broad shoulder. He gave Win a judgemental look from above.

"Meow."

Matthew pulled the kitten off his shoulder and held him suspended on one large palm. The kitten's paws dangled free in the air. "Odysseus, meet Win. Win, Odysseus."

"You have a kitten?" It didn't fit. If Matthew was to have a pet, it should have been an attack trained German Shepherd. Or maybe a cobra. Not a small poof that could easily conceal himself in a toy store's stuffie aisle.

"In his opinion he has me, but yes to the substantive part." He set

Odysseus onto the bed. "He showed up at the building's front door one rainy day about a month ago, and we've come to an understanding."

"What's the understanding?"

"Mostly, that he is in charge and I exist to provide food, a clean litter box, and a lap to curl up on."

"Lucky cat." Realizing she'd said that aloud, Win slid off the bed and, ignoring the ton of pain stabbing her leg, and limped as quickly as she could to the attached bathroom.

After the unexpected foray into Matthew's arms that morning, Win didn't think she could look the SEAL in the eyes again without melting into an abyss from embarrassment. By the time she'd come out of the bathroom, her hand braced on the wall for balance and support, he'd been blissfully gone from the room. That was when their mutual silence had taken hold.

Fortunately, Win's laptop had made it to Matthew's place. Spotting her Macbook Pro salvation in the living room, Win dove into it with the desperation of a drowning woman scenting air. Within ten minutes she'd spun up her VPNs and hopped the virtual distance from Matthew's apartment. It didn't actually insulate her from the lethal SEAL sitting with his own computer not ten feet away, but it was the next best thing. Matthew's mere presence sent too many thoughts through her. Too many confusing emotions. Especially given the fact that she still wore his shirt and scent.

Slipping into her *@DocPhantom42* skin, Win kept herself busy for the rest of the day by catching up on research simulations while playing a side game of capture the flag and keeping half an eye on the forums. Matthew was asking about some experimental anti-seizure drugs. *@DocPhantom42* told him to get his facts in order and sent him enough research publications to make him rub his temples while looking at the screen. Whatever Matthew was trying to do on the dark web, he was an amateur who was going to get himself in trouble.

They had just started on a day of exchanging minimal words while Matthew watched Win's every movement when Cullen Hunt appeared in the doorway. He had coffee in one hand and a bag of her clothes hanging on his shoulder. "Sky thought you could use some of your own things," Cullen said, handing the bag over to Matthew, who'd moved in to intercept. "How are you feeling, Doc?"

"I'm fine," Win answered from the couch. She knew little about Cullen beyond him being the Tridents' unofficial leader and the Chief Operating Officer of the Denton Memorial Hospital where she'd started all this trouble. Like Matthew, Cullen was powerfully built with an aura of command radiating from him in all directions. It made Win want to press deeper into the cushions. Was he the one from whom the punishment Yarborough alluded to would be handed down?

Cullen weighed Win with his gaze then turned to Matthew. "How is she?"

Matthew sat himself on the armrest of the couch—as far away from Win as the piece of furniture allowed—and left the chair for Cullen. "Like you'd expect after a group of bikers jumped her, but… better than it could have been."

"I'm sorry," Cullen said to Win. "The small good news I came to share was that Tank, the ring leader, was picked up by PD. With some luck, they are going to make an assault and battery charge stick."

Win drew in a long breath and instantly regretted it. Matthew shot her an assessing look, but turned back to Cullen. "By 'some luck' I presume you are talking about me assaulting the assholes back?"

Cullen leaned back in the chair, extending his long legs in front of him. "I've seen the video footage. I think any civilian jury we put that video in front of will say you were justified and acting in defense of Dr. Carrell's life." He paused. "Fortunately, we've no cameras in the treatment room where you smashed his face in."

No cameras, but Cullen plainly knew what had happened. And wasn't pleased about it.

A silent alert pinged on Win's screen and she opened the forum window she'd had monitoring anything within the Denton Valley geofence she'd set up as much from prudence as from curiosity. The mens' voices disappeared into the background as she followed the alert, then backtracked to the sender.

"Someone is looking to make that footage disappear," Win said, not looking up from her screen.

The mens' voices stopped.

"That footage is in a secure room within the hospital," Cullen said. "There is no way someone is breaching that. Certainly not a bunch of bikers."

"They don't need to breach the hospital, just the network," said Win.

"We have IT for that," said Cullen.

Win looked up at that, staring at the SEAL incredulously. "No offense, but your security IT is about as good as my IV placement. And in case you are still wondering, that means not very good."

Matthew moved off the armrest and came to sit beside Win and peered over her shoulder at the screen. Every fiber in Win's body woke at the sudden proximity, and the spot where his knee accidentally brushed against her thigh. Win swallowed and tried like hell to give no indication that she was aware of his presence.

"Just how much are you exaggerating?" Cullen asked.

Win pulled up a new command screen and started typing. A minute later, Cullen's cell phone rang.

"Hunt," Cullen answered. "They what? No, I didn't. Wait." He lowered his phone, his face slightly pale as he looked at Win. "Do you by chance know why all the security monitors are now saying—
"

"Welcome to the Death Star, please check in with Cullen Hunt?" Matthew read off of Win's screen. He winced. "That's the only part on there that's in English."

"Yeah," said Cullen. He closed his eyes for a moment and took a deep breath before bringing the phone to his ear again. "Sorry, Bert. I'm on it. Yeah. No. I understand. It's fine. Give me a minute."

He hung up and stared at her intensely enough that Win shimmed further into the couch. It was too much like the glare Matthew gave her when she balked about going into a trauma room or did something that went contrary to the attending's wishes. A perverted shadow of one Tank had thrown at her before exploding. An uncomfortable chill gripped her spine. This is what happened when her computer self and pathetic real self intersected.

A small growl escaped Matthew's chest, his body angling so slightly between her and Cullen. "Back off, Hunt."

Cullen blinked and shook himself, that glare gone. "My apologies, Doc," he said. "My thoughts were about the gaping security hole I hadn't realized I had, not your demonstration. Though, if you could clue me in to how you did that, I'd be grateful."

She swallowed, still watching the SEAL's face. Matthew squeezed her shoulder and a whole new wave of anxious energy raced through her at the touch. At the masculine scent that now coiled around her. "The firmware on some of the camera hardware is outdated," she said, looking back at her computer. It was easier that way. "It's a common issue. Anyway, I exploited it. But I'm undoing it now." She took the message off Bert's screens. "It's not all so cut and dry, but you get the point."

"You, Doc, are one scary woman," Cullen said with no hint of condescension.

"Impressive work," Matthew muttered beside her. Win's stomach did another belly flop.

"I'll have the PD prioritize pulling the footage into evidence," said Cullen. "Unless you are about to tell me that's not secure either?"

"I don't know. I've never looked at Denton PD. But… You lot are working on taking down the whole Satan's Armada chapter, right? Would it be helpful to you to know their banking information?"

"Of course it would," said Cullen. "Why?"

Win started typing. Yes. Yes, that would work.

Matthew touched her arm. "Win? What were you saying?"

"Oh. I just offered to do the camera job for the Armada." She opened three new windows. "If I negotiate this right, I'll have some numbers for you shortly."

SONIA

"I don't think you should go," Casey said for the fourth time as he and Sonia got ready to attend the private get-together last night's chat with Nero had gotten them invited to. "You've seen how they treat women. How I'd have to treat you."

"Like property, yes," Sonia said with a great deal more calm than she felt. "Like you said, I was there. I remember the subtleties."

That last hour when they'd joined Nero and the Armada had been anything but forgettable—or subtle. Casey had pulled Sonia onto his lap, idly fondling her shoulder and knee and then—god—her inner thigh, which he'd somehow managed to access through the slit in Sonia's dress. He'd been so damn casual about it, as if fondling her was just something to keep his hands occupied with while they talked. While the men talked.

Not that Sonia would have been capable of carrying on a conversation even if she'd been invited, not with Casey's fingers tracing lazy circles on her sensitive skin. Each brush of his fingers sent jolts of erotic need through her body, no matter how much she ordered said body to cut it out. They'd been in public for heaven's sake. Had been noticed. Sonia felt the eyes of guests and staff stray over to them. Except instead of dousing her inconvenient arousal, the feeling of being watched had heightened it instead. Which was wrong and depraved in all manner of ways, but no less true for being so. Fuck. Something inside Sonia was utterly broken.

It was a miracle of the first order that Casey hadn't ventured just a few inches higher to discover just how wet he was making her. A miracle that her wetness hadn't slithered lower from her panties. By the time they were thirty minutes into the little get together, she'd found it difficult to think straight over the adrenaline and need pulsing through her body.

Sonia had raced for the shower the moment they'd returned to the stateroom. She'd had to turn the water to ice cold and swiftly take care of herself before she dared to face Casey again. By the time she'd emerged, Casey was changed into sweats and a t-shirt and was ready for his own evening routine.

They didn't talk, Casey not even throwing his usual teasing jabs at her. Instead, he'd put a pillow between them on the bed. A barrier. Because they weren't really engaged or into each other or connected in any way other than operational.

"Of course I'm going," Sonia said, likewise for the fourth time. She took one last look at the computer screen with Briar's intel up and closed the laptop. "We are partners."

"Worried that I might have to seduce other women and cheat on you?" he crooned, back to his usual cocky irritating self as he slipped a pair of gold cufflinks into his shirt. The diamond studded initials, *C.M*, caught the light.

"I'm surprised you haven't gone into withdrawal from not sharing a bed with several women at a time," said Sonia. "But aside from monitoring your fidelity, I'm hoping to talk to the women. From their expressions last night, I didn't get the sense they were beloved girlfriends so much as—"

"Forced sex slaves being taken out for a spin?" Casey finished for her, all humor fading from his face. "That crossed my mind. Especially since Briar's facial ID didn't match anything. My guess is they aren't citizens and the Armada has their documents."

Sonia shuddered. She knew such things happened. Theoretically.

But seeing it up close, knowing someone she used to share class notes with was involved? It was a new level of disturbing.

"I don't like the thought of you in the Armada's stateroom. And I don't like..." he shook his head, a flash of vulnerability crossing his gaze. The cufflink he'd been threading into his cuff escaped his fingers and tumbled to the floor. "I don't particularly like you seeing me with them either. Seeing me behaving like them."

Sonia strode over to Casey before he could go after the cufflink and put her palm against his cheek. There was a slight evening scruff to his warm skin and the familiar scent of cologne wafted from him. His gray eyes looked haunted, but he remained still as she turned his face toward her.

"I know exactly the kind of asshole you are, McKenzie," she said, running her thumb over his tight jaw. "It would take too long to describe everything that's wrong with you, but I know for certain you are not *that* type of asshole."

Casey's throat bobbed as he swallowed. He put his hand over hers, the gesture somehow more intimate than all of yesterday's strokes put together.

"You are playing a game, Casey," Sonia whispered to him, willing him to believe her. "I know you are. I am, too. So, we play. And then we come back to the stateroom and shower it off. Alright?"

He swallowed again, then nodded. "If something doesn't feel right today, squeeze my arm twice and I'll get you out of there, come hell or high water."

"Got it," Sonia said, though she knew full well that she wasn't going to use that parachute for anything short of nuclear war.

"Squeeze three times to tell me you are alright."

Sonia put her free hand on Casey's hard bicep and squeezed three times.

He snorted with soft reluctant amusement. Good.

She crouched down to pick up the fallen cufflink and threaded it through Casey's sleeve. She never imagined giving Casey a pep talk. Never imagined that he might need one. That beneath the rock hard muscle, lethal grace, and that damn arrogant bravado, he was human.

Sonia made herself smile brightly for both their sakes as she held up two skimpy outfits for his inspection. "I'm not bringing Duane in to help with this one, so tell me, which of these says *mindless toy* better? The sparkly black with no back, or the maiden white with too many buttons and too little skirt?"

Fifteen minutes later, Sonia and Casey were walking down the corridor toward the Armada's suite. Sonia had gone with the white dress and Casey with an ankle holster, now hidden beneath expensive fabric. There'd be no cameras for Briar to watch inside, but Casey had the earpiece in for audio input. When they reached the door to the suite number Nero had given them last night, Casey slid his hand possessively around Sonia's waist and knocked.

Popeye answered the door. In black jeans and a t-shirt, he was a mountain of muscled flesh with a bald head. His deep set eyes gave the pair of them a once over.

"Let them in," Nero's voice called from behind Popeye. Popeye's mouth twisted in a sneer of disdain, but he stepped aside obediently.

Unlike the stateroom Sonia and Casey shared, the Armada occupied a suite, with a common living space and several bedrooms. Music blared loudly, though the speakers were positioned facing the outer door, as if their true purpose was to mask whatever conversation was taking place inside.

Inside... Sonia tried not to cringe as she beheld Razor sitting on the white couch with his thighs spread apart while a woman clad in a thong and nothing else worked his cock with her mouth. Razor raised his drink in greeting to Casey and went back to his conversation with Mammoth, occupying the armchair opposite the couch. Two more women knelt on the floor at Mammoth's feet, the man's open fly suggesting he'd been recently amusing himself with them. Patriot, the fifth man in their group, was busy with a laptop and a beer.

On the left side of the room, where a wet bar was set up, Nero cradled a phone between his shoulder and ear. Like Casey, he was dressed in a suit, though his jacket was gone. He motioned a fleeting greeting, then turned his back, barking into the phone.

"No, you aren't getting out tonight... What the fucking hell did you think you were doing? In the parking lot of Denton Memorial? I don't give a fuck about what respect your fat ass thinks its due... You don't fuck up business..." Nero pulled the phone away from his ear and turned around.

"Sorry, McKenzie," he said while the voice continued to talk on the other end. "Just a bit of a mess to clean up."

Casey shrugged. "Anything we can do to help?"

Nero shook his head and went back to his phone. "Listen to me, you fucker. You are going to stay behind bars until your initial hearing and you are going to be the best fucking inmate Denton has ever seen. Let me work out the law on this. What's the evidence? Alright, so no evidence. I'll work on it. You do nothing. And then you will continue to do nothing so we can get real work done."

Nero hung up the phone and it was all Sonia could do to not ask him for details. Denton Memorial. That's where Win was.

"That sounded exciting," Casey said, sounding utterly bored. He started toward Nero, but Popeye blocked his path.

"Arms up, legs spread," Popeye demanded.

"Lovely. But I've brought my own cock reliever with me," said Casey.

Popeye moved the hem of his jacket aside to show a pistol.

"It's standard practice," Nero said from the bar. "Always check wires, weapons, and whores. Words to live by, my friend. You understand."

CASEY

*C*asey shrugged, but stepped away from Sonia to let Popeye pat him down.

The biker grunted as he found the ankle pistol. "What's this?"

"Glock 26," said Casey. "You press the little button there and things fly out of the barrel here. Would you like a demonstration?"

Popeye gave him an unamused glare. "Safe is in the coat closet. Lock it up. You take it back when you leave." He turned to Sonia. "Your turn, sweetheart. Spread those thighs for me."

Casey's arm shot out between Sonia and Popeye. "You touch her, you lose that hand."

"*Calm the fuck down,*" Briar said into Casey's earpiece, making Casey regret putting the damn thing in.

Popeye raised his chin in challenge. "No dice. You want to come play, you play by house rules. Or is there something about her you don't want us to find?"

"There is a great deal about her that I don't want you to find," Casey purred.

A small, exasperated sigh escaped Sonia and Casey felt her squeeze him three times. She was fine with being searched. Good for her. Casey wasn't fine with Popeye—or any of these men's—hands on her.

Not after he read their files. And especially not now that they were alone in the asshole's suite.

Sonia squeezed him three times again, this time hard enough to bruise, and set her nails against his skin in warning for what she'd do next.

The pitbull was too tough for her own good. Certainly too tough for his comfort level.

Casey grunted, then pulled Sonia in front of him. "We'll compromise," he told Popeye. "You don't touch my things, but I'll be a team player and play a little show and tell."

With Sonia safely in his control, Casey pulled the top of her dress tight around her skin, demonstrating the lack of weapons and wires hidden behind the thin material. Then he crouched down, demonstratively running his hands from her ankle, up up up to the hem of her dress. "Good enough?"

Popeye looked like he was about to object, but Nero waved them inside. On the couch, Razor came with a disgusting grunt into the woman's mouth then slapped her ass roughly to send her to the other end of the room. Casey was already regretting having Sonia anywhere near this.

Casey locked up his gun, then picked the empty armchair next to Mammoth, and sprawled in it, pulling Sonia into his lap. God, it felt good to have her soft body pressed up against him. Still, he'd happily give up the comfort to have her safe.

Taking a breath, Casey reminded himself that Sonia wanted to be here. Being a part of the mission was the only reason she'd let him touch her to begin with. So he adjusted her more comfortably on his lap and slid a hand beneath that short dress of hers, stroking her inner thigh casually. Out of the biker's sight, the thumb of his other moved in soothing circles along her back.

Mammoth grabbed one of the girls by the hair and shoved her head into his crotch, as casually as if lighting a cigarette. The girl's neck muscles tightened in pain, but she made no sound before going to work. Not that she had much choice, even if she weren't being held prisoner. Mammoth was well over six feet and built like a small tank.

A thick gold chain hung around his neck, holding up a pendant of a skull in a top hat with blood dripping from its mouth.

Casey didn't look at the women. With luck, the Armada would presume he didn't consider them worth the attention one usually granted human beings instead of the much less convenient reality that the sight made Casey's gut turn. Their vacant look, the bruises he'd spotted on their wrists and necks. Only one was stripped down, but the others' long sleeves spoke volumes on their own. How many times had his mother chosen her clothes with strategic care? He still remembered the smile that never touched her eyes as she laced her arm around his father's, heading out to some fancy function. The abuse hadn't looked like this, but it was still the same.

Casey longed to call off the whole operation and tear the assholes' heads off right then and there. Longed to drag Sonia out of this hell. But Casey was smart enough to know that neither was going to happen, not now that Nero had uttered those fateful words about Denton Memorial.

"So," Casey said, addressing Nero who was now making his way from the bar to join the group around the coffee table. "You've some business you want to run by me? Though it sounds like you might have your hands too full with my hometown to consider expansion."

Mammoth chose that moment to start grunting and yanking the woman's hair.

Sonia shuddered.

Casey lowered his mouth to the top of her ear and sucked, luring her mind to take a small holiday from the room. She shuddered again, this time for a different reason altogether. She'd probably try to castrate him for this later, but he'd take the chance.

Nero swirled his vodka and sat on the love seat. The top of his shirt was unbuttoned and he looked slightly haggard, but in control. He even saluted Sonia with his drink before looking toward Casey. "The Denton incident is a non-issue," he said dismissively. When Casey didn't budge, Nero shrugged one shoulder. "A low level hot head got his feelings hurt and started a fight. He'll cool his ass off in a cell for a night or two, but it will end there."

"You sound certain," said Casey. "I wouldn't be. I heard something about Denton Memorial. That's Cullen Hunt's place and he'd have cameras all over it."

At the back of the room, Patriot snorted, the first indication he'd given of having been paying attention to anything but his computer. That man worried Casey a great deal more than Razor, Mammoth and Popeye. "The footage is being taken care of," Patriot said.

Nero winked at Casey and ordered Popeye to get him a drink. "Patriot has cyber connections, shall we say. And I've my own people in the PD, with more coming aboard."

"Old fashioned," Casey called to Popeye then returned his attention to Nero. "If you say so. I prefer to run my work with better control."

"Who doesn't?" said Nero. "But there is always low level bullshit. Dumb fucks who will measure their cocks first and think later. But that's why I'm being brought into Denton. To make sure nothing interferes with the business. You can ask Mammoth and Razor about our work in New York. Our *ongoing* work there." Nero smiled enigmatically, baiting the question. Since New York was *Belle Nuit's* port of call, it was no small bait.

"*Looking into it,*" Briar said into the earpiece.

Ignoring Nero's opening, Casey accepted his drink from Popeye and sank deeper into the chair. "What is it that you want from me?" he said, with reluctance that was only partly staged.

"Simple. You run a nightclub. I want to increase your cash flow."

In other words, I'd like you to launder our money please. "How much are we talking?" Casey asked, settling in to let the men pitch him. "And spare me the bullshit about this being a no risk, all reward proposition. If you find an idiot to buy that, I have a bridge to sell."

Nero toasted Casey and started spinning the story, Razor and Mammoth joining in with promises and numbers, with examples from New York. Half an hour later they were still at it, the careful dance always focusing on the money. How it would come in. Go out. How much of it there would be. Never on where the funds came from.

Casey strung out the conversation as much as he could, but

beyond stories of personal greatness and sexual prowess, no specifics he needed were forthcoming. It was time for a push.

"*Don't*," Briar said into Casey's ear, as if feeling what Casey was about to do. For someone who wasn't in the room and had all the social skills of a grizzly, Casey's twin had a lot of opinions.

"Lucrative as you make it all sound, frankly, I'm not seeing enough in it for me." Casey casually surveyed the women around the stateroom, leering at them in a way that left him disgusted with himself. "What the Vault really needs is a bit of a competitive advantage in the tits and ass department."

"*Subtle.*" Casey could see Briar rolling his eyes, but Sonia was with Casey. He felt her shift in his lap, all her attention on the room. On the women. Yeah. Neither of them wanted to end the evening without some kind of lead to put a stop to this.

"You want pussy?" Mammoth said, showing two gold teeth and he pointed with his chin toward Sonia. "Here I was starting to think that cunt of yours had you whipped."

"Mi casa, su casa," Razor agreed. He snapped his fingers at the thong-clad girl and pointed to Casey. "Just tell Lolly here what you'd like."

Lolly's face was neutral as she hurried over and knelt at Casey's chair.

One arm still around Sonia, Casey took hold of Lolly's chin, being as gentle as he dared—which wasn't gentle at all. "Thanks, sweetheart. But you aren't my type."

"What is your type?" Nero asked.

"Someone without STDs and leftovers," said Casey. Releasing Lolly, he ran his hand through Sonia's hair and breathed in the scent of her fruity shampoo. "Which is why I've decided to buy instead of renting." He traced a finger along her neck, earning a delicious shiver. "I wasn't asking for me, but rather my patrons. The ones who enjoy... variety."

"I don't think I like where you are going with that," Patriot said from his computer screen. "I'm offended."

"I didn't know that was possible," said Casey.

Patriot clicked a few buttons and turned to Nero, ignoring Casey all together. "Video from Memorial is taken care of. So are the feeds from some nearby businesses. You want to see what your problem child got himself into?"

Nero winced. "No. But I should."

Patriot turned the laptop around. Denton Memorial's staff parking lot blinked onto the screen, comotion already in progress. Thankfully there was no sound to accompany the sight of Win getting jumped by a half-dozen bikers before Matthew came onto the scene, death incarnate all the way to that blade. Casey kept his expression mildly neutral and was proud as hell of Sonia who didn't so much as draw a sharp breath at the sight.

"Who's Prince Charming?" Nero asked.

"Doctor Matthew Jennson. Military, obviously," Patriot turned the screen back to himself. "I'm running facial recognition to try and get more."

Mammoth leaned forward, his meaty forearm on his thighs. "It's your call, Nero, but I'd splash this shit all over the media instead of burying it. Go after the doc for attempted murder, and get the hospital on the line, too. They'll pay through the nose to make this go away."

"And Tank?" asked Nero.

"He isn't even fully patched in yet. Let him take the lumps."

Nero considered Mammoth's proposal, then turned to Casey. "This is your home turf, McKenzie. What do you think?"

"I'm afraid I'm helplessly biased," said Casey. As much as he'd love to have Satan's Armada dragged through discovery, he doubted Nero was that stupid. As far as facial recognition, he wasn't worried. There was little derog to find since—with the exception of the fake marriage and ultimate intentions—everyone involved was exactly who they claimed to be. "You getting into legal shit with Denton Memorial does nothing for me. The doc is going to argue self defense, and he'll have a good case. Whether you are so desperate for a few dollars to bring heat to yourself is only for you to know."

"And what about you, Counselor?" Nero turned his oily smile at Sonia. "How would you advise me to proceed?"

"You don't have me on retainer," Sonia answered sweetly from Casey's lap.

All the men's gazes swung to Casey in silent expectation that he would deal with her disrespect.

Sorry, kitten. Tilting Sonia's body toward him enough to expose her outer hip and thigh, Casey delivered a swift spank against her bare skin. The cracking sound, followed by Sonia's yip of pain, echoed through the room.

Nero laughed. "Dancer has always had a bit of spice," he told Casey. "I'm pleased to see she's finally found her match." He gave Sonia a wink as if they were somehow in on a joke together.

Patriot, however, seemed in not nearly so charitable a mood. He was back at the computer screen, his face dark. "You might not be on our retainer, Ms. Dancer, but you do seem to be on Trident Security's."

"She's an attorney," Casey drawled, not daring to draw Sonia closer. "Did you expect her to be working at an ice cream shop?"

"Trident Security has a history with Obsidian Ops." Patriot turned toward Nero. "They also do protection details, often for government witnesses. She could be a pig."

Since Sonia's attendance at Yale Law was always to be the pretext for their presence on the *Belle Nuit*, there'd been no reason to mess with her history, but Patriot's line of thought was becoming inconvenient.

Casey snorted and turned to Nero. "Is he assigned to play paranoid or does it come naturally?" Glancing back at Patriot, Casey added, "Give her a gun and a target, and you'll rule her out as anything resembling a cop."

He did pull Sonia tightly against his chest then, and stroked her like the kitten he called her. That she didn't elbow him for it, especially as he rubbed a gentle circle over the red spot on her hip, lifted a small weight from Casey's soul. He hated hurting her, even if it was just a spank that was more noise than painful.

"Don't worry about Dancer," Nero said. "I know her and she is as much an undercover cop as I'm a fairy godmother."

"You aren't the only person in the room," Patriot, who was proving annoyingly more intelligent than Casey liked, now turned to Razor and Mammoth. "I for one want some assurance that we aren't being played. That it's not the little girl here pulling McKenzie's strings like a puppet instead of the other way around."

"Funny," Casey said with a lethal voice.

"*Get out of there,*" Briar said into his ear.

Casey stood, setting Sonia's feet on the floor as he turned to Nero. "You invited me here, not the other way around. Get your dogs in order, and maybe we'll talk again. Until then, I've better places to be."

Nero got to his feet as well, his hands up. "Everyone take a breath. McKenzie is right, he is here at our invitation."

"At your invitation," Mammoth said thoughtfully.

"What's that supposed to mean?" Nero demanded.

"Only that your expertise lies with the law, Counselor, and mine with scum," Mammoth said. "Fortunately, your new friends can do a little something to put our minds at ease right now."

Casey contemplated whether he could make it to the door before Popeye could draw the gun his hand was already hovering near. He couldn't. He smiled at Mammoth, showing his teeth. "What do you have in mind?"

"Fuck her," Mammoth told Casey, then glanced at Nero. "You know one thing undercover pigs *don't* practice ahead of time? Fucking each other. But a man and his beloved fiancée..." A grin split Mammoth's face, it's mirror now on Razor's.

Casey's chest tightened. "We are done here."

Popeye drew his gun.

"Fuck her for us, McKenzie," Mammoth ordered, and this time Nero only nodded along. "We want to see if this little partnership is really what it seems to be."

SONIA

*S*hit was about to break loose. Sonia could see it in the set of Casey's jaw, the way he shifted his weight. He was about to make himself into a one man army, taking down the Armada right there in the *Belle Nuit* suite. Except he wouldn't be able to take them all, not before lead started flying. And even by some miracle he and Sonia did escape without bullet holes, those women here certainly could not.

At which point Mammoth and the others would take their fury out on them.

Which was not happening. Not on Sonia's watch.

Casey took a step toward the door, his body blading between Sonia and the gun. "We are done here."

A safety clicked off.

Sonia grabbed Casey's arm. "But I don't want to leave," she said, a little pout in her voice as she squeezed three times. Not a lie. She *was* alright. Unlike the other women here, she had agency. And with Casey, she felt safe. Sex or no sex.

His gaze dropped down to hers, his usually gray eyes were near black with rage. She'd usually appreciate the sentiment, but at the moment the overprotectiveness was starting to turn into testosterone poisoning. Sonia ran her tongue over her lower lip and whispered, loudly enough for the room to hear, "I like them watching."

Not a complete lie either. She liked them watching more than she liked seeing Casey shot or leaving here without the in they came for. The Armada certainly was trafficking women. Forcing them. Sonia had not been able to protect herself from assault once, but she could now protect them. Or at least try to. She squeezed his arm three times again, praying he hadn't forgotten the signal. Or how to count to three. With that rage in his face, he might have.

A soft chuckle sounded behind them. "If your man can't keep you satisfied, Dancer, just let me know. I'll be happy to help out."

That was not the right thing to say. Casey's body vibrated with fury. She hoped to hell Briar was shouting in his brother's ear right now. Though even if he was, it didn't seem to be doing much good. She needed to do something. To get Casey to refocus. Getting up on her toes, Sonia recklessly pushed her mouth against his. *Come on, play along*, she thought at him. *Pretend I'm sexy and you want me.*

For a moment, Casey did nothing, his whole body rigid. But then he opened for her. Slowly at first, then with growing intensity as his lazer focus shifted from the men to her. Fully and wholly to her.

His large hands swept down her back, to steady her or to hold her still, Sonia didn't know. What she did know, was that one instant she'd been the one in control of the kiss and the next... she was not. Casey's mouth took charge with the same ferocity he did everything, sweeping in with powerful claiming strokes.

A wave of relief went through her. Then something else. Something a great deal more primal that sent jolts of sensation all the way to her core.

Casey's hand came up, tangling in her hair. The edge of tingling pain morphed to pleasure, sending a streak of heat down her spine. His lips moved hungrily against hers, and his hand tightening at the base of her skull. Maybe he meant the intensity in warning, a way of telling her to brace for what was to come, but her body was quickly switching to autopilot. Everything inside her responded eagerly to his touch, a warm liquid pooling in her abdomen and seeping along her inner thighs. One more stroke of his tongue and Sonia was unable to keep back the soft moan that escaped her lips. Her mind might know it was all a game, but her body was quickly forgetting the message.

"Do you need some instructions on what fuck means?" Popeye asked with a barked laugh.

Casey's shoulders tightened, but he took his time pulling away from Sonia. His hand slid from her hair to her cheek, his thumb tracing along her skin. She smiled at him, her lips felt deliciously swollen from the kiss.

"Excuse me a moment, kitten." Casey's voice was oddly calm as he spoke, but his eyes blazed. Suddenly, he twisted to Popeye and wrenched the pistol from the man's grip. Before anyone could react, Casey dropped the magazine from the weapon, then disassembled the rest into pieces. He let them fall to the floor like chattel and squared off with Popeye.

No one spoke. Even the Armada knew better than to push just then.

Casey towered over the other man. Despite the expensive suit, the seemingly casual stance, Casey took up all the air in the room. Gone was the forever amused, arrogant nightclub owner who swiped drinks from waiters' trays. There was nothing of him in the man facing down the Armada's goon. Nothing even of the attorney who'd played cruel games with Sonia in court. No. The Casey who glared down at Popeye was a trained killer.

Popeye had the good sense to look scared.

Faster than Sonia could follow, Casey's hand shot out and grabbed Popeye's neck.

"Casey," Sonia breathed.

"I believe I am capable of taking my fiancée without your guidance." He enunciated each word while Popeye clawed at the grip holding him. Casey must have had his fingers in just the right spots because the man's face was already starting to turn dark. "So, how about you sit down, shut up, and enjoy the show."

Popeye somehow managed to nod and Casey tossed him to the floor. Straightening his cufflinks, Casey turned to Nero. "Switch the music. I'm feeling... classical. Piano."

For once, the expression on Nero's face echoed Sonia's own sentiment. She gave Nero a *yeah, that's Casey* kind of shrug.

Mammoth opened his mouth, objection starting on his face, but Nero cut him off. "Mr. McKenzie is here as a future business partner. We can be good hosts." Accommodating as the words sounded, there was also steel behind them. Casey had already pushed the Armada to the breaking point. They'd play his music, but they expected their demonstration.

Casey turned back to Sonia and a nervous shiver ran along her spine as his undivided attention once more settled on her. The violence of the last few moments still hung around her and she swallowed nervously at Casey's approach.

His gray eyes tightened, marking her movement, but he said nothing as he stopped in front of her. Instead, as Beethoven's notes filled the air, he reached out and traced a finger along her jawline. Her pulse quickened as his finger moved downward, tracing the column of her throat before coming to rest on the little hollow just above her collar bone. Casey leaned closer and breathed out a soft sigh against her skin before pressing his lips against the curve of her shoulder. As if they had all the time in the world.

"Still with me, kitten?" he murmured, his teeth scraping her skin. He had her backed almost against the wall now, his body a barrier between Sonia and the others.

A shiver of a different sort rushed over Sonia's skin. "Yeah."

He grinned and bit down.

Fuck. Sonia couldn't help the moan that escaped from between her lips as fire unfurled inside of her. She stepped into him, her hands splaying on his muscled chest. She'd never been with a man like Casey and the feel of him beneath her fingers, the leashed power and muscle and gorgeous body, it was making heat fill every crevice inside her. Especially the ones lower down.

Sonia drew a ragged breath. This was a game. Casey didn't actually want her, he was just pretending to. Like they'd agreed. Would he even find her tolerable enough to -

Casey pressed his hips against her. He was hard. For *her*. Her eyes dashed to his, the disbelief in her mind at odds with what she felt pressing against her belly. A small smile was playing on Casey's lips as he leaned down to purr into her ear. "Oh, that's all for you, kitten." He pressed forward again, making sure she felt his hardness. "I'm very ready for you."

Sonia's mouth watered. She was quickly losing all care about where they were or with who. About anything but how much she wanted to lick Casey like an ice cream cone. Before she could make good on her desire though, Casey gripped the top of her dress and pulled it open.

The buttons broke off one at a time, each making a tiny ripping sound as it shot away from the fabric and landed on the floor. *Ting. Ting. Ting.* Cool air caressed Sonia's skin as her white maiden dress fell open for him. He pulled her out of her bra. His hands went to her breasts next, caressing the orbs before sliding the calloused thumbs over her nipples.

The buds bunched, drawing all the attention. Sonia's nails dug into Casey's shoulders, probably bruising the skin beneath that suit. Not that she cared. She was hot and horny, the heat of his body wrapping itself around her.

One of Casey's hands dropped to her thigh and slid up, up, up. Toward the hot wetness that Sonia knew he'd find there. She wasn't supposed to be enjoying this god damn it. But her treacherous body... Casey's hand found her soaked mound and he grinned with unabashed triumph.

Sonia's eyes and desire flashed together. Two could play this little game. Heart pounding with excitement, she gave Casey no warning before dropping to her knees in front of him and undoing his fly.

He sprang out, hard and velvety and so long that she didn't know if taking all that inside her would even be possible. But her mouth watered as badly as her sex. She lifted her face, finding Casey's wide eyes. Yeah. For once she got the upper hand on the arrogant gorgeous prick. His hands gripped her shoulders, his desire flowing through his tense touch, echoing through her. He swallowed hard and Sonia knew she had only a heartbeat before Casey would take charge again. One heartbeat to stake her claim. And damn it, if she had to be here, having sex in front of all these people, she deserved to give Casey a bit of his own medicine, didn't she? For the good of the mission.

With a wicked grin, Sonia took him into her mouth. Casey tensed as his cock slid along her tongue, twitching against her lips. He moaned in pleasure, making everything inside Sonia tighten. The taste of him was salty and warm. Even better than she imagined.

"Kitten." His nickname for her fell from his mouth, a plea and a warning.

She suckled.

Casey made a strangled sound that was as exquisite as the music rolling from the speakers. His hands tangled in her hair, trembling as she worked his shaft. The feel of him in her mouth was intimate and intimidating and absolutely glorious.

Casey made that delicious sound again then cursed under his breath and began to thrust. Sonia wrapped her hands around his thighs, pulling him closer. Beyond the hard panes of Casey's stomach, Sonia caught a fleeting glimpse of Lolly's face in one of the mirrors. The woman's eyes were no longer vacant, but wide and intense. Like she knew that this intimacy, this connection between Casey and Sonia, it was nothing like the world she lived in.

Casey's hand tightened on Sonia's hair and the rest of the room disappeared from relevance. She didn't have time to consider anything now because Casey's thrusts were becoming more urgent. Shorter.

Sonia prepared for him to come in her mouth. Her sex clenched. God she wanted him so badly that she might come right along with him, just from the taste.

His cock pulsed. Casey shook. The muscles of his thighs bunched into a rock and -

Casey pulled back and sprayed against her breasts.

Sonia glared up at him, letting him see her wrath at being denied.

The hand he had in her hair pulled her head back a little further, making her back arch. "I've other plans for you, kitten," he said, his grin absolutely feral.

CASEY

Sonia was wrecking him. Whatever self control Casey could boast had disappeared completely. Despite having just found his release, he was already hard for Sonia again, and the things he wanted to do to his kitten was making his blood sing. She was gorgeous and giving and she made his whole body sing with need.

But that she'd somehow managed to get him off first? Unacceptable.

With a small growl, he reached down and lifted Sonia onto his hips. Her legs went around his waist on instinct and her eyes widened in clear delight as she felt the hardness already pressing into her. Beethoven's Moonlight Sonata had yielded to Casey's favorite Mozart piece, and he felt himself playing a phantom piano as he held Sonia. The beat echoed through his soul along with the feel of her pounding heart and his pulsing cock. Nothing else mattered. Nothing else existed.

He lowered his head to her neck, licking her skin right over her carotid artery. "Naughty, kitten. I'm going to make you scream," he promised wickedly, enjoying the shudder that went through her. One hand beneath Sonia's backside, Casey reached under her dress with the other and ripped the soggy panties away before letting his fingers roam freely through her hot wetness.

She squirmed slightly, then tightened all together as he grazed her clit.

God. Sonia was the most responsive woman he'd ever been with. Just the thought of that made him painfully hard. He flicked that clit again, his mouth over hers to swallow Sonia's moan of sinful delight.

"Brace yourself, kitten," he whispered into her ear as he lined his cock up against her entrance. Then he nipped her earlobe lightly and thrust inside.

She arched into his body, nails running down his back, her mouth going slack under his as he fully seated himself inside her. When he pulled almost entirely out, she moaned again, tiny little cries of need that shot straight to his pulsing cock. He groaned.

"More," Sonia begged and he obliged, thrusting as he braced her back against the wall for extra support. Her whole body quivered, bowing into him. Her eyes were glazed with need and intensity, as drunk on their connection as he was becoming.

He thrust again, his finger stroking the edges of her sensitive swollen clit. Again. *Thrust. Thrust. Thurst.* The force of each connection vibrated through him. Made him see stars.

"Oh god," she moaned softly, her channel clamping down on him. Tight and hot and needy.

In the background, Casey could hear stifled groans. Someone was enjoying himself too much. The fucker. Casey didn't care about an audience, but Sonia... he didn't want anything to shatter her delicate pleasure. Especially not the assholes in this room. She'd given too much of herself already and Casey would be damned if he let her give one more morsel.

"Hold on for me, kitten," he whispered against her neck, his finger going in circles, making her hips buck.

Sonia whimpered and her hands clamped on his shoulders, nails digging in through the fabric of his suit.

"Not yet," Casey panted though need gripped every fiber of his body. His balls felt hard enough to explode.

Sonia tightened around him, squeezing him like a fist, her muscles going rigid, every part of her body pleading for release.

Still, he stroked around the hood of her clit, pushing her higher and higher, up and up, toward the edge of the abyss. Only then, when Sonia's eyes were so glassy that Casey was sure she no longer knew or cared where she was, only then did he scrape the tip of his blunt nail right over that swollen nub. "Come for me, kitten."

He felt her break, her body shuddering against him. Her mouth opened to cry out, but he covered it with his own and pushed her into the wall, swallowing her delicious scream. It took all of Casey's will power to hold himself back, and he barely held in his groan of desperation as he stroked Sonia's sex again. He milked her pleasure, waiting for her shudders to just start easing before moving his ministrations back atop that engorged nub. Casey rolling her clit between his thumb and forefinger as he thrust into her again.

She shattered again, spasming around him. Casey still held himself in check, his teeth grinding against each other as he *thrust thrust thrust* into her. The music was picking up, too, the notes rushing in a crescendo of sound. *Ta da dee, ta da dee, ta da da dee dee.*

Sonia came for a third time, this time crying Casey's name. The sound of it on her lips undid him entirely. He surrendered to his own release just as she did and it slammed into him like a fucking freight train. Casey's whole body tightened until pleasure became pain that morphed back into bliss. It was all he could do to hold Sonia against the wall as they both rode the spasms of each other's pleasure.

Once the last wave of Casey's orgasm finally eased, he pulled out of Sonia and lowered her feet to the floor. Her legs shook so he dared not let go, even as she leaned a hand onto the wall for support. He pressed Sonia's face into his shoulder to keep her from seeing the stateroom around them, which was now coming into distant focus, one sound at a time.

Someone was breathing heavily. Two men murmured. A bottle popped open and a bubbling liquid poured into a glass. The music was still there, a soothing melody, as if the piano somehow knew what was needed. For another moment, the lingering musk of Sonia's arousal mixed with the fruity scent of her shampoo overpowered all of Casey's senses, but then the reality around him solidified.

The five bikers were all watching them. Popeye had reassembled his gun, which was back on his hip. The women sat tensely.

Slowly, rhythmically, Nero began to clap. The others joined. All except the one girl who was looking away, trying and failing to conceal a strange mix of envy and hope.

"Well," Nero said, lazily stretching out his legs and making the bulge in the front of his pants painfully obvious, "either the Denton PD is a lot more interesting than we imagined or else we have no card carrying members in our midst." He looked to Mammoth and Razor for confirmation and the two nodded reluctantly.

Mammoth's attention had already shifted to the women and he looked inclined to indulge himself all over again.

Casey's arms tightened around Sonia. She was utterly spent, with flushed skin and eyes slightly unfocused. Every fiber inside him vibrated with possessive intensity, the kind he never felt after sex. He was supposed to have fucked Sonia for the sake of their lives. Instead, he'd given his soul over to her.

And that... That was utterly unfair to the woman he'd promised he'd keep safe. Not just from the bikers, but from himself. She was so damn brave. And he'd... he'd given into his need for her and went unforgivingly too far.

"Today's meeting is over," Casey took off his suit jacket and wrapped it around Sonia's shoulders. His seed still glistened on her chest. At least he'd had the wherewithal to pull out when he did. The fact that he almost failed still filled him with shame.

"What about our business?" said Nero. "The merchandise you wanted?"

Casey bared his teeth at him. "Another time. I suddenly have had a shift of priorities for the evening." His mouth pulled into a smile that Casey knew didn't touch his eyes. "And my evening is only starting. Titillating as you all are, I think I'll continue it in private."

"*Gun.*" Briar, who'd thankfully been silent throughout Casey's escapades, now spoke up.

Casey's jaw tightened at the thought of letting Sonia go, even for a moment, but Briar was right. Setting Sonia gently against the wall, Casey adjusted his clothes and retrieved his weapon from the safe, checking it over before putting it into his holster.

"Oh come on, McKenzie," Nero leaned forward with a hint of annoyance on his face. "We're docking in New York tomorrow. There isn't time for this."

Razor nodded. "Lawyer's right. Dump the cunt in your room if you must, and we'll get you something to tide you over while we talk. It's a mens' conversation anyway."

Casey's hand tightened on the gun he was securing.

"*Cool off,*" Briar barked, as if he had a fucking camera on him.

Leaving his gun in the holster, Casey adjusted his pant leg over the weapon and walked back toward Sonia. "Like I said, I've other plans tonight. Maybe I'll find the time tomorrow." He herded Sonia toward the door, pausing only to look over his shoulder. "And Nero, if your dogs don't control their mouths and muzzles next time, we are done. There is only so much disrespect I'll tolerate, even for the sake of business."

Without waiting for Nero's answer, Casey guided Sonia out and back to their cabin.

Casey led Sonia directly into the bathroom, which had a private tub large enough for two—a luxury feature in a cruise stateroom that was as valuable as the floor to ceiling windows. He narrowly resisted flushing the earpiece down the toilet, and settled on just shutting it off before running warm water into the tub. Duane had thoughtfully left a bubble-bath jar on the bath shelf and Casey poured a fair amount into the water. The extra foam would give Sonia some privacy while he cleaned her up... and hide the erection that Casey was certain would hit him again.

Sonia protested weakly when he unbuckled her high heels and lowered her into the water in what remained of her dress. She was spent and still in a mental fog that made her trust him in a way he didn't deserve.

He stripped off only his shoes before getting in with her, the water now lapping the tops of her breasts that floated in the water. He'd ripped the top of her dress, so there was nothing to check them except the thin half-bra she'd worn beneath.

Casey lathered a washcloth with apple scented soap and gently scrubbed Sonia's upper body, washing his seed off from between her breasts.

"You don't need to do that," she said, reaching for the soapy cloth. "I'm alright."

Casey pulled the cloth out of her reach and captured her arm. "Good to hear." Arrogance he felt none of filled his voice. "Though I was rather hoping for 'wow, Casey you fucked my brains out and I can barely stand,, but if you don't bring me back to reality, then who would?"

She smiled faintly, her eyes vulnerable.

He slid the remains of Sonia's dress off her and soaped up her arm, careful not to scrub too hard and hurt her. Or hurt her more than he already had. When he'd helped Sonia into the tub, he'd seen the pale pink spot on her hip, where he'd struck her.

He'd hit Sonia.

Her skin bore a mark from his hand.

The million excuses that bubbled up inside Casey all sounded like his father. *It was her own fault. She made me do it. It was just a slap.*

Yeah. He'd fucked up royally, and not just with that strike. Casey had known that something happened in Sonia's past that left her fragile as hell about her body, and touch and sex. It had been his job, his responsibility, to protect her. She'd been so brave, so game to keep up their roles and their mission, that she'd given all of herself. But she shouldn't have had to.

Casey should never have brought her to the Armada's suite. Even without the Armada's test, Sonia should not have had to watch the abuse Casey knew would be happening there. But he hadn't wanted to upset Sonia by leaving her behind. He'd wanted her to *like* him. And look where it got her.

It got her raped.

Because ultimately, that's what he'd done. Consent given under a barrel of a gun wasn't true consent. And even if, *if,* he could convince himself that he'd had no choice about the sex, he knew its intensity had been his fault. He could have—should have—made it fun and light and meaningless. But he hadn't. He'd wanted Sonia too much and so he took all of her.

That day back in the penthouse, he'd promised Sonia no pink parts. Well, it didn't get more pink than his heart and soul.

A soft sound escaped Sonia's lips and Casey saw that her eyes were closed with drifting sleep. He finished washing her, then wrapped her in a towel before carrying her to bed.

Tomorrow, he would get himself as far away from her as she deserved.

WIN

"The account is at the Bank of Denton," Win said into the speakerphone on Matthew's coffee table. Talking to the Tridents was a lot easier when none of them were in the room and she could sit on the couch with her computer in her lap and her eyes firmly on her screen. "I've tracked nearly twenty transfers into it in the past three days."

Once *@DocPhantom42* had received payment for getting rid of the surveillance video, tracking the financials was relatively straightforward.

Cullen's voice asked on the other side. "Could these be payment for a large drug shipment?"

"Umm... Not unless the Armada has a payment plan." She switched to the right-most window. She only had three things running this morning, so she could give the Trident's more attention—Armada's financials; a convo Matthew didn't know he was having with her about experimental anti-seizure meds; and a hacking algorithm to backdoor into big pharma data. "A few thousand dollars in each transfer, all round numbers."

"Blocks placing individual orders for something?" Eli mused on the other side of the line, his British accent smooth and easy to make out. Win knew Eli in passing. SEAL turned CEO, he was the quickest of the Tridents to smile and lend a hand. "Or just moving money around to make it harder to track?"

Win shook her head.

Matthew, sitting a few feet away on the other side of the couch, cleared his throat. Right. They wouldn't have seen her headshake.

"I don't think those are covert transfers," Win said aloud. "Hey, get off!"

"That was to the cat," Matthew clarified.

Odysseus recently made a habit of jumping onto Win's keyboard and trying to curl atop it. She kissed him between his fuzzy ears and set him on the floor before resuming her thought. "They want to use crypto currency to cover their tracks and have hired me to set up a system for them. Frankly, they don't know the difference between a tumbler and a drinking class."

"Neither do the rest of us," Matthew muttered, but there was a hint of amusement and pride on his face. She didn't understand why, but it was good to see him getting his color back. He'd been pale this morning and Win was willing to bet her computer he'd had a seizure in the early hours. "Most likely your first theory is right, Aiden. We are seeing multiple customers placing an order for something."

"Got it," said Cullen. "That tracks with the Armada establishing business here. At some point these twenty buyers will need to go to a physical location to collect their goods, and that gives us something to work with. Nice work, Doc."

"Thanks," said Win.

"Just please don't make them *too* good at hiding their tracks, mate," said Eli.

"I'm keeping copies of all the keys," Win said with a smile. "Promise."

The line disconnected.

"You know he has no idea what you said about keys, right?" Matthew said, getting up from his end of the couch. He was wearing a pair of blue jeans and a plain tan t-shirt which was stretched taut over his muscled chest. It was still strange seeing Matthew in normal clothes, especially ones that showed off his arms and shoulders and thighs in casual detail.

Win realized she was staring and quickly made a non-commital noise, swinging her attention back to her computer.

He snatched the laptop right out of her hands.

"Hey!" she let out an indignant squeal. "Give that back."

Ignoring her, Matthew closed the computer and set it on the kitchen counter. His blue gaze scanned her from head to toe, his face shifting into an expression that Win knew all too well from the hospital. Matthew was going into his doctor mode. "You've been camping out on this couch for two days. Time to move around. And I want to take a look at you while we are at it."

"I'm in the middle of something that a whole bunch of your friends seem to think is important." She motioned toward the phone they'd just been using. "So, how about you put off playing doctor until this evening?"

Matthew raised a brow.

Win realized what she'd just said. Heat rushed to Win's face, her eyes opening. "I didn't mean it that way. You know that."

A corner of Matthew's mouth twitched. "Which way did you mean it exactly?"

He was doing it on purpose. The man could be as diabolical as his cat when he wanted. Win reached deep into herself, past her blazing cheeks, and gripped the academic voice she used when discussing genetic findings. "I meant, you can examine me—"

Matthew's mouth twitched again. "This evening. You'd like me to do an exam on you this evening?"

Win shut her eyes, her hands on her flaming face. That was just not fair. She could feel Matthew's amusement dancing in the air between them, only that somehow made everything even worse. Did he know she had a crush on him? Younger sister has a crush on brother's best friend. Did it get any more cliché? "Can I just have my computer back now, please?" she whispered into her palms.

Matthew chuckled. "No."

Win put her hands down and sighed. "I'm serious, Matthew. I don't want to play. Please give me my stuff back."

The mischief melted from his face, which was no less beautiful in its serious state. "I'm sorry," he said, squeezing her shoulder. "I'll stop with the teasing. As for the rest though, I do mean it. Either I take a look here, or I can give you a ride to Denton Memorial and you can see one of the other docs. I'll take no offense if that's what you'd like, but it is one or the other. And you know as much."

She did. Which did nothing to alleviate the wave of unwelcome anxiety that churned in Win's stomach.

"I want my computer back," Win said.

Matthew's eyes softened. "I know." As if that exchange had somehow decided something, he brought over the black backpack he usually brought to the hospital and upturned it over the coffee table. A field hospital worth of stuff spilt out.

Win's brows rose. "Michelle is going to kill you."

"I think she actually stuffed a few things in," Matthew said over his shoulder, fishing his stethoscope from the pile. He sat beside her on the couch. "How do you feel?"

Like a bunch of bikers kicked me around two days ago. Win gave Matthew a shrug. "Fine."

"How is the pain? Anything unexpected or alarming?"

"No."

"You know that I know you are lying, right?"

"I'm not lying." She was lying. Her knee was stiff, her ribs ached, and the laceration hurt sharply enough that Win wondered whether it wasn't infected despite the antibiotics she took as a precaution.

"Right," said Matthew, palpating the lymph nodes in her neck as he spoke. He often started his exams that way, but the familiar routine did nothing to put Win at ease. Especially because she had no bra on. Win was small enough to hardly need support and with the stitches... Matthew put the stethoscope into his ears. "Deep breaths."

Win tensed as Matthew reached under her shirt, the round head of the stethoscope cool against her skin. He'd braced a hand against her back and the heat from his palm seeped into her at the same time. Hot and cold. Just like everything else about him.

A part of Win pined for the feel of Matthew's hands along her bare body. The other part trembled in fear of pain. The only thing her body and mind wholeheartedly agreed on was that she was a pathetic girl with a crush who was going to explode from humiliation at any moment.

"Lungs are clear, but you are keeping your breaths too shallow. I know it aches to expand your chest, but try anyway." Matthew frowned, watching her face. "Am I hurting you?"

"No." *Not yet.*

"Alright," he said, but concern danced over his unfairly perfect face. Win wished he was a little less observant. With no ceremony, Matthew slid his thumb under the hem of Win's loose t-shirt and lifted the material with practiced competence. The shiver she barely suppressed had little to do with the chilly air. Though Win knew he'd seen her half bare in the ER, it felt different here on the couch. To her. Matthew's movements were as professional as always as he slid probing fingers around her breasts to probe her ribs.

He was gentle, but there was no escaping what the Armada's boots had done. Win bit her lip, fighting back whimpers that threatened to escape every time he probed too deeply.

"Except for the expected soreness, the ribs look fine. Let's check the laceration." Matthew slid off the couch and nudged Win to lie back, which made everything a thousand times more exposed. It didn't really, Win knew. But it felt like it. Matthew in his doctor mode was scary sexy. Intimidating in a wholly different way than he was as her attending.

He crouched beside her and pulled away the dressing. It had stuck to the wound and the hot zap of pain that shot through Win's side made her flinch. Tears pricked at the corners of Win's eyes. She felt like a wounded animal, helpless and exposed in a way that made all the parts of her feel raw and vulnerable under his touch. God. The only thing worse than falling apart from a little pain, was doing so in front of a SEAL you had a crush on.

Matthew stilled. His fingers remained on Win and the sensation of his touch lingered along her skin. He seemed to be debating something internally as he stared down at her body. Then Matthew did the last thing Win expected—he shifted and lightly touched her cheek with the back of his hand. The gentleness of the caress was enough to take Win's breath. "It's alright," Matthew murmured.

It wasn't. The thing was, Win had always been a coward, ever since she was little. She was the kid who'd refused to take her turn as goalie for fear of the ball—to her father's utter disgust. That kind of thing, well, it wasn't something SEALs had much time for.

"It's infected, isn't it?" Win said, purposely misunderstanding what Matthew was talking about. Maybe if she brought them back to professional ground, she'd be able to pull herself together. Doubtful.

Matthew pulled his hand back. "A bit," he acknowledged. "The razor blade in the biker's boot appears to have been less than sterile."

For a heartbeat Win thought he'd touch her again, but Matthew pivoted to face the medical arsenal. "I'll get you something for it."

Great. More sharps coming her way.

"I'm sorry," she said toward Matthew's broad back.

"For what?" His muscles shifted slightly beneath his stretched shirt as he drew up an antibiotic from a vial.

Might as well say it. "For... you know. Being a wimp about all this."

He looked over his shoulder at her, his brows high. "I've a list of things I wish you were sorry for, starting with an absolute lack of situational awareness in parking lots, but cowardness isn't on the list."

"I've too much self-respect to appreciate placating lies, Matthew."

"Placating lies?" He turned to her, his attention wholly on Win's face. "Do you truly think me so much of an idiot as to judge people on whether they like sharp things stuck into them? Is that some new paragon of character I wasn't aware of? I certainly hope not, or we'd have to get rid of half the SEALs in special ops."

She sighed. "Matthew—"

"No." He tossed the syringe he'd drawn up back to the table and draped his forearms over his knees, balancing with feline grace. "If Eli Mason ever came to you for help, would you treat him differently?"

"Eli?" He'd been on the conference call earlier. Gorgeous, deadly and actually nice. "What does Eli have to do with anything?"

"Man's so terrified of needles I had to order the nose spray version of the flu vaccine for him from pediatrics." Matthew snorted softly. "He was so pitiful, I didn't even give him a hard time over it. Do you think less of him now that you know that?"

"Of course not."

"Are you sure? Because by your logic—"

"I get it." Win winced. "It just still feels weird. Me, I mean."

Matthew let out a long slow breath, and brushed Win's hair from her face. His attention stayed on his hands, as if he were avoiding her gaze, which was so unlike Matthew that it made Win's chest tighten. "When I see you wince, or pull away, or say that you are fine when I know you aren't, I'm not thinking that you are a coward. I'm thinking how it's my fault you are in this mess to begin with. And I'm thinking how..." Matthew's throat bobbed. He still didn't look at her. "I'm thinking how much I hate doing anything that hurts you. I'm thinking how much I wish I could hold you to at least make myself feel better." The last came out in a whisper.

Win stared at him, her heart thumping. What he'd said... She'd think it a lie, except that seeing him with his head bowed, his shoulders tensed as if bracing for a blow, it was undoing everything inside her. Win shifted, rising on her elbow, and grazed her thumb along Matthew's wrist.

It was the first time she'd touched him, instead of the other way around, and his intense blue eyes snapped up to her face.

"I'd very much like it if you held me, too," she whispered.

Matthew slid back onto the couch and pulled Win easily onto his lap, his warmth enveloping her like a blanket. She melted into him and he tightened his arms around her, resting his chin on top of her head. Matthew's palm settled along her waist, just under her shirt. There was nothing professional in that touch and Win's pulse quickened with guilty pleasure at the feel of his skin against hers.

"I feel better already," she said.

"Mmm." She could have sworn Matthew was smiling into her hair. "Better, but not fully pain free yet?" There was a tiny tease in his voice, so subtle that Win wasn't sure whether she imagined it.

She shifted to see Matthew's face, and heat pooled in her chest and belly and thighs at the sight of him watching her.

"No, not yet," she whispered. "I think I might need something more for that."

"Indeed." He brushed her hair from her face, his thump lingering on her cheek. Then he stopped, holding perfectly still in that near preternatural way of his. His gaze was intense, searching her face as if waiting for her to take back her words. When she didn't, he leaned forward until only breath remained between his mouth and hers. "Maybe this will help."

Win's heart fluttered, her lips parting.

That was all the invitation Matthew needed to close the whisper of distance that had remained between them. His mouth covered hers, his tongue sweeping into her more gently than she imagined someone as strong Matthew was capable of. He tasted like mint and coffee, cool and hot.

She wrapped her arms around his neck, not caring about her aching ribs. The hair at the base of his neck was silky soft, so unlike the rock hard thighs and body that held her.

Matthew's hand traveled up the length of Win's spine, settling at the base of her neck as he pulled her even closer against him. He was everywhere—in the heat of his mouth on hers and in the way his chest rose and fell with each contained breath; in the calloused press of his fingers against her skin.

When they pulled apart, Matthew's eyes were half-closed, as if he were still savoring the moment. They stayed like that for several heartbeats, hovering a few inches away from each other while Odysseus meowed his displeasure at being excluded. Then Matthew's eyelids opened fully, and Win saw the same raw emotion reflecting in them that she felt inside.

Matthew cleared his throat. "So... Did that help?"

Win bit her lip, inhaling his scent. "For now."

"We better stay on top of it then," Matthew circled his thumb around Win's naval.

"Mmm," Win agreed and nuzzled against his chest, the *thump thump thump* of his heart like a metronome that echoed through her.

SONIA

Casey was not in bed when Sonia awoke. The weather had built overnight and now foam-tipped waves crashed into the floor to ceiling window of their stateroom, each one making a *thump-woosh* sound as it struck and retreated. She sat up, the soreness from the previous night's activities sending an adrenaline-laced jolt through her body. Last night was... Terrifying. Exciting. Dirty and arousing. Wrong and all too right. A trial by fire. An ordeal. Whatever one called it, it was something transformative.

Not only had she *not* crumpled before the bikers and done what, before yesterday, she'd thought impossible for her, but she'd taken it into her hands and made it her own. Well, into her mouth. Her cheeks still heated at the memory of going down on Casey, of feeling him tremble uncontrollably beneath her ministrations. And the delicious revenge he'd taken for that. Sonia squirmed as heat rushed toward the soreness between her legs. She'd orgasmed. Like really orgasmed. With a man. And all she wanted now was to do it again. And again. And really, why shouldn't she?

That was new, too. She desired sex. For the first time ever, the physical act itself was beckoning her with a siren's song she'd never thought she'd hear. In the years since the assault, sex had been sequestered to being a humiliating little secret. Something to tolerate at best, and dread at worst. She didn't know she was capable of the sensations Casey had given her. And maybe, she deserved them. He'd certainly made her feel like she did. Like her body was something to be celebrated rather than be ashamed of. While nothing would ever erase that day her father's business partner cornered her in his office, Sonia's deep held knowledge of what she was capable of—of doing, of enjoying—had leveled up.

Maybe she should send Nero a thank you note.

Beyond the bedroom wall, she heard shower water, giving away Casey's location. A fresh flash of arousal shot from Sonia's sex to her nipples as she remembered the way he'd lowered her into the large tub last night. How he'd washed her gently. Protectively. Like she had the very value that the bastard of her father's partner told her she didn't.

As explosively wonderful as the sex had been, the care she'd felt afterward was even more potent. Intimate.

The shower shut off. A wave of naughty anticipation coursed through her. She grinned, knowing exactly how she wanted to spend the morning. If sex against the wall had been good, then what would it be like in the luxurious bed without a perverted audience holding a gun to their heads? That this somehow became a logical metric in her life sent a choked laugh through her.

Yeah. She'd fallen through the looking glass. Did that make Casey the Cheshire cat or the mad hatter? Fortunately, either worked in this game they were playing. And though it was all an act, she saw no reason why they couldn't enjoy it fully. It wasn't as if Casey was ever more than a breath away from being ready to jump into bed.

The door to the bathroom opened and Sonia didn't hide her body beneath the down comforter. Casey had helped her dress for bed last night, slipping one of those delicious nightgowns on her. The ones that usually made her blush. Now, Sonia let the seafoam satin show off her body. Even the too small breasts and large hips, which Casey whispered were beautiful as he'd bathed her last night.

She wanted him to see her. To say it all again. To take her. Her pulse sped with anticipation.

Casey stepped out of the bathroom wearing a towel around his hips. Beads of water glistened on his broad shoulders, capturing the light streaming through the windows. He was clean shaven, a tiny bit of shaving cream still clinging to a spot along the strong angle of his jaw. Sonia's mouth watered as she imagined what he might taste like fresh out of the shower. Whether his warm skin was even hotter now.

God. Was she capable of thinking about anything except sex all of a sudden?

"Good morning," she said from the bed.

Casey turned, taking her in. His gray beautiful eyes traced the outline of her nightgown, surely noticing that the covers—for once—were nowhere in sight.

Twisting about, Casey ducked into the bathroom. A moment later he emerged with... with one of the bathrobes.

"Good morning." He tossed the bathrobe to her. He turned to his dresser, digging through his drawer for a pair of boxers that he slid on quickly.

Sonia frowned, but shrugged into the bathrobe. She stood and strode to Casey, catching him in the middle of struggling to pull an undershirt over his still wet body. The thin, tight material clung to the moist skin.

"So, you can disassemble a gun in two seconds flat, but can't figure out how to use a towel?" She caught the edge of his t-shirt and guided it down over his back.

"It's fine." Casey stepped away from her and pulled on a pair of expensive slacks and a fresh button down shirt.

Something uncomfortable skittered over Sonia, but her new found confidence had her stepping right back up to him. She reached for his shirt, helping with the buttons.

Casey caught her wrist. His grip was gentle, but firm enough to get the message across. *Stop.*

Sonia stepped back, her arms hugging her chest, which suddenly felt exposed despite the bathrobe. "What's wrong?" she asked.

Casey's brow rose. "Are you kidding?"

"I'm no longer sure," she muttered, her mind spinning in an

attempt to parse out which of the two of them was losing it. *"Would you tell me, please, which way I ought to go from here? That depends a good deal on where you want to get to."* Sonia cleared her throat and managed to keep from quoting Alice aloud. Clearly, hot passionate sex was not going to happen this morning. Pushing her disappointment aside, Sonia reminded herself that they were here to work. She raised her chin and continued in an admirably professional tone that went directly for the elephant in the room. "I thought we handled ourselves well last night. We make a good team."

"You think we did *well* last night?" Casey shook his head in bewilderment.

Another pang of unease gripped Sonia's chest. "You don't?"

"My god, Sonia." His usually amused voice dropped to uncharacterized sincerity. "If you think that what happened last night fits any definition of *well*, *success*, or *tolerable* then..." He shut his eyes. "I think you should talk about it with Dani."

Eli Mason's wife, a psychologist who now was specializing in PTSD.

"I know something happened to you in the past," Casey continued. "I hadn't realized... I think you are more injured by it than you think. I apologize for aggravating a wound I had no business of playing near."

She pulled the lapels of her robe together, no longer feeling remotely sexy. Casey's words... hurt. More than they had a right to.

"Thank you for the referral," she said tightly.

"I'm clean, by the way," Casey said, returning to buttoning up his shirt. "I get tested regularly, but I'll get another one done as soon as we are on shore for you. Are you on birth control?"

"Yes." Because she couldn't trust men to ask, much less put on a condom, if they decided they wanted something. As for STDs, she almost told him that she'd not been with anyone for over a year, but that was more than she wanted to share just then. "I'll get tested when we return."

She turned toward her closet to keep him from seeing the hurt on her face. "Is there anything in particular I need to wear?"

"Whatever you'd like," said Casey. "I've some business to attend to. Stay in very public places or in the room."

She stopped. "Business? With the Armada?"

"Yes."

Her jaw clenched, the hurt now turning to molten anger that spilt into her blood. She'd been right there with him yesterday. Kept him from losing his shit completely. And now, this morning, he wanted to repay that by cutting her out?

Not caring that she still wore only a bathrobe, Sonia turned on her heels and grabbed Casey's wrist before he could make it to the stateroom door. "I don't know what the fuck is going on with you this morning, but how about you start talking to me like a human being. You aren't usually the twin who has trouble finding words, McKenzie. So start using them."

Casey twisted his wrist against Sonia's thumb breaking the hold with no effort at all. His phone rang just then, the designation for Briar flashing on the screen.

"Put it on speaker," she demanded.

He didn't. "Yeah? New York? Fuck. Alright." Casey's face turned graver with every word he heard.

Sonia's anger shifted to outright fury. The powerlessness of not even hearing the conversation made the cabin feel too tight. When Casey disconnected and headed for the door, Sonia made her last stand.

Getting in front of him, she slammed her palm against the door before Casey could open it. He stopped short, barely avoiding collision. There was no more than a foot of distance between them now, enough for Sonia to smell the soap and aftershave he used this morning, along with the fresh smell of his laundered shirt. She felt utterly naked beside him, but she made herself lift her head as if she were in court. Made herself summon that courage from yesterday when she squeezed his arm three times.

"Talk to me, McKenzie," Sonia said. "We are partners in this, remember? Whatever else you have going through your head, this shit, it's not how you treat a partner."

Slowly, as if each inch of motion hurt, Casey turned his face until his gray gaze caught on hers.

"Since apparently it wasn't clear yesterday, when a thug pointed a gun at your head and threatened to pull the trigger unless I raped you, this 'you and I are partners in this mission thing' is over. This fake engagement is over. You stepping foot anywhere near Nero or the Armada is over. So go to a spa, read a book, eat some chocolate. Plan my gory and bloody death. Do whatever you want, but do it alone. I'm on my way to inform Nero that I've dumped you."

MATTHEW

"Seven, eight, two more." Matthew pressed his hand against Win's shin, giving her resistance as she worked through a set of leg strengthening exercises.

"You are pressing too hard. You are bigger than me, if you've not noticed."

"It's your leg against my arm. You have the advantage."

"Your arm is bigger than my leg." She gave him that irritated pout that made it really hard to keep from abandoning the exercise in favor of pulling Win into his arms. And mouth. He really liked it when he could pull her into his mouth. Matthew cleared his throat, his voice sounding strained. "Come on, pixel."

"I don't think that word means what you think it does."

"I think it's some tiny computer related thing that sounds a lot like pixie."

"Uh huh. And?"

Matthew nodded to Win's leg, waiting for her to continue working it before answering. Her knee was doing well—all her injuries were—and now it was a matter of getting her stronger over all. "And you are a tiny computer related thing that looks like a pixie," he explained. "Hence, pixel."

Win's brows pulled together and she winced as she finished the last exercise of the set. She wore a set of sweats and a crop top, which left a swath of her midsection bare each time she moved. Her mane of golden hair fell deliciously around her face as she collapsed down to the mat. "I guess it's better than Fred. Fred is officially not a thing, right?"

Matthew settled himself beside her and stroked her leg to sooth the lingering burn. It felt unnaturally good to have her here in his apartment, and even better to feel her lean into his touch instead of pulling away. Whenever she did that, the trust made Matthew feel whole. "No more Fred," he confirmed, though he kept the explanation to himself. Fred was something Sith called Win. Once Matthew's feelings for her leapt over brotherly, everything about that nickname felt wrong.

Plus, it made him remember that Sith was going to kill him once he found out. Matthew was supposed to be watching over his best friend's little sister, not thinking of ways to get his mouth on her. Just the thought of that made him harden, and he shifted quickly for a more comfortable position while taking in what had become of his place. The living room was more or less fine, the sparse and simplistic decor only slightly altered with computers and an exercise mat to go along with the couch, coffee table, and two lamps. But the kitchen looked like a crime scene, with most of the counter space covered in knives, bottles, and glassware from when Win tried to make an omelet. She had just squared off with a pepper when Matthew put a stop to the massacre and declared that he was perfectly happy to do all the cooking—and the clean up.

"What are you thinking about?" Win asked, touching his cheek. God. The feel of her finger against his skin was like a jolt of electricity.

"I'm trying to discern how someone can be a brilliant doctor and computer genius, and still lack the life skills of a fifth grader." He shook his head. He didn't care about the cooking so long as she ate, but was still hoping to teach Win a bit of self-defense once she was pain free. Or at least to look up from her phone once in a while in dark parking lots.

Of course if it was up to him, Win would never be in a dark parking lot alone again. Not without him. Matthew had always had a protective instinct, but with Win the need to protect and care had become something more. Something primal.

"Sore?" he asked, and felt a small twinge of pleasure when she nodded instead of giving her patent *fine* claim. He shifted his hand up to Win's thigh and gently squeezed the quivering muscle.

Win's hazel eyes widened. She winced lightly, but the sinful moan of pleasure told Matthew he was in the right. "You keep making noises like that and the neighbors will think we've something else going on."

"You don't have neighbors," she muttered.

That was true. His apartment building had two units per floor, and the other half of his top level was currently empty. He'd considered buying out the other apartment to make a larger space, but there was little point with him and Odysseus living here alone.

An uncomfortable feeling gripped Matthew's chest. He would be living alone forever if he didn't get his epilepsy under control. As wonderful as having Win around was, after her first night here he didn't dare to leave his bedroom door unlocked at night, lest she walk in on him in the middle of a grand-mal. Maybe if *@DocPhantom42* was able to get the experimental drug they'd talked about, things could be different. But for now... For now Matthew was going to enjoy the moment.

Gathering himself, he brought his focus back to the massage, increasing the pressure.

Win purred to match Odysseus and arched into his touch.

"If you keep making *those* sounds I'm going to kiss you," Matthew warned, his voice tight. "And if I'm kissing you, you aren't getting a massage."

"What sounds?" Win asked, her eyes turning glassy. With the next press of his hand, her bare toes curled, her back arching from the mat. If this is what a massage did to her, Matthew couldn't wait to discover what something more intimate would bring. For now though, there was only so much control a man could have over himself.

Scooping Win up, he pulled her against him and covered her

mouth with his own. Her lips parted for him, and he swept inside, taking his time to savor the taste of her. Softness and heat wrapped around him, Win's shy and reactive body sending his senses soaring. Win's hands slid to the back of his head, inviting him to kiss her harder.

Matthew's hand slipped down her back, along that crop top until bare skin met his palm and the tips of his fingers brushed against the waistband of her exercise pants.

Bedeep beep, Win's computer announced just then.

Win stiffnerned and Matthew felt a very violent urge to toss the damn laptop out the window.

Bedeep beep.

He bit back a groan as he lifted his mouth from Win's and looked down at her. He really liked how she fit on his lap. "You really need to check that?" he asked.

"Only if you want to know what Satan's Armada is doing," she said. "That's the alert for them."

Of course she had different alerts for different things. Matthew let her up slowly, but instead of releasing her to the coffee table, he pulled the laptop to them. Win nestled into his body more comfortably as she looked at the screen. Unlike normal people whose screens had pictures, emails, and possibly a document or two, Win's was a mess of black screen with glowing command prompts and rows of scrolling gibbish.

"Well, hello there," she said to the computer. "Really? You don't say." She typed furiously.

"Want to share with the class?" Matthew asked when no more information was forthcoming.

"What? Oh." Win continued typing. "We have a human."

"The Armada delivered a baby?"

"No. But there was just a thirty thousand dollar cash withdrawal from their account in New York, and it was picked up by a real human being. I'm working up details. Anyway, whatever Denton's chapter is doing it looks like it involves paying for something significant in New York today."

Matthew pulled out his phone and dialed Cullen. "Hey. Our boys are buying something in New York today. Isn't that where the *Belle Nuit* is making a port of call?"

"Yeah," came the voice over the line. "I'll make sure Casey and Briar know. Any idea who -"

"Who picked up the money?" Win finished for Cullen. "A Ryon Johnson from Fast Freight Solutions International. I'm doing a scrub on that now. Will let you know more once I've got it."

Matthew grinned into Win's hair. She had no idea how sexy she was when she got into her computer wiz mode. He wished that kind of confidence was with her all the time, but that was a work in progress.

"Thanks, Win." Cullen paused. "While I have you on the line... Richard Merla, that's the real name of the biker who led the assault, made bail today."

Tank. Matthew's hands tightened around Win.

On the other end of the line, Cullen sighed. "I spoke with the prosecutor's office. With the parking lot footage having mysteriously disappeared, there is a good chance he'll walk."

"Win made it disappear, she can make it reappear," Matthew said. "Right, pixel?"

She bit her lip. "Technically speaking, yes, of course I could. But I'm not going to."

"Why not?" Matthew demanded, his muscles tightening as he spoke. "You've done more than enough getting information on the Armada. We aren't putting them ahead of you."

"Matthew isn't wrong," Cullen said gently." Tank assaulted you. He should be punished."

"It's not about Tank," Win said with an exasperated sigh. "It's about my online profile. Reputation is everything on the darkweb, and I'm not going to take a hit of going back on my word."

Silence came from the other end of the line.

Matthew pinched the bridge of his nose.

Finally, Cullen cleared his throat. "I'm sorry, did... I thought I heard Win say that she'd rather see a biker who brutally assaulted her get off scot-free than risk damage to an imaginary person's fictional reputation?"

"Yeah," Matthew said. "That about sums it up."

"You'd think differently if it was your profile," Win said with enough bite that Matthew held up his hands.

"It's your call, Win," Cullen said with admirable restraint, though Matthew could swear he heard a few more thoughts attached to it. "If you change your mind just let me know."

"I won't," said Win.

Matthew disconnected the line and shook his head.

"What?" Win asked.

"Nothing. I was just reminded how much you can drive me up the wall," he said. "Speaking of you driving me insane, we need to stop by Denton Memorial. It's X-rays and paperwork for you and a chewing out for me."

Win's face turned concerned. "Yarborough?"

Matthew nodded. "The stuff in the parking lot is self-defense, but I still have a lashing coming for tormenting patients and assaulting people in the middle of an ER. It's not literal lashing, pixel," he added quickly, seeing her panic. What did she think happened in the modern military? "Yarborough is just going to yell at me for a while and tell me how long this suspension lasts."

WIN

"You are looking a great deal better than when I last saw you." Michelle gave Win a warm hug before pulling out a pile of paperwork. Apparently, when you got assaulted on hospital property, there was a lot of paperwork. "How are you feeling?"

"Well enough to feel bad for Matthew over whatever's happening in Yarborough's office."

Michelle laughed and laid out three more forms for Win to sign. "Don't. Yarborough is the only thing we have in this hospital that keeps the military gods in check. They speak their own language. Sign here to acknowledge workman's comp policy, and this one is to get your medical bills covered. This one says your bloodwork came back clean from pathogens."

Win frowned.

"There was a lot of blood flying about that day," Michelle said gently. "So we test to make sure that nothing from that bastard made it into our people's bloodstream."

Win tried and failed not to flinch. She wasn't sure what to expect when she walked back into the ER, but the sameness of it caught her off guard nonetheless. It was as if nothing had happened. The large square of curtained off beds was the same, as was the backdrop of whirling machines and beeping monitors, and the constant movement of blue scrubs. Busy, but not frantic. Just as it was all supposed to be. And yet it felt wrong. She felt wrong.

"Dr. Carrell?" Michelle asked quietly. "Would you like to finish this up in the staff room?"

"No." Win plastered a smile onto her face. "I'm fine. I've actually missed my workstation. There is only so much power you can squeeze from a laptop. Did you draw labs from Matthew as well?"

"We did."

"Great. I know legal needs to speak to me as well, do you mind if I catch up on a few things here before finishing the rest of this?"

"Of course." Michelle gave her shoulder a pat and disappeared into her neverending duties while Win logged into her account. By some miracle, a simulation she'd had running had continued in the background, but Win skipped past that screen and into the lab's database. A minute later, she was on the phone.

"Dr. Carrell, we've missed you," Albert's voice sounded on the other end. "How are you holding up?"

"To be honest, I'm trying to reclaim my sanity and research. Speaking of, you tested sample PAT-MJ632094 a little while ago. Did you maintain a portion of the original specimen for re-test?"

"Of course. Looks like it's set to be disposed in two days. Was there a problem?"

"No. But I wanted to intake it into my research set. Could you anonymize and run my usual sequencing?"

"Sure thing. What am I looking for?" Albert was always game for research. "I mean what are you looking for?"

"Nice try, but I'm not biasing you."

Albert chuckled. "Fair enough. I've got you, Doc."

Win disconnected the line just as her watch beeped an alarm. The hospital's lawyers wanted to drag her through everything all over again. With a sigh, she headed to the ninth floor.

Three hours later, Win returned to the emergency room with a pounding headache. She'd just pulled out her phone to check messages when something hard that wasn't there a few moments ago slammed into her. Or she into it. Pain shot through Win's ribs and she recoiled, saved from falling on her ass by a set of arms grabbing her back. A familiar scent of ocean breeze shampoo filled her nose.

"You really need to look up once in a while," Matthew said, his voice a mix of exasperation and concern.

"You need to stop popping up in people's paths unannounced."

"I'll work on that," he said tartly, his hands lingering around her a moment longer before dropping away to a more professional stance. Not that muscled arms crossed over an equally muscled frame was likely to give anyone professional thoughts. Win shifted her weight, already missing the feel of him against her back.

Pathetic. She was pathetic.

Which didn't make the heat suddenly pooling low in her belly any less potent. "So how did it go with Yarborough?" she asked.

Matthew's face darkened. "I'm suspended for another week and when I return I'm the new teaching attending for all medical students and first years in the entire department."

A few paces away, Michelle muttered something that sounded like a prayer.

"I can think of worse punishments," Win said. "Like making someone who hates blood exclusive to a trauma service."

Matthew's lips pressed together, but the chuckle was all too evident in his eyes. "Go ahead and ask me how sorry I am about that?"

Win's brows narrowed. "Are you sorry?"

"Not one iota."

"I didn't think so," she muttered.

Matthews' face became more serious. "You won't have to come back to the ER, Win. Yarborough relented on that. You've enough to deal with without having to walk in here."

The embarrassing wave of relief rushing through Win must have been obvious, because Matthew shook his head at her. "You realize that the only thing more painful Yarborough could have done to me is to force me out of acute patient care and stuff me into a white lab coat in a genetics research lab?"

"Maybe."

"Most certainly." Matthew leaned down, his voice a low rumble that tickled against her ear. "I won't miss riding hard on you over trauma calls, though. I find other interactions much more pleasant."

Win inhaled sharpy, a shiver of arousal racing through her in the most inappropriate of ways. She took a step back before Matthew could realize the effect his words had on her, but the smile he gave her, the one full of promises that had no business in a hospital, told her she failed.

"Radiology told me they got updated X-rays of your ribs today," Matthew said, angling his head toward the isolation rooms at the far end of the corridor. "Let's go take a look while we are here."

A passing nurse quickened her pace and Win's cheeks heated. There was no reason to go into a private room to look at chest X-rays and the staff knew it. And so did Matthew.

"You are looking a little flushed, Dr. Carrell," he said. "Are you unwell?"

Win flashed him a glare. "I'm going to reprogram your coffee maker."

"Fighting words." Matthew's fingers grazed Win's lower back, sending shots of electricity through her. She started walking before Matthew could come up with another way of amusing himself.

They'd barely made it to the private exam room before Matthew's hands encircled Win's hips. Lifting her into the air, he carried her easily the few steps to the treatment table and sat her on its edge, his face now so much closer to her own. His mouth so much closer.

"You realize half the nurses think we are here to make out?" Win hissed. The warmth that had kissed her cheeks earlier was back with a vengeance and there was a pulsing need growing between her thighs that she did not want there right now.

"You know what I've learned about ED nurses?" asked Matthew. "They are usually right."

"We are in hospital." She shot a glance at the door. It was closed at the moment, but literally anyone could walk in. A tech looking for supplies, an EMT bringing in a patient, a pair of doctors wanting to hold a private conversation.

Matthew moved in closer, forcing Win to open her knees. *God.*

"Would it make you feel better if we do some hospital worthy things?" he asked. "You can practice blood draws on me. I've been told I have very sexy veins." He pushed up both sleeves of his ribbed shirt, revealing forearms that were strong and toned, the muscles shifting subtly as he moved his wrist. His skin was smooth and warm to the touch, like silk over solid steel.

"Making you hurt and bleed isn't my idea of a good time," she said. Her mouth was dry.

"Hmm..." Matthew considered that. "If you hurt me, I'm sure I can think of a way you could make me feel better. But..." he conceded, "we really should make this about you. And it would be wrong to not examine how those ribs are healing while we are here."

His fingers slid to the top button of Win's shirt, undoing it deftly before moving on to the next. And then the next. Zapping little pulses of arousal shot over her skin with each brush of his finger. She inhaled harshly, the movement too hard and sharp for her still healing ribs.

Matthew's palms flattened along her torso the instant he felt her flinch. "It's alright," he promised. "I have you."

He did have her. Win lifted her face toward him, finding the intensity of his promise etched into each line of his jaw. Never in her life had she felt as safe as she did when he was there, as *seen*. If anyone ever told her that a SEAL would look at a little computer geek with that smoldering gaze, she'd have laughed. But yet here they were.

Matthew leaned down, his mouth brushed hers softly. The moment she opened for him though, the kiss turned claiming. His hand tangled in her hair, his tongue sweeping in hungrily. Win moaned. Her hands found his solid chest, reveling in the heat of his body, the muscles moving under his shirt with every flex of his chest. Her heart thudded faster with each moment, especially when the palm he still had against her ribs slid *down down down* toward -

"What in the fuck's name is going on in here?" A furious voice knifed through the room.

Win jerked, only Matthews's instinctive bracing of her ribs keeping a jolt of pain from piercing through her. He straightened with control and confidence she felt none of as her heart raced so quickly it was difficult to think. To process what she was seeing. *Who* she was seeing.

Yet there he was, standing at the door, Yarborough at his shoulder.

"Sith?" Win asked.

Sith's eyes flashed with fury as he advanced on Matthew. "Get your hands off my little sister. Now."

WIN

Sith. And Yarborough. Her brother and the department chief. A wave of absolute humiliation washed through Win, her swollen lips feeling too large for her face. Sith's gaze raked over Matthew who was now several steps away, his hands raised placatingly in the air—which did nothing to hide the large bulge pressing against his jeans.

Sith took off his sweatshirt and handed it to her, which was when Win realized that her own shirt was still open. Putting his hoodie on was faster than trying to refasten the buttons, if her fingers would even cooperate right now. As the shirt's warmth and her brother's familiar cinnamon scent settled over her however, she finally snapped back to reality.

"What are you doing here?" Win demanded, slipping off the table to wrap her arms around her brother. He looked just as he always did, a black t-shirt and camo pants, with black combat boots and a black tactical belt. Even the watch on his wrist was black, as was the eagle on his right shoulder. Only his golden hair didn't match the rest of the getup. "Matthew said you'd gone dark and -"

"He got hurt," Matthew said flatly. "That's why they sent him home. And why he is self-splinting his arm to his chest."

Blood drained from Win's face. "Sith? Is it true?"

Sith grimaced slightly, but pressed Win to him. "It's all a great deal less dramatic than Jennson is making it sound. I was near something that went boom, and the shock wave wrecked some minor havoc. So the Navy is grounding me for a bit while it heals and figured it doesn't need to be feeding me overseas when I could do it myself at home."

Home. With all of his deployments, Sith's home was wherever Win happened to be. She ran her hands over him, reassuring herself that he was alright. Sith kissed the top of her head.

"What's this I'm hearing about you being on medical leave?" Sith asked.

"There have been some developments," Matthew said. He was still standing to the side, making no move toward her. Which was probably smart, but still hurt.

Sith crossed his arms. "Clearly."

"Several bikers jumped me in the staff parking lot," Win explained quickly. "Matthew got to me before they did any real damage though. He's been watching over me while I recover. He's done a lot."

Instead of looking appeased at Win's explanation, the lines of anger tightening Sith's mouth only deepened with each word. He turned to Matthew. "Let me get this straight, Jennson. I asked you to watch over my sister and you let her get assaulted by a group of bikers?"

"What the hell, Sith?" Win demanded.

Sith ignored her.

Matthew dropped his gaze.

Sith's voice lowered an octave, going from threatening to downright scary. "And now you are getting into her pants? And don't get me started on the fact that you are in charge of her."

"Hey," Win shoved him, which was very unsatisfactory because even the injured Sith didn't so much as rock back on his heels. "First, Matthew wasn't in charge of me at the time. And second, who, when, and how someone gets into my pants is none of your business." Never mind that Matthew hadn't actually managed to make it all the way there.

Sith caught Win's wrist before she could shove him again. "Agreed, Fred. With the one exception being someone who is supposed to be my best friend."

"What does that have to do with anything?" Win asked. "Do you have a monopoly on people now?"

She waited for Matthew to say something, he didn't. Not for heartbeat after heartbeat. And when he did speak, Win wished he'd kept his mouth shut.

"You should also know that Win's been helping the Tridents track down Satan's Armada, thats—"

"I know what Satan's Armada is," Sith's face darkened and he prowled toward Matthew. "Is that who attacked her?"

"Yes," said Matthew.

Sith swung.

Matthew didn't do anything to defend himself, only grunted slightly in pain as Sith's knuckles split his lip. Shock rocked through Win's body as she stared at the blood now trickling along Matthew's chin.

Sith's fist tightened again.

"Do not do that," Yarborough cut in, his voice ice cold and hard as steel. "If any one of the three of you so much as blinks wrong at one another, you will discover just how miserable I can make your existence here. Be you doctor or patient." He glared at Sith, then Matthew, then finally Win.

She stepped back. There was no Matthew behind her this time though. No arms wrapping protectively around her shoulders. A lump formed in Win's throat, the disappointment tasting bitter on her tongue. It wasn't as if she didn't understand. Something had gone wrong with whatever mission Sith was on, and Matthew probably knew better than she did what that could do to a SEAL. And while Sith was an amazing brother, he had a protective streak wide enough to double as an aircraft carrier. She and Matthew had played with fire in the middle of the emergency room and got burned. Right now, this moment was about de-escalation, not a comparison of dick size. She understood all of that.

But the fact that Matthew stood on the other side of the room instead of crossing to be beside her still fucking hurt.

"Am I clear?" Yarborough asked, surveying them all with his gaze again. Though his voice was even, there was no denying the steel behind it.

"Yes, sir," said Sith.

"Crystal," Matthew echoed.

Win said nothing. Not because she wanted confrontation, but because something about the way Matthew had uttered that one word caught her ear. It was a gut feeling really, and she wasn't sure it wasn't her imagination, but it seemed Matthew had stretched that last sound oddly. As if he was suddenly doing two things at once. Being here, and not here.

The whole of Win's attention focused on him, scanning for anything to confirm what her gut warned about. And that's when she saw them, the tiny tells that were growing by the second. A hint of a glaze coming over Matthew's eyes. A drop of sweat on his temple. A curling of his fingers, as if trying to scratch a phantom itch.

Suddenly, Matthew twisted to the door, cutting off whatever Yarborough had been saying to him.

"I need to go," he said at the same time as Win spoke.

"I need diazepam, stat," she said over him.

Matthew's step stuttered, but he continued to the door. Another two paces and he'd be gone, hiding in some corner without help while a seizure wrecked his body. From what he'd told *@DocPhantom42*, the convulsions weren't the pretty kind.

Yarborough shifted his weight, bringing himself in front of the door before Matthew could storm out of it.

"What's going on?" Sith asked as Win yanked the medcart open.

"Nothing," said Matthew.

"Dr. Carrell seems to believe that Matthew is about to have a seizure," Yaborough said. "Which is interesting considering we've no documented history of any kind of combustion disorder. The medication she called for is a powerful anticonvulsant drug."

"We are done here," said Matthew. "I am not sure what game Win is playing right now, but it isn't one that will end with drugs going into my arm."

Games?

"Matthew, do you have seizures?" Yarborough asked before Win could respond.

"No," Matthew said without blinking an eye.

Anger gripped Win's neck. "Oh yeah? Let's wait five minutes and find out."

He turned to her then, and there was nothing, but fury and the sting of betrayal in his blue gaze. The force of it hit Win like a physical blow. Abandoning the medcart she reached toward him. "Matthew—"

"Do not touch me," he said, stepping away. "Not now. Not ever. If you—"

Matthew's body jerked mid sentence, Yarborough moving to catch him before Matthew crashed to the ground. His powerful form contorted, the arms that had once held Win now lurching against the floor.

"This would be a good time for that diazepam," Yarborough said with absurd calm. "I believe this falls under implied consent, Dr. Carrell."

Diazepam. Right. Win rushed back to the medcart and returned, kneeling on the floor beside Yarborough. The older doctor grabbed hold of Matthew's arm and pinned it straight to allow for IV access.

"Good god," Sith whispered, crouching to help hold down his friend's arm. "Good fucking god. Do something Fred. Help him."

"I will." Win's heart pounded as she found the vein while Matthew's body arched violently. She'd suspected his seizures were bad, but seeing them play out, seeing him like this... Her heart tore for him into a thousand pieces. She threaded the needle in, letting out a breath when blood ran into the tubing, confirming placement. She removed the needle quickly, and pushed the meds into the tubing.

For a heartbeat nothing happened, but then the tension coiling Matthew's body eased, leaving him limp against the floor. Win drew his head onto her lap, pressing two fingers against his pulse. Fast, but steady. As was his breathing.

"You have it from here?" Yaborough asked.

Win nodded, not even looking up as Yarborough left the room. Matthew looked so vulnerable laying there, sweat soaked locks of his hair plastered against his forehead. She brushed them aside. "You are alright," she said. "It's over. You are alright."

Matthew blinked, his eyes opening but not seeing. Not yet.

"Matthew?" Sith gripped his friends shoulder, panic laced his voice.

"It's alright." Win glanced up at Sith for a moment and gave him her best calming smile. It was strange to be the one calming him for a change, to be the one taking care of him. Of both the men. "This is normal after a seizure. He'll be back soon."

"How long has it been going on?" Sith asked.

"I don't know." Win stroked Matthew's hair. However long it had been, however long he'd battled it alone, was too long.

"But this isn't the first time its happened, right?" Sith insisted. "That's how you knew to be on the lookout? Why you raised the alarm?"

"It's not, and yes that's how." She frowned. "Why is that important just now?"

Sith let out a long breath. "So these random episodes, they could have been happening for a while?" he insisted, just as focus started to return to Matthew's gaze. "Like when he was deployed with us?"

Irritation brushed over her. "I really don't know, Sith. Does it matter?"

"Of course it matters," Sith snarled with unexpected anger that made Win flinch. "If he knew this happened to him and kept it secret, he put the whole team in danger. He could have gotten people killed. So yeah, it fucking matters."

"I'm sorry." Matthew shifted, his voice quiet but gaining strength. "Sith, I know everything you are thinking, but that's why I left."

"Easy," Win said. "It doesn't matter right now. All that matters is you being alright."

Neither man paid her any mind.

"Yeah, you did leave," Sith said through clenched teeth. "One day you walked the fuck out and never came back. No explanation. Nothing. But you know what? I don't believe that you *excused yourself* as soon as you knew. I think you hung in there, hiding this shit, putting everyone's life on the line over and over and over."

"Sith," Win's voice rang through the room louder than she knew it could. "Stop being an asshole or get out of my treatment room."

Sith blinked, rocking back on his heels. His mouth snapped closed.

Matthew's attention shifted from Sith to her, and it was as if he'd just now realized that Win was cradling his head. His blue gaze gripped her's, the raw pain of betrayal flashing there before a mask of icy calm slid into place.

"Dr. Carrell." Matthew pushed himself up and away from Win. "Do not touch me again. Ever. I believe I've told you as much before."

The words hit her like a blow and Win couldn't move as Matthew got to his feet, straightening his clothes.

"You've no need to worry about me and your sister," he told Sith before walking out, the door slamming shut in his wake.

SONIA

Numbness enveloped Sonia as she sat on the too large, too comfortable chair and stared at nothing. Beyond the window, water lapped gently and there was a gentle hum of the engine creating a fine vibration as the *Belle Nuit* maneuvered through the water. The words Casey had thrown at her before walking out replayed themselves in Sonia's mind. Over and over.

For some time she was certain that Casey would come back at any moment, and with him a wickedly twisted tale that explained away the morning. But deep down she knew it wouldn't. Not with the words he'd said, the fierce anger that lurked behind them.

Finally she padded into the bathroom, turned on a hot shower and got inside. The scent of mint body wash filled the stall as she poured generous amounts onto a washcloth and got busy scrubbing away whatever remnants of the stupid girlish feelings from the previous night that still lingered.

She *hadn't* been wanted. She hadn't been cherished. She had utterly misread everything about the man who had been inside her, who she'd taken into her mouth. Clearly, she'd learned nothing since college. Back then, she hadn't realized a man's intention until he had her cornered. Now she'd erred in a different way, but no less stupidly.

Equal parts pain and anger stabbed into Sonia. Setting the water so hot that it nearly scalded her skin, she sank to the floor of the shower. She welcomed the water's burning pain. Welcomed any sensation that would distract her from the gaping hole Casey had made inside her chest.

The sex last night, it had meant everything to Sonia. She'd allowed it to mean everything. And for Casey... She slapped the wet wall, the sound not nearly as satisfying as she expected.

He'd promised to make her a partner. Had given his word. And then broke it without a second thought. And that bath, the one he'd given her with such tender care, what did he think he was doing then? Washing away evidence from a potential rape kit, apparently.

Yeah. He'd lied. He'd put on a mask. And she fell for it. And the worst part? It wasn't even the first time she'd fallen for Casey's lies.

He'd done the same thing last year during Aiden's trial. They had been partners then too. Co-council on a prosecution team. They sat behind the same council's table, arguing the same case. Sonia had poured everything she had into the courtroom, not knowing that Casey was withholding witnesses and information and strategy. Right up until he descended upon the court like some sort of legal god, taking everyone's breath away and making Sonia look like a fool. He'd come out a god damned hero. She'd been left to pick up the pieces.

She'd vowed to never let it happen again. And yet here they were.

Fool me once, shame on you. Fool me twice...Yeah.

Duane knocked on the door just when she'd gotten out of the shower, his timing as eerily perfect as always. He took one look at Sonia's face, then at the empty room, and pressed his mouth into a tight line.

"I won't need help getting ready today," Sonia told him quietly. "But thank you."

Instead of leaving, Duane pursed his lips and walked right past Sonia to the closet. He came out a few minutes later holding an outfit Sonia didn't know even existed, Duane having assembled it from several pieces.

"Really, I don't think I'll be going out today," Sonia protested as he started laying out the pieces.

"You will," Duane told her. "You *should*. And you are going to look stunning while doing it."

Feeling that it was easier to let Duane have his way than argue, Sonia let him get her dressed, not daring to look at herself until he was finished. Duane outdid himself. A red long sleeve crop top made of a stretchy, form-fitting material accented Sonia's arms while the neckline's off the shoulder style added sensuality to the outfit. The bottoms were a pair of high-waisted pants that hugged her curves and elongated her legs. A zipper detailing at the ankles added a touch of edge to the look, especially paired with the pair of strappy black heels.

Yet it was the belt that truly made the whole thing come together. Leather, with a silver buckle and tasteful embellishments that created a faux rock-chic vibe. With the way Duane looped it high on her waist, the belt morphed her too large hips into an illusion of an hourglass. It was gorgeous, but in a whole different way from the faux maiden dress she'd worn last night or the gown she had on in the piano bar. Everything about this ensemble whispered femme fatale. Strong. Sensual. Confident. It slipped over her like a warrior's shield.

Duane ushered Sonia to the dressing table and spent extra time on her face, drawing out her eyes and lips. He swept her hair back and away from her neck, leaving a few loose strands to frame her cheeks. By the time he was done, Sonia didn't recognize the woman who looked back at her from the mirror.

"Perfect," Duane declared. "And so is the outfit."

"Duane—"

"You should go up on deck, Ms. Dancer," he suggested, sweeping back toward the door. "We are docking in New York shortly and the approach is a sight to behold. As are you, if you don't mind me saying."

The door clicked closed behind Duane just as it had when Casey left, yet Sonia felt as different as she now looked. Heart beating a hard rhythm, she strode over to the safe and pulled out the laptop Briar sent updates to. After last night, she was sure there was more on the drive.

The password prompt flashed front and center. She entered the code. The screen flashed.

Error. Credentials not recognized.

She re-entered the code again, repeating the process several times until she acknowledged what happened. Felt its gut punch. Casey had known she'd go to the laptop and locked her out. God fucking damn it. Sonia tried several more combinations. None of them worked. It was all she could do to not slam the computer against the wall. Fine. She put the computer away, got her phone and called Briar directly.

No answer.

She called him again.

The call went to voicemail so quickly that Sonia knew Briar had actively sent it there. Because twins were fucking twins and once one decided to cut her out, the other one read his mind and did the same. Adding insult to injury, she had no idea where on the ship Briar was holed up, so storming down to his stateroom wasn't an option.

Her hands curled, the nails digging into her palms in frustration. She went to lock the laptop back in the safe but just before she could slam it closed, Casey's earpiece caught her attention. Apparently he'd decided he didn't need his brother in his ear this morning, just as he didn't need her at his side. She turned it on—or hoped she did, because there was no light to indicate that anything had happened—and slipped it into her ear. "Briar, can you hear me?"

Dead silence.

"Briar, please answer. It's important."

Nothing. Either the thing wasn't working or it was off on Briar's end. Or, he was ignoring her on purpose.

She pushed the earpiece deeper into her ear. "Alright. Here is the deal. I'm about to go to ship's security and share my worries about my fiancé's twin, who has a terrible heart condition and has stopped answering his phone. And I'm going to cry and moan about the heart attack I'm certain you are having until security agrees to do a wellness check. Stateroom by fucking stateroom. And then—"

"I get the point," Briar said gruffly into her ear.

Sonia smiled, though it didn't reach her eyes. "Excellent. I always thought you were the smarter of the pair. Now, you and I are going to have a little chat."

Briar grunted in what was probably acknowledgement.

"Oh no," Sonia informed him. "That's not going to cut it anymore. I'm going to go out into the hallway and you are going to use those exceptional skills of yours to direct me to wherever you are holed up, so we can have our talk face to face. Please keep in mind that should an unfortunate comms problem come up and I stop hearing your voice, I am going to veer off to security. Is there any part of this that confuses you?"

"*I'm clear*," Briar said over the earpiece. Nodding though she knew he couldn't see her, she stepped out into the hall.

Briar's voice was the embodiment of even steadiness as he directed her through a convoluted route to a stateroom at the lower decks. The do not disturb sign was displayed outside. Before Sonia could knock, Briar let her inside.

For a heartbeat, she felt her throat tighten all over again. She'd somehow forgotten how much like Casey Briar looked. All gorgeous planes and hard muscles and penetrating gray eyes. Just last night, she touched a body so much like his. Licked it. The strangeness of it nearly made Sonia look at Briar's crotch in wonder if he looked like his brother there too. He probably did.

Briar closed the door behind Sonia, his eyes widening slightly as he took her in. "You look..." He shook himself like a dog, then held out his palm in demand. "I want the earpiece back."

"No."

"You half killed the mic trying to turn it on."

"Oh." Yeah, she'd likely done that.

Sonia handed the earpiece over. Briar examined it briefly, cursed, and connected it to a computer while Sonia took a second to examine the room. In addition to a Casey look-alike in jeans and a t-shirt, the room had several monitors and gaming consoles set up. The cases with weapons she knew Briar had brought were nowhere in sight. With no other place to sit, Sonia perched on the edge of the bed.

"Where did Casey go this morning?" Sonia asked, her voice sounding too calm to her own ears.

Briar didn't bother looking away from the computer screen, apparently more concerned about the possible damage to an earpiece Casey wasn't even wearing now than having a conversation with Sonia. "To meet with Nero and the rest of the Armada."

She'd figured as much. "What's the next move?" she asked.

Briar shrugged. "We are docking in New York today. They will all go ashore together."

A day out on the town, drinking and partying. That tracked, too. But none of it went to the core point she was really here about. She dove for the heart of the issue. "And then what? What happens when he comes back? We are on a cruise ship, bound to cross paths with Nero and the others. We will still need to present a united front for the others, or at least a logical one. And with the shit he pulled this morning, I don't -"

"Sonia." Briar turned to her, and the slight softening of his face made her stomach clench. "Casey won't be coming back to the *Belle Nuit*."

"Wh-What do you mean?" she asked.

"The Armada is picking up a shipping container in New York and accompanying it back to Denton Valley. Casey will go with them and track them to the nest."

At which point the Tridents would likely swarm the place, taking down the whole operation. Sonia stared dumbly at Briar. "What about you? Me? What about that earpiece?"

"You stay on the ship, enjoying the cruise and the reunion sans criminals. I'll leave after Casey is clear and beat him home. As for electronics, Patriot made it clear that's a no go and he'll be looking." Briar shrugged and swiveled away. "That's all I have."

A surreal sort of numbness settled over Sonia. "In other words, you two are tossing me away like left-over lunch."

"On a luxury cruise with an open credit line and old classmates coming for company. There are worse predicaments to be in, princess."

The numbness inside Sonia ignited to icy fury. She rose, dusted invisible specs of dusk from her black pants, and strode for the door.

"Where are you going?"

"To enjoy a luxury cruise and an open credit line, where else?"

Briar was up and in front of her in a heartbeat. It reminded Sonia so much of Casey that it hurt. "Whatever it is you are thinking of doing—"

"Me? Think? No, I don't do such things." She gave him a cold smile and stepped out the door, knowing he couldn't follow. Especially not to the upper deck, where Briar's cameras had shown glimpses of Casey and Nero lounging by the rail. A perfect place for a little chat.

SONIA

Sonia picked up a mimosa from the bar before striding along the upper deck, where many of the *Belle Nuit's* passengers had gathered to watch the approaching New York coastline despite the cold and wind. She'd tapped into that line of credit of Casey's and now wore a long leather jacket fashioned to resemble a trench coat as she met the curious gazes of the meandering passengers. They looked away quickly. Always before she did. Maybe it was Duane's choice of clothes, or the icy anger that simmered low in her belly, but Sonia felt different and the others seemed to pick up on that presence and moved the hell out of her way.

She knew the moment Casey spotted her, his whole body going rigid. His eyes flashed, his upper lip curling up lightly in a snarl that would show off fangs if he were a wolf. Yeah. The warning to stay away from him and the Armada men gathered about him like the cool kids club couldn't have been more clear if he'd shouted it through the ship's loudspeaker system. In another time, in another lifetime—yes, yesterday was that long ago—she'd have heeded the order. But that was back when they were partners working together. Now, they were nothing of the sort.

Taking a slow, luxurious sip of the mimosa, Sonia strode over to the group. They were all dressed in something that she'd call business casual, with khaki pants and sweaters, though she knew that the cuffs of Casey's button-up belonged to the Armani part of the wardrobe. Their jackets were more suited to the weather than hers was, not that she cared much about the chill except as far as it made her nipples bunch—which was of course where Nero's glance went straight away.

Sonia smiled at him, lifting her head and letting him look his fill as she pushed right through the middle of their gaggle, turned and put her back against the railing.

"Good morning, gentlemen." She took a slow sip of the mimosa, the little bubbles racing along her tongue. "I hope you had a good evening after yesterday's... excitement?"

Nero cocked a brow at Casey. "Ms. Dancer doesn't much look like she's been pining over your broken engagement."

Mammoth laughed a full belly laugh and eyed her up and down, which left her skin feeling covered with slime. Popeye said nothing. Sonia got the sense that the man was there in a guard capacity, his eyes moving through the crowd. She didn't know where Razor and Patriot were, but they were probably keeping an eye on the women. Sonia hoped that what she'd done last night with Casey hadn't caused Lola and the other women more trouble.

Sonia turned her attention to Nero. "Me pining?" She brushed the lipstick off her glass with her thumb. "I don't know what tale McKenzie has been spinning for you, but the truth is *I* lost interest in the asshole." She lowered her voice conspiratorially and leaned in toward Nero. "Between you and me, after we got home last night he was too exhausted to get it up. Would you want to stay with a one pump chump?"

Casey choked on his whiskey.

Nero chortled, Mammoth doing the same beside him. Dressed, cleaned up, and in the public eye they put on a good show of being human. Then again, so did Casey.

"Well, well, well," Nero said, shaking his head at Casey. "I knew there was trouble in paradise, but you take trouble to a whole new level."

"I hear we've plans for some sightseeing today?" Sonia said as if Nero hadn't spoken.

"We've plans for sightseeing," Casey's voice dripped with a mix of warning and barely contained fury. A muscle ticked on the side of his jaw and the hand he held in his trouser pocket seemed to have balled into a fist. "The only thing you need to sightsee is the spa."

"Sounds like your kitten has gone feral, McKenzie," Mammoth smacked his lips, his voice low enough to stay within the group. "There are ways of taming her, you know. Not to toot my own horn, but I've been called quite accomplished in such feats."

Bile rose up Sonia's throat, but she let none of the fear and disgust show on her face. She wasn't going to let anything show on her face in front of Casey ever again. But she would see *his* face. That's why she was here, she finally realized. She knew better than to imagine she could get an invite to their excursion or change whatever they planned. But Casey was going to walk off the ship without so much as telling her. And she wanted to see the coward's face when she thwarted that plan. Wanted to make him look her in the eye.

Casey gulped back the rest of his whiskey. "If I wanted her brought under rein I'd have done it myself," he drawled lazily, not even bothering to acknowledge her. "Bitch isn't worth it. And Patriot had a point last night. Too many strings attached to Liam Rowan. Who needs that kind of baggage?"

"Didn't you buy North Vault, your precious club, from Liam?" Sonia crooned.

"Don't confuse business and pleasure, kitten," Casey's voice dripped with venom. "But then again, you turned out to be neither."

Sonia almost flinched, but stopped herself in time. Yeah. Apparently Casey could still hurt her. Which was the stupidest part. But still true.

"You are an asshole," she said thoughtfully to Casey before turning to Nero. "Once you figure that out, feel free to reach out to me and I'll give some insight."

"Hell hath no fury like a woman scorned, I'd be careful if I were you, McKenzie," Nero warned.

"I'm always careful," said Casey.

She tapped her nail against the half drunk mimosa, pushed off the railing and walked off.

"Aren't you forgetting something, kitten?" Casey's voice hit her between her shoulder blades. Then, faster than it was fair for anyone to move, he stepped in front of her and gripped her left wrist. With none of the gentleness she'd stupidly grown used to from him, Casey raised her captured hand and yanked off the ring he'd once placed there. "I was going to let you keep it. But now I think there is a better use for the stone."

"Several uses," Sonia agreed. "Shoving it up your ass comes to mind. Maybe your new friends can help you with that."

This time, no one stopped her from walking away. Sonia didn't stop until she reached the stateroom. Only once there did she let herself sink against the wall. Her legs shook. All of her shook. But at least she'd made Casey break his promises to her face. He owed her that much. And now... now they were truly done.

Grabbing her phone, Sonia dialed one of the numbers she'd memorized before coming on board. Win answered after two rings, her voice thick.

"Hello?"

Everything that Sonia had planned to start with was put on hold as she focused on her friend. They'd not talked at all since Sonia left with the twins, though Briar had said some of the intel he was getting came from her. He'd not mentioned any reason for her to be upset, but in that one word Sonia knew her friend was hurting. "Win. It's Sonia. Are you alright? You don't sound alright."

"Sonia? Shit." Win's voice changed. "Umm, stand by. I'm going to get to you through a different app. Download the link I'm texting you."

True to Win's word, a link arrived and Sonia quickly installed the app her friend sent. And then she settled cross-legged on the floor of her suite and listened. Her blood pressure rose with every word of Win's narrative, from the attack, to her time with Matthew, to Sith's return. She'd known none of it, and she didn't believe for a second that no one told Briar that Win was the one hurt in the Denton Memorial assault. It was just one of the things the twins had decided to keep from her. They were going to leave her on a cruise for another week, getting her nails done.

"I'm so sorry," Sonia whispered.

"Don't be. I mean, what could you do from there anyway?" said Win. "I'm sure they wanted to help you keep your head in the game. Did you know about the payment to New York? Fast Freight Solutions International."

"No, but it makes sense. They are going ashore and not planning on returning." It was her turn to fill Win in, the words becoming a little easier as they fell on understanding ears. "Matthew and Casey were assholes before this whole mess started, is it really a surprise that they are still assholes?"

"Assholes we let get to us." Win growled slightly on the other end of the line. "Whatever happened to our pact? *Survive, grow, don't yield to idiot men.* Remember that one?"

Sonia smiled despite herself, though that day in the Vault seemed forever ago. "I'd like to think that if you and I were together we'd have kept each other from becoming stupid, but honestly, I don't even know."

"So what now?" Win asked. "I am presuming you aren't going to stay on board the *Belle Nuit* and enjoy the spa?"

"I'm not. But I'm done with the Tridents. It's not just Casey. Briar knew too. And I'm done waiting for some guy's approval before making an impact."

"Which means what in, like, practical terms?"

"That I'm coming back to Denton today, joining the state's prosecutor's office full time, and spending my time with someone I truly care about—that's you, if you are wondering. We are going to get roaring drunk, eat all the ice cream and chocolate, watch a stupid movie, and then... and then I'm going to build a case against the Armada. And get Tank back behind bars where he belongs."

"I like it," said Win on the other end. "I'm going to get you a plane ticket from JFK to Denton, so just grab a cab from the dock. And bring a jacket. There is a cold front coming through here. Like really bad."

"They have heating in planes."

"And if you crash? You'll be really sorry if you are hobbling around a crash site without a warm jacket."

Sonia laughed despite herself. "Good point. Warm jacket it is. I'll see you soon."

An hour later, Sonia had a small bag packed and was ready as the ship's loudspeaker came to life.

"Ladies and gentlemen," a man's voice announced, "the *Belle Nuit* is pleased to welcome you to New York. Disembarkment will begin in ten minutes. Please note that we will remain at port until 20:00 this evening. All passengers should return to ship by 18:00 to assure no interruption to your travel plans. For those of you still doing the math, that is six pm. Please note that we are unable to delay departure to accommodate late arrivals. Ladies and gentlemen, disembarkment begins in ten minutes."

She gave the room one last look and took her time going to the disembarkation point. Confronting Casey on deck had been good, but she little wanted to run into him again.

Her phone rang. Briar. She shut him off as he'd done earlier. She didn't really care what he had to say. Instead, bag in hand, Sonia headed for the exit and walked out with the crowd into the Big Apple.

The sheer size of the port took Sonia's breath away. The chilly air was filled with the sounds of seagulls and heavy machinery as towering cranes moved cargo containers on and off ships. In the distance the Manhattan skyline was visible, the Empire State Building and Freedom Tower standing tall and proud. Just because she couldn't help herself, Sonia searched for the Statue of Liberty, finding it across the water. At another time, she might have taken the short ferry ride to see it, but not today. Blending back in with the crowd she headed toward the long rows of vans and limos and taxis waiting to take sightseers to wherever they wished.

"Where to?" The cabbie had an Italian accent and helped Sonia with her bag.

"JFK," said Sonia.

He nodded and pressed the gas, heading out onto the street. If Sonia thought the traffic was bad in Denton, it was nothing compared to the stop and go business of New York. The cabbie talked with his hands as much as his mouth, and seemed unbothered by the fact that Sonia paid him no mind. She was so engrossed in staring out the window and wondering how they'd not gotten into ten accidents already, that when the car suddenly jerked it took her a moment to realize it wasn't just another traffic defying maneuver. Rather, a black SUV had clipped the back corner of the cab.

Great.

The cabbie cursed in Italian and pulled over. While he stormed off to deal with the SUV driver, Sonia checked her watch. The accident was just a next step up from a fender bender and she wasn't sure whether it was more prudent to wait until the drivers exchanged paperwork or grab another cab.

The door on the other side of her opened suddenly, Popeye's familiar face filling the space. He gave her a glimpse of the gun he had pointed at her through his jacket. "Keep your mouth shut, bitch. And get out on my side. Fucking now."

Sonia's heart stopped, her mouth going dry. Popeye made an irritated motion, urging her into movement. The cabbie was still arguing with the SUV driver, who Sonia now saw was Patriot.

"One sound and you are both dead," Popeye said. "Understood?"

Sonia nodded. The moment she cleared the car, Popeye wrapped his hand around her waist, the muzzle of his gun pressing into her side. He would use it. She was sure of it. Her gaze bore into the cabbie, begging him to look up and question what was happening—but Patriot had a bundle of cash out now and was clearly paying for the damages, the two men loudly debating the exact cost.

Popeye opened the door to the SUV and Sonia knew, *knew*, that the worst thing she could do was get inside.

She opened her mouth to scream.

Something sharp jabbed into her neck and the world went dark.

CASEY

～

Casey knew he was being tested when Nero insisted that he drive back to Colorado in the eighteen wheeler Patriot and Razor were taking. A fucking thirty hour trip. He also knew that testing was part of the process. They'd not shown him exactly what was inside the container they hauled with them, but he knew it was nothing good or legal. He'd be charged right alongside Patriot and Razor if the cops stopped them. The assholes didn't need to worry about him though. Casey had every intention of ensuring the ride went smoothly—right into the Armada's nest in Denton Valley. And then he and the Tridents would lay waste to the whole damn thing.

Meanwhile, he had a mask to wear and a game to play. Reclining with apparent ease in the backseat of the eighteen wheeler's cab, Casey briefly wondered whether the two rows of seats in the cab was a normal thing for trucks or just something the Armada had commissioned to carry more people. Then he swung his attention to Razor, in the front passenger's seat, who was running his mouth again. War stories about the club, fucking, the club, more fucking, and the right way to run the country. Casey couldn't even escape into his phone, since handing over his electronics and weapon had been part of the deal.

"We take shifts driving, keep everything moving, and minimize our time on the road," Patriot had told him when they first got in. He was quieter than Razor, but more dangerous. Mammoth and Nero had gone to Denton Valley by air. Casey wasn't sure where Popeye was. Patriot glanced back at him through the mirror. "I hope you can make yourself comfortable in the accommodations."

"I've slept in worse and for less profitable reasons," Casey said.

That had been twenty-five hours ago. Twenty-five hours of being locked up in a tractor-trailer cab with two Armada goons and no communications. There wasn't even anything worth looking at along the highway. Nothing to distract him from seeing that look of fury and betrayal on Sonia's face over and over again. What he'd said to her... the way he left things...

It was for the best. After what happened in the Armada's suite, he couldn't allow Sonia anywhere near these men. They should never have entertained the idea of getting Sonia involved to begin with, not when the mission parameters had changed. And if he'd acted like a piece of shit, well, that was because he *was* a piece of shit. His father's son. But if Sonia's hatred of him would repel her from the Armada, it was worth it.

"Five more hours," Patriot said, taking a sip of his coffee. "Home stretch."

"Thank fucking god," Razor grunted, finishing the last of the potato chips. They'd brought all their food along to avoid pulling into a rest area, making due with trees enroute to see to their needs. "I need a meal, a bed, and some pussy. Isn't that right, McKenzie? Or are you pining over that piece of ass you left behind?"

Casey didn't let Razor see the way his fist tightened, but the need to put his knuckles through the man's teeth was quickly becoming unbearable. He rooted through the grocery bag to cover the flush of fury, but somehow managed to keep his voice casual. "She was a good distraction while it lasted." He pulled out a protein bar and bottle of water. "I did her a favor leaving her on a cruise ship instead of the altar, because god knows that was never going to happen."

That last part was true, if not for the reasons Razor imagined.

Patriot adjusted his rearview mirror, which showed nothing but Casey and the back seat. "The way you fucked her said otherwise."

"True that," Razor agreed. "That bitch has you whipped."

Casey scowled. "What the fuck you trying to start?"

Instead of retreating, Razor stretched, cracking his knuckles. "Just pointing out that you are in fucking love, Romeo. And nobody bought your pussy ass break-up act. Thought you should know that, is all. In case you fooled yourself in the process."

"My head is crystal clear, don't you fret," said Casey lazily, though something in Razor's words didn't sit right. Maybe it was just the talk of Sonia. Well, it was certainly the talk of Sonia. But since when did Armada biker thugs promote self-reflection? "Worry about your own shit. Like whether you are gonna get the clap after sharing with Nero."

"He *is* worrying about his shit," Patriot chimed in, his voice too even. "We all are. As in, we like our shit to stay ours. And when someone comes in and starts lying, it doesn't sit well."

Alarm bells sounded inside Casey's head. Being accused of lying by a pair of armed bikers was never a good thing. Ever. Casey did enough lying in his life to know that. Now, he huffed a laugh. "Twenty-five hours of sitting on each other's laps and now you decide you don't trust me?"

"Didn't trust you from the start," said Patriot.

"And yet here I am. You can lodge your complaint with Nero when we get to Denton Valley."

"See, it's a timing thing," Razor explained, climbing back into the conversation. "So far it's been highway and highway. But now, we are getting closer to home turf. Need to take some precautions to ensure no one does something stupid. You understand, don't you? I can tell from that concerned look on your face."

"That's the look of me being about done with your shit," Casey shifted his weight slightly to get better purchase, though what was he going to do? Start a fight in a tractor trailer rushing down a highway? "It's not my first rodeo, cowboy. You've got my phone and gun, and you've got me. Great company as I am on any cross country joy ride, I figure I'm mostly here so you have someone to throw in front of the cops if trouble starts. Whether that gives you enough piece of mind to sleep at night, isn't my problem. Take it up with Nero or the chapter president."

"You sound defensive," said Razor. "Hey Pat, does McKenzie sound defensive to you?"

"Fuck the games. We're past the perimeter and I don't want drama."

"No drama," Casey agreed, stretching his shoulders. He was stiff from sitting for the day and the miserable weather outside with on and off rain didn't help. The motion did little to release the energy building up inside him though. Whatever was happening, wasn't good. He grinned. "We are all friends here."

"No, we aren't." Patriot glanced at him through the mirror again. "What is it you think we are dragging behind us?"

"Don't know. Don't need to know," said Casey, his voice dropping all hints of polite pretense now. "Don't *want* to know."

"Don't much care what you want. You aren't doing a ride along with the knitting club," Patriot said. "Nero is young. We've been around a while. Consider us your initiation welcome wagon."

Razor pulled a cell phone from his pocket and made a call, Popeye's face filling the screen two rings later. "About god damn time," Popeye said by way of greeting. The video was shaking a bit as if he were in a moving vehicle, but what little of the background Casey could see around Popeye's bald head looked like plain dimly lit metal. "Is Romeo there?"

Romeo. Casey was starting to really dislike that.

"Yep." Razor held the phone where Casey had a good view of the screen.

"Give us a tour of the zoo."

The image flipped from selfie mode and everything in Casey turned to ice. He knew where Popeye was now, and why it looked like he'd been moving. He was moving. Right in the very container their truck was hauling down the road. And the cargo? It wasn't weapons or drugs or stolen crap. There were people in there. Women. All huddled against the far end, pressing into each other for warmth. They'd been there the entire trip, with no relief.

"They may not look like much now," Razor said, "but once you get 'em cleaned up they sell well. Popeye there ensures they stay alive until then. You could probably take prime pick for your club." The last was said with conciliatory tones, as if suspecting that Casey's greatest concern upon realizing that he was a party to the atrocity was his wallet.

Casey's hands tightened around the edge of the seat, as he stared at the screen, his mind racing and all of his willpower going to keep himself from snapping Razor's neck and calling it a day. They'd been on the road for a day. Why tell him this now? Because they were past a perimeter. That's what Patriot had mentioned. Casey was more of a threat to them now that they were close to the operation.

The notion of snapping Patriot's neck surfaced again, but he was driving and might flip the whole thing over and kill everyone. He could go after Razor instead. Scenario variations tracked through Casey's mind, but they always ended with him getting shot somewhere along the way. He was also acutely aware that they were now in Colorado on the last part of the journey. Even if he could safely take control of the truck, which was unlikely, what was he going to do next? Help would take hours to arrive and while the women in the back would be safe and warm in a few hours, it would all just be a minor inconvenience in the grand scheme of things for the Armada.

He needed to get into Denton Valley. Into the belly of the beast. And then carve it up from the inside.

It took strength Casey didn't know he possessed to shrug at the phone in Razor's hand and leaned back. "Which part of I don't give a fuck was confusing?" Casey said. "Getting the cargo safely to the destination is your problem, not mine. And if Popeye there damages anything, that's coming from your pocket too."

"But you've not seen the best part yet," said Razor. "Keep watching. This part is what we call an insurance policy. Just to make sure you don't get any stupid ideas close to home."

"Lookie here, Romeo," Popeye's screen panned across the inside of the container. There was a small space with a lounge chair that must have been his, and then a single figure huddled against the tail end, her bright red shirt and black pants hauntingly familiar.

Casey's heart and breath stopped, and it was beyond him to keep a shudder from wracking through his body. Sonia. They had Sonia in that container. They never bought the claim of a broken engagement and took her to keep him in line.

"This next part is unfortunate, but necessary," Patriot said. "I'll tell you right now you aren't going to like it. But provided you do nothing outside our understanding of proper behavior, it need not happen again. And before you ask, you can have your toy back when the deal is done. In our line of business, we like assurances that go beyond an agreement over drinks at a posh bar."

On screen, Popeye pulled his belt from his pants in a single motion.

Murder flashed through Casey.

"His cock is going to stay where it is," Patriot said very quickly. "We know the line. Right Popeye?"

Popeye grunted.

Casey's nostrils flared, the whole world pounding like a base inside his skull.

On screen, Popeye grabbed Sonia's shoulder. He yanked her around, slamming her chest into the metal wall. Then his arm wheeled back, and the leather came cracking down on the pretty red crop-top. A muffled cry came through the video feed.

Casey would kill them. He would kill them all.

"Don't be stupid, McKenzie," Patriot's voice took on a soothing note. On screen Popeye delivered another blow. "We are in here. Popeye is in there. We all know that he can get to Juliet before you can, no matter what you do. The good news is that so long as everyone behaves, I see no need for additional use of force. We are all on the same team. You want Juliet safe. We want everyone safe. And in five hours, it will all be so. Now, say you understand and we can put this little lesson behind us."

CASEY

He was going to end them all. That was the first and only thought that Casey could hold on to as Razor turned off his phone and went back to small talk, while Patriot tuned the radio to country music. He was going to end them all.

It pulsated, gaining momentum with each heartbeat until Casey finally jerked himself free of its grip and took control of himself. Made the world slow to battlefield precision. To facts. He was aware of his too steady pulse, of Razor's barely concealed grin as he savored his power, of the thick trees that passed along the highway. Casey let himself be aware of everything, and then stripped away every bit that wasn't relevant to the moment. Focused only on what was important.

He needed to get Sonia free. Right now. He didn't care whether that meant forfeiting everything else, his life included.

Except that if he were dead too early, the chances of Sonia getting away were slim. There was no one else on the road within line of sight, but Casey was willing to bet bikers followed. He'd seen them on and off on the road, though none wore patches. Unless Casey moved Sonia off the X, she'd just be recaptured. He couldn't let that happen.

He dug back into the grocery bag, slipping protein bars and water into his backpack. A few more things that were within easy reach. The phone and gun he'd have to acquire by other means. Then he returned his attention to the road. It was mostly straight. But not always. And it wasn't always flat either. Overhead, the sun was close to setting. Which was a double edged sword. But it was a fact, just like all others Casey marked, while his heart kept a steady *thump thump thump* against his ribs.

It was another twenty minutes—twenty god damn minutes—until the highway finally cooperated and Casey marked the sharp turn he needed. Now that it was in sight though, Casey felt nothing as he watched it approach, not even the surge of excitement. He was beyond that. In his head, the piano had begun to play as it often did when something required precise execution. When he was behind a rifle, the scope trained on a target. When he was doing things that were much more close and personal and bloody.

The road turned. The truck slowed to take it. In the front passenger's seat, Razor steadied the cup of coffee on the dashboard.

Casey moved.

Casey's fist hit the side of Razor's head, knocking the man out at the same time as Casey grabbed his backpack and leapt over the seat to the front. Behind the steering wheel, Patriot jerked around, the truck veered hard to the right into the bend. Casey helped it along, steering them into a ditch.

"Are you insane?" Patriot shouted, as he fought to keep the tractor trailer from rolling toward their collective deaths.

"You have no idea." He snatched Razor's phone with one hand while elbowing Patriot's jaw with the other. Grabbing the steering, he course corrected until the wheels found purchase, then pulled the emergency brake into place.

"Holy fu-" Patriot's curse died as Casey hit him again, this time knocking him out.

Casey opened the driver's door and shoved Patriot out before getting out himself, his pack already on. It didn't hold a lot, but it would have to do. He sprinted to the back of the trailer, where hands banged against the mental. He banged back, baiting Popeye into approaching the loading port. To opening it from the inside. The heavy scent of ripe bodies and filth hit the air. The moment the biker stuck his head out the back to see what was happening, Casey was on him. They went to the ground together in a tangle of fists that left a single victor.

"Sonia!" Casey hollered the instant Popeye was down. He rushed back to the truck. Over a dozen terror filled faces stared at him. Casey didn't let himself linger on them though. He wasn't here to save the world. Not now. "Sonia!"

"Casey?"

He zeroed in on her at once. She was on her knees on the floor, near enough that Casey could wrap his arm around her waist and haul her out. A flash of fury and fear at her state rushed through him. He didn't know how hurt she was, and had no time to decipher it either. She was breathing and that would have to do for now.

A gun sounded. Casey folded himself around Sonia. He felt a burn along his back, but his body was already past that, shoving Sonia from where they were at the back of the trailer toward the treeline ten yards away. Just past the top of the ditch the trailer was stuck in. "Go into the woods," he ordered.

Another bang of a gun. Popeye or one of the other two?

Yelling at Sonia to *run run run* Casey wheeled back toward the chaos, drawing the fire to himself. He rolled to make himself a harder target, and caught sight of the muzzle's flash as the weapon fired again. Razor was shooting as he ran toward them.

Casey met Razor just as the biker crested the top of the ditch. He lunged forward, throwing a punch at Razor's face as he grabbed his shooting arm.

The shot Razor was in the middle of firing went wide.

Casey brought his forearm atop Razor's with bone cracking force. The gun fell. Razor roared in pain and swung back. The blow grazed the side of Casey's head, but Casey was already on the offensive again. He twisted, kicking Razor's stomach and head, keeping up the blows until Razor was a bloody mess on the ground.

Crouching to pick up Razor's fallen gun, Casey sprinted back toward the woods. Toward where Sonia was now a glimpse of red amidst the treeline. More gunfire sounded. Patriot and Popeye must have gathered their wits and weapons. Casey fired back as he ran, having just enough wits about him to avoid aiming toward the back of the container, where the women were likely filing out.

He reached Sonia just in time to catch the woman before she collapsed to her knees and pulled them both behind a large tree trunk. She felt so fragile against him. Too fragile.

"We have to keep moving," Casey told her, his voice icy calm. The static of a radio crackled through the air. It was a soft sound, and Casey only picked it out because he knew what it was. One of the bikers was calling for backup. Casey had been right when he thought there might be others on the road. There were minutes left at most before more of the Armada appeared. "Ready?"

Sonia lifted her face toward him, the mix of terror and confusion making her eyes wide. But she nodded. Brave girl. Casey squeezed her shoulder and pointed to a spot deeper in the woods. "Go."

Casey spared another bullet of cover fire as Sonia rushed deeper into the trees, then followed at her heels, keeping his body between her and the Armada. More guns and shouts were coming from behind them now.

"Faster," Casey said. "Sonia, you need to run faster."

She picked up the pace, her bare feet—gods, she had bare feet—hitting the ground. She was still pushing forward when said ground dropped sharply beneath the carpet of autumn leaves. Casey could do nothing as Sonia lost her footing, her body tumbling down the rough, slippery hill.

He scrambled after her, barely keeping his balance along the wet, leaf-strewn forest floor. The wind was cold against his skin, and the smell of wet dirt and decaying leaves filled his senses. In the distance, the sound of thunder rumbled through the air, mixing with the bikers' angry shouts. Yeah, there were more of them now. More bikers and more guns.

Sonia was in a moaning heap when Casey reached her. Sticking the gun into his waistband, Casey hauled her into his arms, taking them both along the rock and dirt formation that stretched along this part of the quickly darkening forest. Spotting a small cavern-like opening, already black with shadow, he pulled the pair of them inside and set Sonia gently on the ground while he took stock of the potential shelter.

The cavern was deeper than he'd dared hope, stretching at least eight feet into the rock, but not high enough that he could straighten to full height. And it was dark. Very very dark. Good enough. Settling himself and Sonia against the back wall, he took out his gun and aimed it at the opening.

Voices were coming, the ray of a flashlight flashing against the darkening forest. There'd be no more running. If they were found, they'd be dead. Or worse. Casey pulled Sonia against him.

"They went this way," a man's voice called. Patriot. "Had to. Went down the hill."

"It's fucking darker than my asshole," another man responded. A new voice that Casey didn't know. More curses and steps and cracklings of branches approached. Flashlight beams scanned the woods. Sonia shook against Casey's side, but held her breath now, not making a sound. One wrong move, one crunch of a twig.

"This is pointless, shit. Get back to the cargo before we lose that."

"You go, I'm gonna do another pass." The man who'd said that was within a foot of the cavern mouth, but kept going. This wasn't the biker's familiar terrain, which was scant as far as advantages went, but Casey would take it. Silence followed after that, neither Casey nor Sonia daring to breathe too loudly. Heartbeats of quiet turned to minutes. When a quarter hour had passed since the last sound, Casey released Sonia and slid out for a recon pattern. Unlike the Armada, he at least knew how to move silently through the woods. Still, darkness was darkness and it was an effort to not break his neck as he finished the perimeter before returning to the cavern.

"They are gone," he said, coming back to Sonia. "At least they aren't looking for us. I caught the truck lights and some engine noise. They are trying to get back on the road." Bracing his hands on his thighs, Casey let out a long shaking breath. "Sonia?"

No answer. In fact, she'd not uttered a single word to him since calling out his name just once back at the truck. Fear stabbed Casey's chest. He knelt beside her. She was conscious and breathing. Holding herself up somehow. "Talk to me," he whispered. "Sonia, please say something."

She trembled, but said nothing. It was shock. Or pain. Or both. Casey drew her onto his lap. Gods, she was freezing and all wet. "How badly are you hurt?" he asked softly.

No answer. Only the chatter of her teeth. It had been raining on and off and she must have rolled through a puddle of some kind.

Swallowing a curse, Casey pulled out Razor's phone, careful to conceal the deadly beacon of light coming from the screen. "Shit. No signal," he whispered, quickly turning the device off to save battery. "We'll need to get to better ground."

But that wouldn't be now. Not in the darkness, with the Armada nearby. "I'm going to get you through this," he promised, pulling off his backpack. It had a hole in it. And blood. His back hurt. He didn't care. What he did care about was the sweatshirt he'd managed to stuff in there. "Step one is getting warm and human again. I need to get your wet clothes off. Tell me if I'm hurting you."

Working by feel, Casey started to peel the wet cotton from Sonia's body. It was like undressing a doll. Except... except she wasn't a doll. And he... Casey hands gripped the hem of her shirt and stopped.

"Tell me it's alright to take this off," Casey whispered into the silence, because he knew that it might not be. That Sonia might chose hypothermia over him, and that he fucking deserved it. His eyes stung. "Please, Sonia. I... I love you. I need to help you. Please."

SONIA

I love you.

Casey's words broke through Sonia's haze. He was saying something else, something more, though it was hard to concentrate through the cold and pain and terror. Plus, all the mental focus Sonia had was going toward one thing: not crying. She didn't know when or why that one thing had prioritized itself as the most vital, but it had. Maybe because it had been the only thing in the world that had remained in her control after she woke up in a metal container with Popeye grinning down at her.

"No little law school friends to fawn over you now, are there bitch?" Popeye grabbed her hair and shoved her against the wall. It had taken her a few minutes to realize where she was. That there were other women in the container. None of the others spoke English though, and had even less protection from Popeye than she did. She'd tried talking to the man, arguing, pointing out the folly with this plan.

Then he'd shut her up with a backhand that filled her mouth with blood. There had been more pain after that. Discipline. And only the knowledge that he wasn't raping her despite taking the other women freely made Sonia believe that she was there for a different purpose than the rest. Then there was that call, and Sonia learned she was right.

Casey's calloused palms ran over her. "Sonia. Please. Talk to me. Tell me I can take this off."

Sonia nodded.

Casey's body seemed to sink with relief. Then he was pulling off her clothes, everything done by feel. He wrapped something warm and dry around her before stripping away her pants. A sweatshirt with his scent. Then he shifted, setting her back on the ground.

Sonia's fingers dug into him.

"I'm just setting your clothes to dry," he whispered. "I'm not going anywhere."

She released him reluctantly, but true to his word Casey only shifted to the other side of the small shelter then returned. "Come here," he said and lifted Sonia back onto his lap. His muscles were rock hard and pressed against her bruises. Her teeth chattered.

"God, you are still freezing. Hold on." Casey pulled off his jacket and shirt, draping both over her. Then he unzipped the hoodie he'd had over her already, and pressed her chilled skin against his warm bare chest. There was nothing sexual about the act, but it was so intimate that it made Sonia want to cry all over again.

I love you.

Casey's arm wrapped around her while he was rooting around in the darkness with the other. He pressed something crinkly into her hand. "It's a protein bar. Eating will help with the cold. Can you try to eat?"

Sonia shook her head. She didn't remember the last time she ate and she knew her body was starving. But the notion of putting something in her mouth now made her nauseated. Casey cursed softly, but readjusted her to fit better into the crook of his shoulder. "Alright. For now we need to stay warm until morning. Hopefully, the Armada is gone by then. If not, we'll need to move to get a signal. You can sleep, kitten. I'll keep watch."

Kitten. That word. The one that she'd started to believe meant something more. She'd been an idiot. She'd forgotten they were pretending.

I love you.

Was that another game of his? Anger and tears pricked her eyes. "I hate you."

"I know," Casey said without a trace of anger. If anything, he seemed to agree with the sentiment. "As you should. And once we are out of here, once you are safe, you don't ever have to see me again."

That wasn't the answer Sonia wanted. She did want to see Casey again. So she could kill kim. And punch him. And kiss him right before kneeing him in the balls. Just as he'd done to her. Popeye had lashed her with leather. What Casey had done hurt so much more.

"You can't leave now," Casey said quietly. "I know you want to be as far away from me as you can, but you have to stay with me until the morning. It's too dangerous to go alone. I'm sorry." He sounded like he really meant it too.

Sonia shoved Casey's chest, not that she could get much momentum behind the blow given that she sat in his lap, the body heat seeping from his skin into hers.

Casey took the blow with an intake of breath that he shouldn't have needed, but he only readjusted the sweatshirt around Sonia's shoulders in retaliation. His arms wrapped her in a cocoon of warmth and safety. She belatedly realized that he was stroking her back gently and had been for some time. Soothing the welts and bruises.

He knew they were there. Some of them had been laid for his benefit. "How did you get to me?" she asked.

"I was in the cab of that truck the whole time." Casey's voice was flat. "Once we entered Colorado, Patriot and Razor decided I needed a reminder of the rules. That's when... You know what happened then."

"Did you know there were women in the container you were hauling?"

"No," said Casey.

"Did you try to find out what the *cargo* was? Did you even ask?"

"No," said Casey.

Sonia's fingers tightened into fists. "You knew the Armada trafficked women and you were alright with not even bothering to check what you were hauling cross country in a metal box? You were alright with all that?"

"Of course I wasn't alright with it." Casey's entire body tightened. "But I needed to follow the container to its final destination so everything could be taken down at once."

"But you could have done something earlier. Called the police. Sabotaged the truck. I don't know. Something."

"Yes," said Casey. "But I didn't."

Except when that call came. That had been the Armada's mistake. They'd meant to use Sonia to ensure Casey's cooperation and instead he'd driven the whole truck into a ditch, broke her out, and started a firefight. A new wave of emotions, one that Sonia didn't know what to do with, shot through her.

Casey had betrayed her on the *Belle Nuit*. He was to blame for the pain that coursed through her. He had to be. His fault. All of it was his fault. "So did you just change your mind, McKenzie?" she snarled. "One moment you are take-no-prisoners on mission and the next you decide that all of it—the intel gathering, the women in the container, the whole taking down the Armada in Denton Valley—it isn't all that important after all?"

"I did," Casey said. He didn't even sound sorry.

She twisted in his lap, hating that she was sitting there, hating that her body would not allow her to get away from the warmth and safety of his body even though she wanted to stab him. "You want to run that one by me again? Because I can't figure out where your bullshit starts and ends."

She felt him tighten, and even in the darkness Sonia felt his intensity even before he spoke, his words burning into her like a brand. "I saw them hurting you. So I put a stop to it."

"At what cost?"

"At any cost," said Casey. He shifted, his hands leaving her torso to take hold of her face, his thumbs pressing along her jaw. "There are many things I wish I could take back, kitten. Many things that I've done that no apology will ever make right. But taking you out of that container isn't one of them."

"And if the Armada -"

"I don't care if the entire Satan's Armada encamps in Denton and we go on an all out war with them," Casey's voice was ice cold. "I am not sorry for a single second for getting you out. And I'd do it again. I'd roll the whole damn truck before I'd allow that bastard to touch you again."

Insane. Casey had gone insane. And the fact that his words pierced Sonia's chest and made her want to cry again didn't help matters. If she didn't get some distance between them, she *would* cry. And that she didn't want. "I'm warm enough," she said, yanking against his hold.

Casey grunted but held on. "No, you are not."

"You don't get to—" she trailed off. There'd been little power behind her pull, and wasn't that strong in the best of circumstances, so why had he grunted? Why had he inhaled so sharply when she'd shoved him before. Why was there something wet on the shirt he'd taken off himself for her.

There had been gunshots. But none of them hit, did they? They couldn't have, not with all the running and moving around Casey had done since. And yet… "Are you injured?" she asked.

"I'm fine."

"That's not a no."

An anger of a different sort spilled into Sonia's blood. She twisted, straddling Casey's lap as her hands roamed over his bare skin. He was a study in anatomy but she felt no wounds, not on his chest or along the six-pack of his abs or along his shoulders. "Pull away from the wall," she ordered. "I want to feel your back."

Casey didn't move.

Sonia gripped Casey's chin between her thumb and forefinger. "No more games. Move your god damn back away from the rock. Now."

To her surprise, Casey did as ordered, and Sonia's hand fell away from his face. She reached behind him, her palm sliding along his shoulder blade and into sticky wetness. "You are bleeding?" she whispered. "You got shot and you've been bleeding. And you didn't tell me?"

"It's just a graze," said Casey. "It doesn't matter."

"You'll forgive me if I make my own decisions on what does and doesn't matter," Sonia said.

"Decide away," Casey said with eerie indifference. "But the graze still doesn't."

"Why the hell not?"

"Because I deserve it and more. And because nothing matters beyond getting you safe," said Casey, the sincerity in his weakening voice twisting Sonia's gut. "Least of all me."

MATTHEW

The banging on Matthew's front door was loud enough to shake the hinges. Matthew was inclined to let it continue nonetheless—and would have—if Odysseus hadn't started adding his own meowing harmony of disapproval to the noise. Matthew sighed, and tossed aside the medical journal he'd been reading on the too empty couch. The short time Win had stayed with him had felt so right that Matthew had forgotten what reality was like.

Long story short, reality was a bitch.

Reality was flopping around like a helpless fish on the hospital floor while everyone looked on. Reality was your best friend throwing the truth of your own incompetence back in your face. Reality was a woman who'd gotten so close to your soul, that it was hard to breathe.

The banging continued.

"Go the fuck away, Sith," Matthew called. It was a guess, but it was a scientifically sound one considering the force and persistence of the idiot in the hall.

"Open the damn door," Sith demanded.

Matthew started to turn away then thought better of it. Sith wasn't going to go away and the door was innocent. Might as well get this shit over with. Sliding open the bolt, Matthew crossed his arms over his chest and let the door swing open.

As predicted, Sith stood in the corridor. Despite the cold autumn day, he only had on a Navy-issued t-shirt over a pair of blue jeans. That and a baseball cap. Sith was one of those assholes who was never cold. Something that worked against him in the sandbox, but was pretty enviable otherwise. Now, he stuck his hands into his pockets and gave Matthew a scouring glance from head to toe.

He and Win had the same color eyes.

"You look like shit," said Sith.

"Understood." Matthew was in a pair of well worn jeans and a long sleeve shirt. "Have a good rest of the day."

Sith put his foot into the door before Matthew could close it. "You weren't answering your phone."

"Yep." He'd turned it off when he'd left the hospital. Given that he was suspended, he had no obligation to Denton Memorial until next week. And with zero interest in seeing anyone, there was no need to have the thing on. So he hadn't. "Are we done?"

"No. Grab your coat. I need a drink."

"Then get one." Matthew's jaw hardened. It was hard to look Sith in the eye, but he made himself do it. He owed the man that much. "Look, you don't want to get a drink with me. And I'm not in the mood for getting one with anybody. But yeah, I got your message loud and clear. You've nothing to worry about with Win. So go enjoy the night."

"I didn't say I *wanted* to get a drink," Sith said, a shadow flowing over his features. "I said I need one. And since you are a whiny little bitch in the cold, I'm telling you to get a god damned jacket."

Matthew didn't move.

Sith twisted and punched the wall, leaving a gaping hole in the plaster covered drywall. That was... Matthew lifted a brow. He'd not seen Sith that way since... never. He'd never seen him that way. Sith withdrew his fist and stuck it back into his pocket, his broad shoulders heaving with heavy breaths. Matthew knew better than to ask after the man's hand.

"I lied to Win," Sith said, knocking the toe of his boot against the floor. "When I told her I was back for minor recovery."

"Shocker." Matthew let out a slow breath, his attention now fully on Sith. "How bad is it?"

"Me?" Sith laughed without humor. "It's not. Not compared to… I'm the only one."

"The only one?" Matthew echoed. Sith wasn't making sense. "The only one who got sent home?"

"No." He swallowed, a lump bobbing over his throat. In the overhead lights, his eyes looked shiny. Lined with silver. He raised his face up to the ceiling as if trying to hold himself in check. Trying not to shed the tears that had lined his eyes. "We all got sent back. The whole unit. I was the only one to ride in a seat instead of a box."

The world stopped moving, then filled with a long devastating hum that echoed through every fiber of Matthew's body as he stared at Sith. For a few heartbeats all he could do was turn the words around in his head, sure that there was a catch. But he knew there wasn't. He could see it in Sith's face. And in the hole that now decorated the wall.

Turning on his heels, Matthew grabbed his coat and car keys. "A drink sounds right," he said, leading the way out. "I know a place."

The North Vault felt strange with Casey and Briar both away, but compared to the news Sith had just dropped on him, that was the least of Matthew's concerns. They settled with beers in a back booth, away from the dance floor where guests moved to upbeat music while professional dancers showed off on pedestals. Matthew kept his mouth shut, letting the backdrop of conversations and the occasional rousing cheers fill the silence while Sith decided whether he wanted to talk.

He didn't. Not for a while. But then the waitress came over with a second round of beers, and the words came.

It wasn't a story. Sith spoke into his beer, sounding like he was reading a summary report. One fact after another.

There had been an explosion, just like he'd told Win. Sith had been too close. The shock wave's impact got him grounded. So, when a mortar round took out the unit the following day, he'd not been there. That was it. Now he was alive and no one else was.

Matthew ran his hand over his face. He'd known some of the SEALs who'd died, but not everyone. He didn't know what to say, or how to ease the undeserved guilt in Sith's eyes. Shit. Did Win know? Matthew would wager anything she didn't. Sith would have wanted to protect her from that, to pretend everything was alright. Except it wasn't.

It was Sith who broke the silence though. Taking a swig of his beer, he leaned forward, his forearms braced against the edge of the table. "It was bullshit," he said. "The crap I said in the hospital."

Matthew stiffened, the branded words as clear in his mind as when Sith had spoken them. *You put the whole team in danger.* It was past time to own up. Squaring his shoulders, Matthew met Sith's gaze. "It wasn't bullshit. You were right."

Sith slammed his palm on the table with a sudden violence that would have spilled both beers if Matthew hadn't rescued the drinks.

"Have you not listened to a word I said?" Sith demanded. "That odd chance of you having a seizure? It didn't fucking matter. Wouldn't have mattered. It was a mortar round. That's what killed them. Us. A shit-ton of explosives. Nothing else."

"Doesn't excuse what I did."

"No. It does put it in perspective though, doesn't it? The probability game. The reality." Sith grabbed the beer Matthew had rescued and drank it. "Anyway. I was angry. Things weren't supposed to happen as they did. And then seeing you trying to get into my sister's pants? For that I'm still going to rip you limb from limb."

"Yeah," said Matthew. He'd take it, too. "Don't think you need to worry about me and your sister anymore though."

"You were an asshole to her," said Sith. "I'm going to rip you apart for what you said to her, too."

Matthew cocked a brow. "You need to make up your mind. Are you mad that I went after Win, or that I backed off?"

"Both," said Sith. "And since I want to rip your limbs off for both, I don't need to bother working out the details. It's like the whole mess in the sandbox. It's just a mess. I'm here and you are here and no one else is. So that's what we've got. But yeah. You hurt my baby sister. So as soon as I finish getting drunk, you and I are going to have a conversation about that."

"Go to town," Matthew waved his hand. "But I'm not exactly fond of your baby sister right now, so there is that."

"That's because you are an idiot." Sith motioned for another beer. He looked well on his way to his desired state of inhibition.

"No argument on that front." Matthew nursed his beer slowly, knowing he'd be driving. As for Win… His chest squeezed painfully. She had no business knowing about his epilepsy. Telling the whole world about it. Humiliating him. It was his own fault though, letting her get so close to him. Two months ago, she'd not have dared get in his way no matter what she thought she knew.

Belatedly, Matthew realized Sith was still talking. "Fred isn't like me," Sith said, his finger tracing a pattern on the wooden table. "She's smart. Super smart. But she gets hurt easily. I've told her she needs to toughen up some but—"

A jolt of anger flashed through Matthew. "No."

Sith frowned. "What?"

"Win doesn't need to *toughen up*," Matthew said, his nostrils puffing. "There isn't some prize for how many punches to the face you can take without wincing. Someone put that bullshit into her head, though. Made her think her worth was tied to her toughness. That she was always supposed to be *fine*. That's some messed up bullshit."

Sith's hand tightened around the glass. "You gonna lecture me about what's good for Fred, Jennson?"

"I didn't think I should need to."

"You know nothing about my sister."

"I know she has more heart and smarts than everyone else in the hospital put together," Matthew spat back. "And I know she -"

Matthew's phone rang. He shut off the ringer without looking. It rang again.

"Answer the goddamned thing," said Sith.

Matthew looked at the screen. Cullen Hunt. Not a good sign. Or timing. He gave Sith a hard look but answered. "This is Jennson. What do you need?"

"Welcome to the conference call," Cullen's voice came on over the line. "We've got a situation."

Matthew put the phone on speaker, and slid it to the center of the table. Better Sith hear too, whatever it was.

"Long story short, the twins pissed Sonia off and she decided to go home," Cullen continued. "Except she never made it over from JFK. And Casey missed his check in as well."

Shit. Matthew pushed his beer away. This wasn't just a situation, this was a search and rescue operation.

SONIA

"Good god, I finally understand," Sonia said between grunts as she maneuvered herself around for a better angle. Casey's blood was slick beneath her hands, its coppery scent mixing with the earth and rock smell of the cave. She braced one hand on his chest, feeling around the wound with the other. It had to hurt like hell, but he didn't fight her. Sonia shook her head. "The reason you make so little sense to me, I finally understand what it is."

"Hmm?" Casey winced. "What is it?"

"It's that you are an idiot." Pulling away, Sonia ripped one long strip off of Casey's shirt and folded up the rest into a thick dressing to press against the wound. The god damned bleeding *bullet hole* in Casey's shoulder. With every motion, she forced more of the fog in her head away. She had to. Because at least one of them had to keep their wits about them, and clearly it wasn't going to be Casey. She glanced toward his backpack. "Anything in there that can help?"

"If you are asking whether I made a quick run on the pharmacy before forcing a semi into a ditch, the answer is no." The words were perfectly Casey, but now that Sonia was paying real attention, she noticed that he needed an extra breath to get them all out. He was strong, but he was mortal and he had limits. Casey pointed his chin toward the backpack. "There's food and water. A poncho. A pair of socks you should put on. Some random things on the bottom. Possibly a toothbrush."

"A toothbrush. Good. That's... that's real good." Sonia closed her eyes for a moment, gathering herself together. She wanted to curl into a ball and hide until this was all over, but reality had other ideas. Casey had gotten her out of that container. She needed to make sure he got out of the cave. "Alright, new plan," she said with more confidence than she felt. "Step one, don't freeze to death. That part stays from the original plan. Part two, don't bleed to death."

"No one is bleeding to death."

"Right. You do realize you only have a finite quantity of blood, right?"

"The wound, it's just pain. It doesn't -"

"If you say it doesn't matter, I will hit you," said Sonia. "And that will hurt my hand."

Casey snorted softly. "I see someone is back among the living."

Sonia straddled Casey's thighs to reach around and apply the makeshift dressing. The shirt strip was thankfully long enough to fit diagonally over his chest, but would take some adjusting to make sure it stayed and maintained pressure. Casey made no sound as she worked, but Sonia felt his flinch, the muscles going taut in pain as he held his arms up and out of her way. Whatever adrenaline he'd been high on was wearing off. Or maybe the pain had always been there, but she'd never looked hard enough to see. Not today, not ever.

Like when they'd come back from the Armada's suite and he'd bathed her so carefully.

"Almost done," she said softly, cinching the bandage in the middle of his chest. Her hand lingered on his skin. In the darkness, she was aware of his every movement against her. The rise and fall of his chest, the quick beat of his heart. The fact that he'd sat himself on the cold ground with his injured back against the rock wall so that she wouldn't have to. He'd done it so easily and naturally, pulling Sonia into his lap and off the ground, that she'd not given it much thought at the time. But now... things looked different now that she was paying the kind of attention to him that he'd always paid to her.

Casey was hurting. In more ways than one. The causes of some, like the bleeding hole in his back, were obvious. Others, not so much. Their entire time together, Casey had always twisted things about, making things about her. She'd thought it was simply a ploy to drive her insane. Well, it most likely was—this was Casey—but it also made it too easy to discount him.

Laying her cheek against Casey's chest, Sonia did the one thing she realized she'd never done before. She hugged *him*. She wrapped her arms around Casey and pulled him against her, cradling his powerful body against her own. He seemed to realize the difference, because his breath caught and he hesitated for a moment before letting himself lean into the embrace, letting her feel the weight of him.

"Thank you," Sonia whispered against his skin. Another thing that she'd never said. "Thank you for rescuing me from that place."

"You should never have—"

"No one should have been in that truck. Not me, not you, not those women. But you are the only one who did something about it."

Casey tensed for a moment, but his muscles softened slightly and he laid his chin atop Sonia's head, his arms wrapping tightly around her. No not arms, one arm. He kept his injured right side immobile now. Had probably been ten times the idiot for not doing it sooner. Hell, he'd helped Sonia strip off her wet clothes with that arm.

"You need to eat," Casey said. "Protein bars are in the backpack. Also, socks. Put them on. What happened to your shoes anyway?"

"Took them off," Sonia said. "I wasn't exactly expecting to be running through the woods. Not that the heels would have helped."

"Fair enough. You need to eat."

Yeah, there he went again. But he wasn't wrong. Sonia twisted around and groped in the darkness for Casey's backpack, taking stock of their supplies as she pulled them out. The fact that he'd had the presence of mind to bring it was impressive. There was a box with half a dozen protein bars and two bottles of water inside, still in a plastic grocery bag. She took out the bars and laid the plastic bag aside, in case it came in handy with the rain. Below the food, she found the folded poncho Casey had mentioned and what looked like a change of underclothes. Socks. T-shirt. Underwear. A toothbrush and toothpaste.

"If this was my purse, there would be Advil in here," she said. "And some tissues."

"If this was your purse, it would have a briefing on the legalities of lawn gnomes inside."

"Yes. Very possibly. Lawn gnome rights have long been overlooked." Sonia pulled on the socks then climbed off Casey's lap. He made a sound of disapproval at that, but if they were going to call this cavern home for the night, it needed to become more hospitable.

On her hands and knees, Sonia swept her hands all over the ground of their shelter. A few years of summer camps failed to impart a love for the outdoors in her, but she did remember how to make outdoor existence less miserable than it could be. Now, she moved the small stones and broken branches away, layering all the fluffy dry leaves she could find onto the ground. She covered the pile with the unfurled poncho. It wasn't much, but it was better than sitting on the cold ground that would likely get wet soon.

As if to punctuate that thought, the rain outside increased to a steady pattern.

"Lie down," she told Casey.

"You eat two protein bars first."

Sonia picked up a bar and bit into it. "Chocolate covered cardboard. Delicious. Lie down."

Casey removed the gun from his waist belt first, then lay down as instructed. Sonia slid the empty backpack under his head then took off the jacket he'd given her and draped it over him.

"I am planning on making use of your body heat," she said tartly before Casey could protest. She snuggled down at his side, opening her hoody so as much of their skin connected as possible. "Not only are corpses cold, but I'd rather you warm me, not the whole cave. So I'm being practical."

Casey made a harumph sound, but pulled her close, his bare skin pressing against hers. She didn't know how he was moving his injured side as much as he was and hoped it meant the wound was less painful than it looked. Of course, that could also mean the puncture didn't hurt enough, and Casey was now making things worse with every shift of his muscles. With him, it could go either way. Sonia had stopped shivering at some point, probably once the wet clothes had come off, but it was only getting colder as the night settled. She burrowed closer to Casey. The beat of his heart vibrated through their connected bodies, a contrast to the rain, and his warm breath tickled her hair.

"Sleep," Casey told her, his heavy arm resting on her bare skin.

Yeah. Sleep would be a good thing. Sonia knew that. But she also needed to know something, and that something felt easier to ask in the darkness, when Casey couldn't see her face.

"Did you..." she started, then stopped. This was stupid. And inappropriate. But what Casey had said, what he claimed to feel about her... Sonia opened her mouth again. Closed it in surrender. "Never mind."

"No dice," Casey said, sounding amused. "You started, you have to finish. And since I can actually feel your face heat, this is bound to be good."

"You are an ass."

"And yet here we are."

"Kidnapped, shot, and hiding out in a cave from bikers who want to kill us?" Sonia clarified.

"Semantics." He poked her in the ribs. "What were you going to ask?"

She huffed. *Fine.* Her face burned and she said the words as quickly as she could. "Do you remember when I, um, took you into my mouth?"

"I'm not dead," Casey said.

"What does that have to do with anything?"

"Yeah. I remember."

Right. She let out a breath. "Did you... Did you dislike it?"

A choking sound came from Casey. "Kitten, I'd have to be dead to *not* enjoy being in your mouth. Or, in any other part of you, if you are wondering."

Well… shit. Another flash of embarrassed warmth slid through Sonia, making her especially glad for the darkness.

"What in that mess of a brain of yours made you think otherwise?" Casey asked. Unlike her, he was clearly enjoying this.

"Well, lots of things," she said defensively.

"Lots of things?"

She needed to just say it. Gods. She did it. She should be able to say it. What was she, in high school? "You didn't let me, um, finish. And then you, you know, went all crazy the next day."

Casey was quiet for several heartbeats, enough that Sonia's own pulse started to speed up. She braced herself, but instead of pushing her away, Casey blew out a long breath. "You had a gun pointed at you, kitten," he said quietly. "I didn't imagine for a moment that you *wanted* to finish. I thought I was doing a good thing, for once in my life, believe it or not."

"I did." She couldn't believe she was saying all this aloud. "Wanted to finish. Is that bad? Do you… Do you think I'm all manner of messed up for enjoying it?"

"Gods no," said Casey. "I think you are exquisite and delicious for enjoying it. What I did on the other hand, that was the unforgivable part."

Huh? "Which part exactly are we talking about?" Sonia clarified. "Just so I know. For research purposes."

Casey tensed against her and there was no humor in his voice when he answered. "I hit you."

"What?" Sonia's head jerked, though there wasn't much space to move. "The swat on my thigh? To begin with, I made—"

"Do not say that you *made me* do it." A sudden simmering fury came out of nowhere and spilt into Casey's voice. "I've heard that lie too many times to ever want to hear it again."

Sonia opened her mouth to protest, to say that she had—in fact—absolutely made him do it. They'd been playing a game and she'd known that her mouthing off would have had to have consequences.

That didn't bother her. Of all things that had happened, the swat was so low on the shit list, that she'd forgotten about it the moment it happened.

But Casey hadn't.

So instead of saying all that, Sonia ran her hand along Casey's shoulders instead. He was so tense, he nearly vibrated with it. "Where did you hear that?" she whispered, her voice gentle "Tell me."

"My father. It was... It was the excuse for every bruise and broken bone he'd left on Mum. That she'd made him do it. That it was all her fault."

Sonia kept quiet, her hand moving rhythmically along his skin. Giving him the time he needed to find the words.

"He'd hurt her and then blame her for it. And she would... Fuck. She'd apologize. Every god damn time. She'd say she was sorry. And the most fucked up thing about it? She actually believed it. He let her believe it." Casey drew a ragged breath. "So when you..."

"Where are they now, your parents?" Sonia asked.

"Scotland," Casey said curtly. "Probably. Mum passed away about ten years ago, so I know she's there. I don't give a damn about what happened to the bastard who sired Briar and me, but he's got enough businesses going that I'd have heard something if he finally went to hell."

Sonia pressed her forehead into Casey's chest. His reaction, his anger with himself made sense now. He was wrong, utterly and completely wrong, but he made sense. And so, Sonia used the only thing in her arsenal that had a chance of breaking through the wall of misconception Casey had erected.

The truth.

"I liked it," Sonia told him. "Not just having you in my mouth, but the sex, too. And Nero and the rest of them watching? I'd never have chosen that voluntarily. Ever. But... once we started, with you, I... it was titillating. It made me feel like maybe I was worth something, sexually speaking. That I wasn't a fat ass on a stick."

"What the hell?" Casey pulled away enough to grip her face, lifting it toward his own. "Why in the world would you ever think yourself undesirable?"

"Because that's what Wade told me. My father's business partner." Sonia spoke quietly, the words spilling out like a confession. She told Casey about being home from college. Being cornered in her dad's office. What Wade had said when he forced himself on her.

"And your father?" Casey's voice was ice cold. "What did he say when you told him?"

"He didn't believe me," she whispered. *Sonia, honey...* Her father's words repeated in her head, as clear and potent as when he'd said them those years ago. *If Wade wanted a girl, trust me that he could have his pick of ones that look like centerfold models. It makes no sense. You... There is just no reason.*

Casey's rumbling growl threatened murder. "Where is he now?" he demanded. "Where are both of them?"

"I stopped talking to my family after that," said Sonia. "Paid my own way. That's why, well, you saw where I live. I didn't have much time for financial planning. So, loans it was, at whatever rate I could get on short notice."

Another soft growl came from Casey.

"Anyway," Sonia pulled her face away from his hand and buried it back into his chest. It was simpler to talk that way. "Not that I would ever recommend it, but that night in the Armada's suite, it was... I don't know. Liberating? I enjoyed it. And I enjoyed knowing they were watching. That they were..." she blushed again.

"Aroused?" Casey offered.

"Yeah." She muttered. "Them and you, too."

Casey chuckled. "Not the brand of therapy generally endorsed by the American Psychological Association," he said against Sonia's hair, "but if it helps you get that bullshit out of your head, we can have sex on the stage of the North Vault every Friday night. And the other days too."

"No," Sonia said quickly. "Very utterly not necessary. I'm good. One time in front of an audience was more than enough."

Casey pressed his chin onto the top of her head. "And what about without an audience?" he murmured. "Would you be interested then?"

Gods. How could this still be embarrassing? "Umm... Would you?"

Casey shifted, nuzzling Sonia's cheek and neck before finding her mouth. He brushed his lips over hers, the touch feather soft and yet intimate enough to send sparks cascading through her body. When she opened for him though, he swept in with heart wrenching intensity. Their mouths moved with one another, Casey holding her tightly as he explored each velvety corner of her mouth. Claiming it.

Sonia wrapped her hands around his neck, as pure emotion surged between them like a wave crashing on the shore.

"Does that answer your question?" Casey asked against her lips when they finally came apart. His hand slid along Sonia's belly and traced a line just above the line of hair curling around her sex. "Or should I demonstrate in other ways?"

A thrill raced over Sonia's skin, taking her breath away. Casey's hand dipped further, his fingertips trailing along her inner thighs that were growing damp in response. She moaned softly, biting her lip as he found the sensitive bundle of nerves at the top of her sex. God. This was so inappropriate right now.

Casey's fingers dipped between Sonia's folds and she shuddered, her hips pressing forward into his hand.

His body vibrated with a deep chuckle. Turning Sonia around so that her back and backside pressed into him, Casey continued his exploration. Deft, calloused fingers played inside Sonia's folds, each flick and brush sending jolts of sensation all the way to her breasts and toes and backs of her legs. A piano. He was playing her like a piano. And the hardness now pressing into Sonia's back promised that he was enjoying every moment.

"You should get some sleep," Casey murmured wickedly into her ear.

Sonia whimpered.

"Sounds like you may need a little more help relaxing." A finger slipped inside Sonia, then back out.

She gasped at the sensation, her head rolling back against his chest as he dipped into her again. And again. Each stroke of his finger sent pleasure rippling through her, and her hips undulated of their own accord, desperate for more and more of Casey's attention. She rode his hand as he added a second finger inside her, curling them with tantalizing precision.

"God." She bit back a scream that would likely summon the Armada as she shattered against his hand, orgasmic pleasure cascading over her body in wave after wave. Her breath came out in short gasps as she clung onto his arm, feeling his lips brush against the back of her neck.

"You are beautiful when you come," he whispered into her hair. "You are beautiful all the time, but especially when you come. When we get home, I'm going to do this all over again in daylight, so I can watch your face. We could invite Briar to watch if you'd like."

Sonia could hear that damn smirk in his last sentence.

"Not necessary," she said. "Really not necessary."

"Are you sure?" He brushed her clit as he spoke and her treacherous body spasmed all over again, rising to a pinnacle then toppling into an abyss of pleasure that left her panting for breath. Casey nipped the top of her ear. "I think you'd enjoy it."

"No. No no no."

"I think you'd enjoy many things you've not yet considered," he mused.

"I'm going to kill you."

"Unlikely. You like my hands too much."

God damn it. Sonia didn't know how it was still possible to be embarrassed, and yet here she was, blazing with heat.

Casey chuckled, readjusting Sonia against him. "Sleep. Before I start researching what else that body of yours can do."

Sonia was still holding onto Casey's arm as she drifted off to sleep, safe and comfortable despite the cold ground and the sociopathic gangsters camping out in the ditch by the road. Which was, logically speaking, absurd. But everything to do with Casey was absurd, so at this point, Sonia was just going along with it.

She woke sometime later, when the rain had stopped and streaks of light peeked into the cavern entrance. Behind her, Casey's breathing was louder than she remembered, his body too hot against hers. The arm he had around her had gone slack.

She scrambled up quickly, getting up on her knees beside him. Pale too-hot skin. Ragged breaths. The dressing she'd put on yesterday was soaked with wet blood. "Casey?" she called softly, her hand on his shoulder. "Casey, wake up."

He opened glassy eyes, focusing them with visible effort. "Are you alright?"

"Key question is whether you are alright," Sonia said. "And the answer to that is no."

Casey shifted and grimaced. "I'll be fine. I'm just... Just cold. Or hot. I'm not sure."

"You have a fever," she said. "And not enough blood from the looks of it."

"I'm fine," he sat up, swayed, fell back down—catching himself on his bad side and swallowing a shout of pain.

Grabbing Casey's shoulders, she eased him back down to the ground on his uninjured side. "I'm going to take the phone and look for a signal," she told him, sliding her now mostly dry clothes back on.

"No. You stay. I'll go."

Sonia put a hand in the middle of Casey's chest, keeping him down. "Stay here and don't die."

"I'm fine," he insisted. "I just need a minute."

He wouldn't be alright in a few minutes. And certainly not in a few hours. She wasn't coming back without help. Taking the phone, Sonia gave him a bright smile. "Excellent. I'll be back in a few minutes and you take a turn then. If it looks like the Armada is still here or it doesn't feel safe, I'll come back even earlier."

He glared suspiciously, but Sonia stepped out before he could reply.

The cold forest greeted Sonia as soon as she stepped out into the morning light, the wet ground soaking her socks. A spot of the bright red painted cab of the Armada's tractor trailer flashed between the trees. The Armada was still here. Sonia wondered what story Patriot,

Razor, and Popeye had spun for their masters to explain the delay. Apparently, that was a lesser risk to them than calling in aid and admitting the problem.

Wrapping Casey's hoodie against the chill and wind, Sonia headed for high ground away from the Armada's encampment, her heart pounding against her ribs. Most of the rain had stopped, but the remaining drizzle still made her hunch herself like a turtle as she trudged along, begging the little bars on the phone's screen to appear. Even just one. Something.

Beep.

The phone's sudden tone made Sonia jump. She looked down quickly, trying to turn off the volume. But the sound had to be a good thing. Except... There were no bars. Instead, the phone was flashing a low battery warning. "No." She whimpered under her breath. "No, no, no."

"Quiet." A large hand clamped over Sonia's mouth, a strong male body grabbing her around the waist before she could scream.

SONIA

"Quiet," the man holding Sonia repeated, the order leaving no room for negotiation. His voice sounded familiar and the grip holding her was hard, but not painful. "Do you understand?"

She nodded, her heart pounding too quickly to think.

The man released her at once, and Sonia spun around to find herself looking at… Matthew. Except he didn't look like the scrub-wearing Matthew she was used to seeing. No, this Matthew, with his camo clothing, long gun, and bullet-proof vest, looked ready to assault a small country. His sharp blue eyes scanned her briefly then returned to the treeline, his hands on his weapon.

"What—"

Popping sounds came from the direction of the Armada's truck. Like loud firecrackers. Moving faster than Sonia thought possible, Matthew grabbed her again, curling his body around hers as he moved them behind cover of a large tree.

He put one finger to his lips, the other going to his ear, where Sonia now saw the clear cable of an earpiece.

More popping sounds came and Sonia felt her stomach lurch. Gunshots. Those were gunshots overthere. Beside her, Matthew looked too calm to be rational as he covered her body with his, sandwiching her between himself and the tree trunk. The scent of his shampoo filled her nose.

As quickly as he'd covered her, Matthew stepped back, his shoulders relaxing. "Site secure," he said quickly, before depressing his radio and speaking in a quite clear monotone. She caught something that sounded like GPS position and the word *friendly*, which probably meant her. She hoped it meant her.

Grabbing Matthew's arm, she forced the man's attention back to her. "Casey," she said quickly. "He's hurt."

"Show me," Matthew said, the eerie calm around him spreading to her.

Sonia turned in a circle, hoping she remembered how to get back to the cavern. The forest looked the same no matter where she looked. She drew a deep breath, reaching for logic. She couldn't have walked far enough to really get lost. They'd been in a cavern, so that meant large rocks. Which were behind her. Hoping she wasn't losing her mind, Sonia led Matthew forward.

A wave of relief hit Sonia as she found the mouth of the cavern where she'd left Casey. Matthew walked forward ahead of her, crouching to fit.

"Don't move," the click of a gun cocking echoed through the space, Casey's silhouette pointing the pistol at Matthew's head.

Matthew raised his hands. "It's Jennson. Don't shoot."

"Yes, please don't do that," Sonia added quickly.

Casey hesitated, lowering the weapon slowly before stepping out into the light. His eyes looked glassy as they went to Sonia first. "Are you alright?" he asked.

"Really, that's your first question?" Sonia walked over to Casey, slipping her arm around him before he could fall. "Not *what's Matthew doing here and why were there gun shots?* Because that's what I still want to know."

Matthew caught on quickly, bracing Casey as he helped the man sit down on a large stone. "Long story short, the pair of you went off grid and so we started looking. Briar knew the license plate of the truck and Win did something highly illegal to get into the EZ pass toll system to get the trajectory. Then there was a lot of driving and looking. A tractor trailer in a ditch was a bit of a marker." Matthew peeled back Casey's jacket and wound dressing, swearing under his breath.

"You took the truck?" Casey asked Matthew through gritted teeth.

Sonia laid a hand on Casey's good shoulder, feeling his hot skin.

"Affirmative," another familiar voice said, Liam appearing through the trees. He was dressed much like Matthew, though the gaze with which he swept over the scene was a great deal harder. "If either of you are wondering why Dancer was supposed to stay home and no one was to get into a god damn truck with no comms, this is your answer."

Sonia flinched and Casey's arm wrapped around her protectively.

"I think this bullet made the point better than you can hope to," Matthew said mildly. He'd opened a small medkit attached to his vest and was now packing something into the wound. Casey shook slightly, but made no sound.

Liam's look said he disagreed, but he jerked his head toward where the Armada's truck was still hunkered. "We've control of the down vehicle. One hostile is down and Eli is having a chat with the others. They've been calling in excuses for lateness to Denton while trying to conjure a way to get that truck out."

"There is going to be a major auction of sorts in Denton," Casey said. "That's where they were taking the women. Take down the nest and Armada's foothold in Denton will crumble."

Liam nodded. "We've called in victim services for the women, a tow for the truck, and whatever SWAT teams Denton has. We'll turn the truck into a trojan horse and take this viper nest out from the inside." He turned to Sonia, his voice softening. "It's over. I'll yell at you later—a lot—but for now, catch your breath. I know what they did to you, but you are safe now. We are going to get all these bastards. Alright?"

Sonia gave him a shaky nod.

Liam pulled off his vest and jacket, laying it over Sonia's shoulders. "How is he?" he asked Matthew.

"Fine," said Casey.

"Call MedFlight," said Matthew. "He needs blood."

"He needs brains," Liam said, but the concern in his voice sent a shiver along Sonia's spine. He crouched in front of Casey. "Briar is your blood type, I presume? He's dealing with the mess over there now, but I'll send him over. We'll get something into you en route."

"You need him with you. You are already short me and Matthew." Casey closed his eyes. "Don't tell Briar. Tell him… just figure something out."

"I'm a universal donor," said Sonia.

Casey's head snapped to her, his eyes opening. "No. Absolutely not. You've been through enough."

Sonia turned toward Matthew. "Can you draw blood off me to infuse in-flight?"

Matthew looked between her and Casey, calculations running through his gaze. "Yeah," he said finally. "Yeah, I can do that."

Casey started to protest, but Sonia took hold of his face, her palms pressing against his heated cheeks. "You need my blood. And I *want* to give it to you." Leaning in, she pressed her mouth against his, not caring who else was there and watching. "Take it. Alright?"

The MedFlight helicopter came faster than Sonia expected and the medics and Matthew helped Casey climb inside. Casey waited only long enough for an IV to be started on him before pulling Sonia against him. He held onto her, pressing his lips against the nape of her neck as Matthew started a line to collect blood.

She didn't know when she started shaking, but it was sometime after the pint of blood was dripping into Casey's veins and she'd been covered with a blanket, a box of orange juice held tightly in her hand. Casey's eyes were closed. Somehow, in the middle of all this, he'd fallen asleep. Or passed out.

Matthew slid over to Sonia, his fingers pressing firmly against the pulse in her wrist. "I'm fine," she said into the headset they all wore. Matthew gave her a questioning look, then reached over and flipped something in the controls. A moment later, his voice came over the headset.

"It's a private channel," he told her. "You and I are the only ones to hear each other."

"I'm..." She sighed, looking out the window at the ground streaking beneath them. "It's over, isn't it? Everyone will be fine now?"

"It will take a bit for the Tridents to arrive at the target and secure it, but yes, you are no longer trapped in a metal container." There was no sarcasm in his voice. "You aren't alone. And neither is he—since that is clearly of consequence now."

Sonia brushed her hand over Casey's face. A stray bit of hair was stuck to his sweaty forehead. "Yeah. It's been... complicated." But it wasn't any more. Or rather it was, but mostly because too many emotions were sweeping over her too quickly.

I love you. Casey's low voice caressed her soul, warming her all over again.

She touched her fingers to his lips. *I love you too.* She hadn't said it. She should have. Sometime before he passed out. No, fell asleep. He'd just fallen asleep. It was so hard to tell with Casey because of all the fronts, all the games. "He will be alright, right?" she asked.

"His system is in overload," said Matthew. "The body can be pushed and it compensates, but there is a limit. And nothing is free. Eventually, you have to pay back what you took. That goes for you too, by the way." He put a blood pressure cuff over her arm, and it tightened. "The stress of being held in a container, starved, abused, and dehydrated isn't something that magically disappears with a kid-size box of orange juice."

"You seem to know quite a bit of what happened."

Matthew shrugged one shoulder. "Eli is a persuasive interrogator."

Sonia leaned her head back against the seat. "I talked to Win before I left the *Belle Nuit*," she said.

Matthew tensed.

"You are an asshole."

"Am I?" Matthew removed the blood pressure cuff and clipped a probe onto Sonia's finger. On the monitor, an oxygenation reading began to flash.

"You are," Sonia confirmed.

This time, Matthew didn't respond at all. Instead, he flipped the comms switch back to the general channel and asked the pilots for an update.

A team was already waiting on the helipad when MedFlight touched down on the roof of Denton Memorial Hospital. Casey woke with a wince of pain as he was moved out of the chopper and didn't settle until finding Sonia.

"You shouldn't be walking," he said. "You still don't have shoes."

"You shouldn't be talking," said Sonia. "You still don't have common sense."

Casey chuckled then looked at Matthew, his humor fading. "You cutting me up?"

"There is no exit wound," Matthew said. "I'll know more when we get some X-rays."

"That isn't a no," said Casey.

"It isn't," Matthew confirmed, his attention snagging on a small woman sprinting toward them from the elevator entrance. He pivoted just in time to get out of Win's way as she launched herself at Sonia, hugging her tight. Matthew cleared his throat. "Sonia donated blood en route and she's been through—"

"I got her, Dr. Jennson," Win cut him off without looking away from Sonia. "She's my patient now."

A muscle ticked in Matthew's jaw. "Last I checked you were still a resident."

"I still am." The chill in Win's voice could freeze a lake. "And you are suspended with no privileges here, so that makes me the doctor and you, well, a visitor. You can check in at the nursing station and get a badge."

Win held Sonia back, letting Matthew and the rest of the crew take Casey into the elevator ahead of them. The moment the door closed, she threw her arms around Sonia again, holding her tight. "I heard what happened," she said, calling the elevator again. "Sith was too drunk to head out with the Tridents, but they were in touch and he told me. And... God. I'm so sorry."

The elevator opened again and Win led Sonia to the ER, nudging her toward a private room where... Sonia's eyes widened as she caught a whiff of the smell. "Is that Chinese food?"

"I couldn't subject you to hospital food after all that," Win said, closing the door. "I have some clean clothes, too. And hot chocolate. And wine. I wasn't sure what you'd be in the mood for. But it's all here."

Sonia's eyes stung.

Win quickly held out a box of lo mein and chopsticks. "First food, then I check you out, alright? I can't promise that you are actually getting out of here tonight, but we're together all the way."

"Casey—"

Win hopped onto a computer, clicking quickly through a few screens. "Casey is... Here we go. He's heading to the OR to get a bullet out of him, so he's going to be busy a while. In other words, you are stuck with me. And food. Will you please eat something?"

Sonia didn't know what it was with everyone determined to feed her, but she made herself smile and picked up the takeout container. She really wasn't hungry though, at least not until she opened the lid and heard her stomach growl. Alright. So maybe she was hungry. And tired. And unable to trust her body to tell her the truth about anything.

"How are you and Matthew?" she asked, stirring the noodles.

Win's face darkened. "There is no me and Matthew. He made that clear enough because I had the audacity to try and help him. The stupid thing was that I'd actually thought we had something going. And by something, I mean trust. But it's not trust when it doesn't go two ways, you know."

Sonia nodded. Maybe before Casey she would have tried to explain Matthew's behavior away, but Win was right when she spoke about trust. "So, is it over? The, well, whatever it was you had?"

"He said to never touch him again. That's pretty binary there." Win swallowed and pulled over a second container of chinese, keeping a companionable silence while Sonia ate.

A couple of hours later, Sonia had showered, convinced several doctors that she was not about to collapse, and was starting to consider a jail break when Win reappeared at the door.

"Casey?" Sonia sat up so quickly that her head spun.

"Awake and mouthing off," Win said with a grin. She held up a pair of sneakers in her hand. "Borrowed these from one of the nurses, size eight. Better than hospital socks. There is something that's just dehumanizing about all the stuff we make patients wear."

Sonia slipped the shoes on quickly and followed Win toward the ER exit, making it into the main treatment area just as Matthew was walking in. Win turned on her heel mid-step and set course for the nursing station.

Matthew followed. "Really?" he said. "Are we in pre-school to be playing this game?"

Win ignored him. "This way. We can take the back -"

Win's words got cut off by a popping sound that reminded Sonia so much of what she'd heard in the woods that, for a moment, she forgot where she was. Then a chorus of panicked screaming filled the ER.

"Everyone down on the floor, now," a man shouted, firing his gun again. Someone cried out in pain. "And shut up, all of you."

Matthew shoved himself in front of Win and Sonia. Twisting toward the sound, Sonia saw three bikers in Armada leather jackets swaggering inside, their patches stark in the bright lights. As she watched, the one in front leveled his gun at an orderly and fired.

Sonia gasped.

"Tank," Win whispered behind her. "That's Tank."

WIN

Win fell to the floor behind the nursing station, Matthew's shove hard enough to leave her knees bruised. Her bad knee screamed and it was all she could do to swallow the pain. Beside her, Sonia's muted gasp said she'd fared the same, but the cabinets making up the large square structure shielded them from the three Armada bikers who'd come in. It didn't shield them from having a clear view of the dead orderly, whose vacant eyes seemed to watch Win accusingly. As if this was all her fault.

And maybe it was.

She'd been the one who'd pissed off Tank to begin with, and then chose to let him walk away from charges rather than ruin her online reputation by letting the security footage resurface. And now Tank was back, and that patient, Satan, with him. She didn't know the third man, but Tank had called him Salt. Tank, Satan, and Salt. A numbing kind of fear raced through her. She was in the parking lot again. Tank and the other men surrounding her. Kicking her. Except this time, they had guns.

"Everyone shut the fuck up, get down, and stay down," Tank's so familiar voice boomed over the emergency room, overpowering the beeping monitors and sobbing patients. "You, lock the ER doors and cover the glass. Tell them you've an infection or some shit like that. I see a cop, I start shooting people."

Win didn't know who Tank had grabbed, but a few moments later Michelle came on the loudspeaker, announcing the ER going on quarantine. Beside her, Sonia had a mixed look of terror and resolve, as if she were about to do something stupid. Like get up and tell the Armada off. And then she'd be hurt, too. Or dead, like the orderly. Win's throat closed, the panic flooding her blood making her dizzy. She gripped Sonia's arm to keep her friend at bay.

"No one goes in or out," Tank said. "Anyone tries, and they die. Anyone reaches for their phone, they die. Anyone fucking looks funny, they die."

Die. Die. Die.

"Win, look at me." Matthew's voice pierced through the onslaught of terror flooding Win's thoughts. She hadn't realized she had closed her eyes, but once she opened them Matthew's blue ones were there to catch her gaze. He nodded his approval and spoke with soft calm, "Deep breath. Good. Another one."

Win obeyed, her wits returning a little more with each dose of oxygen.

"Can you do your tech thing to get the word out about what's happening?" Sonia asked.

Win swallowed. "To who? The hospital rent-a-cops? The only people with the skills to deal with this are on the other side of town, taking down the Armada's human trafficking ring. Sith is passed out at home." Even Yarborough was away, helping with a complex procedure in Denver. Win found that out when she tried to get him to work on Casey.

"Hospital security will work out something is wrong shortly," Matthew said. "But we need to give them eyes into here."

The ER did have security cameras, but for privacy reasons they were always off when patients were present. "I need a hospital computer to turn them on and push the feed," said Win. Useless. She was useless again.

"Here are the rules," Tank announced. He sounded so close. "You gather up all the oxy, fentanyl, and whatever else you hoarders keep around here. Then we walk away, and you do too. See, simple." He let the words sink in. "I don't need to hurt anyone. But I want to. So give me half a reason, and it will be you."

"They won't leave without hurting people," Sonia whispered, her face pale. "Not the Armada. They... they will hurt someone. And enjoy it."

The dead orderly's eyes bore into Win.

Matthew drew himself up into a couch and pressed his finger to his lips. He was still dressed in the same camo as when medflight arrived and looked every inch the warrior Win wasn't. Calm. Brave. Collected. Useful. "I'm going to thin the herd," he mouthed quietly. "You both stay down and stay quiet."

Before Win could protest, he slid forward and opened one of the rolling cart drawers, pulling out a scalpel. Then he was moving again. A dart out from behind the cover of the cabinets, a quick step behind the treatment bay privacy curtain, a silent jog toward the front of the room, and out of her sight.

"Can you see anything?" she asked Sonia.

Sonia nodded. "In a reflection. I think he's moving toward the biker nearest to the door. He has a spare gun in his belt."

Win pressed her back against the cabinet panels, trying to keep her breaths in check. The bikers had guns. They already killed one person. One trigger press and Matthew would be on the floor next. She needed to do something. To at least get the word out. To get help moving. She reached for her phone.

"Don't," said Sonia. "They'll kill you."

Win pulled her hand back. Sonia was right. On the other side of the nursing station, Tank was already pissed off about how long things were taking. Michelle's explanation that the controlled substance dispenser only gave out one dose at a time was met with a resounding slap and a cry of pain.

"Where is the cunt who fucked me up?" Satan said suddenly. "The little one. Who claimed to be a doctor. I want to have a chat."

Shit. Win's eyes darted about, but there was no place to hide that she could get to.

"Let's take a look-see," Tank barked. His steps tapped against the linoleum floor of the emergency room. "Where are you, whore? Come out, come out wherever you are." The *tap tap tap* of the boots against the floor grew louder. Suddenly they were in Win's line of sight.

Tank grabbed Win's arm, wrenching her to her feet. "There you are."

"Let her go!" Sonia scrambled up beside Win, grabbing Tank's arm. He wrenched it easily out of Sonia's grip and elbowed her in the face. She stumbled back with a choked sound, blood staying from a nose that Win prayed wasn't broken. She tried to go to Sonia, but Tank's grip returned quickly and harder than before.

He grinned cruelly, his overgrown beard framing a mouth of bad yellow teeth. "Let's have a chat while we wait for my things to be delivered. What should we talk about?"

Win swallowed. Sonia was down, one of the nurses tried hurrying forward with a towel to staunch the bloodflow. On the other side of the ER, Matthew's silhouette was making progress toward Salt. If Win could wait out just a few more minutes, give Matthew a little more time, things could change. They had to.

Tank shook her. "Answer when a man speaks to you."

"No, I-I don't know," Win managed to say. Matthew was almost at Salt's back now. She needed to keep Tank and the others distracted long enough to buy him the opportunity to act. "What do you want to talk about?"

"Respect," Spittle appeared at the corner of Tank's mouth. He pulled something familiar looking from his pocket and waved it in front of Win's face. A rubber like band with a box and two prongs attached to it. Win frowned, Was that?... Yeah. It was an electric dog collar. Her stomach sank. Tank had planned this out. He'd brought a dog collar. He'd always intended to torment her.

"Respect?" Win asked, hoping the prompt would keep him talking rather than doing.

"It's about respect," he confirmed. "Which is something this fucking excuse for hospital needs to learn. And you? You need that lesson in particular, don't you? How about we start with putting that mouth to good use." Tank shoved Win down to her knees, and this time she couldn't hold in the howl that escaped when her right kneecap slammed into the floor. Agony shot through her body, the whole room spun from the pain. Only Tank's grip—now on her hair—kept Win from falling.

"Did that smart?" Tank laughed, pulling her up by her hair with the clear intention of slamming her down again.

"Let her go," Matthew stepped out from behind the curtains, just a few paces from Salt's position. His hands were up in the air in a gesture of surrender. "It's not her you want to teach your lesson to, it's me. And here I am."

No.

Tank's face lit up. "Well well, what do we have here? Two for the price of one."

Salt's gun swung to point at Matthew.

One hand still on Win's hair, Tank turned to his new captive. "On your knees."

Matthew complied, his blue eyes finding Win's. The promise that he would protect her, that she wasn't alone, shone in them with iron certainty. Win's heart squeezed.

Tank tossed the electric collar to Matthew. "Put this around your neck, like the bitch you are."

Matthew again did as he was told. "Let her go. This is between us," he said. "The men."

"You aren't a fucking man." Tank let go of Win to pull out a remote he had hanging around his neck. Matthew's whole body jerked as an electric shock surged through his nerves. More electricity than any dog collar should ever have. The bastards must have modified the thing. Tank grinned. "What do you think of my toy? So many settings to experiment with."

"Can't wait," Matthew said once he could talk again. Win, who'd scrambled away from Tank, longed to go to him. But she knew better. Hell, even if the Armada wasn't there with guns, Matthew would not want her to. Now, he lifted his chin and looked fearlessly at Tank. "You have me to do with as you please. You don't need the others. They are a liability to you."

"I call them collateral fodder," said Tank. "In case someone decides to misbehave."

"The seventy-five year old with diarrhea won't bring anything, but irritation. Neither will the women. Let them go and you'll have better coverage. I'm a doctor here. I can help get you what you want. The women can't."

"You want to help me now, Doc?" Tank swaggered forward, his eyes narrowing. "What an interesting turn of events." He triggered the dog collar again, and this time the current brought Matthew down to the floor. Tank motioned to Satan. "Zip tie this helpful fucker's hands."

Satan made short work of wrenching Matthew's hands behind his back and locking them together. Even with the collar no longer shocking him, Matthew's muscled body was still twitching slightly. A small seizure triggered by the current.

The next hour unfolded in Win's mind with the clarity of a computer simulation. Outside, someone was figuring out that something was wrong. Maybe one of the hostages called 911 or just hospital operations following up on the strange announcement. Either way, someone would eventually call for a hostage negotiator and tactical team, only to discover that no one was there. They'd argue about what to do. Who else to call. They'd go to the rent-a-cop security station and force the ER cameras on. That would make them realize that the bikers could spray half the ER with bullets if someone barged in. So they'd wait.

Meanwhile, Tank would keep torturing Matthew. Settling his score and pride. The pleasure he took in depressing that button said he was here for his ego at least as much as for the drugs. As for those, sooner or later they'd realize the ER simply didn't have the quantity any self-respecting drug dealer wanted. Then all hell would break loose.

Simulation after simulation rushed through Win's thoughts too quickly for her conscious mind to process. No matter what variable she picked at though, there was always the same outcome: Tank wasn't going to walk out of here without doing damage. It would take moving a mountain to stop him. And right now, the only person available to move the damn thing, was her.

Win gave Sonia an encouraging look and then stepped right toward Tank.

"You need the pharmacy," she said, her voice sounding too small in the large room.

"What?" Tank turned around, the barrel of his gun aiming at her chest.

Win's mouth went so dry it took two attempts before she could form words again.

Matthew had recovered enough to glare at her, everything about his face screaming to get back and hide.

Win raised her chin. "That glorified vending machine will take another forty minutes to dispense everything." She pointed toward where Michelle was dutifully getting the drugs out one-by-one. "And even then, you aren't going to have much to show for the time. The hospital keeps quantity in the pharmacy."

"What are you saying?" Tank demanded.

Win thought she'd been rather clear, but apparently not. "If you want a lot of drugs, someone from the pharmacy will need to bring them up here for you."

"Bull fucking shit," said Tank.

"Why would I lie?" Win asked. "You want to get your drugs and leave. I want you to leave. So the sooner you can have the drugs the sooner you can leave. Right? Or better better yet, look for yourself at what the machine holds."

Tank squinted at her as if the catch to the whole thing was written somewhere on Win's face.

"Stay out of this, Win." Matthew managed to say.

"I'm trying to speed things up," said Win and turned back to Tank, managing to look at his face instead of the gun. "If you want, I can call the pharmacy—"

"You aren't fucking calling anyone," said Tank.

"I can send an order through the computer then," Win offered. "You can watch me and approve it before anything goes out. The hospital knows something is up by now, but you can control entry through the back door. It's small, not like the front. And you can see the tech that brings the stuff. Is that acceptable?"

Tank considered Win's words then had Satan walk over to the drug dispenser to confirm the contents. Finally, he grunted. "Fine. But one wrong move and I start shooting hostages. Understand me?"

"Very much so," Win said. Her heart pounded as she walked over to the workstation that had been set up for her work, and she savored the familiarity of the computer keys to ground herself as she logged in with her credentials. Despite all the simulations she'd run in her mind, the pressure of getting everything right was making her hands shake. Or maybe the shaking was because of the gun Tank now pressed into her back.

The computer screen blinked obediently in recognition of the user, then a black screen with white letter of the command prompt filled the large display.

"What the fuck is that?" Satan demanded, looking over Tank and Win's shoulder.

"The hospital's computer system is super old," said Win as she typed commands that had nothing to do with her words. "I'm checking the pharmacy inventory." She pointed to a line of code. "See, that says morphine is low, but both oxy and fentanyl stock numbers are coming in good. What do you want? Fentanyl will have the highest street value of anything we carry, unless your business extends to HIV meds? Let me check those." More lines of code went in and Win sent a prayer of thanks to any god that was listening that none of the bikers moonlighted as computer scientists. "Yeah. Full stock on those. They are under patent and expensive as all hell—if you have the buyers."

"Stop," Tank barked, grabbing Win by the hair. "When I want your fucking commentary, I'll ask for it."

Win pulled her hands away from the keyboard. "So, what do you want brought up?"

"Everything," Satan said. "And you better type that in one sentence because I don't like this shit."

Win waited until Tank released her hair, then moved slowly toward the computer. She typed *bring everything* into the screen. "Is that alright?" she asked.

Satan elbowed her out of the way. *Back door. One person. No cops. Or people die.* "Send that," he instructed.

Win hit enter and stepped away, not meeting anyone's eye. She'd done what she'd hoped, but whether it would work depended on a man who might still be drunk on anesthesia.

CASEY

Casey's room erupted in a cacophony of alarms, each so loud and persistent that for a moment he wondered if he wasn't, in fact, dying. Or hearing an air raid warning. Certainly nothing short of those events seemed a logical explanation for the frenzy. Hell, even the television screen was flashing as if trying to acquire a signal. Or give someone a seizure. Hospital equipment was rather predatory.

A team of nurses rushed inside with a resuscitation cart, their white coats flapping behind them like wings. The group skidded to a halt when they spotted him on his feet, pacing the room. They looked confused. Yeah. Welcome to the club.

"What the—," the male nurse in front swallowed a curse, though the beeping machines were going to swallow it anyway.

Erin, the young woman who'd been taking care of him since he'd woken up from having a bullet dug out of his back, went over to silence the monitors. The ensuing quiet was such a welcome contrast that Casey let out a breath.

"You look remarkably well for a dead guy," said Erin.

"Thanks." Casey massaged his shoulder. The wound was near the scapula but his whole side still ached. "Does that mean you are letting me out?"

"Not a chance. You –"

The phone at Casey's bedside table rang, cutting Erin off. He picked it up. At this point, why the hell not?

"It's Jackson at the pharmacy," the male voice on the other end of the line sounded panicked. "Sorry for the delay. Took me a minute to work out who Dr. Carrell needed me to call."

Casey rubbed a hand over his face and tried to get his thoughts in order. "Why didn't she just—shit." Casey's gaze landed on the television screen, which had stopped flickering and now streamed security camera footage from the top of the nursing station at the Emergency Room. A chill settled over him.

Around him, the few nurses still in the room finally looked up as well, blood draining from their faces as they too realized what was happening.

"What's going on?" Jackson asked.

"Best I can tell, a few armed jokers have taken the ER hostage." Casey pinched the bridge of his nose, fighting off the remaining grogginess from the anesthesia. Fortunately the team used conscious sedation and hadn't needed to put him under the whole way. Now, he studied the screen intently, unable to keep from searching for Sonia. There. On the floor. Was that blood on her?

Casey's heart rate quickened as the possibilities for what could have happened to her rushed through his head, but he caught himself in time to keep from getting drunk on the fear. The only way to help Sonia, to help everyone down there, was with a cool head.

"What was Win's message?" Casey asked into the phone, the earlier sound explosion now making sense. The little computer genius had needed to get his attention, and took significant risks to do it.

"She needs a bunch of controlled substances, including loose fentanyl—which, excuse my language is dangerous as fuck—brought to the ER," Jackson sounded shaky now. "What you have to do with this I don't know."

"Fair to say fucking is significantly less dangerous, but I get your meaning." Casey studied the screen again. Three men. All armed with long guns. At least one victim. Matthew looked incapacitated.

"What do you have to do with anything?" Erin asked Casey, echoing Jackson's question.

Casey kept his attention on the screen. "The Tridents and all tactical teams are out of pocket and Yarborough is in Denver. I presume I'm the closest this hospital has to a trained response."

"But you are in no shape to be tactical." Erin waved her arms around in her own impersonation of what tactical meant.

"Feel free to find someone better," Casey said mildly. He didn't disagree, but at the moment Denton Valley Memorial had slim pickings. Holding up a finger to halt Erin's further commentary, he returned to Jackson. "I'm going to be your drug courier and you've about five minutes to tell me everything I need to know about what I'm carrying."

"Um, yeah. Ok." Jackson sounded shaken. "There was one other part to the message though, but I don't get it. It just says O2. Like oxygen. Except the ER has more oxygen than you can shake a stick at, so I don't know why she'd want more in there."

"Understood." He didn't really, but Jackson had no need to know that right now. One step at a time though. Casey looked up to catch Erin's gaze. "The five minutes with Jackson is going to take about as much time as you have to bind my wound for greatest stability. And someone get what passes for security up here." He wasn't hopeful on that front, but there was a chance of setting them onto a half decent perimeter. Plus, they had guns and Casey needed one of them. "A map of the place wouldn't hurt either."

It was time to work.

WIN

Win sat on the floor next to Matthew, their shoulders touching. She didn't dare speak with him, but heat from his body seeped through to her with a steadying presence. Proof that he was alive. That so was she. For now.

She'd gotten her message sent. Whether it was received and understood was a separate matter altogether. But they'd know soon enough either way.

Tank, Satan, and Salt all paced up and down the ER floor, leveling their weapon randomly at patients and staff. Like children tormenting bugs. Sobs came from the different bays, the monitors beeping in protest as blood pressures and heart rates rose. Stopping in front of one such monitor, Tank sent two bullets into the thing.

The patient attached to it screamed, but the beeping stopped. "That's better," said Tank, then twisted to Win. "How long is this going to take?"

"The pharmacy needs at least fifteen minutes to pull the meds together, and another fifteen to bring them in here."

"One person comes," Tank said. "Any more and I'm shooting people. Clear?"

"Crystal," said Win, as if she had some telepathic connection to enforce Tank's order. "There is a peep hole at the door you can look through before opening."

Tank grunted, appeased for the moment.

Win leaned her head back against the wall and fought for deep even breaths. Sonia was still on the other side of the room, looking dazed and holding a towel to her nose. Michelle stood with a hand on the nurses station counter, as if it was the only thing holding her upright. Keeping a lower profile than Win was. Win didn't dare draw any more attention to Sonia, but Matthew she needed to speak with. To at least try and let him know what she'd tried to do. Hopefully he'd worked out that she'd done more than just sent a script to the pharmacy, but he'd been so out of it earlier that she wasn't sure.

She pressed her knee against his.

He pressed back.

"Will lure to Isolation B," she muttered as quietly as she could.

It was not quiet enough. Tank spun toward her. "No talking," he barked. "What did you just say?"

"I didn't," Win said quickly.

Tank pressed the button on his remote. Matthew jerked from Win a split second before his whole body went taut from electric shock.

"I'm going to increase the settings each second that you don't tell me what you said," said Tank.

Win's mind spun. Tank turned the dial. Matthew's scream tore a hole through Win's heart.

"I told him I loved him," she shouted, the tears streaking down her face. "I wanted him to know that, in case we didn't make it out of here."

Tank snorted, but let go of the trigger and Matthew slumped to the floor away from Win, drawing gulping breaths. Win's pulse hammered. She didn't know whether Matthew had heard the lie that wasn't a lie. Whether he believed it. She told herself it didn't matter, because Tank had bought the words.

Win started toward Matthew to help him up, but a jerk of Tank's gun made her back away. Now there was nothing to do but wait, and the passing seconds on the clock were as nerve wracking for her as they must have been for Tank. She closed her eyes and tried to escape in her body's rhythm. To pretend this was all a computer simulation with inputs and outputs and a command prompt of which she was god. That it could all be ended by pulling a cord from the wall. But Win was terrible at lying to herself. Today's ending would be a great deal more bloody than a computer game.

The buzz of the back door bell jerked Win to attention so sharply that she nearly hit her head on the wall she leaned against. Recovering herself, Win got to her feet. She could feel Matthew watching her every move, but didn't dare look at him. She didn't think she could look into his bright blue eyes and hide the horror she intended to unleash.

"That's your stuff," Win told Tank. Everyone in the ER went quiet, their attention rapt on this new moving part.

"Lead the way," Tank ordered.

"I'll do it." Matthew got up to one knee then another. "Let's let the men finish this out."

Tank set off the collar by way of answer, bringing Matthew back to the floor. "If he acts up, shoot him," Tank told Satan and Salt. "If I'm gone too long, shoot him. If anything smells wrong, shoot him. Understand all that."

Satan patted his gun and the extra ammo he had sticking out of his pocket. Salt looked at Michelle and licked his lips. "Might have some fun first."

"Keep your cock in your pants," Tank spat. "Don't need you with your pants around your ankles while I'm gone." He nudged Win with the tip of his gun. "Move."

Win limped on her injured knee as she obediently led Tank to the back door, one that was right beside Isolation B. Tank put his eye to the viewport, grunted in apparent satisfaction, and pulled open the door.

"I'm from the pharmacy. I was toh-oh-old to bring this," Casey said, holding up a duffle bag with his left hand, his right being in a sling around his shoulder. For a special forces guy, he did an impressive job of looking pitiful, his shoulders hunched protectively under a white lab coat. Win didn't know where they'd found something Casey's size, but it, combined with the stutter, was impressive.

Tank reached for the bag.

A corner of Casey's mouth twitched.

Tank pulled back. "You open it."

Casey pointed with his chin to his bound arm. "Doh-oh-on't have two hands."

Tank moved his gun to point at Win's temple. Win caught Casey's gaze, then cut her eyes toward the isolation room. Her pulse pounded in her head. How much of the message had he understood?

"I'll take it in there," Casey said quickly, moving toward Isolation B. "Will lay it all out o-o-on the table. Is that alright?"

Win's eyes widened as she caught on to the pattern in Casey's new stutter. The oh. There were always two extra "oh". O2. Oxygen. Tank had cut Win off before she could clarify what she needed, so Casey was now asking.

"On." Win whimpered. "On-on the table. Please hurry."

Casey shuffled into isolation, nearly tripping over his own feet as he went. "Sorry," he muttered, catching himself on the oxygen output valve to keep from falling. By the time Casey recovered his balance, the lever was shifted all the way on. "I'm clumsy when I'm nervous."

"Get on with it, or you'll give you something to get nervous about," said Tank.

Casey put the duffle bag onto the table and opened it. He tilted it up to show it stuffed full of plastic bags with pills of various types and even one with a loose powder substance. Enough to show that the bag held something, without giving a full view of what. Win's breath caught in her chest as she waited for Tank to take the lure. To take a step into that room.

He did.

Casey got the hell out.

Win hit the isolation lock, the door sliding closed with a hiss. A mix of relief and anxiety flooded Win's nerves, Tank's furious glare sending shots of fear through her. The thick protective glass drowned out the man's words, but his sentiment and intentions were being made clear enough with his gun.

"Don't shoot! You are in a negative pressure isolation room," Win said quickly into the intercom. "And it's full of oxygen."

Tank looked unimpressed.

Casey leaned toward the microphone, his voice now cold and professional. "That means one spark will make the air around you explode."

Tank dropped his weapon so fast that Win screamed. If that gun had gone off, Tank wouldn't be the only one to die. Not with them so close.

"Guns fire when you press the trigger, not on their own," Casey said calmly. "You alright, Doc?"

"No."

Casey pulled her against him with his good arm, his clean scent filling Win's lungs. "One down. Two to go." Something hard pressed into Win ribs. "I've got a handgun in my sling," Casey said into her ear. "One of the security guards kindly lent me his baby Glock."

"You can't use it," Win said quickly. "Not near the oxygen. Don't fire."

Casey snorted softly. "Yeah we went over that in demolition 101. And with you, about ten seconds ago."

"Tank, you alright back there?" Satan called from the main ER.

Shit. All the comfort that Casey's presence had brought Win disappeared like so much smoke. Tank's orders were to shoot if he doesn't answer, and they would certainly start with Matthew. Turning on her heels, Win sprinted toward the main ER, jolts of searing pain shooting through her knee with each step. Tears she couldn't keep back streaked her face, but she paid them no mind. She couldn't afford to.

It was worse than when she'd left it a few minutes ago. Fear so thick it saturated the air, coating the inside of her mouth with a coppery taste. Salt held Michelle by her hair, using the tip of his gun to move loose strands back from her face. Muffled crying and whimpering was now an endless backdrop of sound.

Matthew was still on the floor, but at least awake and alert. Watching her. Satan watched everyone.

"Tank closed himself in with the fentanyl," Win shouted to Satan. "I think... I think he's high. You can see for yourself. Don't hurt anyone. Please."

Salt growled, letting go of Michelle to stalk toward Win. He grabbed her arm and jammed his gun between her shoulder blades, the spot already bruised from similar treatment. "Show me," he ordered. "If you are lying, I will make you hurt."

Win led Salt back toward isolation, hoping that Casey had some idea of what to do with the man. Each step felt like a march toward execution. The only question was who'd die.

Win knew the instant Salt saw Tank pounding on the glass.

"What's going on?" he demanded, bringing his gun toward Win's face.

"Don't shoot," Tank said through the intercom, which Casey must have flipped back on. "The bitch rigged a fucking bomb. One spark and we are dead."

Salt tossed his gun down and grabbed Win by the throat, lifting her in the air. She choked, clawing the hand holding her, her feet kicking fruitlessly against meaty thighs. Salt didn't need a gun to kill. Hell, he didn't even need both hands. The pressure on her neck tightened and the things she never got to do or say raced regretfully through her mind. Like telling Matthew she loved him. That the lie hadn't been a lie at all.

A streak of white cut through Win's darkening vision, the tail of Casey's lab coat spinning so quickly that it looked like a weapon.

The pressure on Win's neck released and she crashed to the floor. Salt staggered, but Casey was already spinning again, his leg making a clean arc toward Salt's head. It connected just as a crashing sound filled the hallway.

Tank had grabbed a space oxygen tank and was beating the glass with it. The material was durable, but it was never meant to withstand impact. A crack formed at the point of impact, spidering all around. Tank struck again. Again.

"Win, run," Casey ordered.

She did. Tried to. Her leg gave out, the would-be sprint turning into a pitiful limp. Still, Win pushed through, trying to block out the pain and fear. She needed to get to her workstation. The sound of a gunshot echoed from the ER, followed by screams.

Satan had opened fire.

Win rounded the corner into total chaos. A herd of patients and staff streaked toward the main ER doors, trampling each other in the process. Matthew was on his feet, blood soaking his shirt sleeve as he squared off against Satan, whose gun was now on the floor. Matthew's hands were free, the scalpel he'd grabbed earlier now on the floor, but he moved slower than usual. As if still recovering from a seizure. Beside him, Satan towered like a linebacker.

Matthew's eyes raised and focused on Win, as he was somehow aware of her arrival. "Behind you," he shouted.

Win twisted in time to see a group of five panicked people rushing toward the exit, stepping on anything and anyone in their way. She tried to get out of their path, but her knee slowed her movement and Win went down hard, her head hitting the side of the counter.

The world blinked. Matthew shouted. Sonia was at her side, holding her up.

"Get her out of here," Matthew ordered Sonia.

"No." Win said. "Computer."

Sonia looked between the two.

"Please," Win said. "My workstation. Girl power."

Sonia nodded and slipped her arm around, steering Win where she needed to be. The moment Win got to the computer, her fingers were already moving. Pulling up the remote connection to the resuscitation equipment in Isolation B.

"Is Casey back?" Win asked.

"No," said Sonia.

"I need him to get away from the isolation rooms," Win said to Sonia. "Whatever you need to do."

Sonia looked at her for a second, then smiled. Raising her face she shouted the one thing that had a chance of getting Casey to leave a fight. "Help! Casey! They have me! Casey!"

The answering promise came a heartbeat later, as Casey's booming voice filled the air.

"Tell me the moment you see him," Win ordered, not daring to take her eyes off the screen. She'd already established a remote connection to the Lifepak defibrillator in the room. Its remote access was intended to send EKG tracing directly to cardiology, but the virus Win just finished uploading into its system would send the lifesaving device into electrical overload. Creating enough spark to set the oxygen being pumped freely on fire.

"I got him," Sonia said into Win's ear.

Win sent the execute command and Isolation B, together with Salt and Tank, exploded in a rush of flame.

SONIA

Three hours after isolation B went up in flames, Sonia sat on Casey's lap in his living room. Her head throbbed. Casey tightened his left arm around her for a moment then slid it up her back to massage the base of her neck. The divine pressure spidered from his touch, sending tendrils of such intense pleasure down her nerves that she nearly purred, despite their company and the fact that Casey had no business being outside the hospital. Then again, neither did a bunch of people sitting around them.

The Tridents had returned from taking down Armada's human market and now joined the hospital escapees—her, Casey, Win, and Matthew—at the twins' penthouse. Win sat in an armchair, knee elevated and covered with a bag of ice. A similar bag of ice was draped over the right part of Casey's back. At the kitchen island, Cullen stitched up Matthew's forearm, Eli looking on with twitching fingers. When it came to the Tridents, there was never a shortage of medical supplies or medical people vying for the chance to play with them.

"Isn't there a better venue for that?" Briar asked, pointing at the blue suture drape Cullen had set up.

"The mini-doc blew up the hospital," said Casey. "This is more comfortable."

"I did not blow up the hospital," Win said.

"Not for lack of trying," said Matthew.

She glared at him.

"What he means to say, is thank you for saving all our asses," Sonia told her, Casey nodding his agreement. She tilted her face up toward him, and he leaned down, brushing an unapologetic kiss over her lips.

"You two need a room?" Aiden asked.

"We have a room," said Casey. "You lot just happen to be in it."

Aiden laughed and toasted with his beer. "Fair enough mate."

Briar crossed his arms stiffly and shot him and Casey a disgruntled look. Yeah, Briar was unhappy with, well, with everything. That the Tridents' takedown op had left their homebase unprotected, that Casey played one-armed rambo, that Sonia ran off from the *Belle Nuit* to begin with. The list went on and on.

"I should have been there," Sith said, his hand tightening around a bottle of beer that he'd not touched. He had a haunted look about him and ran concerned glances over his little sister whenever he thought she wasn't watching.

"Too bad you were out the day the SEALs issued clairvoyance and telepathy," said Win, sounding exasperated. Plainly, this wasn't the first time she and Sith had had this conversation. "Next time a pissed off low life decides to be stupid, I expect you to know at least two days in advance."

Matthew scowled. "This isn't funny. You could have been killed five times over."

"Thanks, I was unclear about what the guns meant," she snapped back at him.

Matthew and Win's eyes locked across the room, enough electricity crackling between them that it was a miracle the lights weren't flickering. They'd been at each other's throats ever since the ER debacle ended—at least, when their eyes met. When they thought the other wasn't looking, they expended just as much energy covertly assessing each other's injuries. Sonia considered pointing that out, but for the safety of Casey and Briar's penthouse decided against it.

There was more for those two to work out than could—or should—be addressed in company.

"Speaking of viruses and trojans," Sonia said, changing the trajectory of the conversation, "can someone give a better account of what happened at the Armada's human market than '*site secured, no casualties?*'" She leaned forward, her attention darting between Briar and Liam, who she knew best. "Was Nero there? Razor? Did you kill them?"

She meant to sound, well, normal, but her breath hitched, the memories of that container threatening to overtake her. Casey brushed a kiss along her temple and some of her muscles eased. She was safe. It was over. She'd helped bring the bastards down.

It was Eli who answered, his British accent and general good nature at odds with his words. "After Patriot and his mates gave me some background on their business and then finished shitting their knickers over Casey's reincarnation," he gestured to Briar and smirked. "We came to an understanding with one of them."

"Which was?" Sonia said.

Eli shrugged one muscled shoulder. "He radios in that all is well, explains away the delay as a minor mechanical issue, and drives us to the intended destination and past the perimeter control."

Sonia's brows narrowed. "And in exchange?"

"He gets to keep at least one of his balls."

Sonia started. "You didn't really…"

A darkness passed over Eli's face. "I didn't. But I still think I should have."

Liam cleared his throat. "Fortunatuntly, that let us breach their auction site without shots fired."

"I wish I could have seen their faces when the backdoor opened and a bunch of armed bastards came out instead of frightened girls," said Casey.

"There was a wee bit of chaos," Aiden said, joining in the conversation with his Scottish brogue. "But it all ended with about fifty of them face down on the floor. Sellers, buyers, power players. We almost ran out of zipties at one point. Fortunately, Tara had spares." He winked at his wife.

"Someone had to be responsible," Tara answered.

"And Nero?" Casey asked, his thumb now making slightly inappropriate circles along Sonia's thigh.

"Tried to make off by saying that he wasn't part of the group, but rather the attorney representing them," said Liam. "I believe he is still arguing that part from behind bars."

That sounded right. Sonia's stomach tightened. The sleazy bastard would twist around the legal system like an eel, and there was nothing any of the Tridents could do about that.

But she could. "I want to prosecute him," Sonia said, her quiet but strong words drawing the attention of everyone in the room. "I want to be the one who takes him down in court."

Liam and Cullen exchanged glances Sonia didn't understand, but behind her, Casey seemed utterly relaxed. As if he'd never expected anything different. She loved him for that alone. She turned toward her boss.

"I've been doing some work with the prosecutor's office," she told Liam defensively. "I realize this will be a bigger trial than I have experience handling but—"

"There are no more capable hands I'd rather be handing the case to," Liam said, toasting her with his can of diet coke. "I was just moping over losing a great attorney from my team—and was betting Cullen was thinking the same about losing all the help at Denton Memorial."

Cullen nodded in agreement. "Make them pay," he said, lifting his beer.

"Here here," everyone echoed.

"I bet you'll even be able to do it without blowing up a building," Matthew added, earning a furious glower from Win.

About an hour later, the gang started to thin. For a minute, Sonia thought that Matthew would try to corner Win into a conversation, but she turned her back on him and quickly left with her brother instead. Matthew's jaw tightened, but he didn't follow, while everyone around pretended not to have noticed anything amiss. At least until the place was empty except for Sonia, Casey, and Briar.

"What's going on with the two docs?" Casey asked, closing the door after Liam, who was the last to leave.

"Don't know, don't care." Briar gave Casey and Sonia a salute and strode off to his room on the other side of the penthouse.

"I wasn't really asking you," Casey called after his twin, even as he put his hand on Sonia's hips and turned her toward him. She knew she looked like hell and had been lucky to escape without a broken nose, but Casey's gaze held nothing but appreciation. "You know though, don't you, kitten?"

She tried to glare, but it hurt her face. "I have an idea," she admitted. "Let's just say they have some deeper issues to work out."

"Deeper issues?" Casey's eyes sparkled wickedly. "Just how deep are we talking?"

"Oh my god. Really? That was your takeaway? Can you be any more juvenile?"

"I absolutely can. Want to see?" He nipped at Sonia's bottom lip, his teeth grazing her in a way that sent tiny shivers of arousal all the way to her core. And then down.

Her breath caught.

And then stayed there, in her chest, as reality finally settled. Casey was playing and teasing, but he was *Casey*, that's what he always did. But everything that had forced them together was over now. The unified enemy, the pretend relationship, the need for survival. Did the words Casey had said to her in that cave, the ones about love, still apply now that no one was bleeding and freezing?

"It's late," she said, quietly gathering her dignity. "I should go."

"Why?"

"Because I don't live here," Sonia said. *And you probably have hookers waiting in the North Vault to bring up.*

"Why not?"

Sonia lifted her face to study his, and found no amusement

dancing there. Instead, Casey's gray eyes held hers with an intensity that gripped each fiber of her body and soul

"I don't want you to leave," Casey said. "Not now, not ever."

Not now, not ever. Did he mean?... No, of course he didn't.

Casey's left hand came up to take Sonia's chin and then he pressed his forehead gently against her. "I love you, Sonia. I want you."

Everything spun. Her thoughts, her emotions, her logic. "You... want me?" She sounded like a parrot or an idiot or both. "Want me how?"

"A little tipsy would be good just about now," Casey muttered, then took a breath and pulled his face back enough to grip her gaze again. "Let's try this one more time. I want you to marry me, Counselor."

Sonia froze, her eyes widening.

Casey wanted her. Forever. A warmth spread over Sonia, mixing with the avalanche of emotions already cascading into her blood. Adrenaline and need and love and... It was a lot. Too much. Just right. She pressed her mouth against Casey's, finishing the kiss that he'd started, her tongue sweeping inside and making itself at home.

"Just so I'm clear," Casey said, pulling away for a moment, "that's a *yes*, right? Not some diversion tactic to make me stupid while you run away?"

Sonia laughed. "It's a yes."

"Thank fucking god," Casey breathed. "Now there is one thing that I need to do to make this perfect. Before making this official." Lifting Sonia with one arm, Casey carried her to the baby grand piano and set her atop it. The smooth piano top brushed the back of Sonia's thighs. Casey surveyed her hungrily. "Yes. This is exactly where I want you. Except your shirt is all wrong."

"What's wrong with my shirt?" asked Sonia.

"That you aren't wearing one of mine," he stepped between her thighs, which parted to let him in, and brushed his hand along Sonia cheek. The soft scrape of his calluses along her skin sent tiny jolts of sensation though her. Casey leaned in, his lips grazing her ear. "On second thought, it's that you are wearing one at all."

Dipping under her shirt, Casey laid his palm flat against her belly and whispered all the wicked plans he had for the night.

Sonia's face heated with each word, but her sex already pulsed with need.

WIN

Win stood in the hospital hallway, leaning against the painted wall. The cellphone in her hand felt like a brick and she'd typed and erased the same message into the screen several times.

I have your package ready to go.

This time she finally pressed *send*, shooting the missive from *@DocPhantom42* to Matthew. In the two days since the disaster in the ER, that was the only place Win had had contact with him. He'd tried to reach out several times, both directly and through Sith, but Win held on to her decision with all the willpower in her body.

She'd stupidly fallen in love with Matthew Jennsen and she couldn't go back to the casual game he wanted to play. *Shit or get off the pot.* It was one of Sith's favorite sayings and it was all too apt. A relationship, the only kind she could have with him now, had to go two ways. Either Matthew trusted her with his own pain, fears, and weakness, or he didn't. And he didn't. He'd made that clear. So that was that.

Win looked down at where the cursor was blinking on her screen and quickly added the basics. *Where do you want it sent? Payment due prior to mailing.*

"Dr. Carrell, you have a patient in exam two." Appearing out of nowhere, Michelle thrust an iPad in front of Win's nose.

Win started and jammed the phone into her back pocket. "Sorry, didn't see you."

"It's a skill I've learned working with doctors," Michelle told her. "If you can see me, you can run. And I need the patient in two seen."

Win couldn't help the small chuckle. She shook her head, regretting it a moment later. Her neck was tight. All of her was tight and bruised and hurting. She doubted Michelle was any better off. "Why are you at work?" she asked. "You should be home, decompressing a bit. How do you feel?"

"Like shit, but it feels better to be doing something than sitting and brooding." She raised a brow. "I can ask you the same question, by the way. Especially since you aren't even supposed to be assigned to the ER anymore."

"The ER is short staffed until Dr. Jennson returns. I'll move on once he is back."

"Where are you going?" Michele looked like she might say something more, but then just pressed the iPad forward. The nurse was haunted. They all were. Healing would take time no matter how brave a face everyone put on everything. "Exam two. That's now across the hallway and to the right, by the way. We've reconfigured since you redecorated the place."

Win winced. "I hadn't meant to do quite that much damage—"

"Don't you dare apologize." Michelle spun around. "You saved lives, Doc. And you have all our thanks. Mine in particular." She took a breath, gaining control of herself with visible effort. "But if you feel like contributing to the cause today, the sooner you can clear Exam two for me, the better."

"On it," Win promised, though Michelle was already on her way, hurrying off to keep the world turning the way nurses always did. Win looked down at the chart in her hand. A John Doe with arm pain. So anything from a splinter to a heart attack. Given that the patient had trouble with his own name, the vague complaint was unsurprising. Triage usually did a better job of ferreting out the details, but today... Today everyone was just doing the best they could.

Win limped toward the room, her hinged knee-brace restricting her motions. In her pocket, her phone started to vibrate. From the hepatic pattern, she knew it was Matthew's message. Win paused, reaching for the phone—then stopped. Matthew, and the experimental drugs he'd rather be ordering from the dark web than talking to Win about, could wait. Should wait.

Opening the door to Exam two—so identified by a handmade sign on the door—Win scrolled down the chart to see if anyone had managed to get any other info on the patient. Appendectomy was listed, probably someone noticed the scar and surmised as much. Detective medicine. Win liked that actually. "Good morning," she said brightly, her attention still on the chart. "I'm Dr. Carrell. I understand you are having some arm pain?"

"Yes."

Win's jerked at the sound of the familiar voice, her balance wavering.

A firm hand caught her elbow before she could fall on her ass, Matthew's fingers hot against her skin. "You could try looking at your surroundings once in a while," he muttered.

Win pulled out of his grip, her stomach clenched so tightly she was surprised she could still draw breath. "Whose idea of a joke is this?"

"Mine, mostly. But Michelle helped." Matthew retreated back to the bed and sat on the edge. He wore a pair of blue jeans and a t-shirt, the material falling loosely over the hard body that Win remembered in more detail than she wished. Matthew ducked his head sheepishly. "Honestly, I was worried you'd not see me if you knew who I was."

Win stepped back toward the counter, which was as far as she could get from Matthew in the small room. Not that it helped. His presence filled the space, the scent of his clean male musk already filling her lungs. All the effort she'd put in to *not* think about him these last days, to give them a clean break, it was all for nothing. He was here, and everything inside Win longed for Matthew to draw her up in his arms and hold her tight. She knew he'd do just that if she let him.

But it would never be the other way around.

The band around Win's ribs cinched tighter still. "What do you want?" she asked.

"A medical clearance to return to work."

He wanted her to lie for him.

"I recommend you find another doctor." She tossed the iPad onto the counter. "I know more than you'd like in your file."

"I don't want another doctor." Matthew's jaw tightened, a muscle ticking on the side of his face. "You are on duty. I'm your patient. You can't actually refuse to see me."

"Really? That's the angle you want to play?" Win pulled the rolling chair over for herself and turned on the computer. "Fine."

"Win—"

"Let's start a review of your medical history, Mr. Jensson. I see you had an appendectomy. Do you have any other medical history? Any medications you are taking?" She paused, her finger poised over the keyboard. She had him cornered, and they both knew it. The only way for Matthew to keep his medical record free of his secrets was to lie outright. To admit that this whole exam was a farce.

Silence stretched and Win smiled to herself without humor. Yeah.

"I also have epilepsy."

Win flinched. She'd not expected to be playing chicken with him, but so be it. Instead of turning back to him like he no doubt expected, she clicked right into the medical chart. "Epilepsy," she typed into the screen. "When was the onset?"

"Two years ago. Self-diagnosed."

She twisted on the stool, finally turning his way. "You really want me to write that in? Once I press enter, there is no going back."

Matthew didn't waver. "Then press enter."

Win closed her eyes, her world spinning. She was too tired for games. Too hurt. She didn't want to play chicken anymore. Didn't want to play anything. "Can we stop please?" she whispered. "Just tell me what you want. I know it isn't to ruin the medical record you've worked so damn hard to keep clean. So please—please—just, tell me what the endgame here is."

"The endgame is to prove that I'm honest with you," Matthew's voice was soft, but confident. He was always confident. "So, go ahead and write it all down. I started having seizures approximately two years ago. No known triggers and they've become progressively more common. They usually last from seconds to minutes, often with full tonic clonic activity." There was a pause. "But you'd somehow already figured most of that out."

She opened her eyes. Matthew had leaned forward, his hands braced on the edge of the exam table, his attention boring into her.

"I'm..." Her shoulders sagged. She really didn't have any fight left. "I'm sorry for sticking my nose into your business. I know you didn't appreciate it and it won't happen again."

"I hope not." Matthew raised his chin. "Because I want it to be *our* business, not just mine. If you'll give me another chance." He paused for a moment, then continued, his words tripping slightly. "It *was* us for a while, Win. And I miss us. I miss you. I miss holding you. I miss cringing every time you walk toward the kitchen and threaten to make breakfast. Miss you explaining computers to Odysseus. I miss how grounded I felt when you were in my life. I love you."

Win's breath caught, her entire body suddenly paralyzed. She stared at him and Matthew stared back, every chiseled line of him seeming to vibrate as he waited for her answer.

Except what was she supposed to say to that? *When all else fails, try the truth.*

"You don't love me, Matthew," she said softly. "You love having someone to protect. But protection, it's not the same as trust. You'd rather have a tonic clonic seizure in some dark corner of the hospital over letting me help you, for god's sake. What am I supposed to do with that?"

He ran a hand through his hair, looking a bit abashed. "I was hoping you might just call me an idiot and give me another chance. Come stay with me for a few days. Let me make you feel safe. Make me feel..." he trailed off.

"Grounded?" Win guessed gently. "I'm not an electrical wire."

Matthew jaw snapped shut, his face closing off. A darkness fell over him, like a computer shutting down, the screen closing with finality. He slid off the exam table and tucked in his shirt. "I was going to say, not alone," he said, all business now, no emotion in sight as he walked past her to the door. "But nevermind. I'm fine with being alone."

"Are you?" she said into his back.

"No," Matthew didn't turn around. "But I'm going to be. I apologize for having interrupted your day."

"Wait." Win felt like she was getting pelted with hail, except she couldn't see the directions the shards flew in from. She didn't even know where to step next, except that if Matthew walked out now, it would be a mistake. And if he stayed... She didn't know what would happen if he did. What she wanted to happen. She wanted so badly to believe him, but how could she? How could she believe any words of togetherness and trust when, even as he said them, Matthew was also chatting with @*DocPhantom42*? Looking for experimental drugs on the darkweb instead of talking to her. "Let's just finish the exam. You are here anyway. And you need the clearance."

"I'll ask someone else." He opened the door.

Win put her hand on it, shutting it before he could leave. "Matthew—"

"No." He twisted, his face flashing with a mix of hurt and determination that she had never expected to see. "I asked, you said no. I'm not going to try to force you back into my life just to make myself whole. We are done."

She straightened her spine, fighting for every inch of height. "I said I want to examine you, not fuck you. So get your ass back on my table."

Matthew's brows jerked up in surprise, but Win's heart was hammering too quickly to bother with blushing. There was too much between them. Reaching up, she curled her hand around his upper arm, just above the elbow. His muscles were coiled tight beneath her touch, his skin warm. Real. "Get back on the table," she said again, gentler this time.

He stood rigid for a moment, then nodded curtly. Returning to the center of the room, Matthew hoisted himself up and found a spot on the wall to look at. Win moved quietly around him, checking the wound on his forearm before covering it with a new dressing.

"Cullen did a good job with the stitches," she said finally.

No answer came at first, but then Matthew nodded. "He did. I was lucky the bullet only grazed me the way it did."

"*Lucky* and *hit with a bullet* shouldn't be used in the same sentence." Win took out a penlight, shining it into one eye then the other. The pupils reacted obediently, shrinking away from the beam to let more of the crystal blue show. Matthew had expressive eyes. He always had.

Maybe Win was being unfair. He'd reached out. Met her halfway. More than. If that wasn't enough, maybe it was a start.

Win brushed her fingers along his neck. The spots where the collar's prongs had zapped him were an angry red, like vampire marks. His jaw clenched slightly when she palpated the area. "Tenderness on palpation," she said. "Any residual neural effects?"

"No." His mouth pressed into a tight line. "Just... seizures as usual."

"Good." Well, no it wasn't *good*. But it was better than it could have been. Win's hand curled into a fist as, for the first time since Tank had stormed the ER, something inside her burst apart. "What were you thinking?" The angry words shot from her, each like a javelin thrown at Matthew's chest. "You were never supposed to hand yourself over. Let them put that collar on you. Do you know what that electricity could have done? Of course you do. You know exactly. Better than anyone. You didn't even fight. You just... just..." The words choked her, making it difficult to speak.

"Win—"

"You could have died. He wanted to kill you. And you were going to let him." She gasped for oxygen that was suddenly lacking. Or exploding. Or suffocating. "How could you? How could you do that, goddamn it?"

Matthew frowned, looking down in gentle confusion. "I couldn't let him hurt you, pixel."

"I hate you!" she tried to scream the words, but the sound came out in a croak. She was back in the ER again, Tank zapping Matthew with enough electricity to send his body into convulsions. An orderly's body lay on the ground, his dead eyes staring at Win. Blue eyes. Just like Matthew's. Win's pulse raced, the room spinning and flashing around her. "It's your fault," she barked. His fault for making her care. For protecting her. For getting hurt. For letting himself… letting himself… Win swung her hand, hitting Matthew's shoulder as hard as she could.

The force of the impact jostled her arm all the way to the elbow, but made no impression on him. She went to hit him again, but this time Matthew caught her wrist in mid-motion.

"I know," he said with gentle firmness. "I know. But watching Tank hurt you was more than I could handle, pixel. It was too hard. It hurt too much. I couldn't let it happen. I'll never be able to let it happen."

Win's face felt wet. She hadn't realized tears had started pouring down her cheeks. She went to wipe them, but Matthew beat her to it, his knuckles brushing down her face.

"What you said before, about me not loving you, that's total bullshit. I love you. I want to be with you. And yes, I do want to protect you. The only place those things are mutually exclusive is in that brilliant scared head of yours. I will always protect you, pixel. But you protect me, too."

"I didn't," Win said. "I just watched as Tank…" The full force of the terror that she'd somehow suppressed earlier, now crashed around Win's ears. Her body shook, a small tremble at first, then more and more as belated fear coursed through her blood.

"But you *did* protect me," Matthew said, the conviction in his voice so strong that it penetrated through the haze of Win's mind. "Your stupid stunt with setting oxygen on fire? Yeah. That's what got everyone out. But even before that. You were protecting me back well before Tank ever came into the ER. I'd just been too scared to appreciate it. You are brave, pixel. Braver than I sometimes wish you were."

Matthew moved closer to Win, cupping her face in his hands and brushing away her tears with his thumbs. His calluses scraped against her wet skin.

Her breath hitched.

Leaning forward, Matthew brushed his lips against hers. Despite the lethal strength that seemed to forever vibrate through every cell of Matthew's body, the kiss was soft, his mouth asking instead of demanding. Yet that was enough to send sparks of electricity searing through her veins.

Win's arms curled around Matthew's neck. She opened for him, and that was the only invitation Matthew needed. He plunged inside her, claiming her mouth with his tongue more fully than she'd thought possible. She held on to his neck, losing herself in the kiss until they finally broke apart, both breathing heavily.

Standing so close, Win still felt the heat radiating off him, the taste of him still coating her tongue. He tasted of courage and determination. And a little bit of fear, too.

She stepped back just a fraction of an inch and locked eyes with him. "Do you still want me?" she asked in a voice barely above a whisper.

Matthew snorted, then scooped Win up in his arms, twisting them until it was her perched atop the table and him between her open thighs. This time, when his mouth descended on hers it was with predatory intent.

He slid his hands down her body, sending shivers running through her. With each caress, a new wave of belonging surged through her. A connection that went both ways between their souls.

Matthew's lips moved down to kiss the curve of her neck, and Win let out a low moan. Wrapping her legs around him, she felt every muscle in Matthew's back as he pressed his hard body against hers. His calloused hands roamed up and down her curves possessively, and Win had never felt so desired or alive before.

The heat between them was overwhelming, the energy an intoxicating force that swept through Win's soul. He held on tightly, her eyes closed, nothing mattering except Matthew's touch. His lips slid back over Win's neck, sliding to her ear.

"Yeah, pixel," he whispered. "I still want you. I always have."

"Sith will be mad."

"Good." Matthew nipped the top of Win's ear. "It's past time I made it clear where I stand when it comes to you. I love you."

"I love you, too," said Win, whispering back.

Matthew tipped his face toward the ceiling. "Thank fucking god."

"Dr. Carrell, is everything alright?" Michelle's voice called from the hallway.

Win jumped, but Matthew only closed his arms right around her.

"All's well," Matthew called back. "Go away, Michelle. This room is… malfunctioning."

"Well can it malfunction somewhere else, I need the space, Doctors."

"I'm just finishing up," Win called back.

Michelle scoffed, but footsteps sounded along the floor.

Win pulled away reluctantly. "We really should finish up. Can you take your shirt off please?"

"Just the shirt?"

Heat rushed to Win's cheeks.

Matthew laughed. It was a good sound.

Thankfully, before everything could go off the rails completely, he complied, letting Win get a full set of lung and heart sounds for the chart. Win was about to put the stethoscope away, when the faint heart sound caught her ear. Win returned the stethoscope back to the spot she'd last held it, her brows pulling together.

"What is it?" Matthew asked.

She closed her eyes, listening to whooshing blood, the heart valves that opened and closed on command, to the small whisper that had no business being there.

Her eyes snapped up to his face. "You have an Elizabethan murmur," she said.

Matthew frowned. "I have a benign murmur. I don't think it's royal though."

Win shook her head, her mind spinning, her instinct flaring with adrenaline. "An Elizabethan murmur has a specific sound. It's a rare genetic artifact. Benign, like you said and I only noticed it because…" Because it was in her field of study. "Lie down and stay still. I want twelve leads."

"You want to share with the class?" he asked, letting her get the ECG tracing.

"Not yet." Win watched the tracing with baited breath. There. In the anterior leads. Twisting back to the computer, Win pulled up the blood sample analysis Jackson had done for her. Seizures. Elizabethan murmur. Anterior lead marker and… She stared at DNA mapping on the screen.

"Win? What is it?" Matthew was up now, standing behind, his voice tight. "Tell me."

"You don't have epilepsy, Matthew." Win swallowed. "You have Vilka Syndrome."

Matthew raised his chin, his attention completely on her. Hints of fear shone in his eyes, but he made no sound while Win gathered her facts together and turned toward him.

"It's one of the rare genetic disorders I study," Win explained. "In Vilka Syndrome, the body doesn't produce Vigabutin. That's an enzyme similar to GABA, but is produced in a different part of the brain and has a different effect on nerve impulses."

"Nerve impulses. Like seizures?"

She nodded. "It looks like epilepsy, but it's not. And Matthew… It's mangeable. Completely. With enzyme replacement, your symptoms are going to disappear. You could go back to the SEALs. To active duty."

Matthew drew a ragged breath, the possibilities of a different future unfurling in his face with a spark of wonder.

Win's eyes stung, but she understood. Matthew was a SEAL. He never wanted to leave the field. He never wanted this civilian life that his seizures forced him into.

"How long would it take?" Matthew asked.

"A few months to get your levels up. You'll need maintenance infusions, but that's about it."

"So, no more seizures?" said Matthew.

"No." Win smiled at him, hiding her own unfair ache.

Matthew grinned back. "You know what that means?"

"You get to crawl through the mud and shoot guns again?" Win put all the excitement she could into her voice.

Matthew put his hands on either side of her face, tipping it up toward his. "It means that I can ask you to move in and not worry I'm going to thrash in the middle of the night and break your nose," he told her. "You are very small."

"But..." Win blinked without understanding. "But you can go back to the SEALs now. Isn't that what you've always wanted?"

"Hmm..." Matthew brushed his thumb along Win's lower lip. "It was. But you have a way of shifting things, always turning my plan on its head."

"You aren't going to go?"

"I'm not going anywhere," Matthew said. "Except to the realtor's office to say that I want to buy out the other apartment on my floor. You know, for when you burn down the kitchen we already have."

"Doctors," Michelle's voice sounded again on the other side of the door. "Get a room. Not mine."

Matthew snorted. "Go on ahead," he told Win. "Unlike you, I still have to work with her."

Win brushed a kiss against Matthew's lips and walked out of the treatment room, pulling out her cellphone to avoid meeting Michelle's gaze.

The screen blinked with the unread message Matthew had sent to @PhantomDoc42 earlier.

Thanks for your help, but I've found a doctor I trust. Your services will no longer be needed.

* * *

You've finished Casey's book - but there are more Tridents to get to know. If you are reading this in ebook version, continue on for a FREE preview.

If you enjoyed this book, you may also like the other stories in the TRIDENT RESCUE Series.

ENEMY ZONE
Cullen and Sky

ENEMY CONTACT
Eli and Dani

ENEMY LINES
Kyan and Ivy

ENEMY HOLD
Liam and Jaz

ENEMY CHASE
Aiden and Tara

If you are reading this in ebook version, continue on for a FREE preview of ENEMY HOLD.

OTHER BOOKS BY THIS AUTHOR:

TRIDENT RESCUE (Writing as A.L. Lidell)
Contemporary Enemies-to-Lovers Romance
ENEMY ZONE (Audiobook available)
ENEMY CONTACT (Audiobook available)
ENEMY LINES (Audiobook available)
ENEMY HOLD (Audiobook available)
ENEMY CHASE
ENEMY STAND

* * *

Writing as Alex Lidell
POWER OF FIVE (7 books)
Reverse Harem Fantasy Romance
POWER OF FIVE (Audiobook available)
MISTAKE OF MAGIC (Audiobook available)
TRIAL OF THREE (Audiobook available)
LERA OF LUNOS (Audiobook available)
GREAT FALLS CADET (Audiobook available)
GREAT FALLS ROGUE
GREAT FALLS PROTECTOR

IMMORTALS OF TALONSWOOD (4 books)
Reverse Harem Paranormal Romance
LAST CHANCE ACADEMY (Audiobook available)
LAST CHANCE REFORM (Audiobook available)

LAST CHANCE WITCH (Audiobook available)

LAST CHANCE WORLD (Audiobook available)

* * *

SIGN UP FOR NEW RELEASE NOTIFICATIONS at https://links.alexlidell.com/News

ABOUT THE AUTHOR

A.L. Lidell is the Amazon Breakout Novel Awards finalist author of THE CADET OF TILDOR (Penguin) and several Amazon Top 100 Kindle Bestsellers, including the POWER OF FIVE romance series. She is an avid horseback rider who believes in eating dessert first. She writes as both Alex Lidell and A.L. Lidell.

Join Alex's newsletter for news, bonus content and sneak peeks: https://links.alexlidell.com/News

Find out more on Alex's website: www.alexlidell.com

Join Alex's newsletter for news, bonus content and sneak peeks: https://links.alexlidell.com/News

Find out more on Alex's website: www.alexlidell.com

SIGN UP FOR NEWS AND RELEASE NOTIFICATIONS

Connect with Alex!
www.alexlidell.com
alex@alexlidell.com

Printed in Great Britain
by Amazon